A Christmas Proposal

Rose Warner, who also publishes as Jen Gilroy, writes historical women's fiction and feel-good contemporary romance. She has been a finalist for the Romantic Novelists' Association's Joan Hessayon Award and Romance Writers of America's Golden Heart® award. Now based in Canada, Rose has dual Canadian/British nationality, and lived in England for many years. She returns regularly to visit friends and old haunts, and to conduct extensive research in the WW2 and post-war periods. As Jen Gilroy she writes sweet small-town romance for Harlequin Heartwarming (HarperCollins) and has also published with Grand Central Forever (Hachette) and others.

Also by Rose Warner

Teacher Evacuees

The Teacher Evacuees
A Christmas Proposal
The Teacher's Secret

A Christmas Proposal

ROSE WARNER

canelo

Penguin Random House

First published in the United Kingdom in 2026 by

Canelo, an imprint of
Canelo Digital Publishing Limited,
20 Vauxhall Bridge Road,
London SW1V 2SA
United Kingdom

A Penguin Random House Company
The authorised representative in the EEA is Dorling Kindersley Verlag GmbH.
Arnulfstr. 124, 80636 Munich, Germany

A CIP catalogue record for this book is available from the British Library.

ISBN 978 1 83598 028 6

Printed and bound in Great Britain by Clays Ltd, Elcograf S.p.A.

Look for more great books at
www.canelo.co | www.dk.com

1

FSC www.fsc.org MIX Paper FSC™ C018179

*In memory of Flight Lieutenant Gordon Stewart Richards,
Royal Canadian Air Force, No. 406 Squadron.*

Born Toronto, Canada, 1 June 1920. Enlisted November 1940 while a student at the University of Toronto. Killed in action 18 October 1943 near Tŷ Croes, Anglesey, Wales.

Lest we forget.

Chapter One

Wednesday, 21 August 1940

'Thank you, Miss Hopson. I'll tell the others straight away.' Beatrice Wentworth ended her call with the headmistress of London's Park Road School and clenched her gloved hands. As much as she tried to conceal it beneath the calm and collected demeanour she'd perfected over her forty-two years, a familiar anger and bitterness bubbled away like a pot left unattended on the hob. Whilst Beatrice genuinely admired and respected Miss Hopson, she couldn't help wondering, yet again, when *she* would have the chance to become a headmistress herself. Not likely, marooned here in the country, possibly for years.

Rearranging her features into what she hoped passed for a pleasant, neutral smile, she left the red telephone box at the far end of Hazelbury's village green and nodded at the foster mums of several of her evacuated pupils who were queued up waiting. 'Yes, it's indeed a lovely day, Mrs Yallop.' Beatrice increased her pace to avoid one of the most notorious village gossips, three of whose children she taught – the result of a teacher shortage which meant that, owing to the village's teacher having left her post, the London school had recently been combined with the local one.

'What did Miss Hopson say about the school inspector's visit?' Victoria McKaye, her friend and colleague who was responsible for the infants' classes, met Beatrice under the shade of a large beech tree near Hazelbury's pub, across from the green.

'Yes, I'm all in a flutter to hear.' At Victoria's side, Nell Potter, the youngest of the three London teachers who'd been evacuated to this small North Norfolk village almost a year before, clutched her satchel, handbag and gas mask box close to her chest as if to shield herself from bad news.

'We can expect Mr Rimmington's visit on Thursday in the third week of September. Just over a month from now.' Beatrice suppressed a sigh and tried to keep her tone cheerful. 'Miss Hopson said we need not worry. Like the rest of us, school inspectors are well aware that there's a war on and we're all doing the best we can.'

Victoria and Nell might not have cause to fret, but Beatrice's situation was different. As the most senior teacher, as well as the erstwhile head of Park Road's junior school, she did not have the title or salary befitting an official headmistress, but she certainly had many of the responsibilities. If the school inspector found fault with the pupils' work or anything else to do with their school life, those faults would be raised with her first. She also had to make sure that all the necessary documentation was in place relating to both lesson plans and pupil progress. Oh, it made her head ache just thinking about it.

'Beatrice?' Victoria touched her arm as the three of them fell into step to walk back to their billet near the village. 'What's wrong? Is it only Mr Rimmington's visit or is there something else?'

Despite the turmoil in Beatrice's stomach, she masked her unease with a practised smile. 'It is only that we shall have extra work to prepare for his visit.' She glanced around Hazelbury's tidy high street lined with brick- and flint-fronted buildings. Here, in this quiet corner of North Norfolk, it was almost possible to forget the war, unless a military lorry rumbled through the village crossroads or aeroplanes thundered overhead.

'Beatrice?' Nell's usually meek voice was even smaller and more tentative than usual. 'If Miss Hopson said anything else, you can tell us, you know. We're all in it together, remember?'

Beatrice *did* remember. She'd said the same thing often enough herself. However, if not for the war, Canadian-born Victoria, and Nell, who'd grown up in London's East End, would never have been anything more to her than professional colleagues. Instead, after being evacuated here with their school in September 1939, and almost a year of living and working together, they'd become unlikely friends.

'Nell's right and we want to help.' As Victoria touched Beatrice's arm again, the large sapphire and surrounding diamonds in the engagement ring she'd received the previous week sparkled in the late-summer sunshine.

'I know you do.' Her friends perhaps knew Beatrice better than she did herself. Victoria especially was so friendly, warm and without guile that despite intending not to, Beatrice often let her guard down. 'I'm afraid it's nothing that either of you *can* help with. Miss Hopson merely spoke about the war and it's unsettled me.'

'The news is perfectly horrid, isn't it?' Nell's voice quavered. 'Gosh, I get scared when I think about London.

We've had enough alarms round here already. My dad says he'd rather die than live to see the Germans take over.' Surrounded by thick dark-brown hair cut into a stylish bob, Nell's pale face flushed as if she'd said too much.

Behind Nell's back, Beatrice exchanged a worried glance with Victoria. There was nothing they could say to reassure Nell that everything would be fine, and the days of thinking the war would soon be over were long gone.

'Oh look, there's Mrs Meldrum.' To Beatrice's relief, Victoria diverted the conversation. 'I wonder if she's heard anything further about us going blackberry picking and making jam at Whittleton Hall? Mrs Bertram mentioned it to me at the last W.I. meeting. It would be good fun. Almost like a party with all us women together.'

'Indeed.' Beatrice tightened her grip on her school satchel. If only she could be more like Victoria, who was so self-assured and always seemed to know the right thing to say and do. And who had an instinctive understanding of and empathy for timid Nell that Beatrice lacked. A quality Victoria shared with Mrs Bertram, wife to a decorated army major and gracious chatelaine of Whittleton Hall, a nearby country house of the kind Beatrice had grown up in.

'Oh, Miss Wentworth.' Wearing a grey-green Women's Voluntary Service summer dress, Mrs Meldrum approached them at the corner by the post office like one of His Majesty's ships going full steam ahead. Beneath her uniform hat her grey hair, worn in tight curls, was rigid despite the breeze and she carried a large black handbag and shopping basket. 'You'll never guess what I heard.' Her gaze darted from Beatrice to Victoria and Nell.

Although another one who was always up on village gossip and, in Beatrice's opinion, took too much unnecessary interest in school matters, Mrs Meldrum nevertheless had a kind heart. Along with her four sons serving in the Forces, she also more than did her bit contributing to the W.I., Red Cross, church, the W.V.S. and numerous other worthy causes.

'No, I'm sure I couldn't guess.' The rolling in Beatrice's stomach intensified.

Good heavens, she had to get a grip. It was unlike her to be so nervy. However, whilst she was happy for Victoria, her friend and colleague's recent engagement had reminded Beatrice of too many things she tried not to think about. In addition to what, in a rare moment of frankness, Miss Hopson had said about the anticipated aerial assault on London, Beatrice was more than *unsettled*. For the first time, she was truly afraid of what might befall them in the coming months – and for what little remained of tradition, decorum and human decency.

'Whittleton Hall is being requisitioned for military use much sooner than Major and Mrs Bertram expected.' Mrs Meldrum's usually florid cheeks were colourless. 'It's to become a convalescent hospital for wounded servicemen. Can you imagine? That beautiful home being used in such a way – but I suppose we must see it as a necessary sacrifice in these perilous times.'

As Mrs Bertram tutted, Beatrice's head spun and she swallowed the bile that rose in the back of her throat. Another beloved family home sacrificed at the altar of war. More broken lives with a plethora of visible and invisible wounds. Scars transcending the war itself, echoing across generations. However, she must remember that this convalescent hospital was nothing to do with her. She only had to nod and smile for a few minutes and then continue on her way.

'The postmistress said Mrs Bertram is recruiting volunteers for writing letters, kitchen work, making tea and such.' Mrs Meldrum took a piece of paper and pencil from her handbag. 'I offered to help by collecting names. We can count on you three, of course.' It was a statement, not a question. 'With our country in such dreadful danger, it is even more important for us all to come together and do our bit, isn't it? And you, Miss Wentworth, can be of particular assistance. I understand from the vicar that you served in the V.A.D. in the last war?'

Beatrice put a hand to her mouth, memories she'd tried to bury deep assailing her. The broken soldiers she'd cared for in the Great War as that girlish member of the Voluntary Aid Detachment. As a V.A.D. she'd only been a civilian nursing assistant, but she'd still seen horrors she couldn't forget. Yet it was her duty, and in wartime especially, everyone had to do their part. So once again she must pretend to be a stalwart soldier on the home front with a cheerful smile so as not to let the side down.

Alex would have wanted her to help, of that she had no doubt. Like Beatrice, Alexander James George Athill had been raised at a particular time, and in a particular class, where expectations of one's moral duty and responsibility reigned supreme. And for that, he'd got himself killed in what they'd all then thought would be the war to end all wars. She'd sacrificed the person most dear to her – and for what? Only to be embroiled in another awful conflict scant decades later. How could she face a convalescent hospital full of young men like Alex? Young men that, if the two of them had been able to marry, could have been her own sons?

'Time permitting, we shall help in whatever ways we can manage.' Ignoring Mrs Meldrum's question about her V.A.D. work, Beatrice forced the words from her mouth, conscious of Victoria and Nell giving her sideways glances of suppressed alarm. 'However, our immediate priority must be preparing for an upcoming visit from a school inspector from the London County Council.' As she spoke, Beatrice was well aware that the inspector's visit would only account for the next few weeks, and it was unlikely the hospital would be up and running so soon.

'I understand. Education must come first.' Still, even as Mrs Meldrum nodded, she waved away what Beatrice had said as if it were as inconsequential as a fly. 'However, I shall add your names to the list, nonetheless. You, Miss McKaye, will, I am sure, take a particular interest because of your attachment to Mr Grainger. Writing letters, providing a bit of conversation and company for men whose families are far away. I expect you'd want some kind soul to do the same for your fiancé should he ever find himself in similar distress.'

'I… certainly.' At Beatrice's side, Victoria gave an almost imperceptible gulp, and her bright expression dimmed as she undoubtedly considered the dangers Louis Grainger, a Royal Navy officer, faced.

'I also thought that the school children could put on some form of entertainment for the home's patients.' Undaunted, Mrs Meldrum turned back to Beatrice. 'What about a Nativity? The little ones would be ever so sweet. Miss Potter is such a marvel with sewing and would, I'm sure, be able to make costumes. It would be splendid, don't you think?'

Nell's mouth opened and closed and she studied her shoes, cowed as always by Mrs Meldrum's forcefulness.

'I shall write to Mrs Bertram this evening for more particulars.' Beatrice gave Mrs Meldrum her best quelling look. The same one that her mother would once have used to reprimand a maid or gardener. 'As you will appreciate, we already have more than enough to do. Given the myriad commitments to our pupils' welfare beyond the classroom and our ongoing war work, any time we can give to the convalescent hospital must of necessity be limited.' With another severe look, Beatrice gestured to Victoria and Nell to follow her. 'Good day, Mrs Meldrum.'

'You didn't half tell her.' Nell's voice was awed, almost a whisper, as she scurried after Beatrice and Victoria towards the lane that led to Hazelbury Manor, the once grand family seat of the Grainger family where the three teachers were billeted. 'I could never be that brave.'

'Although I appreciate you sticking up for us, I suppose we can find time to help.' Victoria sighed. 'Mrs Meldrum's right. I'd want someone to do the same for Louis.'

'If it's only for a few hours a week, we could manage,' Nell said. 'And if it's a convalescent hospital, the men will be getting better, won't they?'

'One would expect so, yes.' Beatrice exchanged another covert glance with Victoria. Victoria was thirty and the daughter of a Scottish-Canadian doctor who'd served in the last war. She couldn't be completely ignorant of wartime injuries. Yet neither she nor Nell could have seen or experienced what Beatrice herself had, and she was even now kept awake at night by memories of the indescribable horror, loss and ruined lives of the last conflict.

As the other two went ahead – Victoria to check the post for a letter from Louis, and Nell to walk the Graingers' dog – Beatrice lingered in the narrow lane. Between the high hedgerows perfumed with summer flowers and the clear blue sky above, she felt safe, protected.

Nevertheless, she already knew that safety was an illusion. She could not even pretend that it existed. She was different from Victoria and Nell. She'd already seen too much of life to share their optimism. When this war was over, no matter the outcome, they'd still have time for marriage and families. And even if the worst happened and Louis were to be killed, Victoria could return to her family in Canada and perhaps find a husband there.

But if the conflict dragged on, what would Beatrice be left with? She'd focused on her career because with her father, brothers and the family fortune gone, she'd had to support herself and her mother. She'd also clung to the idea of becoming a headmistress because, before the war had upended everything again, it was the one thing in her life she'd thought she had some control over. Like her dream of that imaginary cottage by the sea that she was scrimping and saving to buy, helped along by a small legacy from a great-aunt. A place to which she could retire and regain the stability and security that had so cruelly been torn away from her.

Near her feet at the grassy verge, several bees buzzed over a patch of brilliant-yellow goldenrod, intent on gathering nectar. As she continued along the lane, a butterfly soared on fragile wings, and a brown field mouse scuttled across to burrow deep into the hedge. Although she'd begun her life like a butterfly, perhaps she had become more worker bee or agile, adaptable field mouse who found sufficient joy and contentment in doing her duty.

She picked up her pace to rejoin Victoria and Nell turning into Hazelbury Manor's tree-lined drive. Like everyone else, she'd do her part – although that did not include being bossed around by Mrs Meldrum.

Beatrice straightened her shoulders and suppressed a smile. Maybe parts of the woman she used to be were still there. It was useless to ruminate over what might have been. She'd settled into Hazelbury and would continue to make the best of it. Hitler was beyond the pale and had to be stopped. Even if it meant she had to face a convalescent hospital or organise a Nativity play.

Chapter Two

Friday, 23 August 1940

'A spade is used to dig, Ralph. Not to toss soil at others.' Two days later, Beatrice was working with the children in the allotment gardens behind the village hall. 'Well done, Ruby.' She gave the pallid, spindly girl holding out a basket of ripe tomatoes an approving smile.

'Ta, Miss.' Ruby's smile was shy, almost frightened.

'Thank you, Miss Wentworth,' Beatrice corrected, making the reproof as gentle as she could.

Ruby nodded as she repeated what Beatrice had said.

Although the North London neighbourhood from which Park Road School drew its pupils was largely middle-class and prosperous, a reorganisation in 1939 had extended the catchment area to include a pocket of poorer families. Ruby, who'd only arrived in Hazelbury a few weeks before, came from one of the latter, as did Ralph, who'd been part of the first evacuation in September 1939.

'Ralph.' Beatrice raised her voice. 'Stop bothering the girls. If you can't make yourself useful, I shall find something else for you to do. Extra arithmetic problems?'

'Yes, Miss Wentworth. And no, Miss Wentworth. About the arithmetic, I mean.' With a cheeky grin, Ralph resumed digging to prepare the ground to plant the radishes and winter cabbages that would replace the vegetables now being harvested and yield extra food for the coming winter.

'That boy is incorrigible.' Beatrice spoke under her breath to Victoria who'd joined her in the allotments. 'I appreciate you've done your best with him, but I shall have my work cut out for me when he officially moves up to the juniors next month.'

'He's not so bad.' Victoria gestured to their London pupils working alongside the young villagers. 'Along with Ralph, you'll also have Diana.' She indicated the fair-haired girl currently helping several of the smaller infants harvest cucumbers. 'Albert as well.' She inclined her head to the boy planting radish seeds in the holes Ralph had dug. 'I'll miss all three of them.'

Beatrice's heart squeezed as her gaze settled on Diana. She'd welcome the girl to her classroom as she would any other child, but also because her mother, Mary Foster-Dalton, formerly Mary Athill, was Alex's younger sister and, in their schooldays, had been Beatrice's dearest friend.

'You can visit. They'll only be in the village school. It's not far.' She made her tone crisp to hide an unexpected rush of emotion. If things had been different, she would have been Diana's Aunt Beatrice.

'I know.' Victoria gave her a small smile. 'That's the problem with teaching. I get so attached to my pupils and then they grow up and move on.'

'If only that were all we had to worry about.' Beatrice held back an unladylike groan. 'Our stock order is still delayed. I'm aware there's a paper shortage, but what will we do if the children don't have anything to write on when the school inspector visits?'

'Don't fuss. I expect he'll understand.' Victoria's expression was consoling. 'We have enough chalks for them to share, and unlike me in the village hall with the infants, in the school you have a blackboard.'

'True.' As always, Beatrice had to remind herself to be grateful for small mercies. 'It's almost time for the bell. Where's Nell got to?' Beatrice scanned the allotments, but amongst the lush rows of plants there was no sign of her colleague's wide-brimmed straw hat, which Nell had trimmed with a purple velvet ribbon tied into a bow at the back.

'Here I am.' Nell appeared behind them. 'Sorry, I was chasing after two of my new boys. Some of that lot from the village are the most dreadful imps. Collecting bomb fragments, they were. You can be sure I confiscated the one they found.' Nell removed a small piece of twisted metal from her dress pocket. 'I told them I'd put it in the school's metal recycling collection. I take great satisfaction in knowing this horrid reminder of German destruction will go to make aircraft for the RAF.'

Beatrice nodded as she retrieved the school bell from a table they'd moved out of the village hall and rang it. With a shorter summer holiday due to the war, for this first part of the autumn term, she and the other teachers took their pupils outdoors for the afternoons as frequently as the weather permitted. They combined lessons for the entire school, including gardening, games and country rambles.

'Miss Wentworth?' Albert, a boy of nearly eight, with straw-blond hair and a freckled face, tugged at Beatrice's cardigan sleeve. 'I heard the vicar say Whittleton Hall's going to be a hospital. Where will Major and Mrs Bertram go?'

'To one of the estate cottages, I expect.' Beatrice stood at the rear of the crocodile of children filing into the hall whilst Victoria and Nell had already gone indoors to rejoin Ivy Byrne, the vicarage maid, who worked half-days as Victoria's assistant with the infants. 'Wash your hands before you go home. You don't want to make more work for Mrs Russell.' Albert, his older brother Wilf, and Diana were billeted at Hazelbury's vicarage, and Mr Russell, the kindly vicar, was a good influence on the boys, Albert especially.

'But how will the Hall become a hospital with them fancy paintings and rugs and gold-coloured curtains?' Albert lingered at Beatrice's side as the last of the children disappeared into the hall without him. 'I remember when we went there, Miss McKaye said we couldn't touch nothing. Only look with our eyes.'

'Miss McKaye was quite right. The Hall's more valuable furnishings will be packed away and stored.' The Bertrams' treasured possessions wouldn't be sold, their family's memories crushed under an auctioneer's hammer as Beatrice's had been. 'Run along and don't forget those cucumbers for Mrs Russell. They're in a basket on Miss McKaye's desk.'

'Yes, Miss Wentworth.' Albert darted into the hall's kitchen where there was a basin and ewer of water.

In the sudden silence, Beatrice looked around to make sure that no child had been left behind. At school, she was usually too busy to think of anything except her work, but now there was no escaping the task she'd tried to avoid since Mrs Bertram's letter had arrived in yesterday afternoon's post.

A letter in response to her own, saying that if convenient, Mrs Bertram would expect Beatrice at Whittleton Hall after school today to discuss plans for the convalescent hospital, and suggesting how the teachers and pupils might support its work. A letter that had heartily endorsed Mrs Meldrum's idea of organising a Nativity play to bring Christmas cheer to the men in hospital, and offering Mrs Bertram's full support.

As she collected her handbag and satchel from the table that served as Victoria's desk, Beatrice gritted her teeth. Whittleton Hall wasn't a convalescent hospital yet. There would be nothing and no one there to spark any unpleasant or disturbing memories. It had stopped raining, and despite the low cloud, she'd enjoy the fresh air and her bicycle ride there and back along verdant country lanes. It was also Friday, so there were two days off school to anticipate.

She had nothing to fear.

–

'I'm delighted you could join me.' Three-quarters of an hour later, Mrs Bertram ushered Beatrice into the large drawing room at Whittleton Hall, which held the gold damask curtains, paintings and Flemish tapestry rug that had so impressed Ralph. 'As you can see, it's all hands to the pump, as my father would have said. *His* father was a Navy man.' She gestured towards the white-haired butler, who carried a wooden crate, and Major Bertram, who was perched on a ladder removing crystal pendants from a chandelier before handing them to a young woman dressed in the brown corduroy breeches and fawn-coloured shirt of the Women's Land Army. 'Here.' She indicated an alcove with several chairs around a small table. 'We won't be disturbed or get in the way of the workers.'

Beatrice sat down in a rose-patterned chintz armchair while her hostess, in a plain, pale-grey day dress almost the same colour as her hair, took one across from her. A Chinese lacquered tray held tea items on the table between them. A nineteenth-century French mantel clock ticked from a nearby desk, sounding a rhythmic protest against the disorder and activity.

'When do you have to leave the Hall?' Beatrice glanced around the drawing room, where a sofa rested on one side against a pale-gold wall.

'By tomorrow evening.' For an instant, Mrs Bertram's implacable mask slipped, and she sounded younger, vulnerable even. How could she not, when faced with the imminent loss of her home?

'But that's…' Beatrice stopped and pressed her lips together so Mrs Bertram wouldn't see them tremble.

'Yes, we had four days' notice. I gather that some families only had three so we must consider ourselves fortunate.' At Beatrice's nod, Mrs Bertram added milk to a turquoise and gold-rimmed teacup and poured tea from a matching pot. 'It's not unexpected that the government needs our home, and we'll be comfortable enough in what was the head gardener's cottage. It's been difficult telling the remaining staff, but my dear husband managed to ensure that they'll be kept on in some capacity. After all, people will still need to eat, have laundry done, and what's left of the lawn and gardens will need to be cared for.' She darted a glance at Major Bertram who, having finished with the chandelier, was working with the butler to pack several paintings into crates.

Although she'd lived in England for going on forty years, like Victoria, Mrs Bertram had been born and raised in Canada, and in moments of stress, the accent of her home country became more pronounced.

'Still, it must be exceedingly trying for all of you.' Beatrice spoke around a lump in her throat. How 'trying' she knew all too well. 'If there's anything I can do to help...' She swallowed and the backs of her eyes burned.

'That's most kind, but no, thank you. We'll manage.' Mrs Bertram passed her a plate. 'A carrot biscuit? Rather dry, I'm afraid.'

'Aren't they all nowadays?' Although she'd never say so, Beatrice sometimes longed for the biscuits and cakes of her childhood. The mini meringues, decorated petit-fours, macaroons and sponge cakes topped with fruit and whipped cream made by their cook, which had so delighted Beatrice and her brothers.

'Indeed, yes.' Mrs Bertram's laugh was light. 'Still, we must make do. Like me, you undoubtedly remember the sacrifices we all made before.'

'Yes.' Beatrice choked down a piece of biscuit and reached for her teacup.

Unlike Beatrice, Mrs Bertram had married *her* sweetheart, and they had four children together, now grown, and had enjoyed many happy years of matrimony.

She darted another glance at Major Bertram. 'Right romantic,' is what Nell had said after hearing how he'd met and fallen in love with the pretty Canadian who'd been touring Europe and the British Isles with her mother and sister before the last war.

'Well, let me tell you more as to why I invited you here today.' Mrs Bertram moved her chair around the table and closer to Beatrice's.

Beatrice stiffened. Like Victoria, Mrs Bertram had a habit of assuming everyone would be a friend and so behaved accordingly. 'As you said in your letter, I imagine it must be to do with the convalescent hospital. As well as Mrs Meldrum's suggestion of the children putting on a Nativity play for the patients here at Christmas.' She kept her tone cool.

'Yes. Isn't Mrs Meldrum a marvel? So energetic and involved in everything. I must confess that she makes me feel quite indolent.'

Also, like Victoria, even if Mrs Bertram understood British class distinctions, she seemed inclined to forge ahead and ignore them. Whilst Mrs Meldrum had undoubtedly married up, as the saying went, her husband had owned a number of drapers' and haberdashery shops before selling them at what was reputedly a tidy profit. As such, she was not someone with whom Beatrice's family would have mixed.

'We each contribute in our own way.' Beatrice set her teacup back on its saucer with a precise click.

'Exactly.' Mrs Bertram's smile was trusting, as if the two of them were confidantes and she was prepared to unburden herself. 'When you wrote asking for more information, I was truly delighted.'

Beatrice's heart seemed to sink to the soles of her practical, black lace-up shoes. 'But Mrs Bertram, you must understand that none of we three teachers have much time to spare.'

'Say no more. You already do so much, but I'd hoped you'd be willing to make an exception. It's such a worthy cause.' Mrs Bertram touched Beatrice's wrist.

She was tactile like Victoria too. 'We do want to help. All three of us.' Beatrice took a steadying breath. She'd vowed to conquer her fears. 'A Nativity would be lovely for the children as well as the hospital patients. Goodness knows, there's little enough these days to make the Christmas season special.'

'We could involve some of the adults as well.' Mrs Bertram beamed. 'Perhaps Mrs Meldrum? Any final decisions would naturally rest with you, given you've been so involved with amateur dramatics.'

A vision of Mrs Meldrum presiding over the play as the angel Gabriel popped into Beatrice's mind, and she quashed a shudder. She'd enjoyed amateur dramatics since childhood and had joined the Hazelbury Drama Society in an attempt to become part of village life and meet some of the foster parents of her pupils informally. But now she wondered if she had been drawn to acting because it offered an acceptable way of temporarily becoming someone else.

'The first step will be to gauge interest in the village.' Beatrice made herself sound more agreeable than she felt, pushing the troubling thought of escaping her own life to the back of her mind.

Mrs Bertram nodded. 'You're highly capable, and I shall defer to your wisdom and sound judgement.'

'It's more the convalescent hospital. As you may know, I trained with the V.A.D. in the last war and… it was difficult work. I shall do my best but…' A chill surged through her, and Beatrice tried to compose herself. What was the matter with her? She prided herself on never losing control of her emotions and she'd verged on doing so twice within hardly a quarter of an hour.

'You don't need to explain. I saw more than enough myself. And my home…' Mrs Bertram looked around the rapidly emptying room. 'Even if Sidney and I are able to return here one day, it won't be the same.'

'No, it won't.' Beatrice had never spoken about the loss of her own home. 'But that's part of the reason why I want to try to assist the hospital. Even if it's only rolling bandages or clerical work for a few hours on a Saturday.' For Alex – but also for herself. Even if you tried to ignore them, fears didn't lessen, and maybe there was something to be said for facing life – and obstacles – head on. That's what Victoria did. Although at first Beatrice had been dismayed by her colleague's forthrightness, as they became friends, she grew to respect and admire her enthusiasm and positivity.

'Good.' Mrs Bertram gave her a small smile. 'Although I won't have any formal say in how hospital volunteers are assigned, I can certainly tell Matron that you'd prefer to be in an office rather than on a ward or attending an ambulance triage station.'

'You'd do that for me?' Beatrice's breath caught.

'Why not?' Was that amusement in Mrs Bertram's eyes? 'One of the advantages of growing older is that one is not daunted by matrons, no matter how starched their uniforms.'

'I see.' There was that lump in her throat again. 'Thank you, Mrs Bertram.'

'It's a pleasure, my dear. Now, tell me what you think you will need for this Nativity, and I shall do my best to help.'

As Beatrice took the notes she'd made out of her handbag, a new warmth suffused her heart.

Except for her engagement to Alex, she'd never been the sort of daughter her mother wanted. Beatrice had accepted that fact long ago, even in early childhood. Perhaps that was where her lack of confidence and the closing off of herself – her thoughts and emotions – had begun. But maybe it wasn't too late. Thanks to living and working with Victoria and Nell, she wasn't the same Beatrice who'd left London almost twelve months ago. And maybe Mrs Bertram, twenty-odd years or more her senior, could help show her the next part of the way.

Chapter Three

'I'm not certain I wish to hear the news, although I suppose I must.' With a frown, Nell pulled her chair closer to Beatrice's as they gathered around the wireless in Hazelbury Manor's wood-panelled library on Friday evening. 'After the Germans dropped a bomb on Harrow, who knows where in London could be next.'

'Harrow was likely an accident.' Miss Hetty Grainger, the elder of the two white-haired sisters with whom the three teachers were billeted, took her knitting from a floral tapestry bag. 'The Luftwaffe would hardly target an ordinary London suburb. They were undoubtedly aiming for an airfield.' She shook her head and gave Nell a reproving look. 'You must not let your imagination run rampant. The same goes for you, Addie.' She turned to her younger sister. 'Remember what Mr Churchill said in his speech to the House of Commons this week. There have been far fewer casualties in the first year of this war than the last time around.'

Except, Beatrice thought, Mr Churchill had also said that 'never was so much owed by so many to so few'. Retrieving her own knitting, Beatrice shivered. Although Britain remained poised for a German invasion, it was the brave fighter pilots and bomber crews from the Royal Air Force and other Allied nations who'd defended them against the summer's Luftwaffe aerial assault. 'We have sufficient time before the news. I want to tell you about my meeting with Mrs Bertram after school today.' She glanced around their small circle and at the empty chair between herself and Miss Addie where Victoria usually sat. 'I thought—'

'Sorry, here I am.' Victoria burst into the library with the Graingers' golden cocker spaniel, Lady, at her heels. 'Those letters to pupils' parents took longer than I expected.' She settled into her chair with a bright smile.

The Misses Grainger gave her gracious nods. Since Victoria's engagement to their great-nephew, Louis, she was considered by them to be almost family, and accorded the respect and deference due to her as their beloved great-nephew's fiancée. Whilst Miss Hetty and Miss Addie seemed to accept Louis's choice, Beatrice's mother would certainly have had something to say if one of her children had become affianced to a person so decidedly middle class as Victoria. And yet the world was changing, and somehow or other everyone had to change with it.

'Right, since we're all here, I have agreed with Mrs Bertram that we shall organise a Nativity play with our pupils, and perform it for the men and staff at the Whittleton Hall convalescent hospital.' Beatrice couldn't let any of them guess she'd been strong-armed into it or that she found Christmas more a trial than a cause for celebration. 'I also confirmed with her that the three of us would volunteer at the hospital, but only as and when our time permits. I emphasised that, as teachers, we have numerous other responsibilities.' Goodness, she sounded as severe as Miss Hetty often did. 'I hope you agree?' Now she sounded tentative, which was worse.

'A school Nativity will be lovely.' Victoria clapped her hands and dropped her knitting. 'Especially since we didn't have one last year.'

'We couldn't, not with the kiddies going back and forth between Hazelbury and London.' Nell, who was the most skilled and fastest knitter of all of them, didn't glance up from the blue scarf she was making. 'I'll start looking out bits and pieces for costumes and scenery and such.'

'I'll help you.' Miss Addie's face flushed pink with pleasure beneath her soft, white hair. 'Daddy's old brown wool overcoat might be just the thing for a donkey, don't you think, Hetty?'

'I suppose so.' Miss Hetty glanced at Beatrice. 'For the convalescent hospital itself, did Mrs Bertram say how many volunteers will be needed?'

'No, I should have asked.' Beatrice hadn't enquired because she'd been more concerned with her own feelings. 'I forgot.' Along with those unexpected emotions, it was also unlike her to be anything less than thorough.

'I am not surprised.' Miss Hetty was still studying her. With the blackout up, the library was cloaked in shadows, the only light coming from several oil lamps. 'I applaud your commitment, but it is also time for Addie and myself to become more involved in war work beyond the W.I. and Red Cross. The convalescent hospital would be—'

In the distance, the village's air-raid siren wailed, and Lady scooted beneath Miss Hetty's chair, tucking her tail between her legs.

'Lights.' Beatrice sprang to her feet as the others gathered up their knitting and began to extinguish the lamps. She clicked her torch on, ready to lead the way to the manor's cellar. 'Here, Lady.' She coaxed the trembling dog out from under the chair, affixed a lead to her collar and pointed the torch towards the door. 'All set?'

'Yes.' Nell's voice quavered as she and Victoria each took one of the older ladies' arms. 'Do you think it's another false alarm?' Nell also collected the flask with the tea she'd made earlier, forgoing their usual teapot as if half-expecting there would be a raid this evening.

'Undoubtedly.' Beatrice tried to keep the fear from her voice. 'Why would the Germans bomb Hazelbury?' Except, if like Harrow, it was an accident. They were near an air base and several bombs had fallen in the vicinity throughout the summer, but the others were depending on her. She couldn't be nervy.

Chin up. Don't let the side down. Come on, old bean.

As the siren continued to wail, she could almost hear her father's voice. He'd meant to encourage his children and maybe it had worked for her brothers, but Beatrice had been timid by nature. *Like Nell.* Her heart gave a painful thud, and she clutched Lady's lead harder.

As they left the library and walked the short distance to what had been the servants' staircase, Miss Hetty's voice rose above the siren. 'Thank you, Victoria. No, I am not at all unsteady or feeling faint. Carry on.'

Their shoes clomped on the uncarpeted stairs and Lady tugged at the lead. Two flights down, and then Beatrice opened the cellar door, the familiar dank scent greeting her. Although the space had been cleared and made into a basic shelter months ago, she didn't feel safe here. Only trapped. Her breathing sped up as she made her way to one of the wooden benches.

'Well done, Beatrice. I think that was our fastest time reaching shelter yet,' Miss Hetty said as she took charge of Lady.

'Beatrice?' Victoria sat beside her. 'Blanket and cushion?'

'Yes, no, I don't…' She gripped the edge of the bench as the cellar and Victoria's face seemed to spin around her.

'Here.' Miss Hetty sat on Beatrice's other side and put a cushion behind her back and a blanket over her knees. 'Addie, would you please find the biscuit tin? Nell, the tea flask and a cup? Breathe through your nose, Beatrice. That's right.'

Nell put a cup of tea on a small table in front of Beatrice, and the biscuit tin rattled. Nowadays, since the raids were so frequent, they kept a tin of biscuits in the cellar, replenishing it weekly.

'I'm sorry.' Beatrice raised her head and took the cup to have a sip of the strong tea, the hot liquid warming her chilled body. 'I don't know what came over me.'

'It's the ruddy Germans, they're what's coming over all of us.' Nell gave Beatrice a biscuit and gestured upwards where the sound of enemy aircraft droned overhead, interspersed with the echo of local ack-ack guns.

Beatrice stared at Nell as unexpected laughter burbled. Maybe the two of them were more alike than she'd ever considered. 'I'm all right now.'

'Splendid.' Miss Hetty's nod was brisk. 'Where's the tablecloth, Nell? I brought one down earlier – linen with Battenberg lace embroidery in a floral pattern. Our housekeeper did it when I was a girl. You can't serve tea from that dreadful bare table. I'd expect it of one of the village girls, not you. Now, how about a game of cards?' As Nell found the tablecloth, Miss Hetty produced a pack from her cardigan pocket. 'Victoria still hasn't learned to play whist properly. Sit down, Addie. There is no need to flutter about. We'll likely be here for a while.'

Beatrice straightened and pressed a hand to her forehead where a headache had begun to throb behind her temples. She should be mortified, losing her composure like that in front of the others, her colleagues and subordinates – let alone the Misses Grainger. Yet none of them had judged her or seemed unduly alarmed.

'It will be all right, you'll see,' Victoria whispered. Under the cover of starting the card game, one of her hands briefly covered Beatrice's. 'We're all facing things together, remember?'

Although it was almost a wartime mantra, for the first time Beatrice truly believed it.

Chapter Four

Monday, 26 August 1940

'No, you may not have another pencil.' On the following Monday afternoon, Beatrice shook her head at the fifth child who'd asked her for some kind of school supply in the last quarter of an hour. 'We're still short of stock so you must share.' What that meant for the school inspector's visit, Beatrice still couldn't let herself consider.

'Yes, Miss Wentworth.' The girl hesitated for several seconds, as if she wanted to say more, then turned away and went back to her desk.

Beatrice pinned a loose strand of her hair back into its knot and then glanced from the clock above the schoolroom door to her pupils, ranged in rows. The school inspector wasn't to be feared. From past experience, most of them offered advice and support, not criticism. However, this was her first official school inspection in wartime, when the usual educational expectations and administrative processes that had once governed Beatrice's professional life were upended.

She studied her pupils again. From a boy in the back row who slouched in his seat with his eyes half-closed, to a girl who chewed her pencil top and tapped one foot in a rhythmic motion, they were all tired, fretful and anxious.

Even the arts and crafts lesson she'd taken such care to plan hadn't captured their interest. It wasn't surprising – not after a weekend when both Plymouth and central London had been bombed, and aeroplanes from RAF Whittleton and the Luftwaffe had rumbled overhead for three nights running. Yet, somehow, the children had to learn and meet a prescribed standard, and it was Beatrice's responsibility to teach them.

'What is it, Jimmy?' She turned to the ten-year-old who seemed to have grown an inch or more in the past few weeks and now stood head and shoulders above the other boys his age.

'I were reading this book.' He held out the illustrated Norfolk and Suffolk travel guide Beatrice had borrowed from the manor's library to supplement their history and geography lessons. 'I'm drawing a boat, see, and I were looking for pictures.'

Jimmy Clarke, one of the local children who lived on a nearby farm, struggled with reading. Whilst Beatrice and Victoria and more recently Nell gave him extra tuition, apart from the illustrations and photographs, the guide would be well above his ability to tackle.

The three teachers had also often debated how frequently to correct the children's grammar. While at first Beatrice had attempted to correct every instance of incorrect speech, she soon learned it was futile. Although Nell was all for letting the children express themselves in the way that came most naturally – which they'd learned at home – Victoria proposed a compromise: correcting their written work but not always insisting on precision otherwise. Despite Beatrice's initial reluctance, that compromise turned out to be the right approach, even though she still had to remind herself not to interject.

'What pictures did you find in the book?'

'Some good 'uns' – Jimmy gave a solemn nod – 'but I seen there weren't nothing about Hazelbury in it. There's photographs of buildings and rivers and such from other villages, but I reckon there's history and geography right here as good as anywhere else.'

'Of course there is.' Beatrice looked out one of the tall classroom windows to see that the earlier rain had finally stopped and weak sunlight was filtering through patchy clouds. She'd been racking her brains to come up with some way for the pupils to showcase their work to the school inspector. What if they did something that also showcased Hazelbury? Since there were a number of new children recently arrived from London, such an activity would also help them settle into village life. She glanced again at the clock, which showed there was still an hour until dismissal. 'You may finish your art tomorrow. Please put away your things while I speak with Miss Potter.' Nell taught in the classroom across the hall and, from what Beatrice could hear, her pupils were similarly lethargic.

Amidst the clatter of desk lids and books and papers being stowed, Beatrice crossed the narrow corridor separating the two rooms in Hazelbury's village school and gestured to Nell.

'What's the matter?' Nell had an ink stain on her chin, chalk residue on her navy skirt and wore a harassed expression.

'Nothing. Rather, nothing out of the ordinary.' There was a great deal the matter but most of it Beatrice couldn't solve, so – as they all did these days – she tried to make the best of things. 'The rain's stopped, so let's take the children outdoors. I've had an idea.' She briefly explained the notion of a 'Hazelbury project' for the school inspector's visit. 'With the shortened holidays and longer autumn term, it's not as if we're starting more formal lessons until next week anyway, so why not?'

'Why not indeed?' Nell started as a clatter sounded from her classroom. 'We have to do something. With hardly any stock, the kiddies so upset with all the aeroplanes and hearing dreadful war news from their elders, I don't think my lot have learned anything today.'

'They'll have learned more than you think – but go on.' Beatrice waved towards the sound of raised voices coming from Nell's classroom. 'I'll meet you outdoors in a few minutes.'

As Nell ran to deal with whatever latest calamity had befallen her half of the juniors, Beatrice returned to her own classroom, put on her hat and gloves and then led the older pupils outside the school. 'Wilf and Pauline' – she gestured to two of her most studious and responsible pupils: a boy who'd been evacuated from London in September 1939, and a girl who was the daughter of a Hazelbury shopkeeper – 'I shall need your help.'

'Yes, Miss Wentworth.' Wilf nodded and then, as Nell and her class joined them, he and Pauline organised the two groups into pairs.

'Right, we are going to do something called "fieldwork".' Beatrice distributed several of the precious sheets of paper and two pencils to Wilf and Pauline. 'We shall collect information about what we see in the village and record and analyse it. We will then present our findings to Mr Rimmington, the school inspector, when he visits us from London.' If he was impressed, having such praise on her record couldn't hurt Beatrice's chances of becoming a headmistress. *After the war. But what if Hitler couldn't be stopped? What if they all ended up under Nazi rule?* No, she couldn't let herself think of such things.

A low murmur went around the assembled children. Finally, she'd reached them and, she hoped, managed to divert their attention from the large number of people who'd been killed and injured in Saturday's Plymouth bombing. Whilst she and the other teachers tried to keep talk of war out of the classroom, their older pupils – unlike the infants – had a greater understanding of what was happening in the world beyond Hazelbury. They were also more attuned to adult worries. So, from playground games to arithmetic, reading and music, there were times when, despite Beatrice's best efforts, the war seemed to infiltrate most aspects of school life.

'Observe and take turns writing down what you see.' As the children moved along the road that bordered the school, the humid August air filled with excited chatter. 'Yes, Jimmy, nature counts as much as the built environment. Yes, the Scout hut counts as a building.' She gestured to the small white cottage that sat at one corner of a country lane near the school.

'Will you ask Miss McKaye to take part with her infants?' Nell fell into step beside Beatrice as they walked behind the groups led by Wilf and Pauline.

'Certainly.' Although the teachers used first names between themselves, in front of the children they were careful to maintain formality. 'It must be an entire school affair. It will also give us an opportunity to see how our new London evacuees and village pupils work together and to consider how best to assign Nativity parts.'

During the hours she'd spent sheltering in Hazelbury Manor's cellar this past weekend, Beatrice had made additional notes and worked out several scenes. Thankfully, she hadn't had a recurrence of the terror that had seized her on Friday night or any other 'emotional spells'. As she was apt to remind herself, control of one's emotions was a result of willpower, as well as remembering that there were many others considerably worse off.

'Miss Wentworth?' Ruby, who'd started out with Victoria's infants several weeks ago but had been moved up to the juniors when they'd discovered she was older than she appeared, hovered at Beatrice's side. 'What's that there ambulance doing?'

'Where? Oh.' As they reached the village crossroads, Beatrice saw the drab, olive-coloured military vehicle with the red crosses on the sides and roof. 'It must be on its way to the convalescent hospital at Whittleton Hall.' Her heart gave a painful thud.

How many men were inside? Were they stretcher cases or able to sit up unaided? It didn't matter. They were all casualties of another terrible war – one that Beatrice had never expected to see again. For an instant, she swayed, and the children's voices faded.

'Miss Wentworth?' Nell's voice this time. 'Shall we stop here and wait in the shade? It's a scorcher, isn't it?'

'Yes, of course.' Beatrice shook her head to try to clear it. *Willpower.* 'It appears that the ambulance is the first of several.' She gripped her satchel. *Lives ruined. Families destroyed. Women bereft.* The thoughts swung back and forth like the pendulum in the longcase clock in Hazelbury Manor's gracious front hall.

'Miss?' Ruby's small, hesitant voice pulled Beatrice out of her stupor. 'What does "convalescent" mean?'

'It is someone who is recovering from an illness or injury.' Unlike Alex, these men would recover from whatever wounds the war had inflicted upon them. 'Whittleton Hall will help brave soldiers, airmen and sailors become stronger.' *God willing.*

'That's good then, aren't it?' Ruby's warm hand slid into Beatrice's gloved, yet still cold, one.

'Yes, it's very good.' She should gently and discreetly take her hand away from the child's clasp. While she'd grown used to being part of the evacuees lives beyond the schoolroom – from hospital visits to sorting issues with billets – Beatrice still kept her distance. It was right and proper. She was their teacher, not their mother, and at least some standards had to be upheld.

'I'm glad, Miss.' Ruby squeezed Beatrice's hand, and her pale-blue eyes shone. 'Do you think the poorly men would like flowers?' As Ruby said it, the word came out sounding more like 'flares'.

'I expect they would, yes.' As the last ambulance passed, Beatrice exhaled but still kept hold of the child's hand. There was something comforting about that trusting grasp, and it wasn't doing any harm. Ruby must be troubled and uncertain here in the country, away from her family and where everything was new and strange. It was Beatrice's professional duty to support her.

'Then I'll pick some flares for 'em.' Ruby gave a decisive nod with her pointed chin. 'We all got to help. That's what the vicar said in church on Sunday.'

'He did.' Beatrice's heart squeezed. 'If you pick some lovely flowers, I'll take them to the hospital for you' – it was the least she could do – 'I shall soon be volunteering there.'

'You're good, Miss.' With a final squeeze, Ruby dropped Beatrice's hand and ran to rejoin several other girls.

Although Beatrice didn't always feel that she was good – some of her uncharitable thoughts about Mrs Meldrum came to mind – she always tried to do her best.

Perhaps that was enough.

Chapter Five

Tuesday, 3 September 1940

'Ladies, ladies. If I may have your attention, please.' At the front of the village hall, Mrs Meldrum's voice rose above the clamour of chatter.

'Surely the W.I. could do without us tonight. We really shouldn't be at this meeting with so much preparation still to do.' Sitting in the middle of a row of chairs between Beatrice and Nell, Victoria's voice was low. 'Not with Mr Rimmington arriving in just over a fortnight.'

'You don't think he might come early, do you?'

'Certainly not.' Beatrice shook her head at Nell's wide-eyed pallor. 'School inspectors have a timetable. We're not the only school he'll visit in this part of Norfolk.' Although it often seemed they were isolated in Hazelbury, with thousands of evacuated children and teachers from all Britain's cities and large towns scattered across the country, a network of officials from various government departments were responsible for checking on them. 'If anything changes, I expect someone would send a letter or, in case of urgency, a telegram.'

Which might happen if the Germans turned their attention to an aerial assault on London. Beatrice prided herself on being both pragmatic and a realist. Those were useful qualities when it came to educating young minds, but they also gave her too many wakeful nights spent worrying. *Would death from a bombing be instant or would one linger in agony? What might happen to those unfortunate enough to be caught in the street or trapped under rubble in their homes?*

As the room settled again – a debate over whether it was 'better to be fat than thin' having become somewhat heated – Mrs Meldrum introduced the final item on the evening's agenda: an update on Whittleton Hall's convalescent hospital.

As their president's voice slid over her, Beatrice's thoughts wandered. That debate had been ridiculous. With food rationing, they were all thinner than before. As for the hospital, an update was hardly necessary. With ambulances and other military vehicles rolling through the village on a daily basis, Hazelbury talked of little else. At the first W.I. meeting after the August break, it would have been far more useful to discuss how they, as a village and led by the W.I., could best contribute to the government's war savings scheme.

'Miss Wentworth and the other teachers are supporting the convalescent hospital. Miss Wentworth, would you care to say a few words?'

Beatrice raised her head. Mrs Meldrum stared at her expectantly, rather like the bright-eyed red squirrel that lived in a hollow tree by the school. No, Beatrice didn't 'care to say a few words'. In truth, she'd rather not say any words at all.

People in our position must set an example, Beatrice. Her mother's voice echoed in her head. But what example did her mother set these days? Ensconced in a distant cousin's decaying Oxfordshire country house near Henley, Mrs Wentworth lived in a world of her own imagining, one which had changed little since the summer of 1914.

'Of course, Mrs Meldrum.' Beatrice stood, forced a stiff smile and gave a brief summary of the plan to celebrate the Christmas season with a school Nativity. 'We hope that by holding two performances, one here in the village hall and the other at Whittleton, our efforts will give pleasure to the men at the convalescent hospital as well as everyone in Hazelbury.' Mrs Bertram had subsequently suggested two performances, and it was a good idea. With two different audiences, they could take up a voluntary collection at each to raise money for the Red Cross or another charity.

'How delightful' – Mrs Russell, the vicar's wife, clapped her hands – 'it will certainly lift spirits at such a difficult time.' Her smile slipped. 'Mr Russell and I will be pleased to help in whatever way we can.'

With their eldest son having been killed when his plane was shot down by a German bomber earlier in the summer and no body recovered, Christmas and New Year would undoubtedly be 'a difficult time' for the vicar and his wife. Yet, as always, they thought of others before themselves and, unlike her mother, inspired Beatrice to do the same.

'The W.I. might organise a party for the patients, children and their families after the performance at Whittleton. What do you think, ladies?' Miss Addie darted a nervous glance at Miss Hetty to whom she usually deferred.

'Whilst it could not be anything of an elaborate nature, I would support such an activity.' Miss Hetty nodded. 'All in favour?' She glanced around the room at the raised hands. 'Motion carried.'

Mrs Meldrum opened and closed her mouth as if, for once, the wind had been well and truly taken out of her sails. 'I suppose that adjourns our meeting.' As she gathered up papers, she glanced at the women who'd already begun moving towards the tea urn, many congratulating Victoria on her engagement.

Although it did indeed end the meeting, in an odd way, Beatrice had a modicum of sympathy for Mrs Meldrum. She knew what it meant to be left out. That sense of exclusion, even when part of a group. She'd felt it as a child and later as a young woman, as a teacher too, having to make her way in a changed and often hostile world. The only place she'd ever truly belonged was with Alex, the childhood playmate who'd become a sweetheart as soon as they were both old enough.

'Miss Wentworth?' At Victoria's side, surrounded by well-wishers, Nell waved. 'Do come and join us.' As Beatrice reached her, Nell held out a plate. 'You must try Mrs Russell's honey biscuits. I set one aside for you. I'll get you a cuppa as well.' She lowered her voice. 'Shame on Mrs Meldrum putting you on the spot to talk about the Nativity. It's more than three months until Christmas. As if you don't have enough to think about.'

'It's all right.' Beatrice took the biscuit plate and curbed a smile at Nell's outraged expression. 'If the W.I. gets involved, we'll have more help and bring more joy to the children. In the end, that's all that matters.'

'True, but the cheek of that woman beggars belief. No, Mrs Yallop' – Nell turned away – 'I'm making a cup of tea for Miss Wentworth first. I won't be a moment.'

Beatrice wasn't the only one who'd changed since arriving in Hazelbury. Victoria was engaged, and Nell was learning to stand up for herself, but the biggest changes were the invisible ones.

Beatrice took a teacup and saucer from Nell and touched Victoria's shoulder to get her attention. 'War began a year ago today. So, to us.' She raised her cup and clinked it against Victoria's.

'To us,' Victoria and Nell murmured as they joined in the toast.

As she looked around their small circle, Beatrice's heart warmed. She was no longer alone or left out. She belonged here, with Victoria and Nell.

Chapter Six

Saturday, 7 September 1940

Four days later, on Saturday afternoon, Beatrice cycled up the long, curving drive to Whittleton Hall. Since her last visit here, the surrounding grounds had changed almost beyond recognition. Between military vehicles, tents and several Nissen huts on the front lawn, everywhere she looked it was evident that the Hall was no longer the Bertrams' home.

'Are you one of the hospital volunteers, Miss?' A fellow in a khaki uniform who hardly looked old enough to shave, let alone join up, greeted Beatrice near a green door in a wall which, she remembered from previous visits, led to the kitchen garden.

'Yes, I'm indeed a volunteer.' She dismounted from her bicycle and took a deep breath. She was here to do clerical work, nothing more.

'Leave your bike in the shed' – he gestured to what had once undoubtedly been storage for garden tools – 'then go in through the back way and ask for Matron.' The lad waved her towards the green door before an ambulance pulled up and he darted away.

Beatrice wheeled her bicycle into the shed, took her handbag and cardigan from the basket, and then made her way through the kitchen garden and into the house via a narrow, propped-open door she'd never encountered on previous visits, when she had entered by the front door. Coming into a corridor with a stone-flagged floor, she paused to try to get her bearings. She'd only ever been 'upstairs' at Whittleton Hall but, judging from the clatter of pans and voices, she must be near the kitchen.

She looked around, unsure of which way to go. If Victoria or Nell could have come with her, she'd have felt more at ease. However, Victoria was giving Jimmy Clarke extra reading tuition and Nell was baking a cake for a young people's meeting at the church.

Beatrice straightened her shoulders beneath the short-sleeved, pale-blue shirtwaist day dress with its delicate lace-trimmed collar. Nell had made the dress from fabric Miss Addie had found in Hazelbury Manor's attic. Even before the war, it had been years since Beatrice had had a new dress, so this one would have been a novelty anyway. But, used to receiving a cousin's cast-offs in colours and styles that, albeit still serviceable, rarely suited her, Beatrice had hardly recognised herself when she looked at her reflection in her glass-fronted wardrobe earlier.

'Are you lost, then?'

She turned at the female voice, ready to say she wasn't lost, but then hesitated. Maybe not asking for help when she needed it had held her back. And maybe part of this new start meant she needed to open herself up to others as Victoria did. 'I'm here to volunteer in the office, so yes, I may be lost.'

The brown-haired woman looked to be near Beatrice's age and wore the blue-grey dress, white apron and cap with a red cross that designated her as a nurse in the

Voluntary Aid Detachment. 'Come with me.' She had a broad Norfolk accent and gave Beatrice a cheery smile. 'I'm new as well. Only started yesterday, so I'm still training. I live in Whittleton. You?'

'Hazelbury.' Beatrice returned the smile. Whittleton was the village several miles from the Hall and adjacent to a large RAF base of the same name.

'This way.' The trainee nurse guided her towards a stone staircase. 'Straight up the stairs and then to the right. The office is the first door. You should find Matron or Sister there.'

'Thank you.' Beatrice paused to introduce herself, but the woman had already disappeared. Although the V.A.D. trainee wasn't who Beatrice's mother would have called 'our sort', Beatrice had intended to be sociable – and that was what counted.

At the top of the stairs, she reached the main reception hall. The flower-filled Chinese cloisonné vases had disappeared, along with most of the ancestral portraits – lighter spaces on the walls marking where they'd hung. Muddy footprints marred the black-and-white chequerboard-tiled floor, and an empty stretcher sat in front of the massive front doors, open on this warm day. Outdoors, army vehicles and ambulances parked on the gravel drive disgorged military staff and patients.

Turning right, Beatrice glanced at one of the few remaining paintings: a mountain scene with rugged peaks rising into clouds, surrounded by an ornate gold frame. The Scottish Highlands? She stepped closer to try to make out the artist's name. As a keen, although largely self-taught artist, she thought the piece looked Victorian. Since she didn't recognise the signature as that of any well-known artist, perhaps it had been painted by a member of Major Bertram's family. She squinted and was about to retrieve her spectacles from her handbag for a better look when a cacophony of voices sounded outside the front door.

All talking at once, a grey-haired nursing sister and several men in British Army uniform brushed past Beatrice, and she shrank against the wall so as not to be knocked over.

The voices came closer and Beatrice clutched her cardigan and handbag as her entire body froze. She should leave immediately, but her feet seemed stuck to the floor. Aircraft rumbled overhead, almost drowning out the voices and the clang of an ambulance bell.

'Oh, here you are. I'd wondered where you'd got to.' The door to Beatrice's right opened and Mrs Bertram came out of what she assumed was the office. 'I walked up to the Hall to welcome you and… are you all right?'

'Fine, thank you.' Beatrice forced the words out.

'I wanted to introduce you to some of the staff. I've been recruited, as you can see.' Mrs Bertram pointed to her own V.A.D. uniform.

Beatrice swallowed. Even the sight of that uniform evoked things she'd rather forget. *A boy of eighteen, the son of a family friend, swathed in bandages with just his eyes visible. Permanently disfigured due to debris from an exploding shell. An officer she'd danced with at a ball, his face burned beyond recognition by mustard gas.*

And Alex. She'd been on duty wearing that uniform when the telegram from his father had come. Fearless Alex. Was that what had got him killed? He'd been determined to keep his men safe, his commanding officer had said, so he'd left the trench first and that move had proved deadly.

'Are you and the major settled in the cottage?' As long as she chatted about ordinary things Beatrice truly would be fine, so what she'd said wouldn't be a lie.

'As settled as we'll ever be, I expect. It's rather a squash but we're managing. Sidney says it's like being in barracks, so he's in his element.' Mrs Bertram glanced at the front door and then back at Beatrice. 'Matron's doing rounds, but why don't you come into the office with me and I'll—'

'You over there? Can you give us a hand?' A man's voice rang out, seemingly to hail them.

'Of course.' Mrs Bertram moved towards the entryway, ushering Beatrice with her. 'How may we assist?' As the two of them stood inside the open front door, the St John Ambulance crew carried several injured men on stretchers up the steps.

Sweat dripped down the back of Beatrice's neck and her breath stuck in her throat. Whittleton Hall was supposed to be a convalescent hospital for men who'd been discharged from more acute care. Not a place which received emergency cases.

'What on earth's happened?' Mrs Bertram's voice was calm and controlled and she stood as straight as an officer reporting for duty.

'Accident at the air base, ma'am. We brought the lads here as one of the fellows might not make it to hospital in Norwich. A medic should arrive shortly.' The first ambulance crewman gestured as the nursing sister, who'd reappeared, directed him to what had once been the dining room.

Already rolling up her sleeves, Mrs Bertram glanced at Beatrice. 'They're short-staffed. I hate to ask but, like me, you were trained in the last war. There are several spare uniforms in the office: one's sure to fit you. I have to set an example, you understand?'

Once again, her mother's voice reverberated in her head. It was also Beatrice's duty, no matter how difficult and unpleasant.

-

After what felt like hours, but was only about ten minutes later, Beatrice, dressed in a V.A.D. uniform of her own, stood at the top of Whittleton Hall's imposing front steps waiting for the medic the St John Ambulance crewman had mentioned. *The uniform was a shield, a form of protection, and the real Beatrice was somewhere else.* As long as she kept that reminder at the forefront of her mind, she'd be all right.

'No, you may not park there. That space is reserved for the doctor.' She marched down the steps and waved at the driver of a small, mud-spattered Morris saloon. With four doors and under all the mud and dark-green paint, it was the kind of car Beatrice could imagine her brothers driving when out on estate business. *If either of them had lived long enough.* No, she couldn't let her mind go there either. Not now, not ever – especially here. 'You must not have heard me.' Approaching the driver's side, she gesticulated at the dirty window. 'There are plenty of spaces to park elsewhere and—'

'Keep your hair on.' The driver's door was flung open and a tall, hatless man with windblown brown hair clambered out of the vehicle. 'I *am* the doctor' – he retrieved a battered black medical bag and gestured to it – 'and I had a devil of a time getting here.' He slammed the door and sprinted lightly up the front steps, taking them two at a time. 'If you'd be so kind as to show me to my patients?'

'Of course.' Her face burning, Beatrice trailed in his wake. 'Do forgive me. I was expecting one of the local doctors or someone from RAF Whittleton.' She knew all the local doctors – if not personally, then at least by sight – and an RAF doctor from Whittleton would have been in uniform and in a military vehicle. And surely no doctor would have turned up in a white, open-necked shirt and blue trousers torn at the hem like this stranger?

'I'm Dr David Stanley. From London.' As they entered the house, he spoke to her over one shoulder. 'Or rather, I *was* from London.' He stopped near the dining room door. 'Is there somewhere I can wash? I had a puncture and had to change a tyre and, as you can see…' He held up his grease-stained hands, finely shaped with long, tapered fingers.

'Certainly.' Beatrice's stomach lurched and her face grew hotter. She'd been wrong about him not being a doctor and too quick to jump to conclusions. In fact, although painful to admit, she'd behaved exactly as her mother would have, not giving the man any benefit of the doubt.

She wasn't her mother. Wouldn't be like her mother. She was here. Her mother wasn't.

As Beatrice took Dr Stanley through the main hall and into the dining room, which had been set up as a makeshift hospital ward, she also studied him covertly. On closer inspection, his brown hair was flecked with silver, and on his squarish face, lines ran between his nose and mouth and across his forehead. He wasn't in the first flush of youth and must be near her own age, a man in his middle years. Whilst doctors had initially been a reserved occupation, due to a shortage of medical staff for the armed forces, since April they had also been subject to being called up. Was that why he was here?

Mrs Bertram left the side of one of the young men who'd been brought in on the stretchers. 'Oh, thank goodness, Dr Stanley.' As she reached them, she lowered her voice. 'I'm afraid Aircraftman Griffiths is in a bad way. Before he slipped into unconsciousness, he was delirious and calling for his mother, poor chap. He's only a boy. Sister and I did what we could but…' She took the doctor over to a basin and ewer sitting on a sideboard and darted a glance at Beatrice. 'I see you've met Miss Wentworth. She is assisting us this afternoon.'

'We've not been formally introduced.' Water splashed as the doctor scrubbed his hands with carbolic soap and then rolled up his shirtsleeves to wash his lower arms as well.

'Miss Wentworth is a teacher in Hazelbury. She was supposed to be helping in the office, but since she trained as a V.A.D. in the last war, well, we all have to do what we can, don't we?'

'Indeed.' Dr Stanley's voice was brisk. 'Gown?' He held out his arms for Mrs Bertram to cover almost his entire body with a voluminous white surgical robe. 'Can someone tell me what happened?'

'If I may, sir?' The first ambulance crewman, who was stocky with a ruddy face, stepped forwards. 'Two aircraft collided mid-air and crashed. On a training exercise they were.' His bushy eyebrows furrowed. 'Me and my crew had just finished delivering first-aid instruction to a group in Whittleton, so we saw the whole thing. Lucky we were nearby but…' He bowed his head. 'The medic on the base had been called out earlier, so there weren't anyone but several nurses and us lot to help. We treated the lads as best we could in the field where they fell and brought the worst-off ones here.'

Dr Stanley nodded. 'Good work. I'll take over.' He scanned the row of cots with patients lined up along one of the dining-room walls, several V.A.D.s – including the trainee whom Beatrice had crossed paths with earlier – moving quietly between them. 'AC Griffiths first, I expect?'

'Yes, Doctor.' The nursing sister bustled towards the cot at the nearest end of the row. 'From what I can gather, he was thrown from the aircraft's tail when it broke apart on impact. Dreadful business.' Her plump face creased into a grimace.

'Miss Wentworth?' Mrs Bertram touched Beatrice's arm. 'If you could assist me please, in making sure all the surgical instruments are ready for use? I made a start but was then needed elsewhere.' She inclined her head towards the cot where Dr Stanley was already examining his patient.

Beatrice made her frozen limbs move, aware of the guttural moans and cries emanating from the various cots, juxtaposed with Dr Stanley's voice asking more questions and issuing short, urgent instructions to the sister, now joined by Matron. 'Will Aircraftman Griffiths pull through, do you think?' she asked. Reaching the white-draped table where various medical supplies had been set out – some still in cases to be unpacked – Beatrice turned her back on the men in the cots.

'If he does, it will be thanks to Dr Stanley.' Across from her, Mrs Bertram consulted a typewritten list. 'He's from University College Hospital in London. Very skilled and an all-round first-rate fellow, my husband says. Up on the latest research and techniques as well. He's even published papers in *The Lancet*.'

What was a man like him doing here? Perhaps he had some connection with Major Bertram. However, his accent hadn't sounded like that of a Londoner. More northern on certain words, Yorkshire maybe? But the inflection was muted, suggesting he'd lived in the south of England for some time.

At a scream, Beatrice turned, dropping the bandages she'd picked up.

'Morphine, please. And can someone hold this lad's hand until we get him into theatre? If there is one.' Dr Stanley's voice was steady, with no hint of the impatience he'd shown upon arrival.

'I will.' New resolve rose up inside Beatrice, giving her the courage she needed. She glanced at Mrs Bertram. 'If you can manage here, I'll hold Aircraftman Griffiths's hand and assist in theatre as necessary.'

'Are you certain?' Surprise flashed across Mrs Bertram's face.

'Yes, I am.' For herself – as well as Alex, her brothers and poor Griffiths – she needed to show that London doctor what Beatrice Wentworth was made of.

Chapter Seven

Monday, 9 September 1940

'Try not to worry. Ruminating over what might have happened does not do you or your family any good.' Beatrice glanced at Nell's grey, drawn face as the three teachers walked to school together on Monday morning. Despite the mellow golden haze of the fields, pale blue sky and the usual country sounds from birds and nearby cattle, everything was far from ordinary.

'If something had happened to my family, I'd have had a telegram, don't you think?' Nell's mouth was pinched.

'Of course. I'm sure your mum and dad and brothers and sisters are fine.' On Beatrice's other side, Victoria was quick to reassure the younger woman.

Beatrice pressed her lips together so she wouldn't say anything to distress Nell further. At the weekend, the Luftwaffe had launched their long-anticipated aerial attack on London and, from everything they'd heard so far, casualties and damage to homes and businesses were high.

'Now, more than ever, we must keep our classrooms a safe and comforting space for the children. If compelled, we shall have to supply whatever facts we are certain of, but it is our duty to discourage rumours and idle gossip.' Was that what their headmistress, Miss Hopson, would say? Beatrice didn't know – but it was what she herself believed and, without other guidance, she had to show leadership. As the vicar and Mrs Russell had done at church yesterday, and Mrs Bertram and Dr Stanley on Saturday at the convalescent hospital. Even the Misses Grainger, who, seemingly galvanised by the prospect of Mrs Meldrum 'taking over and getting ideas above her station', as Miss Hetty put it, were throwing themselves into war work and village life with new and unexpected vengeance.

Yet, despite so many worthy examples, since Saturday afternoon – although they'd only exchanged a handful of words, none of them personal – Beatrice had found herself thinking of the new doctor more than was wise. She restrained a shiver at the memory of the badly injured airman and how she'd held his hand and, with no thought of herself, done whatever Dr Stanley and Matron had asked to try to keep him alive.

And when she'd left Whittleton Hall in the cool, purple dusk, she'd breathed a silent prayer heavenwards. If there truly was a God – although after the last war she was no longer certain – she'd prayed he would let Aircraftman Griffiths live or, if not, give him a merciful death.

'Sorry. What did you say, Victoria?' Until recently, Beatrice had always been focused and not easily distracted, but since hearing about the convalescent hospital at Whittleton Hall, she'd been preoccupied and, after Saturday, off balance even. While she'd tried to tell herself the emotional upheaval was because of the London bombings, she'd already been flustered and decidedly unlike herself before those news reports came through. No, it was being at Whittleton Hall, the encounter with Dr

Stanley and then that inexplicable, impulsive offer to assist with surgery. Whatever had she been thinking? She hadn't thought – that was certain – and although she'd held her nerve, it was an experience she had no wish to recall.

'I asked if you thought the school inspector will still visit? Given, you know... recent events.' Victoria darted a sideways glance at Nell.

'Since Mr Rimmington is not due until next week, I suppose we shall have to wait and see what may happen,' Beatrice said. 'For the present, we will continue as planned with the fieldwork project and all our other work.'

Would the Germans continue to bomb London, or would they direct their attention elsewhere? As with Nell's parents and siblings, someone would presumably send a telegram if one of their pupils' families had been injured or killed, or if Park Road School was damaged or destroyed. In the meantime, it was no good imagining the worst – which, in the middle of the night and despite the wise advice she regularly gave Nell and Victoria, Beatrice was all too prone to do.

'Miss Wentworth?' In the village proper, at the junction where Victoria turned to go to the village hall and Beatrice and Nell continued on to the school, a male voice stopped her.

'Yes?' She put a gloved hand to her head to straighten her hat. 'Oh, Dr Stanley. Good morning.' As he stopped in front of the teachers and tipped his own hat, Beatrice summoned a stiff but welcoming smile and introduced him to Victoria and Nell. 'Is there any news about Aircraftman Griffiths?'

'He's holding his own. Under other circumstances, I'd transfer him to a proper hospital for specialist care, but it's too risky at present for him to travel anywhere.'

'I understand.' More than Dr Stanley knew. Alex had also needed specialist hospital care, something unavailable to him in the muddy trenches of the Western Front. And when proper medical help finally arrived, it was too late. 'What about his family?'

'Matron reached his mother, and Mrs Griffiths travelled from Cardiff yesterday.' An unexpected smile softened what Beatrice had first thought was a certain taciturn severity in Dr Stanley's features. 'One must never underestimate the positive impact a mother's love and care may have on a patient. Modern medicine can only do so much, but mothers – well, they often work miracles.'

Some mothers – but not Beatrice's. Despite trying to check the mean-spirited thought, a snippet from one of her mother's recent letters popped into Beatrice's mind.

> *Now, more than ever, you must be mindful of whom you associate with and keep your distance from inferiors. I should hardly have to remind you that one does not make friends of the lower classes or confide in them. Whilst circumstances have forced you together with Miss McKaye and Miss Potter, you need not take such obvious pleasure in Miss McKaye's engagement or Miss Potter's domestic capabilities. It is most unseemly, Beatrice, and I expect better of you.*

'Mrs Griffiths coming to see her son so quickly – that's good news, then.' She forced the memory of her mother's letter away to focus on Dr Stanley. Why hadn't Beatrice noticed his eyes? A warm hazel, were they flecked with springtime green, autumn gold or both? And wearing a smart suit and tie, and with his face clean-shaven, he looked eminently respectable.

'Let's say I'm cautiously hopeful. Thank you again for all your assistance on Saturday. I'm most grateful.' With another smile and gentlemanly touch of his hat, he said his goodbyes and continued towards the village green.

'You mentioned you'd helped a doctor but you didn't… Dr Stanley's nearer your age than most other men round here and he's…' Victoria gaped at his retreating back and then looked at Beatrice with a knowing expression.

'He's right handsome, isn't he?' Nell gave Beatrice a teasing smile. 'Must be a real tonic to his lady patients when he puts a hand on their fevered brows.'

'I didn't notice, and you've read too many silly romances. Besides, he undoubtedly has a wife and family.' Even as she shook her head, Beatrice felt her face warm. 'We'll be late for school if we don't hurry.'

'I don't read romances. It's Victoria who— Oh, those boys. Albert, Ralph.' Nell darted ahead to where the two evacuees were tossing a ball behind Mrs Meldrum's back, narrowly missing her feathered hat.

'Don't mind Nell and me. It's all in fun, and goodness knows fun is in short supply these days.' Victoria patted Beatrice's arm. 'I'll begin assigning parts for the Nativity today, shall I? The older pupils will take the main roles, but I want to get my little ones used to the idea of being lambs and such. If Dr Stanley is living in Hazelbury, maybe he'd like to get involved?'

‘I don’t know where Dr Stanley is living.’ Although Beatrice had wondered. ‘He’s also likely to be too busy with his work.’ She schooled her features into what she hoped was a disinterested expression.

Yet, as she followed Nell, Albert and Ralph towards the village school, managing to avoid one of Mrs Meldrum’s ‘little chats’ on her way, she couldn’t deny that Nell was right.

Dr Stanley was indeed handsome, but, even if he was unmarried, of course he wouldn’t be interested in a woman like Beatrice.

And she wouldn’t – couldn’t – be interested in or, heaven forbid, attracted to a man like him. Whilst certainly respectable and in an established profession, he wasn’t of her class. For a start, his accent – albeit pleasant and unexpectedly appealing – did not have the same ‘cut glass’ tones as hers or that of the Misses Grainger. It would also have been unusual for any young man in her circle to become a doctor. Instead, following in the footsteps of their fathers as landowners and estate managers, they were also expected to become leaders in other spheres, primarily politics and business.

A doctor was still very much middle class and, while she might like to think such distinctions didn’t matter – after all, she’d made friends with Victoria and Nell who weren’t of her class either – a more intimate association was different.

Or was it?

Beatrice’s mother would certainly not entertain her daughter ‘lowering herself’ by being attracted to such a man. However, Beatrice had done her utmost to try to separate herself from her mother’s fixed opinions and snobbishness. *Good heavens, what was she thinking?* She wasn't attracted to Dr Stanley, and she'd already given him more attention than he merited.

Her focus should be on her pupils. Anything else, even the convalescent hospital, was an unnecessary distraction.

Chapter Eight

Tuesday, 17 September 1940

In the front hall of Hazelbury Manor, Beatrice folded Miss Hopson's letter back into its envelope and turned to Victoria and Nell. 'We are to expect Mr Rimmington the day after tomorrow, as planned. He's staying in Norwich for several nights in order to make as many visits to evacuated schools as possible.'

'Hopefully that means he won't linger at ours.' Nell grimaced as she took off her hat and knelt to greet Lady. 'I suppose it's encouraging school inspections are going ahead, despite what's happening in London. My mum's postcard said they've been sheltering in the underground station every night for almost a week. She sounds sick with worry over it all.'

Beatrice could only imagine. She felt sick with worry too, and neither she nor her mother or any other family were even in London. Yet, as German bombers continued their assault on the British capital, she couldn't help but remember the city she loved. The place where, after the last war, she'd built a new and independent life. Summer picnics on Hampstead Heath. Art exhibitions at the Royal Academy. Selfridges and the shops on Regent Street at Christmas time.

And, even earlier, memories of the Wentworths' town-house overlooking a leafy Belgravia square. Walks with her nanny each afternoon, rain or shine. And, when her parents held one of their frequent parties, she'd leave the nursery and crouch at the top of the stairs to glimpse the people below: the women with their glittering jewels, her mother the most beautiful of all – as befitted the most celebrated debutante of her year – on the arm of Beatrice's dashing father.

A world which, even before this war, had gone forever.

She gathered up the rest of her post, noting her mother's handwriting on one of the envelopes, and tucked it at the bottom of the pile to read last. 'Any news from Louis?' Beatrice glanced at Victoria, who sat on a hall chair, engrossed in a letter of her own.

'Only a brief note, but he's still in England. He can't tell me where, but I so hope it's not London.' Victoria looked up. 'This letter is from my youngest sister. One of our cousins has enlisted in the Royal Canadian Air Force and will be coming to England soon. She writes that Stewart wants to visit me when he gets leave. While I long to see family from home, I wish it wasn't happening in such a way.' She stopped and brushed a hand across her face. 'Stewart was only a boy when I left Canada. I may not even recognise him.'

'We'll welcome him as if he were our own family,' Nell said. 'Which in a way he is, seeing as you're family now.' She gave Victoria's shoulder a comforting squeeze.

'Girls.' Miss Addie came into the hall. With a checked apron over her faded, floral-print house dress and a kerchief almost covering her hair, she looked more like an older version of Marjorie, the daily help, than one of the ladies of the manor. 'I thought I heard your voices. I was polishing silver in the scullery. We shall have guests to dine with us for Sunday lunch.' Her cheeks were pink and her blue eyes sparkled. 'Hetty wrote to Dr Stanley and he has accepted our invitation. The vicar and Mrs Russell will also join us. Dr Stanley is a widower with no children, Mrs Russell said, and with accommodation in such short supply, at present he's lodging in one of the rooms above the pub.' She adjusted her kerchief. 'Whatever shall we give them to eat? Should we sacrifice a chicken? With the meat ration as it is, we can't offer a proper roast, but a carrot-and-potato hot pot does seem rather mean.'

As the others clustered around Miss Addie to discuss the merits of various savoury pies, crumbles and vegetable versus cabbage soup, Beatrice climbed the stairs to the first floor, her feet heavy.

When she reached the sanctuary of her bedroom, she put the post, her handbag and satchel atop the dresser and sat on a skirted slipper chair to remove her shoes. Then, still in her school clothes, she lay on top of the eiderdown and stared at the busy floral wallpaper.

Making herself imagine Dr Stanley with a wife and children meant that, in the past week, Beatrice had been able to put him out of her mind. But now, she had to face the truth. She was inexplicably drawn to him in a different way than she'd been to Alex.

Then, she'd been a girl and they'd grown up together. Now, she was a woman – and a middle-aged one at that. One of those 'surplus girls', the unmarried women whose chances of marriage and families of their own had been dashed by the carnage of the last war.

Beatrice had long thought she'd accepted there would be nothing more for her than making a busy and useful life because, after all, what other choice did she have? But maybe, deep down, she still yearned for something more than becoming a headmistress and then retiring to that solitary cottage by the sea.

She rolled onto her side and stared out the window into the verdant garden below. The Great War and its aftermath had taken everything of consequence from her. Not only Alex, but her father, brothers, male cousins, several uncles and her family's fortune, home and the way of life that had come with it. Unlike her mother, she'd tried not to brood on those losses, but maybe that had been a mistake, and she'd only given lip service to the changing world.

Oh, it was all too confusing. Beatrice put a hand to her head as if to force herself back into the strictures of her usual no-nonsense practicality. It was only Sunday lunch, and Mr and Mrs Russell would be there as well. In her girlhood, a lunch invitation to the local vicar would have been part of her family's duty. Whilst her mother would never have included the village doctor – he was only invited to their annual garden party – the Misses Grainger had done the right thing. Beatrice also had to stop thinking about what her mother would or wouldn't do. It was because she had spent a few days' holiday with her in August, mere weeks before, that Clarissa Wentworth's outdated strictures kept coming to the fore.

I am telling you for your own good, Beatrice.

Posture, deportment, etiquette, maintaining appropriate connections. All of her mother's unsolicited advice was supposedly meant to 'help' Beatrice, but Beatrice was no longer a child, and she refused to be treated as one. Still, neither appeasement nor standing up to Mrs Wentworth had ever made any noticeable difference, so Beatrice simply tried to make the best of things – and kept her Oxfordshire visits brief. And since neither Hazelbury Manor nor the cousin's country house where her mother resided had a telephone, calls were, of necessity, infrequent, superficial and brief.

Besides, first things first. Unless he or his house were flattened by a bomb, Mr Rimmington would arrive in her classroom in less than forty-eight hours. An icy chill slid through her. Previously, school was the only part of her life over which Beatrice had some control, but war had transformed that as well.

And a man neither her mother nor any member of her circle would ever recognise socially held Beatrice's professional future in his hands.

Thursday, 19 September 1940

'Thank you, Albert. Now you, Diana. Please present the last part of our fieldwork study to Mr Rimmington.' From behind her desk in the village school, Beatrice gestured to Diana to come to the front of the room.

The entire school – her pupils having been joined by Nell's and Victoria's children for this part of the day – sat at desks, in extra chairs and on the floor, in unnatural silence. Like their teachers, the children were on edge, unsure of what this stranger from London might say or do.

As Diana reached the front of the classroom, Beatrice permitted herself a small breath of relief. When she wrote to Diana's mother, Mary Foster-Dalton, at the weekend, she would give her a full account of the ease with which

Diana had settled into this next part of her school life after moving up from the infants' class.

Once upon a time, a child from a family like Diana's would have been educated by a governess at home and then sent to boarding school as Beatrice and Mary had been. But no longer. Thanks to what Beatrice's mother termed Mary's 'ill-advised choice of husband', Diana was here in Beatrice's classroom amongst children who would formerly have been considered 'beneath' them both.

As Diana spoke about North Norfolk's history of brickworks, with Jimmy Clarke pointing to drawings Beatrice and the children had pinned to the classroom walls, Mr Rimmington gave an approving nod, and a faint smile creased his thin face. Upon their first meeting that morning, Mr Rimmington had reminded Beatrice rather of a clothes peg with his thin frame, sandy hair, sparse moustache and stiff, unsmiling demeanour. However, as the day had gone on, and now, in this last lesson, he'd unbent somewhat. That must be a good sign, but she'd given up trying to read him.

Beside Beatrice's desk, Victoria and Nell sat ramrod straight in two extra chairs borrowed from the manor, their hands folded demurely in their laps. Just as with Beatrice, Mr Rimmington was here to judge them too, but ultimately, his rating of their school – and whether they'd been judged to have succeeded or failed – rested on Beatrice's shoulders.

'You will see many examples of North Norfolk's red brick and flint buildings in Hazelbury and the surrounding area. The bricks were made locally.' Diana's clear, confident voice, with its crisp diction, held no hesitation or fear.

Beatrice glanced around the classroom, where even their liveliest pupils sat goggle-eyed, as if overcome by the importance of the occasion. Except for Ruby. What on earth was the girl doing?

Beatrice half-rose out of her chair and gave the child a quashing look, but Ruby's twitching – almost bouncing – in her seat continued. Exchanging alarmed glances with Victoria and Nell, Beatrice stood and, as quietly as possible, walked around the edge of the classroom until she reached Ruby's desk.

'Is there something wrong, Ruby?' She bent and spoke into the girl's ear while, at the same time, gesturing to Diana to continue.

Ruby's frightened blue eyes met Beatrice's, and her voice came out in an audible hiss. 'There's something in me knickers, Miss.'

A low titter went around the classroom and Diana stopped speaking.

'Here, come with me.' Beatrice held out her hand as a piercing shriek rent the air. 'What on earth—'

There was a clatter as chairs overturned, more children cried out, and Victoria called for order.

'It's a snake, Miss Wentworth. Under Edith's desk.' Albert's voice rose above the hubbub. 'Must have come in after lunch. Do snakes come out when it rains? It was pouring down with rain earlier.'

Beatrice straightened as Ruby's hand gripped hers. 'Go into the other classroom, children. Follow Miss McKaye and Miss Potter.' Without Beatrice having to ask them, and despite the smallest girl sobbing and clinging to Victoria's neck like a limpet, she and Nell were already marshalling the pupils into rows.

'It's likely only an ordinary garden snake. I do apologise, Mr Rimmington. I'll return shortly after attending to Ruby and our uninvited visitor.' She waved in the direction of Edith's desk, where the floor was surrounded by scattered books, papers and chairs.

'I shall attend to the snake myself, Miss Wentworth.' Mr Rimmington was already on his feet with Jimmy Clarke hovering at his side. 'The children's welfare is your immediate priority. You there, Albert, isn't it?'

'Yes, sir.' Albert stared at Mr Rimmington, his mouth partly open and his face pale beneath his freckles.

Half-carrying a now crying and still-squirming Ruby, Beatrice gave Albert a reassuring smile.

'You and Jimmy look like reliable young lads. You may assist me with this snake or whatever it is. You must have a bucket or some such receptacle, as well as a broom.' Was that a hint of a smile twitching at Mr Rimmington's mouth beneath the moustache?

'Here you are, sir.' Jimmy darted to the back entryway and retrieved the specified articles. 'Don't worry, Miss Wentworth. Albert and me will help Mr Rimmington and the snake too. I knows all 'bout snakes. We've lots at our farm. Real interesting, they is.' He sent her a cheery smile over one shoulder and then closed the connecting door.

As Ruby's sobs increased in volume and the girl refused to let Beatrice lift her dress, Beatrice opened the rear door and took the child outside into a small playground area and along the path to the lavatory. 'Hush, dear. Whatever it is, I'll sort it out and you'll be fine.'

A cold chill slithered up her spine. She'd been too preoccupied with the immediate crisis to consider what the snake drama and Ruby might mean for Mr

Rimmington's evaluation of Park Road School. *Oh, dear heaven.* Not only might she never become a headmistress, but she could also be sacked. Still, she couldn't let herself think about such things at present.

'No, I's not goin' in there by myself.' Ruby clutched Beatrice's hand and dug her heels into the ground outside the compact, brick lavatory building. 'One of the big boys said there's a crocodile in it who waits for little girls to eat 'em.'

'There are no crocodiles in Norfolk, nor even in the whole of Great Britain.' Not in the wild, anyway, and neither she nor Ruby were likely to visit London Zoo in the near future. If they hadn't been killed, as many venomous creatures had been to avoid the danger of them escaping should the zoo be bombed, any crocodiles would have been transferred to Whipsnade Zoo for safety, along with other valuable animals, birds and reptiles. 'All right, I'll come into the lavatory with you.'

If she managed to keep her job, after dealing with whatever 'big boy' was terrorising Ruby, Beatrice should plan several science lessons about reptiles. Like the other teachers, she frequently had to adapt the standard curriculum, and Miss Hopson hadn't ever raised any concerns. However, Mr Rimmington seemed the sort who might.

'What's the trouble? If you won't look yourself, you have to let me do so, dear.' Beatrice wrapped her arms round Ruby's heaving shoulders to try to quieten her. 'I won't hurt you.'

'Me mum says I'm never to let anyone 'cept Doctor look down there.' She pointed to her knickers. 'It's private.'

'Your mother's quite right, but I'm sure she didn't mean *you* weren't to look there. When did you last take your knickers off?'

'When I went in them there bushes behind field at lunch. I were too scared to go in here.'

Ruby's tear-stained face was solemn, and something in Beatrice's heart shifted and softened. 'Well, I'll hold your dress and you take your knickers off again and look.' Would she need to ask Dr Stanley to check on the child? Could Ruby have worms or some other kind of infection? Children from areas with poorer hygiene often had multiple ailments, but Ruby had been in Hazelbury almost a month. Surely any such infection would have shown up by now? 'I'll write to your mother tonight to explain the difficulty.'

'Yes, Miss.' Ruby gulped, hiccupped and then bent forwards and pressed the hem of her faded print dress into Beatrice's hands. Fabric rustled, and then a pair of mended but clean knickers landed on the lavatory floor at Ruby's ankles, followed by a collection of leaves and twigs. 'Oh, Miss. I fell over, after you know...' She paused. 'And I were in a hurry because you were ringing the bell and calling us to be quick so I didn't notice. I'm sorry, truly. I didn't mean to be bad.' She raised frightened blue eyes to Beatrice. 'Are you goin' to take a belt to me?'

'Of course not. I'd never hit you with a belt or anything else. You couldn't know something was wrong until those bits started... moving around. We'll say no more about it.' Anger spurted inside Beatrice. Was Ruby accustomed to being beaten? She made a mental note to visit her foster family. 'Once you're ready, we shall return to the school so you can wash your hands and tidy yourself. I expect the boys will have taken the snake outside. Like you, it must have been very frightened. Just as we didn't want to be near it, I expect the snake would also rather have been far away from us.'

'Yes, Miss Wentworth.' Ruby straightened her clothing and then tucked one hand back into Beatrice's. 'Thank you, Miss Wentworth. I's all right now.'

'Good, I'm glad.' Beatrice opened the lavatory door and the two of them went back out into the September afternoon towards the now-quiet school.

Even though she still had to face Mr Rimmington, Beatrice truly *was* glad. It was natural that Ruby and the other children had been frightened and, despite what it could mean for her personally, Beatrice would stand up for her pupils *and* Victoria and Nell.

If Mr Rimmington or anyone else tried to remove her from her post, she would stand firm. For as long as the war lasted, these children and her colleagues needed her. She wouldn't let them – or herself – down.

Chapter Nine

Saturday, 21 September 1940

Beside one of the blackberry bushes in the lane behind Hazelbury's parish church, Beatrice adjusted the wide-brimmed straw hat she'd borrowed from Miss Hetty to shield her face from the Saturday afternoon sun. After what had felt like an exceptionally long week, the weekend, although filled with its own tasks, offered a welcome break from the classroom. Several hours picking blackberries with the W.I. felt more like a holiday than a chore. She glanced with satisfaction at her shallow basket, almost full of ripe, dark-purple fruit.

'Can you imagine if Mr Rimmington had stayed for more than a day? He was decent in the end, but I was never so glad to see the back of anyone.' Nell plucked several plump blackberries and dropped them into her own basket.

'All's well that ends well, although I suppose we have to wait for his final report to be certain.' Victoria made a face. 'I hardly knew what I was doing in the classroom yesterday, nor did my infants. We were all worn out.'

Beatrice nodded and tried to make her voice encouraging. 'Mr Rimmington was understanding, and remember that when I spoke to Miss Hopson, she said all the commotion with the snake and Ruby might help rather than hinder our evaluation.'

In his closing address to the school, Mr Rimmington's previous stiffness had all but disappeared. And when Diana had presented him with a jar of Mrs Meldrum's strawberry jam and Albert's pencil drawing of the school, the inspector patted Diana's head in a genial, almost fatherly way. He also asked after Ruby and privately commended Beatrice and the other teachers for their calmness in taking charge of what might otherwise have been an even more discomfiting situation for 'the little lass'.

Still, despite the headmistress's reassurance, Beatrice's worries over her job hadn't quite dissipated. She popped a ripe blackberry into her mouth, savouring the sun-warmed, juicy goodness. Whilst she'd considered herself resigned to life in Hazelbury, she wasn't – not truly – and another of her mother's weekly letters in this morning's post hadn't helped. In addition to the familiar complaints about food shortages, rationing and the tediousness of being 'marooned' in the country without adequate staff or petrol, the missive also mentioned several of Beatrice's contemporaries – girls who, despite the last war, had still managed to make 'good marriages' rather than undertaking 'demeaning work' like teaching.

'You're doing splendidly, ladies.' Further along the row of blackberry bushes, Mrs Meldrum's voice boomed out. 'Many hands make light work, and we shall remember this happy day when feasting on blackberry jam this winter.'

'You'd think picking blackberries to make jam was her idea rather than Mrs Bertram's, wouldn't you? If Mrs Meldrum dared, she'd cut Mrs Bertram out of things entirely.' Nell set her full basket on the verge, and wiped her stained hands on one of the clean rags she'd brought with her. 'I expect that's why the Misses Grainger are having Dr Stanley and Mr and Mrs Russell for lunch tomorrow – to get in first.'

Beatrice bit back a smile. The same thought had occurred to her and was then quickly dismissed, but it would be unbecoming of her to let Nell suspect such an idea. 'Miss Hetty and Miss Addie are merely welcoming Dr Stanley to Hazelbury.' The more Beatrice considered their invitation – one she'd been careful *not* to mention in her own weekly letter to her mother – the more she appreciated the social concession the ladies of Hazelbury Manor had made. 'Given their position in the village, the Misses Grainger would not concern themselves with what Mrs Meldrum or anyone else might do.' For Miss Hetty and Miss Addie, that line would never be crossed, no matter how much the world changed.

'I wish Louis could be here. I do long to see him, and he would also somewhat even out the men around the table.' Victoria gave a light laugh. 'Listen to me being so foolish. As if we don't have more important concerns than equal pairings for Sunday luncheon.' She dropped more blackberries into her basket. 'We've almost picked these bushes clean.'

'Irrespective of the absence of men, and even this late in the season, there *will* be enough blackberries for jam *and* for me to make a crumble for tomorrow's lunch.' Nell gave them a happy smile. 'Dr Stanley looks too thin, don't you think? Living alone, the poor man likely doesn't eat right, and as a doctor he must always be rushing round. I'll send him home with a loaf of bread and some carrot biscuits.' Nell tutted. 'Mrs Meldrum says the house next to the school only has army recruits staying temporarily. I wonder if Dr Stanley might eventually lodge there?'

'I expect he'd want to be nearer Whittleton, what with working at the convalescent hospital.' Victoria shrugged into the cardigan she'd hung on a nearby branch of the hedgerow. 'When I went there after school yesterday to help some of the men with letter writing, I could hardly believe the transformation in the place. You'd never think that Whittleton Hall was so recently a family home.'

'Yes, it's quite extraordinary.' A lump rose in Beatrice's throat. Like her own erstwhile family home, Whittleton Hall had stood almost unchanged for centuries. Yet, in only a few weeks, hundreds of years of gracious living had disappeared as though they'd never existed. She shivered and, as the sun went behind a cloud, reached for her own cardigan.

'All done?' Mrs Bertram joined them and stood beside Beatrice. 'I was visiting the wife of one of our tenant farmers this morning, so I missed seeing you at the Hall. How did your shift go?'

'It was fine. I worked in the office filing paperwork and answering the telephone.' Undemanding, repetitive tasks which should have been precisely what Beatrice wanted but somehow wasn't. Or was it because Dr Stanley hadn't been there? Against her better judgement, she'd found herself looking for him. 'Any news of Aircraftman Griffiths? I didn't see Matron to ask.'

As the W.I. women dispersed into small groups, and Victoria and Nell went ahead together, Mrs Bertram fell into step with Beatrice. 'He's doing much better than anyone expected. Dr Stanley says he'll soon be stable enough to be transferred to Norwich for further treatment. I do hope that at some point he'll return to the Hall to convalesce. I feel rather invested in the boy's well-being, almost as if he were one of my own.' Mrs Bertram's lower lip trembled, and she looked away towards the tranquil village green.

'I understand.' To her surprise, Beatrice felt the same way about many of her pupils. Although initially, teaching had merely been a respectable job and a means to support her mother and herself, in the past year it had become something more – almost a true vocation. And Ruby was… well, Beatrice couldn't let herself think too much about that child. All seemed well at her billet, and when she'd visited Ruby at her foster home yesterday after school, the girl had been happily working in the garden with her foster mother. 'It's welcome news that we're still able to use the Hall's kitchen to make jam. Since the Hall was requisitioned earlier than expected, I mean.' Over the past week, she'd managed to steer clear of emotional matters and wouldn't let herself veer down that path now.

'It is.' Mrs Bertram's brown eyes twinkled. 'I had a word with the major about it, and *he* had a word with Matron. Given it's a domestic rather than hospital matter she'd likely have said no to me, but Matron has great respect for military men— Oh, look, there's Dr Stanley. I arranged to get a lift back to Whittleton with him. He's on an evening rota. Let's hope it doesn't extend to all night as it did yesterday. We don't want him to wear himself out when he's only just started, do we?' Mrs Bertram waved her arm vigorously until the doctor's car rolled to a stop outside the village hall.

'Mrs Bertram, Miss Wentworth.' Dr Stanley tipped his hat and spoke through the open window. 'Do wait, Mrs Bertram, I'll—'

'I'm quite capable of opening a car door. Don't trouble yourself.' In an instant, Mrs Bertram was in the passenger seat. 'Carry on. I don't want to keep you.'

'Certainly. You're most kind.' As Dr Stanley checked over his shoulder for traffic – unlikely, as hardly anyone had a motor here and petrol coupons were saved for essential trips – his gaze caught Beatrice's.

She drew in a breath, and her face heated. His hazel eyes held amusement, warmth and something that made the palpable attraction she'd tried to suppress roar back at full force.

Those flecks of colour in his eyes weren't gold, but as green as the hedgerows in midsummer. Although why that detail was important she wouldn't – couldn't – let herself imagine.

Chapter Ten

Sunday, 22 September 1940

'Thank you, Miss Grainger, Miss Adelaide.' As Sunday luncheon in the formal dining room at Hazelbury Manor drew to a close, Dr Stanley stood and helped Miss Hetty with her chair, as the vicar did the same for Miss Addie. 'I very much appreciate your kind hospitality.' His smile included Beatrice, Victoria and Nell, and Beatrice's heart beat faster. 'The publican at The Crown does his best, but being here, in your family home, is a great pleasure.'

Miss Hetty gave a gracious nod and glanced around the table upon which – from the roast chicken they'd indeed sacrificed to the potatoes, carrots, peas and Nell's blackberry crumble – not a scrap of the meal remained. 'Shall we take a walk around the garden?' She gestured to the vicar to join her.

Beatrice suppressed a sigh. Unlike the Sunday luncheons she'd grown up with, there was no staff to cook and serve the meal or clear it up afterwards. Today, there wasn't even Marjorie, the daily from the village, as Sunday was her day off. So, after their guests departed, she'd have to pitch in along with the other teachers and the Misses Grainger to do the washing up and restore the dining room to its usual order. While she smiled and joined

Victoria and Nell in taking cleared plates to the scullery, bitterness left a sour taste in her mouth.

'I'll make a start in here.' Nell gestured to the crockery and cooking paraphernalia piled on every available surface in the scullery.

'No, Miss Hetty's invitation to walk in the garden was extended to all of us,' Beatrice said, standing in front of the hooks where the aprons hung. 'Why should you be the only one to hang back?' She motioned to Nell to roll her sleeves back down. 'I know it looks like a mountain, but we'll tackle it together later.'

'Of course we will. Many hands make light work.' Victoria glanced between them. 'Once we get our hats and gloves, we can join the others outside.'

'I'll get Lady from the drawing room and catch you up,' Beatrice said. 'She'll be glad to go into the fresh air, and I left my hat and gloves by the front door after church.' Earlier, in deference to the luncheon guests, Beatrice had shut the sometimes too lively dog in a separate room.

Leaving the scullery and going through the green baize door – a shortcut to the front hall once used by the manor's servants – she took her hat and gloves from the table and put them on, then found Lady's lead before opening the drawing-room door. 'Come here, girl.' The dog darted towards Beatrice, wagging her tail and making yipping sounds of pleasure. 'There you go' – she clipped Lady's lead to her collar – 'behave nicely. No jumping up, do you hear me, Miss Lady?' She closed the door on the gloomy apartment, a room which held the piano but was otherwise mostly shut up and unused, with the furniture covered in dustsheets for the duration of the war.

'Surely a dog named Lady must be both charming and well-mannered.'

Beatrice started at the voice from behind her. 'Oh, Dr Stanley.' She turned to him, and Lady tugged on her lead. 'I didn't see you there.'

'Miss Adelaide asked me to collect her shawl. She left it in the morning room.' He nodded to the doorway beyond the dining room, where they'd gathered for a glass of sherry after church. 'I'm sorry if I startled you.' He came closer to pet the dog, holding Miss Addie's silvery-grey shawl (which Nell had knitted for her birthday) safely out of Lady's reach.

'It's fine.' Beatrice gave him a stiff smile. 'Lady, *no*.' She gathered up the lead to bring the dog closer and stop her from nosing the doctor's hand.

'She's all right, aren't you, girl?' He straightened and held out one arm. 'Shall we?'

'Thank you.' Beatrice rested her gloved fingertips lightly on his forearm. It was providential, really, that she had the opportunity to speak with him alone. *Because of Ruby, not for any other reason*, she reminded herself as he held the front door open for her and they left the house. Victoria and Nell must have used the rear stairs to go up to their bedroom and then outdoors, as there was no sign of them and the manor was silent. 'It's a lovely day, isn't it?' She gestured to the sunshine that filtered through the trees lining the drive and made a lace-like pattern on the gravel.

'Yes, very fine.' Dr Stanley nodded. 'Shall I hold the dog's lead for you?'

Wordlessly, Beatrice transferred Lady's lead to him and took Miss Addie's shawl in return. She had to find a way to introduce the subject of Ruby – but how? None of her mother's dictates about how to speak to gentlemen – with flattery, deference and judicious charm – were suitable. Nowadays, apart from Louis Grainger, the vicar, a shopkeeper or a pupil's parent, Beatrice was also unused to speaking to men.

'Has the new school term started well?' Dr Stanley began the conversation, which Beatrice appreciated.

'As well as possible, I suppose.' As they walked along the drive, a light breeze rustled the leaves in the tall oak trees overhead. They seemed to be following Lady, who followed her nose towards the rear of the house where the 'gardens', like those at the front, now grew vegetables. 'Actually, I would appreciate your advice. Medically, I mean, for the children – or rather, one child in particular.' She turned away, ostensibly to admire a proliferation of pumpkin vines, a plant Victoria had insisted they grow as a reminder of her Canadian home. Beatrice had no need to be nervous or awkward. She was consulting Dr Stanley on a professional matter.

'Of course. How may I help?' As they reached one side of the manor house, where a gravel path branched off in two different directions, he stopped and waved Victoria over from where she stood with the others near Miss Addie's herb garden. 'Miss McKaye? Would you be so kind as to deliver Miss Adelaide's shawl to her? I need to have a word with Miss Wentworth. We'll join you shortly.'

'Certainly.' Victoria approached and took the shawl from Beatrice, raising her eyebrows with an amused sideways glance.

Beatrice took her hand away from Dr Stanley's arm under the pretence of adjusting her straw boater. She knew that look all too well. Since Victoria was so recently engaged, she had romance on her mind. Yet Beatrice couldn't let herself be diverted. She'd put any thoughts of romance out of her mind and heart years ago, and that wasn't about to change.

'Right, where were we?' Dr Stanley held out his arm again and guided Beatrice and Lady along the path leading to an old brick summerhouse topped with a thatched roof.

'It's about one of my pupils. Ruby Parker.' As she explained Ruby's home situation, Beatrice let her hand settle on Dr Stanley's arm. He didn't only have a pleasant speaking voice; his singing voice was very fine as well. Not that she'd paid particular attention, but he'd sat behind the manor pew at this morning's church service, so she couldn't help hearing his voice raised in the familiar hymns. 'Ruby's family clearly isn't well off, but it's not that. Even the poorest families can love and care for their children as devotedly as those who are wealthier. Sometimes more devotedly.' Beatrice's heart pinched at the memory of her own childhood which, albeit rich in material things, had lacked parental attention and affection. 'Ruby seems fearful, though, and I suspect she may have witnessed and experienced violence at home. I visited her with her foster family, and nothing seemed amiss there. Ruby is billeted with an elderly widow, Mrs Fisk, and she's a gentle soul. I know her from the W.I., and there's naught to suggest she's anything but kind to Ruby. However, as her teacher, I'm responsible for the girl – and I don't know what to do to help her.'

'It sounds a troubling case.' Dr Stanley rubbed his free hand over his chin, which was well-defined and strong, complementing the fine proportions of his face. 'I don't think there is anything you *can* do at present. Perhaps with time and loving care, Ruby will settle, and she may even talk with you about her London family. I can take a look at her to rule out any medical issues. You said she's pale and thin?'

'Yes. As if a light wind would blow her away.' Beatrice stared across the sunny garden. Overhead, puffy clouds dotted the crisp, blue autumn sky and, with the absence of aircraft, it was almost possible to momentarily forget the war. 'Insofar as rationing permits, Mrs Fisk tries to tempt her with extra food and little delicacies, but she said that Ruby hardly eats enough to keep a sparrow alive.'

'Have you written to Ruby's parents?' There was a comforting warmth to Dr Stanley's voice that made Beatrice feel she could confide in him – a sense of calm that eased the tightness in her chest and shoulders. What would it be like to have someone like him by her side to share life's burdens?

'Yes, I've written several times but, as yet, haven't had any response.' Beatrice forced her attention back to Ruby, the reason for this conversation in the first place. 'I suppose it's not surprising I haven't heard. Reports of the bombing raids are truly dreadful. Even if the family home is still standing, the post must be disrupted.'

Beatrice and the other teachers often felt guilty here in Hazelbury, an oasis of relative peace and tranquillity, while their pupils' families faced the might of the Luftwaffe nightly. 'I gather that Ruby's father died before the war, when Ruby was hardly old enough to remember him, and her mother has since remarried. Ruby has mentioned her mother on numerous occasions, but never her stepfather.'

'Does Ruby have siblings?' As they turned the corner of the path near the summerhouse, Lady stopped to sniff a cedar hedge, burrowing into it until only her tail stuck out from amongst the dense foliage.

'Not that I know of. She's never spoken of any.' Or had the girl, like Beatrice, lost a brother or sister? Not through war, but – along with accidents and malnutrition – there were any number of infectious diseases that could prove fatal. Perhaps it was for the best that Beatrice had never had children of her own. There were far too many things for mothers to fret over.

'Why don't we visit Ruby at Mrs Fisk's after school this week? Would Thursday suit you?' Was there a hitch in Dr Stanley's voice? Could he be as affected by Ruby's situation as Beatrice was herself?

'Yes, that would be ideal.' Beatrice bent to see what was occupying Lady. 'Why don't you come by the school around four on Thursday? I'll also speak to Ruby beforehand to prepare her.'

'Good. It's settled, then.' Dr Stanley's voice was brisk. 'I've also been intending to speak with you about Aircraftman Griffiths. He'll be sent on to hospital in Norwich soon. Possibly as early as next weekend. If you're free, I know he'd welcome a visit, as he speaks of you with great fondness. I gather he considers you rather as an "angel of mercy" after having comforted him during those hours when he hovered between life and death. After seeing Ruby, I could take you on to Whittleton Hall in my car and then bring you back here? I'm not scheduled to work at the convalescent hospital that day, but I do try to keep an eye on my patients.'

'I'd like that very much.' With effort, Beatrice kept her voice steady. She'd done her duty holding the young man's hand and assisting in theatre, nothing more. There was nothing angelic about it or her, but still, warmth crept around her heart. 'Come out of there, Lady.' She fussed with the dog, brushing twigs and grey-green leaves from her brown-and-white coat. As for accepting a lift from the doctor, it was a practical solution and would save her a great deal of time cycling. It wasn't as if Dr Stanley was suggesting anything remotely resembling courting. It was entirely proper and professional. 'How wonderful that Aircraftman Griffiths is doing so splendidly.'

'He still has a long journey ahead of him, but with time, he should be able to live a relatively normal life.' Dr Stanley studied the tips of his polished black shoes. 'Whatever "normal" will mean for any of us. After the last war, I'd hoped…' He stopped. 'Well, I also wanted to apologise to you.' His voice changed; that brief moment of almost intimacy between them was gone.

'Apologise for what?' As they continued along the path to rejoin the others, Beatrice tried to tamp down her curiosity. What had he been about to say about the Great War? He'd have been the right age to have joined up. Had he served in the medical corps or in one of the fighting forces? Either way, he'd have seen even more of the war's carnage than she had.

'I wasn't very polite to you at our first meeting. Between the tyre puncture, trying to find my way with no road signs and my concern for the men in those aeroplanes, I wasn't myself. In addition, I'd only just arrived from London when the call from RAF Whittleton came through to the pub.'

'It's no matter, Dr Stanley.' Beatrice toyed with one of the buttoned cuffs on her dress. 'Your confusion was natural. Indeed, although I now know this area well, I took several wrong turns myself when cycling to visit an evacuee's host family last week.' With the expectation of a German invasion, the government's decision to remove place name and navigational signs from the roads made sense. However, until they'd disappeared, Beatrice hadn't realised how much she'd relied on such directional aids to find her way to the more remote farms that housed several of her pupils.

'Thank you, Miss Wentworth. You are most kind whereas I, even given the circumstances, was uncivil.' Under the brim of his grey fedora, Dr Stanley's face looked slightly pink.

'It is forgotten.' My goodness, he was formal – stilted even – but she wasn't a great deal better. 'I, too, was sharper than I should have been when I assumed you were not a doctor.'

'Not at all.' He dismissed her attempt at an apology. 'It was a natural mistake given my appearance and how I conducted myself that day. I didn't realise until much later I'd torn my trousers whilst wrestling with that punctured tyre.' He paused as if he wanted to say something else entirely. 'I'm glad we understand each other.'

Did they? Apart from his brief reference to the last war, they'd only spoken about Ruby, Aircraftman Griffiths and superficial matters. As they reached Miss Hetty – strolling sedately alongside the vicar and wearing an elaborate feathered straw hat – Beatrice stole another glance at the doctor.

In a part of herself she thought was gone forever, she could admit she wanted to get to know him better. In time, they might even become friends. He was of her generation, and in that sense, they already had something in common.

However, there could be nothing more than friendship between them, even if she foolishly might want there to be.

Chapter Eleven

Wednesday, 25 September 1940

On Wednesday afternoon, Beatrice sat in the Grainger family pew at the village church. She often joined the choir, but having missed several recent practices due to preparing for the school inspector's visit, she sat with the rest of the congregation today, as she had last Sunday.

She bowed her head and clasped her black-gloved hands together as the bishop's voice intoned a prayer for the deceased. *Gilbert Rupert Edward Russell.*

Beatrice had only met the vicar and Mrs Russell's eldest son briefly, so, unlike the villagers and other mourners who'd come from as far afield as Cromer, Sheringham, Norwich and even Cambridge, she couldn't say she'd known him well. However, he'd evidently been a well-liked and much-admired young man, as the church was packed. Even the extra chairs that had been brought in weren't sufficient for the crowd, so many – mostly men in RAF uniform – stood at the rear. Sitting with their foster families, some of her pupils, solemn and dressed in their Sunday best, were also part of the congregation. With Miss Hopson's approval, Beatrice had given the children and teachers the afternoon off from school so that the pupils who were old enough could attend Gilbert's funeral.

Gilbert was the first of Hazelbury's citizens to be killed in this war, although he likely wouldn't be the last. As the prayer ended, she raised her head, and her gaze drifted to the large framed photograph beside the altar. Whilst Gilbert and all his crew but one had perished when their aeroplane was shot down over a month ago, village gossip – courtesy of Mrs Meldrum – held that no individual remains had been found intact or identifiable enough for burial. As a result, although Mr and Mrs Russell had never addressed local chatter, they were holding this memorial service instead of a funeral.

The backs of Beatrice's eyes stung as Nell's beautiful soprano voice rose in 'Abide With Me'. It should have been comforting. It *was* undoubtedly comforting to the rest of the congregation, but to Beatrice it would always evoke memories of Alex.

As was then the custom, he'd been buried in a military cemetery in France near where he'd fallen in 1917. However, some months later, his family installed a memorial window in the local parish church and held a service to bless it. A family friend, a professional soloist well-known in prominent London and continental circles, had been invited to sing 'Abide With Me' to an audience of the great and good of British society. From the aristocracy to Parliament, and the worlds of arts, letters and military leadership, all were represented. Whilst Alex would have scoffed at the fuss, both his mother and hers were in their element.

Digging in her handbag, Beatrice fumbled for a handkerchief. Unlike that soloist, Nell hadn't had formal musical training or sung on the stages of European concert halls. Yet, somehow, in this small and unremarkable place of worship, surrounded by Gilbert's family and friends, her rendition of the beloved hymn was the more touching one.

'Here.' To her right, Miss Hetty handed Beatrice a starched linen handkerchief while keeping an identical one clutched in her other hand. The older woman's usually stern expression was softer, and her forget-me-not blue eyes might even have held a hint of dampness. As one of Gilbert's godparents, it wasn't surprising that Miss Hetty would be moved by this service, but – like Beatrice's own mother and aunts – it was most unusual for her to display any sign of emotion.

Beatrice nodded her thanks, and as Nell finished her solo and returned to her place in the medieval choir stalls beside Victoria, she discreetly wiped her eyes.

After a scripture reading, more prayers, the laying of a wreath by Gilbert's three younger brothers – one in uniform – several hymns, and then the benediction, it was over. At only twenty-three, Gilbert's life had been snuffed out, and his family didn't even have the comfort of a grave at which to mourn him. Beatrice had been able to visit Alex's grave, and his simple white headstone, identical to the hundreds of others stretching along a quiet French hillside, was a tangible place to remember his life and acknowledge his death.

Putting the handkerchief in her handbag, Beatrice straightened her shoulders. She had to be thankful for what she had, not lament what she didn't.

'So affecting, wasn't it?' With a white handkerchief edged in black lace half-covering her face, Mrs Meldrum stopped at the manor pew. 'I can hardly imagine how the Russells must be feeling. And Mr Gilbert's poor young lady, Miss Hammett.' She darted a furtive glance at Gilbert's fiancée, a delicate-featured blonde in a Women's Auxiliary Air Force officer's uniform, who'd sat with the Russell family in the vicarage pew.

'The service was most moving, yes.' Murmuring an apology, Beatrice excused herself from Mrs Meldrum. Perhaps it was cowardly, but she couldn't face her or anyone else at present. Although never prone to feeling faint, she found the crowded church stuffy, and the scent of the garden flowers – aromatic asters, late-blooming roses and phlox, which she'd helped arrange the previous evening – was suffocating.

As for Miss Hammett, Beatrice hoped she wouldn't be expected to meet her. What could she say? What, indeed, could anyone say that would be of any comfort? And yet Miss Hammett would have to nod and accept sympathetic offerings in the spirit in which they were meant, all the while screaming inside and wishing she could be anywhere but here.

However, Miss Hammett wasn't Beatrice. Maybe, beneath her calm exterior she actually *was* calm, accepting Gilbert's death as God's will. Maybe, in due course, she'd meet someone else, marry him and have a family. Or if she didn't, life was different for girls nowadays. Miss Hammett might join the civil service, or if her family had money, she'd be able to travel. No matter her specific circumstances, she'd still have more opportunities than girls like Beatrice had had during and after the last war.

Desperate for air, Beatrice loosened the top button of the black jacket which matched her skirt and made for one of the church's side aisles, trying to school her features into an expression that was suitably mournful whilst also appropriate for a teacher. Goodness, she was tired of always having to be so respectable, doing her duty and whatever society expected of her. She'd never kick over the traces, but oh, sometimes how she wished she could.

Keeping her head down, she tried not to make eye contact with any of her pupils' foster mums who, despite being in church – and at a memorial service – were undoubtedly likely to try to collar her about one or more of the seemingly endless problems related to their evacuees. Straight ahead, the church door lay open to the bright afternoon. Received wisdom was that funerals were easier if the weather was fine, but for someone who was truly grieving, what did the weather matter?

'Miss Wentworth?' At a brief touch on her arm from Dr Stanley, she stilled. 'You look rather pale. Is there any way in which I might assist you?'

'No, thank you. I'm...' Beatrice stopped. Even though she wasn't about to faint, she wasn't fine. The lie stuck in her throat.

'Shall we go out of doors and away from the crush?' As Dr Stanley's keen and intelligent eyes studied her, Beatrice's gaze dropped again.

Still keeping her eyes averted, she nodded and let him take her arm. What was he doing here? Had he known the Russell family before coming to Hazelbury? Questions swirled in her mind as Dr Stanley led her outside and around the building to the rear, amongst the oldest gravestones in the churchyard. 'I'm all right now,' Beatrice said, forcing a bright smile. 'It was warm in the church and...' Once more she stopped, but this time, when she met his gaze, it was because of the expression in his eyes and on his face. The understanding and compassion.

'You don't need to pretend with me.' His voice was low, steady and discerning.

'I'm sure I don't know what you mean.' She tried to brush away what he'd said, glancing along the row of headstones, many half-sunk into the ground, their worn inscriptions illegible.

'I think you do.' He took his arm away, and when Beatrice turned back, he stared at the tall hedgerows bordering the lane that ran alongside the churchyard. 'Like me, you've known wartime loss, haven't you?'

'I have' – her breath caught – 'but it was a long time ago.'

'The grief may fade but it never truly goes away.' He fiddled with his watch. 'Especially at funerals and memorials. I knew Richard Russell at Cambridge. We weren't in the same year, but I counted him as a friend.'

'I'm sure that Mr and Mrs Russell appreciate you being here today.' When Beatrice's gaze returned to his, she trembled. She wasn't sure of anything at present, except that her heart was supposed to be buried with Alex in France. And yet… she was inexplicably drawn to this man. It was all so confusing. 'Dr Stanley, I must get—'

'David. Please call me David, at least when we're not with others or at the hospital.' He took a step closer. 'We're alike, you and me. I feel it, and if I'm not mistaken, you do as well.'

'Yes, I do.' Her supposedly grieving, numb heart throbbed as if in agreement with what was impossible to deny. 'David.' She tried out his name, sweet on her tongue. 'I am Beatrice.'

'Beatrice' – an almost boyish smile spread across his face – 'bringer of joy. Blessed. I studied Latin,' he added at her puzzled expression. 'The name suits you.'

'I was named for a great-grandmother.' She'd never felt especially 'blessed' but to many others – Ruby and Nell, for example – she supposed she would be. Nor had she ever considered herself a 'bringer of joy' – more an imparter of knowledge – but maybe it wasn't too late to live up to her name.

'I was named after a great-uncle. In photos, he looked like the quintessential stern early Victorian, but according to my mother, he had a playful side. David means "beloved", which also appealed to her. Still does, actually, as she never fails to remind me when I visit.' His smile widened. 'I say, if we go out that way, we can have a ramble in the lane.' He gestured to an old wooden gate set into the hedge which, before the village had grown in the opposite direction, had once served as the churchyard's entrance. 'Unless you intended going to the vicarage for refreshments?'

Beatrice had indeed, because it would be expected of her. Yet, given the crowd in the church, she wouldn't be missed, and unlike Victoria and Nell, she hadn't volunteered to pour tea or pass around plates of sandwiches and biscuits. 'I don't need refreshment.' For once in her life, she wanted to do something unexpected – unconventional, even. Although missing a post-funeral gathering wasn't radical or rash, it was still in direct conflict with the norms of the world she'd grown up in. 'A ramble in the lane would be lovely.' Thinking of her mother's appalled reaction, she suppressed a smile. 'I can tell you more about Ruby,' she added, in case she'd sounded too bold or misinterpreted David's invitation – Ruby offered a plausible and innocuous conversational topic.

'I'm looking forward to meeting Ruby tomorrow' – David extended his arm for Beatrice again – 'but right now, I'd rather get to know *you*.'

As Beatrice took his arm, her fingers tingled and a pleasing warmth flooded her body.

She wanted to get to know him too. *Beloved*. The meaning of the name 'David' wasn't significant. How could it be? Yet Alex – *Alexander* – meant 'protector of men', which had cost *her* Alex his life.

Although Alex would always be in her heart, she couldn't live for him, her family or anyone else. Besides, it was only a ramble down a country lane.

Chapter Twelve

Half an hour later, Beatrice and David had walked along the winding lane and reached the countryside proper. In the warmth of the sunshine, she'd first unbuttoned her jacket and then slipped it over her shoulders. He did the same, as well as loosening his tie. Here on higher ground, farm fields spread on either side of the lane in golden autumn splendour, and above them, flocks of migrating birds soared in graceful arcs.

Beatrice drew in a lungful of air, rich with the earthy scents of autumn mixed with the sweetness of buddleia and other late-blooming flowers. Here in the open – unlike in the church – the fragrance was pleasing, not suffocating.

'It's not the Yorkshire moors, but the feeling of openness is similar.' David extended his arms and turned in a circle.

'Is Yorkshire where you grew up?' Beatrice had wondered about his accent the day they met and it seemed she'd been right. So far, she'd done most of the talking, but he'd seemed genuinely interested in her opinions of current books and music and had asked thoughtful, intelligent questions about her work as a teacher.

'Yes, in a village in the heart of the moors, the North Riding, but also not far from Robin Hood's Bay.' He took off his hat and ran a hand through his thick hair. 'I'm still a Yorkshire country lad at heart.'

Here, with only the two of them, that northern accent was stronger, as if he could truly be himself. 'I've never been further north than Shrewsbury to visit a school friend.' Instead, before coming to live in Hazelbury, Beatrice's life had been firmly rooted in London and its nearby counties. Any other travel had been either to the south coast or abroad.

David laughed. 'I expect you've been to lots of places I haven't.'

Whenever their conversation had verged into the more personal, she'd steered it back into neutral waters, being careful not to say much about her family. However, David wasn't a fool and with his tousled hair, ruddy cheeks and loosened collar, he looked like an older version of the 'country lad' he professed to be.

Ignoring his comment about where she might have travelled, she gave him a stiff smile. 'We should start back. It may feel like summer, but the night draws in quickly at this time of year, along with an autumn chill. We also don't want to be caught in the blackout.'

'Of course' – he put his hat back on – 'I hope I didn't say or do anything to offend you.'

'You didn't. It's me.' She put a hand to her mouth, wishing she could take the words back. As measured in her manner as in her speech, Beatrice always thought before she spoke.

'What about you?' David asked as they started down the low rise and a rockier part of the track. He kept one hand outstretched to steady her if she stumbled.

'Our families are different.' It had to be said. Get it out of the way, so to speak, because if they became friends, the village would talk. She kept her eyes on her feet, ostensibly so she wouldn't fall, but also to avoid his too penetrating gaze.

'I certainly didn't grow up in a family such as yours.' His voice was clipped, formal. 'My father owned a shop and did well, but *his* father started life in a crowded four-room cottage as the youngest son of a labourer. My grand-mother went into service as soon as she left school, and before she married, rose to become a parlour maid. I'm not ashamed of my background, even though when I arrived at Cambridge, some there tried to make me feel that way.'

'Nor should you be ashamed. That's not what I meant.' Beatrice's heartbeat sped up. She'd inadvertently got into a dreadful muddle and somehow she had to extricate herself from it. 'My family isn't what it once was. I need to make my living as you do.' *Despite her mother's objections.* As always, the hypocrisy of it made Beatrice's blood boil. *Where would her mother be without the money Beatrice sent her each month? Their cousin's generosity extended only to providing a room, not food, clothing or the little luxuries Clarissa Wentworth insisted she couldn't live without.* 'My two elder brothers were killed in the last war. My fiancé was killed as well, and my father died in the Spanish 'flu epidemic in November 1918. The house that had been in my father's family for more than three hundred years had to be sold. Whatever money was left went to pay death duties. Now it's only my mother and me. She lives with a cousin in Oxfordshire, and I support her as well as myself.' She took a deep breath. 'All I meant is that, since we come from different worlds, perhaps we may not have a great deal in common. For instance, I know little about the medical field.'

'Nor I about teaching but isn't variety the spice of life?' David walked more quickly and Beatrice hastened to keep up. 'Or so William Cowper would have us think.'

'Oh yes, the poet. I just wanted to be honest.' But by doing so, she'd likely destroyed any chance of even friendship between them.

'Then let me be honest with you as well.' As they drew within view of the village, the church tower rising through the trees, David stopped. 'Mrs Meldrum, whom I met in the post office, took me aside soon after I arrived here and told me about your family. She saw us speak that day when you were on your way to school and you introduced me to Miss McKaye and Miss Potter.'

Of course Mrs Meldrum had spotted them, and she'd also likely made Beatrice's family sound considerably grander than it was. Beatrice started to speak, but David cut across her.

'No wait, let me finish.' His voice was low but firm. 'My father died when I was at Cambridge. It was sudden, and although he left my mother "well fixed", as Mrs Meldrum would put it, I still consider myself responsible for her comfort and well-being. My elder sister died young and there were only the two of us. My wife died giving birth to our first child, who also died, while I was serving in France. Much as I wanted to protect and keep Maud and our baby safe, in the end, I could not.' He brushed a hand across his face. 'Since then, my work has been my life, and I have never let anyone or anything else interfere with that. Not family, friends or even hobbies.

But when I saw how you sat for hours with Griffiths and your patience and kindness to him, and then how you spoke of Ruby and today at Gilbert Russell's funeral, I recognised something in you. Something that transcends those "different worlds" as you called them. I regret I was wrong.'

'No, you weren't wrong. And I'm truly sorry about your wife and child. How utterly dreadful for you.' Losing Alex had been bad enough, but losing a child as well? Almost unthinkable. 'As for Mrs Meldrum, I expect she was looking out for you. She's a kindly soul, truly. Until recently, my life has been my work too. When I lived in London, I kept myself busy, but I didn't have any real friends. Now I do, and thanks to Miss McKaye and Miss Potter and becoming part of the village, my life has a richness I could never have imagined. We three teachers come from different worlds, too, and it doesn't matter to our friendship. But with you… I…' Beatrice stopped, on the verge of saying too much.

'I'd like us to be friends, Beatrice.' She trembled as he said her name. Had anyone ever said it with such sweet gentleness? 'That means I'd like to get to know you. I suspect there aren't many others like us here in Hazelbury. Without a family, I mean.'

'There aren't, but not like us in other ways, either.' They were betwixt and between, as the saying went. His family had come up in the world whilst hers had tumbled down, but perhaps they might meet somewhere in the middle. 'I'd like us to be friends as well.'

The class difference wasn't important, and it didn't matter what her mother or anyone else thought. Beatrice had moved beyond being so small-minded and snobbish, even if she still had anything to be snobbish about – which she didn't.

'Good.' He gave her a smile that once again transformed his face, and a dimple she hadn't previously noticed indented his right cheek. 'I'll see you home. No, I insist,' he said, waving away her objections. This time, when he took her arm, she let it rest in the crook of his.

When they reached the village crossroads and turned towards the manor, several aircraft from RAF Whittleton roared overhead.

David drew her closer so his warm breath grazed her cheek.

Although she always put on a brave face with Victoria and Nell, when faced with any aircraft – even RAF – Beatrice feared both the machines and what they represented. Yet somehow, David had sensed her discomfort and sought to reassure her.

She quivered as even when the aeroplanes had gone, rather than releasing her, David continued to hold her close, his strong arm and broad shoulder like a bulwark against the world.

It *had* only been a ramble in the lane, but the foundation of Beatrice's world – one she'd built and fortified more than twenty years before – had shifted. Or maybe that shift had been in progress over the past year, and David had helped her acknowledge it.

From the first, she'd been drawn to David in a way that went beyond friendship, and today's walk had only strengthened those feelings. So, although David had offered friendship, would it be enough? That was the bigger question, and she was no closer to answering it now than she'd been before this afternoon.

But either way, she knew she'd never be the same.

Chapter Thirteen

Thursday, 3 October 1940

'Ruby's a dear little girl, so quiet and obedient, but she's almost too well-behaved.' Just over a week later in the front room of her neat-as-a-new-pin cottage, Mrs Fisk's worried gaze met Beatrice's.

Although David had planned to see Ruby the day after Gilbert Russell's memorial service, a new group of convalescent soldiers arriving at Whittleton Hall meant he hadn't had a day off since. Beatrice had visited Aircraftman Griffiths on her own, cycling to and from Hazelbury, and had even missed seeing David at Whittleton since he'd been in meetings when she was there. Still, it wasn't as if Ruby could be called an urgent case. She attended school as required and, from what Mrs Fisk said, was in all respects a 'model' evacuee.

'What do you mean by "too well-behaved"?' Beatrice could guess, based on how Ruby was at school, but she wanted to hear from Mrs Fisk what the child was like at home.

'Even though I try to encourage her, she doesn't want to run and play like other children. Although me and my husband were never blessed with young ones of our own, I still remember my own childhood. Between wanting to climb trees and gates and joining my brothers in games, I was rarely still. Drove my poor mum to distraction, I did. And I see other children in the village. Ruby's not anything like them.'

Outside, October rain lashed against the small-paned windows, and a gusty wind whipped the tree branches into a frenzy. Indoors, a fire burned in the grate and its flames cast light around the low-beamed room, softening the lines on Mrs Fisk's wrinkled face.

'Let's see what Dr Stanley says.' Beatrice put her cup back on its saucer on a side table and declined more tea. Given the weather, it was lucky she hadn't had to cycle here. Despite being only a few miles from Hazelbury, Mrs Fisk's cottage seemed more remote, tucked into the deep hollow of a narrow lane and almost hidden by surrounding trees. 'How is Ruby managing the walk to and from school?'

'She does all right. Goes with the Legerton girls across the road.' Mrs Fisk gestured to the window. 'Ruby never complains, mind, so if she were to get tired, I suppose I wouldn't know.'

Beatrice held back a sigh. Some of her pupils complained too much, whereas with others, such as Ruby, she had no idea where to start in helping them.

'Ah, here's Ruby.' Beatrice stood as the girl came into the room, a large brown-and black patterned tabby cat cradled in her arms. 'And Dr Stanley.' She took a step forwards to greet them, but not before straightening the elaborate knitted lace antimacassar on the back of the armchair where she'd been sitting. Although the subject hadn't come up, Mrs Fisk must have once been in service – not a housekeeper, but certainly, given the cottage's pristine order, trained by a good one. A person who was fastidious and to whom details mattered.

'Dr Stanley checked Kitty too.' Ruby gave Beatrice a shy smile and held out the cat for her inspection. 'He said she's in tip-top form.'

'She is indeed,' David said, gesturing to Mrs Fisk to stay seated. Despite his otherwise grave expression, his hazel eyes were soft with kindness. 'As for this young lady, several dietary changes are in order. A carrot a day will be a good start, along with as much milk as she can drink. I've also prescribed cod liver oil, and I'm going to have a word with the district nurse and local authority. See if we can rustle up some extra eggs and increase her meat ration temporarily.' Over Ruby's head, his gaze connected with Beatrice's. 'Make sure she gets her milk and orange juice at school and eats the lunches Mrs Fisk packs. And for the next while, let her rest whenever she needs to during break time and games.' He glanced at Ruby, who was playing with the cat and chattering excitedly to Mrs Fisk. 'As a start, she needs to be built up. Only light chores at home as well.' He put a gentle hand on one of Ruby's thin shoulders. 'It's admirable that you want to help Mrs Fisk, but I don't want you bringing in wood for the fire or doing anything strenuous in the garden. Stick with things like washing up, easy dusting and picking a few vegetables.'

'Goodness, no' – Mrs Fisk's eyes widened – 'one of the Legerton boys does the heavy work. I wouldn't think of asking Ruby to do it.'

'Still, she seems to think it's needed.' David's mouth was strained. 'I'll pay another visit to her in a month and then let's see how things are. With loving care and the right nutrition, I expect Ruby will soon be a different child.'

'Why would I want to be different?' Ruby looked between them. 'I likes who I is.'

'Dr Stanley meant that you'll shortly feel even better in yourself,' Beatrice said. 'You'll have more energy to run and play, that's all. But you're exactly right as you are.' She knelt to Ruby's level. 'Mrs Fisk, Dr Stanley and I are here to help, but you also need to tell us if anything doesn't feel right or if you're troubled in any way.'

Ruby pursed her lips and then gave a quick, solemn nod. 'Me mum would say Doctor's alright.'

'He is.' Beatrice held back a smile.

'Thank you, Ruby.' Although David remained similarly solemn, his eyes danced with fun. 'I hope you still think I'm all right once you have your first dose of cod liver oil. I'll arrange for the chemist to send it out to you. He sometimes makes deliveries if necessary. No need to go into the village.' His keen scrutiny narrowed in on Mrs Fisk. 'You make sure you're eating right as well. No skipping meals to give Ruby extra.'

'No, Doctor.' Mrs Fisk's pale cheeks flushed, suggesting she'd been doing exactly that.

'Are you able to get out to church, W.I. meetings and such? Ruby tells me you're often troubled by rheumatism.' He approached Mrs Fisk's chair and, as Beatrice had done with Ruby, crouched at the older lady's side.

'I'm not as sprightly as I once was to be sure, but Mrs Meldrum takes me to church and suchlike in her car. If she can't, the vicar and Mrs Russell are ever so good as well. Folk are kind.'

'Mostly.' There was a bitter note in David's voice as he straightened. 'If you're ready, Miss Wentworth, we can be on our way.'

'Certainly.' Beatrice collected her handbag and school satchel from where she'd left them by her chair.

'Wait.' Ruby set the cat on Mrs Fisk's lap and then darted to Beatrice's side. 'The Nativity. You's said Father Christmas will come, except I bet the real Father Christmas will be too busy. That's what happened at my last school. One of the big girls' dads from our road dressed up as Father Christmas instead. I knows 'cause I heard her talkin' about it. Doctor'd be perfect, don't you think? He's not fat enough, but you could stuff some feather pillows under a suit for a big tummy. I won't tell nobody.' Her blue eyes shone.

Beatrice worried her lower lip. She *did* need to find a Father Christmas, and between the young ones who'd been called up and their elders who were involved in voluntary war work alongside their other jobs, suitable men were in short supply. She couldn't ask the vicar, as his voice was too recognisable – likewise Major Bertram. But David was as busy as anyone else – likely busier – and he also worked unpredictable hours. However, this was the first time Ruby had voluntarily spoken up or shown such interest in anything. She didn't want to discourage the child or dim her excitement.

'Ruby, I—'

'I'd be delighted to be Father Christmas at your school's Nativity,' David interjected. 'But you and Miss Wentworth have to help me practise.' He summoned up a faint 'Ho, ho, ho,' making Beatrice and Mrs Fisk laugh.

'You need to be louder.' Ruby studied him with her hands on her hips. 'Like this.' Her 'Ho, ho, ho,' came out in a high-pitched squeak.

Beatrice swallowed an unexpected lump in her throat. 'We'd be happy to help you practise.'

'And I have plenty of feather pillows. I've already been digging through my sewing basket for other costume fixings. Young Ruby's to be an angel *and* a robin,' Mrs Fisk said, her expression brightening.

'We're having a somewhat expanded Nativity,' Beatrice said. 'In addition to the usual parts, there are some non-traditional ones.' With so many pupils from the village and London schools, and wanting to include them all in some capacity, Beatrice had added several 'winter elements' to the usual Nativity play. Alongside Mary and Joseph, the Wise Men, angels, shepherds, sheep, the innkeeper and the donkey, other scenes featured a Victorian Christmas sketch, carol singers and a scene with small animals and birds celebrating the Christmas season in a snowy garden.

'Albert's bein' a Christmas cake,' Ruby explained. 'Miss Potter's making his costume out of old cardboard and we're all helpin' paint it. And Miss McKaye's mum and other ladies she knows have sent the school a box of things from Canada for Christmas. When it gets here, Miss McKaye says we'll have what she called a "box opening" with biscuits, but we're not allowed to open the parcels inside until the day school breaks up before Christmas. They have to go under tree.'

'It sounds grand.' David picked up his medical bag. 'I shall look forward to taking part.'

'We're having two parties. One at Whittleton with the poorly men, and one on last day of school. Aren't we lucky?' Ruby took one of David's hands and squeezed it. 'I've never had such a Christmas.' She then took one of Beatrice's hands too. 'Miss Wentworth and the other teachers always make nice things for us. I 'spect it'll be my best Christmas ever.'

Standing between them, as Ruby looked up, her small, angular face animated, the backs of Beatrice's eyes stung. Wartime life, with its myriad restrictions, was hard. Only the night before, she, Victoria and Nell had lamented the difficulties associated with putting on any kind of Nativity at all, with material – even old sheets to use for angel costumes – in short supply.

Now, she mentally berated herself for being caught up in trivialities. She needed to focus on what this Christmas would mean to Ruby and all the others who were far from their families amidst the ongoing horror of bombs raining down on London.

'We'll certainly try to make this Christmas your best one ever, Ruby. All of us.' She squeezed the girl's hand.

Thanks to Ruby, Beatrice found herself reminded of the true meaning of the celebration. Since losing Alex and her brothers, Christmas had been cheerless – an occasion to be endured rather than enjoyed. But it should be about hope and joy, no matter where or how you found it.

And love.

She gave David a quick sideways glance as he listened attentively to Ruby telling him how he needed to prepare for being Father Christmas.

Could she risk letting love into her heart again? Love for Ruby, who so clearly needed it both within and beyond the classroom. And maybe even love for David, someone who, like Beatrice, carried his own sorrows and with whom she had much more in common than she'd expected. A man who was kind and good. One whom any woman would be fortunate to have by her side.

Chapter Fourteen

Monday, 14 October 1940

'It's a squash, but we shall have to manage. We have no other choice.' Beatrice surveyed Hazelbury's village hall, which currently held the juniors' as well as the infants' classes. Amongst the many possibilities she'd tried to prepare for when it came to teaching in wartime, an infestation of rats in her classroom had not been one of them.

Victoria paused, still holding the exercise books she'd been handing out when Beatrice, Nell and their pupils had arrived a few minutes earlier. 'I suppose we could talk about Princess Elizabeth's radio broadcast. I expect most of the children listened to it yesterday. If we then focus on music, art, games and Nativity practice, that would be suitable for the different learning levels.'

'It would,' Beatrice replied. Once again, she was grateful for Victoria's level-headedness and ability to solve problems. 'It is far too soon to deliver a natural history lesson on rodent life.' She shook her head. 'For the most part, the children remained calm. It's not as if they haven't seen rats before, but it was still unnerving.'

Maybe for Beatrice most of all. Although uncomfortable, she had to acknowledge the truth. In her teaching, she'd always been more rigid in her thinking, adhering to the standard curriculum and relying on order and routine. However, this first year of war had shown her that she needed to be flexible, adapting lessons to whatever situation might present itself.

'Good, it's settled.' Victoria gave Beatrice an encouraging smile. 'Don't fuss. There's no school inspector here today.'

However, Beatrice still felt the weight of responsibility that came with being the most senior teacher. 'I shall have to record this morning's events in the school logbook and also write to Miss Hopson.' It was part of the seemingly never-ending administrative work that filled her days in between actual teaching, lesson preparation and evacuee care within and beyond the classroom. When had she last taken her sketchbook out for pleasure? It had been weeks, maybe even as far back as the summer holidays, but drawing had always been an important part of who she was. Without it, Beatrice felt off balance and unlike herself.

As Victoria clapped her hands to get the children's attention, Beatrice marshalled her class together to sit on the floor around the infants, who were ranged on mismatched chairs on both sides of two long tables. 'Ah, here you are, Miss Potter.' She nodded at Nell who'd gone outdoors to retrieve several pupils who, amidst the general disruption, had taken the opportunity to wander off to the garden allotments. 'We shall resume our lessons, albeit to a slightly different timetable. No, Albert, we shall not be breaking early for lunch and please raise your hand if you wish to speak. How many times have I told you not to shout out?'

'I dunno, Miss. Lots?' He gave her a cheeky grin.

It had been a rhetorical question but no matter.

'Sorry, Miss Wentworth.' In response to Beatrice's most severe look, Albert settled beside his friend Ralph and several boys from the village.

At least she could always rely on Diana. Her gaze drifted to the girl who sat by Ruby and had a consoling arm around her, the two of them looking at a picture book.

Diana was a good influence on Ruby and, like her mother, had an instinctive empathy for those less fortunate. As with her art, it had also been too long since Beatrice had written to Mary, now living in North Wales with her husband, who had been evacuated there with his government office. Mary had married 'beneath her' as Beatrice's mother called it, but she seemed happy enough.

Besides, marriage had given Mary a daughter as well as two stalwart sons. If one considered it from that perspective, Mary, not Beatrice, was the more successful. Mary was more comfortable in material things too, since she didn't have to survive on a teacher's salary and support her mother as well.

And most important of all, Mary had a loving husband who was devoted to her comfort and well-being. Nothing else truly mattered, did it?

As quiet descended on the village hall, Beatrice went to the front and stood by the table that served as Victoria's desk. 'How many of you listened to the *Children's Hour* programme on the wireless yesterday and heard our lovely young Princess Elizabeth addressing us from Windsor Castle?' Beatrice adopted the sort of reverent expression and tone one took when mentioning members of the royal family.

Every hand went up, including Ruby's.

'We teachers listened as well and were moved by how the princess spoke directly to those of us whom war has separated from our families. Like many of you, Miss McKaye, Miss Potter and I are also far from our loved ones.' However, for Beatrice, being separated by the war from her mother in Oxfordshire had been something of a blessing in disguise. With her mother living so near London, Beatrice had made almost weekly visits before the war. Now, an annual visit had to suffice. 'Princess Elizabeth and her sister, Princess Margaret Rose, also thanked the "kind people" like those of you here in Hazelbury who have graciously opened your homes to Londoners.' Some more grudgingly than others, it was true, but it was a considerable imposition even for the most willing of hosts. 'Do you remember anything else from Princess Elizabeth's speech?'

'No, but me dad said someone must have wrote it for her,' Leonard, one of the village boys who was usually in Nell's class, called out.

'Raise your hand, Leonard.' Nell darted an apologetic look at Beatrice.

'Yes, Miss Potter, but my dad still ain't wrong.' Leonard's nod was decisive.

'Whilst someone else *may* have written the speech which the princess delivered, or helped her with it, that takes nothing away from how clearly she spoke and how charmingly heartfelt she sounded,' Beatrice said.

Was it wartime propaganda? Perhaps, but Beatrice preferred to take a more charitable view. Despite what the young princess might think privately, she'd done her duty, and like the teachers did on a daily basis, she'd tried to boost the children's spirits. Why else would Beatrice, Victoria and Nell be doing their utmost to make sure the Nativity was a success?

'The princess spoke to children of the Commonwealth too,' Victoria added, picking up a wooden pointer as she moved to a map of the world pinned on one of the walls. 'In my country, Canada, as well as Australia and New Zealand and—'

The wail of an air-raid siren cut across her words.

'Quickly, children.' Despite the cold chill of fear curling in the pit of her stomach, Beatrice made her voice bright. 'Don't forget your gas masks.' Even though today was the first time the siren had sounded during school hours, they'd all practised for this moment. Whilst the Luftwaffe was still bombing London and other British cities at night, during the day the Germans had also turned their attention to coastal towns, airfields and other military targets. 'Yes, take your cardigan.' As Beatrice gathered up her handbag and stuffed the school's logbook, register and several storybooks into her satchel, she answered questions while doing a headcount as the children lined up in their assigned pairs.

'Stop pushing each other, boys,' Ivy Byrne, Victoria's morning assistant who also helped Mrs Russell at the vicarage, reprimanded Ralph and Albert.

'Right, follow Miss McKaye, Miss Potter and Miss Byrne, and I shall bring up the rear.' She gave Ivy an encouraging and grateful smile. The girl was a great support to all the teachers, not just Victoria.

Once outside, the siren's wail made Beatrice's ears ring. As the four of them marshalled the children towards the pub, villagers rushed past, heading either to Anderson shelters in back gardens, a converted basement, or a trench that had been dug and reinforced to make a communal shelter on the far side of the village green. If Beatrice, Nell and their pupils had been at the school, they would have gone to the latter, but from the village hall, the cellar and adjoining tunnel beneath the pub was nearer.

'Good, good,' Mr Foulger said, Hazelbury's air-raid warden, who met them in front of the pub. 'Pop indoors and down the steps, kiddies. No running. We don't want any of you taking a tumble.' With his steel helmet, blue overalls, armband and ARP badge, he had an air of authority that even Beatrice's most unruly pupils did not dare question.

'I don't want to go down in the dark. I's scared.' Near the front of the group of children, Ruby's voice reached Beatrice.

'I know it's hard, dear, but you have to. Here, put your arms around my neck and I'll carry you,' Nell said.

'But I don't want to.' Ruby started to cry and several other girls joined in.

Every fibre in Beatrice's being yearned to go to the child, but she couldn't. She was responsible for everyone, not just Ruby, so she would be the last to go into the shelter after all the pupils were accounted for.

At Beatrice's side, Jimmy Clarke took a step forwards. 'I'll see to Ruby, Miss. And any others who're scared.'

'Good, lad. I'll help too,' a deep voice spoke from behind them, and then David was alongside the children. His light touch on Beatrice's shoulder and quick smile as he passed, anchored her amidst the mayhem. They also helped calm her own fear – one she'd never admitted – of going into a dark, enclosed space, and the resultant feeling of being trapped with no escape. 'It's all right, Ruby.' In an instant, the girl was in David's arms, her face buried in his chest. 'It's fine, Miss Potter. I'll see to her. You and Jimmy look out for the others.'

Moments later, the ARP warden stopped at the top of the steps as the last pair of children went down them with Ivy. 'Everyone accounted for, Miss Wentworth?'

'Yes. The entire school. We were all at the village hall.' Beatrice gripped the class lists, her handbag, satchel and gas mask box. There was nothing to be afraid of. Although the Luftwaffe were likely targeting Whittleton Airfield rather than Hazelbury itself, she'd still be in more immediate danger if she stayed up here.

'Right. I'll be off then.' The warden touched his helmet and turned to assist a white-haired lady carrying a cage that held a budgie flapping its wings and making high-pitched squawks.

Beatrice took a deep breath. One step at a time.

'Miss Wentworth?' David came back up the stairs and held out a hand. 'All set?'

'Yes.' She jerked her chin as the steps yawned in front of her.

'Here we go, then.' He took Beatrice's satchel and gas mask box, then clasped her cold hand in his warm one. In the moment of crisis and preoccupied with getting the children to safety, she hadn't stopped to put on her hat or gloves. She smiled wryly. As if such propriety mattered in the way it once had, especially now. Yet as David's palm met hers, she trembled – not with fear, but with something else entirely. A reaction to David's closeness.

'Not far now,' he said, guiding her down the steps. 'Bob the publican has provided several torches so it's not too bad. I left Ruby listening to a story Miss McKaye's reading. Ruby and the rest are right as rain.'

'Thank you,' Beatrice spoke through numb lips as they reached the entrance to the cellar under the pub.

David squeezed her hand before letting go. 'I was on night duty at the hospital and had only just dropped off to sleep when the siren went. Here' – from somewhere he retrieved a flask and cup – 'tea? Miss Potter's distributing biscuits.'

'Miss Wentworth?' came Ruby's voice. 'I saved space for you's to sit with me. You and Doctor. Miss McKaye's reading us a book about a family in America who lived in some big woods. One of her sisters sent it to us.'

'It's *Little House in the Big Woods*.' Although the book was popular in England, Beatrice hadn't read it until after Victoria's sister's parcel arrived. Then she'd devoured it in a weekend, marvelling at the way the Ingalls family had lived in Wisconsin seventy years ago. The 1870s weren't in the distant past. Beatrice's mother had been born in 1870, so was close in age to Laura Ingalls Wilder. Yet, unlike the hardships experienced by Laura's family, before the last war Clarissa Wentworth's life in England had been one of privilege. Beatrice made her way to Ruby, conscious of David still by her side, almost as if he were protecting her.

'Is mink like what's Mrs Meldrum's fur hat? The one she wears to church?' Peter, one of the infants, piped up in response to a reference to mink in the story.

As Victoria explained that Mrs Meldrum's hat was indeed made of mink, Beatrice sat beside Ruby, took the cup of tea David pressed into her hand and then a honey biscuit from Nell.

'It'll be all right' – Ruby cuddled into Beatrice's side – 'Doctor said so.' In the dim light from one of the torches, Ruby's face was still pale but it looked fuller and healthier than it had only a fortnight before. 'Doctor also said we can pretend we're all snug and cosy like rabbits in a burrow.'

Aeroplanes thundered overhead and the siren continued to shriek, but Ruby's small body was warm. As Victoria continued reading, Beatrice's breathing steadied.

'All right, Miss Wentworth?' David spoke softly, sitting on Ruby's other side.

'Yes.' Unexpectedly, despite the circumstances, she *was* all right.

An explosion sounded in the distance and, as the ground and cellar and tunnel vibrated, David reached behind Ruby and took Beatrice's hand again.

It was definitely improper. Beatrice was a teacher – the senior teacher – and had to set an example for her pupils and colleagues. But it was dark where they sat, wedged on a wooden bench along one of the stone walls, and between the children listening to the story and villagers playing cards or chatting, nobody would notice or care.

For this brief moment, Beatrice let herself relax into the comfort and reassurance of David's touch. Even though she dreaded when she'd have to relinquish it again.

Chapter Fifteen

'If I cut around the worn patches in this old grey blanket, I could make a costume for the Nativity donkey. Unfortunately, there's not enough usable fabric in the late Mr Grainger's brown overcoat and the tweed's also too thick to shape. The coat's lighter-brown silk lining, though, will do for several of the rabbits and mice, and perhaps the innkeeper's tunic. Those costumes are smaller.' In the library at Hazelbury Manor, Nell held the blanket up for Beatrice and Victoria's inspection.

'Yes, the blanket would make a sort of cape arrangement for the donkey,' Beatrice said, as she nodded her approval. 'You could use scraps for the ears, and either more fabric or knitting wool for the donkey's tail. If Jimmy has some black trousers – or if he hasn't, maybe he could borrow some – he could wear them underneath.'

Beatrice set aside the exercise books of arithmetic problems she'd been marking, took off her spectacles and rubbed her eyes. When the all-clear had finally sounded, and they'd come out of the cellar beneath the pub, none of the children had been in any state to settle to music, art or Nativity practice. So, between first the rats and then the air raid, it had been an even more trying day than normal. She was also more tired than usual, and it was only Monday, so there were still four days of school to go before the weekend break.

'I'm sure there's an old hat of our father's that Jimmy could wear. I'll look in one of the attic chests tomorrow. It will be too large and come down over his face, but that's all to the good, and I think the colour is right.' Miss Addie took one end of the blanket and studied it. 'The donkey's ears could be fixed to the hat's band, and you can cut holes for him to see through.'

'Necessity is the mother of invention.' Victoria laughed, and as she set her knitting aside and stretched, her engagement ring sparkled in the firelight. 'If there's enough left of the worn parts of blanket and they're not needed for rags, my infants could make a fort from them. I want to set aside a corner of the village hall to use for reading and imaginative play. When it's too wet or cold, the little ones can't go out during break, so it's dull for them stuck indoors.'

'I'll see' – Nell spoke through a mouthful of pins – 'I may need the worn pieces for parts of the bird costumes.'

'I'll ask the president of the Amateur Dramatics Society,' Beatrice offered. 'Whilst the majority of their costumes will be adult size, there are likely hats, scarves or other items we might borrow and adapt for the Nativity. There aren't enough members or even time for the society to put on a play this year.' They also weren't having regular meetings, which Beatrice missed, as they'd been a highlight of the autumn and winter during her first year in Hazelbury.

'When we were sheltering during the raid, Peter asked me if we could use Mrs Meldrum's mink hat for a Nativity costume.' Victoria laughed. 'As if.'

'Mrs Meldrum is inordinately proud of that hat. I am often tempted to remind her that pride goes before a fall.' Miss Hetty looked up from her knitting and joined their conversation. 'It is most unseemly, especially in wartime.'

'Now Hetty, you know she got that hat last autumn,' Miss Addie said. 'And she'd ordered it from London before war had even been declared.'

Beatrice refrained from smiling. Gentle Miss Addie rarely clashed with her elder sister but maybe, like Nell, she was developing more of a backbone. They all were, Beatrice included. Or, to draw on another part of Holy Scripture, perhaps the war made her less likely to suffer fools.

'Is there any more news from Whittleton?' Victoria introduced a less charged subject than Mrs Meldrum and her hat.

'Nothing more than that while there were no casualties and only minor injuries, one of the airfields is in a bad way.' Nell stuck pins into an orange-silk pincushion. 'At choir practice, Mrs Russell said the vicar heard that one of the runways can't be used and several aircraft are also badly damaged.'

'If there had been casualties, Dr Stanley would likely have been called out,' Victoria said. 'I don't know when that poor man gets any sleep at all. Between the convalescent hospital, RAF Whittleton being short-staffed, and the lack of local doctors, Dr Stanley seems to be treating most of the area. Do you know the midwife called on him to help deliver two babies, one last night and the other early this morning? I heard him mention it to someone after the all-clear. He said he'd be grateful not to be called to the telephone unless it was another emergency.'

Victoria stood up. 'Speaking of sleep, I'm off to bed. Beatrice, Nell?'

Beatrice shook her head. 'I still need to finish marking this arithmetic and then write to Miss Hopson about the rats.'

Nell put away her sewing. 'Don't work too late.' For a brief moment, her gaze held Beatrice's. 'If you need help with the marking, I can stay.'

'Thank you, but I'm almost done. Go on. I'll take Lady out before I go to bed.' Beatrice forced a smile until Nell took Miss Addie's arm, Victoria took Miss Hetty's and the four of them left the library.

'It's just you and me, Lady.' The dog, who'd briefly raised her head, settled back down in front of the fire as Beatrice returned to her marking.

Several of her pupils should really have the chance to sit a grammar school examination. But even if they did and got a scholarship place, was there a school close enough for them to travel to on weekdays – or could they board, and would that also be paid for? If they stayed here until they were fourteen, how could she challenge them?

Closing the last book and putting it into her satchel, she took out her writing case, a pen and the letter to Miss Hopson she'd begun earlier.

She dashed off several more paragraphs, and then concluded the missive with a brief mention of their plans for the Nativity and an invitation to Miss Hopson to visit Hazelbury in December to attend one of the performances.

If the war should so permit. An innocuous phrase covering all manner of dire eventualities. What would London look like the next time Beatrice visited? Greatly altered, certainly, but even if Park Road School and the local area had escaped bombing, it still wouldn't be the same. *She* wasn't the same.

Beatrice rested her chin in her hands and stared into the fire, caught up in the flickering orange flames. She should douse the fire and fill her hot water bottle. Like everyone else, she'd learned to sleep when she could but often, even when she was tired, rest didn't come easily.

'Oh, Beatrice.' Miss Hetty's voice came from the library door, along with a cold draught. 'I thought you'd have gone to bed by now. I came to find a book. I seem to be wakeful.' In the beam of light cast by a torch, Miss Hetty's smile was wry as she shut the door and came further into the room, clad in a dark dressing gown with a white nightcap covering her hair. 'No, Lady.' She waved to the dog to stay where she was and joined Beatrice by the fire.

'Would you like me to make you a cup of tea?' Beatrice moved to get up.

'It's most kind, but no, thank you.' Miss Hetty shook her head. 'Tea would make me even more wakeful. At night especially, I often find myself remembering what this house was like in my childhood. It was vastly different, as I expect you can imagine.'

Beatrice's throat constricted. She usually tried not to think of her childhood home. The memories were too painful.

Playing croquet on the sunlit lawn. Music spilling from her eldest brother's new gramophone. Charades at Christmas. The lavish dinner parties with eight or ten courses. The way of life she'd never questioned until everything changed.

Miss Hetty stared into the dancing flames. 'My fiancé proposed to me in this library. Right there by that long window overlooking the garden. It was after a tennis match which we'd had to call off partway through due to rain. The butler interrupted him. Mr Jenkins was most embarrassed, but Montague simply carried on. It wasn't the most romantic of proposals, but neither Montague nor I were the most romantic of young people.' Miss Hetty's dry chuckle was like the rustle of autumn leaves in the wind. 'Addie used to despair of me.'

Beatrice knew that Miss Hetty had been engaged, and that her fiancé had been killed in the Boer War. Until now, absorbed in work and the present war, she hadn't drawn any parallels between her own life and the elder Miss Grainger's. Perhaps she hadn't been ready to see herself in a woman who, although they often chatted due to having a similar family background, was of Beatrice's parents' generation.

'What was your fiancé like?' If Miss Hetty was in a confiding mood, Beatrice wanted to encourage it.

'Montague wasn't handsome, but looks fade, and it is inner character which is of greater importance.' Turning to face Beatrice, Miss Hetty's eyes had a faraway look. 'Still, he had a kind face and manner, and together we made a formidable tennis partnership. I've often thought that life is a great deal like a tennis match. One must adapt, no matter the difficulties, and take responsibility for one's actions and choices, but there are also always unexpected events and adversity.'

Beatrice knew she shouldn't grumble, but her life seemed to have had an inordinate share of unexpected events. The last war and now this one, barely twenty years apart for a start, although she was not the only person to experience *that*. 'Did your family approve of… your fiancé?' She couldn't bring herself to call him 'Montague'. It seemed improper, especially with Miss Hetty, but his surname hadn't been mentioned.

'Montague was eminently suitable. He was Sir Montague, you know, and along with having the proper background, he was also comfortably off. At that time, and with a father such as mine, I would not have entertained any man's affections otherwise.' She stopped and fidgeted with her dressing gown cord. 'After Montague was killed, I grieved, certainly. But in remaining devoted to his memory, I perhaps failed to adapt when I might have. Like this house, the world is different. For too long, I refused to acknowledge the inevitability of change.'

Beatrice's thoughts whirled. Miss Hetty had never spoken so freely, but was she only speaking about her own life or attempting to give Beatrice a message? 'My mother is rather fixed in her way of looking at the world.' That was an understatement and perhaps Beatrice should not have shared something so personal. However, there was something about the quiet house and the small circle of light from the fire that invited confidences.

Miss Hetty's laugh was sharp. 'But you are not your mother, are you?'

'No, I'm not.' Beatrice's shoulders slumped. All her life, she'd been unfavourably compared to her beautiful mother.

If only she were more like Clarissa. So unfortunate, isn't it? Still, perhaps Beatrice will grow out of her awkwardness. The words of an elderly visiting great-aunt, overheard and never forgotten, echoed across the years.

Beatrice hadn't grown out of it and, if anything, she'd become more awkward, especially after Alex was killed.

Do sit up straight, Beatrice. Slouching is most indelicate. I have done my best and you could at least try to make some effort. That was what her mother had said on Beatrice's last visit when she'd caught Beatrice listening to the wireless whilst mending – after a day of backbreaking work in the hot sun in their cousin's garden.

Over a lifetime of criticism, overt or implied, almost without noticing, she'd shrunk into herself, fearful of drawing attention, yet still constrained by both familial strictures and societal expectations.

'It is good that you recognise you are not your mother.' Miss Hetty gave a decisive nod. 'Be true to yourself, Beatrice. That is a lesson I learned too late, but for you – well, from my vantage point, you are still young. Make the most of it.' She reached down to pat Lady. 'I may be elderly, but I did not misinterpret how Dr Stanley looked at you when he joined us that day for luncheon. Do not underestimate yourself or your considerable charms.'

'But I… he…' Beatrice stammered.

'Indeed.' Miss Hetty stood. 'After Montague, nobody else was ever suitable. That is what I thought, and by the time I realised I was wrong it was too late. Even now, whilst I'm content living here with Addie, I do sometimes wonder how different my life might have been if I'd shown a bit of backbone.'

'Backbone?' She, too, got to her feet. Miss Hetty had the most backbone of anyone Beatrice knew.

'The inner strength to stand your ground. I know you have it, but perhaps you need a reminder.' Miss Hetty pulled her nightcap more firmly over her head, its ruffled edges giving her face a softer and more feminine appearance than usual. 'I must find a book if I am to get any sleep at all. Maybe one of Miss Edgeworth's novels. I've read them so many times they have the virtue of not holding any alarming surprises. Do take Lady out, won't you? The damp night air is bad for me. And close your mouth. You must have been taught that it is most unbecoming and ill-bred to leave it hanging open.'

'Yes, Miss Hetty.' Beatrice snapped her mouth closed. Whilst it sounded like something her mother might say, coming from Miss Hetty it was different. Not so much criticism as a brusque sort of caring. 'Good night, Miss Hetty.' She bent to retrieve Lady's lead, always kept close at hand given the frequency with which the air-raid siren went off and they had to seek shelter.

She didn't need a man to be content, but how might the companionship of the right one make her life better? She didn't want to end up like Miss Hetty, recognising too late what might have been.

Because even if her mother was unwilling or unable to admit it, most of the men she would have considered suitable lay in the fields of Flanders, their broken bodies turned to dust.

Chapter Sixteen

Saturday, 2 November 1940

Despite her coat, and beneath it a woollen jumper, blouse and vest, Beatrice shivered as she rounded the corner of a gravel path at Whittleton Hall, pushing one of the convalescent servicemen in a wheelchair. The volunteer who usually took him for a walk was needed elsewhere so today the job had fallen to Beatrice. In the half hour they'd been outdoors, Beatrice had at first attempted to make conversation – but since Flying Officer Brown hadn't uttered a word, they'd soon reverted to walking in silence.

The leafless trees that lined the drive creaked in the wind, and the scent of woodsmoke drifted across the crisp air. Winter was coming – the second one during wartime – and still the bombing continued. 'Shall we go indoors? I'd welcome a cup of tea, wouldn't you?' She made her voice cheery as she wheeled Brown up a newly installed wooden ramp that ran along one side of the house to the front door.

Slumped in his chair, the man didn't answer, although he put a hand to the livid scar that cut across his right cheek. His aeroplane had been shot down near the south coast, and he'd been one of the lucky few to have survived. Looking at him now, though, that 'luck' was debateable.

‘Oh, Mrs Bertram,’ she greeted the other woman, who opened the door as Beatrice and Brown approached. ‘I didn’t expect to see you here today. What a pleasure.’

‘I came in to assist Dr Stanley.’ Mrs Bertram glanced at Brown and then back at Beatrice. ‘Are you returning to Hazelbury soon?’

‘Yes, my shift’s just ended, although I’d thought to have a cup of tea before cycling back.’ A nurse approached, and at Beatrice’s nod, she took the handles of Brown’s chair, speaking softly to him.

‘Well, if you can wait for that tea and have it in Hazelbury instead, Dr Stanley has offered me a lift there. I expect he could take you as well.’ Mrs Bertram gave Beatrice a warm smile. ‘I promised Mrs Russell she could count on me to help with the parish jumble sale. They delayed opening until noon because of both the Red Cross meeting and Mr Wright’s funeral this morning.’

Beatrice nodded. ‘The Misses Grainger went to that funeral. I understand Mr Wright worked at the manor when he was young.’ Having been in ill health for the better part of a year, Robert Wright’s death wasn’t unexpected, but the two ladies had seemed most affected by it, almost as if he were a family member.

‘It was before my time but yes, I did hear that he worked for the Grainger family. In the stables, I think, or was it the gardens? I can’t remember. Oh, here’s Dr Stanley.’

Beatrice manufactured a neutral smile. ‘I don’t want to inconvenience him, and I don’t mind cycling.’ However, getting a lift would mean she could get to the jumble sale soon after it opened before items had been picked over. Despite Nell’s ingenuity, there were still bits and pieces needed for Nativity costumes, and Beatrice had also hoped she might find some warmer clothing for Ruby. The child needed sturdier shoes and a thicker coat. Another skirt and jumper wouldn't go amiss either. She wanted to go to the sale for entirely pedestrian reasons, but her breath quickened as David drew near.

'What's this about cycling?' David stopped at Beatrice's side, and as Mrs Bertram explained, Beatrice's face heated.

'I'd be happy to give you a lift back to Hazelbury. You and Mrs Bertram both.' Did David's gaze linger on Beatrice? Before she could respond or raise any objection, he continued, 'It's no trouble, and since I'm taking a military lorry we can pop your bike in the back.'

'It's settled, then.' Mrs Bertram clapped her gloved hands. 'Here.' She directed Beatrice down the front steps to the lorry. 'You get in out of the cold.' She turned back to David. 'Miss Wentworth's bicycle is in the shed outside the kitchen garden door. Slide along the seat, Miss Wentworth, and sit in the middle. My goodness – that wind is bitter.' She got in next to Beatrice and shut the door, continuing to chat about the weather and the jumble sale.

Moments later, Beatrice's bike was in the back of the lorry, and David was in the driver's seat. As he started the vehicle, his arm brushed against Beatrice's. Would he think she'd manoeuvred this seating arrangement to suit herself? She clutched her handbag and studied her gloves as they rattled down the drive and into the quiet country lane. When he leaned forwards to change gear, Beatrice caught a woodsy, soap-like scent – luxurious and comforting.

'Is your car out of service?' Mrs Bertram asked.

'No, but I needed to collect a delivery for the hospital from the train in Cromer earlier. Now that I have more permanent lodgings, I also had my trunk sent up from London.' When David smiled, the creases around his eyes and mouth deepened, giving his face extra character and, if it were possible, making him even more attractive.

'Oh, where will you be living?' Beatrice put a hand to her mouth as the question popped out unbidden.

'Still in Hazelbury. Mr and Mrs Russell have made space for me in the vicarage.' His smile disappeared. 'I didn't want to put them out, but they insisted.'

'They've given you Gilbert's room,' Mrs Bertram said, her voice catching.

'Yes.' David kept his gaze on the narrow lane but a muscle twitched in his jaw. 'They said they'd rather have me in it than a stranger.'

'That's understandable, but still…' Mrs Bertram's voice trailed away.

Beatrice stared out of the window at the muted November landscape, with its palette of greys and browns. Mrs Bertram must be thinking of her own sons serving on land, in the air and at sea – and her daughter in London. There were plenty of civilian casualties in war as well.

'Here you are, Mrs Bertram.' In Hazelbury's high street, which they'd reached much quicker than Beatrice expected, David stopped near the church and parked. Unlike in some villages, Hazelbury's parish hall was part of the church building itself, and from parish and community meetings to jumble sales and other such activities, it was in almost constant use.

'And here's the vicar.' Mrs Bertram waved as Mr Russell approached and greeted them.

'If you're going back to the manor, Miss Wentworth, I can—'

'I'm not, but thank you.' As the vicar helped Mrs Bertram from the lorry, Beatrice moved across to the side passenger seat, putting more space between herself and David. 'I need to visit the jumble sale myself.'

'I understand.' David drummed his fingers on the steering wheel. 'It's only that I've hardly seen you in the past fortnight, and I wondered… You undoubtedly have other plans, but do you dance?'

'Dance?' Beatrice drew in a quick breath. 'Yes, of course I do.' *Backbone. No regrets.* 'I enjoy dancing but don't often get to do it.'

'Well, then, there's a dance next Saturday night in Whittleton. Would you like to go? With me?' He stopped drumming his fingers and instead clasped his hands together.

'I would. Very much. If you don't get called to the hospital.' Beatrice tried to tamp down her excitement.

'I won't.' He smiled with his eyes, not just his mouth. 'I've arranged for another doctor to work that weekend. He's coming from Norwich.'

'Good. I mean, I'm glad you'll be able to have a break.' Out of the corner of one eye, she spotted Mrs Meldrum and several other women from the W.I. observing them from the church porch. 'I must go – but thank you for the lift.'

'I shall look forward to next Saturday. Perhaps we could have supper beforehand? There's a café in Whittleton. It won't be what you're used to, but I'd enjoy your company.' David's voice was low and held an almost intimate note.

'The café will be fine. I am not accustomed to dining out, there or anywhere else.' She darted another glance at the women who'd moved out from under the porch. 'My bicycle. I mustn't forget it.'

Following Beatrice's gaze, David winked at her before getting out of the lorry to come around and open her door. 'Since the rats have been removed from the premises, I'll drop by the school at some point this week to make arrangements for Saturday.' He paused and then raised his voice. 'I'd like to take another look at young Ruby.' His eyes sparkled with fun.

'Certainly.' Beatrice grinned, all of a sudden feeling young and almost carefree again.

She was adapting, and although she'd thought life would never get any better, it just had.

Chapter Seventeen

Wednesday, 6 November 1940

'I seen another rat, Miss.' From the back of Beatrice's classroom, one of the village boys, her oldest pupil, raised his hand as he spoke. 'A big one, it were.'

'Did not' – Jimmy Clarke shook his head decidedly – 'you're lying, you are.'

'Am not.'

Beatrice rapped on her desk with a ruler. 'The rat catcher has assured me that there are no rats in our school.' Although that didn't prevent her from imagining random rustles, scratches and gnawing sounds coming from behind the walls and under the floorboards.

'Not here. I seen the rat outside by the toilet.' The boy guffawed and two of his mates joined in.

'Given you would rather joke than attend to your lessons, the three of you will spend your afternoon break cleaning the lavatory. If you do not complete the job to my satisfaction, you will stay after school to finish it.' Beatrice had never struck a child, preferring other, more constructive forms of discipline, but, nearing fourteen, some of the village boys were already too big for anyone but a strong man to cane. She glanced from her now silent and wide-eyed pupils to the clock on the classroom wall.

'The rest of you may take your break early. The rain has stopped, and since it was too wet to go outdoors this morning or at lunchtime, we must make the most of the better weather.'

Desks rattled, chairs scraped and numerous pairs of feet thundered across the bare wooden floor towards the cloakroom and freedom. More slowly, Beatrice followed them to the classroom door and popped across the corridor to tell Nell so she could dismiss her pupils too. Nell was also on playground duty, a task they divided between them.

Then Beatrice returned to her desk, sat behind it and put a hand to her head. Unlike at Park Road School, there was no staffroom here. No indoor lavatory solely for staff use. And with no proper kitchen in which to make tea, she usually brought hers from home in a flask – which, having overslept, she'd forgotten to do this morning. Why did she let her mother upset her so? Her most recent letter had kept Beatrice awake long after midnight.

You will remember Sarah Stamford-Jones?

Of course Beatrice remembered her. They'd grown up together, and Sarah, with her pink-and-white prettiness and myriad of accomplishments – and suitors – had been something of a thorn in Beatrice's side. A girl her mother had expected Beatrice to emulate.

I had a card from Mrs Stamford-Jones. Sarah is Lady Hossington now and her husband has recently been posted to Washington to serve in some kind of wartime diplomatic role. Like myself, Mrs Stamford-Jones is widowed and alone, so she and Sarah are setting up home at the Hossington family seat in Sussex. It will be such a comfort for them to be together, don't you think? And Mrs Stamford-Jones will have the comfort of her grandchildren too. The older ones, only in the school holidays, but the two youngest are not yet of the age to board. So often I grieve not having the joy that grandchildren bring.

Mrs Wentworth had gone on in the same vein for four closely written pages: comparing Beatrice unfavourably to Sarah, offering unsolicited advice on everything from foundation garments to being mindful of their family's reputation, and finishing with her usual lament that 'poor, dear Beatrice' was not getting any younger, along with a request for money.

> *Just a little extra. I find myself rather short this month, darling.*

Because of having to support her mother, Beatrice, too, often found herself 'rather short'. But what was she to do? Albeit an impossible situation, it was also one she could not change. Besides, sending money was far preferable to bringing her mother to live with her, even if it were possible to do so.

'Miss Wentworth?'

At the sound of the small voice, Beatrice raised her head. 'Yes, Ruby. What is it? Why aren't you out playing with the other children?' Shouts of boys tossing a ball echoed from the yard, and nearer the classroom window, higher-pitched girls' voices rose and fell in a skipping rhyme.

'I made you somethin'. Pressed leaves. Mrs Fisk showed me how to do 'em.' From behind her back, Ruby presented Beatrice with a piece of stiff card on which brilliant red, orange and yellow leaves had been stuck in an approximation of a bouquet. 'I put 'em in Mrs Fisk's big family Bible and then I had to wait a few weeks, but didn't they turn out fine?' Ruby beamed at Beatrice. 'I put my name on the bottom. See?' She pointed to the crooked uppercase letters beneath a red leaf. 'I also collected the leaves special for you.'

'Your work is beautiful, Ruby. Thank you.' Beatrice's throat tightened. 'I shall treasure it. You're a kind and thoughtful girl.' While Beatrice and the other teachers often received bunches of wildflowers from pupils, this token from Ruby meant more. Unlike wildflowers which faded within a day, Ruby's bouquet was one Beatrice could keep. It also represented a great deal of thought and effort.

'I got a postcard from me mum too. I wanted to show you but not the others. Ain't it pretty?' Ruby took the postcard from her skirt pocket and held it out for Beatrice to admire – a coloured illustration of kittens tumbling from a basket.

Although Beatrice had finally received a brief note in reply to her letters to Mr and Mrs Parker, Ruby's mother, whilst expressing her appreciation for Beatrice's care and concern, had not been forthcoming as to Ruby's home situation. Was the woman merely unused to letter writing, or was she intentionally concealing the reality of their life? Beatrice suspected it was both, so she'd decided to continue doing the best she could for Ruby without worrying over Mrs Parker.

'Your mum's card is beautiful too.' Beatrice smiled. In the cosy blue jumper, navy skirt and stout shoes Beatrice had found for her at the jumble sale, Ruby, while still not the picture of health, looked more solid and less likely to be carried away by the wind. Her hair was thicker and its flaxen colour reminded Beatrice of a Norfolk wheat field in midsummer. 'That kitten in the middle looks like Mrs Fisk's cat, doesn't it?'

Ruby gave a solemn nod.

'Would you like me to help you write back to your mum?' Beatrice opened her desk drawer. 'I have some postcards here for you to choose from.' She'd bought several from the village shop for that purpose.

'Yes, please.' Ruby pointed to a card with a single cat in a style similar to the one her mother had sent. 'Mum wrote that, since he lost his job, me dad joined up. With the navy, he is, and Mum's gone to work in a factory making things for the war.'

'I see.' Beatrice hesitated. 'You don't have any brothers and sisters?'

Ruby shook her head. 'I had a little sister, but she got took away by the angels.' Her bottom lip trembled. 'That dad's not my real one. Good riddance to him, I say. I hope he don't never come back and gets drowned in the sea.'

'Ruby.' Beatrice held back a horrified gasp. 'Don't you remember what the vicar said about loving each other?'

'Yes, but he didn't know me dad.' Ruby squared her shoulders and what Beatrice had always considered the girl's meek demeanour was replaced with an attitude of defiance and palpable fury. 'Vicar's a good man. Like Doctor and Mr Fisk.'

'Mr Fisk?' Beatrice seized on the last, most easily addressed part of what Ruby had said. 'Mrs Fisk's husband died many years ago, dear.'

'Yes, but she still talks 'bout him. She showed me his photograph in a frame on the table beside her bed. She said he wouldn't even hurt a fly.' Ruby screwed up her face. 'A "right fine fellow" – that's what the gentleman he worked for called him. Mrs Fisk said nobody ever spoke truer.'

'I expect your stepfather must have some good qualities, but in any case it is wrong to wish harm to anyone.' Unsure as to how – or if – she should raise the child's home situation any further, given that another pupil could return to the classroom at any moment, Beatrice found a pencil and held it out to Ruby. 'What do you want to say to your mother?'

'I hear lots of folk say they want Mr Hitler to cop it.' Ruby took the pencil but continued to study Beatrice. Her eyes were brighter than before and seemed to blaze with blue fire. 'Mrs Yallop said she'd like to see 'im boil in oil 'cause it'd be a long and painful death. Them's her exact words. I heard her right in village shop when Mrs Fisk gave me a penny to buy sweets.'

'I see.' It was evidently time for Beatrice to issue another one of her regular reminders at the next W.I. meeting – without naming names, of course. Children heard and absorbed more than many adults realised. Whilst it was natural for people to talk about the war and Hitler, she and the other teachers tried to remind them not to do so when young ones were present.

'Oh, it's Doctor, Miss Wentworth.' At a knock on the open classroom door, Ruby whirled around and ran towards David with her arms outstretched. 'Me mum sent me a postcard. See?' Ruby waved the card. 'Miss Wentworth's helping me write back to her. Miss Wentworth bought me these new clothes, too. Look.' She gave a twirl.

As Beatrice stood to greet him, one hand went to her hair to smooth it. 'Hello, Dr Stanley.'

'Miss Wentworth.' A slow smile spread across his face. 'And Miss Ruby.' He crouched to the child's level. 'Let's take a look at you in your fine new clothes.' His warm hazel gaze looked Ruby up and down. 'I'm pleased to see you with rosier cheeks. Doing what I said, are you?'

'Yes, Doctor. Even though the medicine tastes nasty.' She wrinkled her button nose.

'Good girl.' He patted her shoulder. 'If your important letter writing can wait, I need to have a quick word with your teacher. Why don't you go outside and join the other children for a few minutes?'

Ruby glanced between them. 'All right. You likes Miss Wentworth, don't you, Doctor?'

'Ruby.' Beatrice felt her face flame. 'Run along.'

'You're quite right, Ruby. I do like Miss Wentworth but please do as she asked.' David looked as if he was trying to keep back a laugh.

With a smug smile, Ruby skipped out of the classroom and the outer door shut behind her.

'I'm sorry.' Beatrice rushed to apologise. 'I don't know why Ruby would have said such a thing.'

'I'm glad she did, because she spoke the truth.' David came closer and took both Beatrice's hands in his. 'I do like you, and if it is not too forward of me to say so, I hope you return the sentiment.'

'I do.' She sounded prim but she couldn't help it.

'Good.' David squeezed her hands before releasing them. 'Now – about Saturday.' As he confirmed the details for supper and going to the dance in Whittleton, Beatrice nodded and smiled like the well-bred woman she was. Yet beneath the surface, her stomach fluttered, her heart raced, and she was hardly aware of Nell ringing the bell to bring the children back in.

David had said he liked her. Twice. Warmth curled around Beatrice's heart. And she liked him.

'Until Saturday, then?' David tipped his hat farewell as Beatrice's pupils thronged into the classroom, Ralph and Albert bouncing a ball between them.

'Until Saturday.' Beatrice caught the ball mid-bounce. 'No ball games indoors, boys. You know the rules.' However, she couldn't make her voice as stern as she usually would or her expression as severe.

She couldn't think of it as a 'date', as such. They were in their forties and 'dates' were for the young. It would simply be a pleasant evening with a congenial and respectable man. That was enough. It had to be.

Chapter Eighteen

Saturday, 9 November 1940

On Saturday afternoon, in a corner of the large kitchen at Hazelbury's red-brick Victorian vicarage – a house known as The Three Chimneys – Beatrice stood between Victoria and Nell chopping parsnips, vinegar-scented steam rising around them.

In her excitement at David's invitation to supper and the dance, she'd momentarily forgotten that she'd promised to join Mrs Russell and several other W.I. members after her hospital shift in a community effort to preserve late-season root vegetables. Even if Beatrice was able to heat sufficient water for the copper tub used for bathing at Hazelbury Manor, she'd likely still carry a whiff of the pickle factory.

Gentlemen expect ladies to be well-groomed. It is our duty to make ourselves pleasing and elegant for them. You are not a servant girl dousing yourself in cheap scent.

Yet another nugget of her mother's 'advice' popped into Beatrice's head. After the last war, there were hardly any 'gentlemen' left to make herself 'pleasing and elegant for', and she hadn't worn scent – what a man like David would undoubtedly call 'perfume' – in years. Still, he wouldn't expect her to turn up smelling as if she'd been doused in vinegar.

Should she say something to him to try to explain? Ladies were also never supposed to discuss personal matters with gentlemen, but David wasn't a 'gentleman' of the sort that Beatrice's mother had referred to.

'Making jam was much more fun,' Victoria said. 'The convalescent hospital wasn't yet fully set up so we had the run of Whittleton Hall and estate.' She passed a bowl of cut up carrots to Mrs Meldrum and wiped a hand across her forehead. 'I remember our hired girl "canning" at home. What you'd call "bottling". I didn't realise it was such laborious, time-consuming work.'

Beatrice hadn't either, but since she'd missed Mrs Bertram's jam-making day because she'd had to write reports following the school inspector's visit, she'd felt compelled to join in today.

'Imagine if we had to do this job at the manor.' Nell's hands flew as she chopped. Although the three of them were wrapped in voluminous aprons and had covered their hair with kerchiefs, Nell had an air of brisk efficiency and competence both Beatrice and Victoria lacked. 'Also, think of how accomplished we shall feel with all these glass jars lined up in the pantry.' She gestured to where they sat on a shelf, waiting to be filled.

Beatrice wiped her hands on a towel. She didn't know about 'accomplished', but she already felt exhausted. Before coming here, she'd spent two hours in the convalescent hospital's office, where the telephone had rung incessantly and there had been a constant to-ing and fro-ing of nurses and other staff. As she'd left to cycle home, several doctors arrived in a military vehicle and rushed up the steps, calling for Matron.

'I had a letter from my cousin in this morning's post.' Victoria began chopping cauliflower. 'Stewart, you know the one in the Royal Canadian Air Force? He should get leave in a fortnight or so and he's planning to visit us. Just think, girls. I haven't seen any of my family in almost three years. It will be like Christmas has come early.'

'It'll be grand to meet him,' Nell said. 'Along with all the other dangers, it must be dreadfully cold in those aeroplanes. I'll start knitting the lad a pair of socks and scarf tonight. You know, I read somewhere that—'

'Miss Wentworth?' Mrs Russell touched Beatrice's shoulder. 'There's a telephone call for you.'

'For me?' Nobody ever rang Beatrice except Miss Hopson or, on her birthday, her mother. Since there was no phone at Hazelbury Manor, those calls were arranged in advance at the village telephone box. Who would know she was at the vicarage to call her here?

'For you, indeed.' A small smile tugged at the corners of Mrs Russell's mouth.

Mystified, Beatrice went into the hall where the telephone sat on a small table next to a straight-backed chair. 'Hello, Beatrice Wentworth speaking.'

'Beatrice.' David's voice was soft and almost like a caress. 'I'm so glad I got hold of you. At breakfast this morning, Mrs Russell mentioned you were one of those who'd be there later today when she as good as ordered the vicar and me from the premises. I'm ringing from the convalescent hospital.'

'But what… why?' He'd promised he'd be off duty this weekend. Along with concern, irritation flickered.

'I know, I am not supposed to be here, but several men were recently transferred here from London.' David let out a long breath. 'It appears they brought influenza with them. We're isolating patients insofar as is possible and closing our doors to the wider community. As the doctor caring for these men yesterday and the day before, I was called in and will have to stay here and isolate with other staff until the danger has passed.'

'Oh.' For an instant, the vicarage hall seemed to spin, and Beatrice grabbed the chair to steady herself. Her father had died of influenza in November 1918, and she'd also lost an aunt and uncle and several friends in that same epidemic. 'Flu was dangerous and not to be taken lightly. 'I'm so sorry.'

'I am as well, especially because I promised I wouldn't let you down.' She could almost picture David's expression – his hazel eyes pleading and brow furrowed in regret. 'It is the life of a doctor, I'm afraid, but the authorities have also cancelled tonight's dance in Whittleton. We must do everything possible to limit the spread of infection.'

'I understand.' Beatrice shook her head as if to clear her muddled thoughts. Her brief disappointment over missing supper and the dance was both ridiculous and selfish. There was so much more at stake. *David*. She couldn't lose him too, not when they were only just getting to know one another. 'You must be careful.' Her voice cracked. 'Please do not take any unnecessary risks.'

'I won't.' He paused. 'It is you I am more worried about. You were at the convalescent hospital this morning.'

'Yes, but only in the office.' Beatrice stared at the telephone, its simple black Bakelite ordinariness anchoring her. 'For the most part, I worked alone, but I spoke to Matron when I arrived, as well as to several nurses. While staff came in and out during my shift, it was brief. The only time I spoke to anyone directly was when we were outdoors in the kitchen garden and never near each other.'

'Good.' David's voice held relief. 'If you have even the slightest concern or experience 'flu symptoms, get word to me. For now, I suggest you return to the manor and keep to your room for the next few days. You don't want to expose anyone, but particularly the Misses Grainger, to danger.'

'Of course not, but what about the school? I can't leave the children, and we don't have enough staff to cover anything more than an absence of a day or two.' Once again, her thoughts whirled. She couldn't ask Victoria, Nell and Ivy to take on additional work. They were overstretched as it was.

'I suspect the school may be closed for several days as well. Think of it as an unexpected holiday.' David's familiar chuckle was strained.

'I understand.' Apart from reading, drawing, writing letters, listening to her radio and sewing and knitting, what would Beatrice do stuck in her bedroom? She'd have time to think – something she made every effort to avoid.

'We'll go to a dance another time. I hear there's one in Hazelbury in early December. What do you say?'

'That would be lovely, thank you.' It would – and Beatrice would hope for the best rather than fear the worst. David would be fine. They all would be. There was no reason to think otherwise.

Chapter Nineteen

Thursday, 14 November 1940

Beatrice flicked through *Little Women*, the book Victoria had left with a luncheon tray outside Beatrice's bedroom door. Rain streamed down the window, and although it was only early afternoon, the garden was shrouded in mist and the day was already drawing in. Louisa May Alcott was right. November *was* a 'disagreeable' month, especially so in wartime, although *Little Women* was set during America's Civil War, not this one.

In addition to the local influenza threat, Mr Chamberlain's death the previous Saturday had cast a pall over the entire country, including Hazelbury. Whilst the former prime minister was not without his faults, his death had silenced critics and many instead saw him as a sincere man who'd done his utmost to achieve peace and avoid war. Yet – here they were, and still the German bombing continued.

At a soft rap on the door, Beatrice turned away from the window and reached for her shawl. 'Yes? What is it?'

'The post has come,' Nell said through the closed door. 'There are several letters for you. I'll slide them under the door, shall I?'

'Yes, please.' Beatrice wrapped the shawl more tightly around her shoulders. Hazelbury Manor was draughty at the best of times, but usually she was at school, where a fire kept the classroom warm. However, they'd all been confined to the manor for almost a week, and Miss Hetty deemed it too early in the season for fires except in the evening. As David had suspected, all the local schools had indeed been closed. 'Has there been any further news from the village? I heard the Land Girls in the garden earlier.' Their two Land Girls lived in a hostel with others on the outskirts of Hazelbury. Since agricultural jobs couldn't be put on hold, Miss Pilch and Miss Carroll arrived daily to do their work as usual, although they spent most of their time in the outlying fields.

There was a soft swishing sound as Nell pushed envelopes under Beatrice's bedroom door. 'There are several cases of 'flu in Whittleton, on the air base and village, but none so far here, thank goodness.'

After thanking Nell for bringing up her post, Beatrice gave a huge sigh of relief. Unlike in 1918, from everything reported so far, the influenza outbreak wasn't serious, and the prompt actions taken by David, other hospital staff and the local authorities seemed to have contained any wider spread. And, despite the boredom of forced inactivity, she had to admit that these few days of rest had been welcome.

As she moved to the door to pick up her letters, her gaze drifted to the drawing pad, sketchbook, pencils and tin of watercolours on the desk. Without the routine of school life and the pressures that came with it, Beatrice had spent many happy hours this week drawing and painting, much as she'd done in her girlhood. While she'd completed the smaller bits of scenery needed for the Nativity – pieces that were too advanced for the pupils to do – she'd still had time for her own work. From studies of the common house sparrows that frequented the garden beyond her window to making pencil sketches from memory of some of her pupils, it had been satisfying to make good use of her art supplies. Mrs Parker would undoubtedly be pleased to receive the sketch Beatrice had done of Ruby, and Beatrice planned to frame a watercolour of Lady as a Christmas present for the Misses Grainger.

She flipped through the post, not expecting much except circulars and possibly her mother's weekly missive. Instead, there were two letters, both with unfamiliar handwriting and one clearly from a child.

Finding her engraved silver letter opener – a twenty-first birthday present from an aunt – she opened the child's letter first.

Dear Miss Wentworth

The carefully formed letters tilted downwards across the paper and several blots of ink highlighted the child's unfamiliarity with writing personal correspondence.

With love from Ruby

Beatrice's breath caught as she zeroed in on the signature.

Dear Ruby. The girl had written to say she hoped Beatrice was staying well, and that although Ruby missed school and hoped to see Miss Wentworth again soon, she was keeping up with her reading and arithmetic with help from Mrs Fisk. She ended the missive with a pencil drawing of Kitty, Mrs Fisk's cat, sleeping on the flagstone hearth in front of the fire. Although a rough sketch, Kitty was clearly recognisable, and Ruby had captured the cosy charm of the cottage scene admirably for an artist of any age, let alone one so young. Did Ruby have a particular interest in art? With so many pupils, Beatrice was not always able to recognise an individual child's talent, but once she did, she tried to nurture it.

Propping the letter and sketch on her desk, she opened the other envelope and drew out a single sheet of pale-blue paper filled on both sides with black, spidery writing. She peered at it through her spectacles to find the signature first.

David. Beatrice pressed a hand to her face. He'd written to *her*. Returning to her chair by the window and what remained of the fading daylight, she sat to read his letter.

Dear Beatrice

She traced her name – the swirl on the final 'e' and the precise circles on the 'B'.

I am on call tonight and writing to you from the desk in the office at Whittleton Hall, where you often sit to carry out your duties.

Although, selfishly, I wish you were here with me, I am glad that you are not and are safe at Hazelbury Manor. One of the men has been very ill indeed but it looks like he will pull through. The others have had milder infections, including the kitchen staff, but the latter has meant we have had to fend for ourselves insofar as victuals go.

With the cook and her staff unwell, Mrs Bertram has been of great assistance and leaves all manner of delicacies on the front steps morning and evening. We've received provisions from RAF

Whittleton as well, so, to be truthful, I can't complain. We have set up a cooking rota and yours truly has pulled his weight, never fear. I must say I've become a dab hand at making stew, but bread is beyond my capabilities.

Naturally, David would 'pull his weight'. As if she'd think otherwise. Beatrice smiled. However, it must be difficult having to feed himself and others alongside working all hours. She returned to the letter in which he told her about various patients she'd got to know. Despite the chill of her bedroom, warmth curled around Beatrice's heart. Perhaps she'd played a small part in their healing. She hoped so.

Fortunately, the Hall's library is well stocked, so in my few moments of leisure, I have been able to read something other than medical journals. One of my patients, Welsh like Griffiths, mentioned Richard Llewellyn's book, How Green Was My Valley. Having an interest in visiting Wales, it sounds like one I would enjoy but the library here does not have it and nor do I often get to a bookshop.

And now, my dear Beatrice, I turn to more personal sentiments. I miss you and still regret we were not able to go to that dance together. I hope you are continuing to enjoy robust health. Please know I am counting the days until we shall see each other again. Do take good care of yourself, my dear.

Your most affectionate friend,
David Stanley

He'd signed his name with a flourish. He'd also called her 'my dear' twice beyond the letter's formal salutation. He was also her 'most affectionate friend'. Her face heated and her heart seemed almost to burst out of her chest.

He'd thought of her and taken the time to write. And not just any ordinary letter. No, whilst he could have written much of it to anyone, both the beginning and end were personal to her. Almost the kind of letter a man would write to a woman he considered his sweetheart – or to whom he wanted to be.

Beatrice's mother would consider it presumptuous, but the world had changed. Beatrice had changed too, and all she felt was pleasure – more carefree girl than staid middle-aged spinster.

Ruby and David. Still holding his precious letter, she glanced at Ruby's note with the drawing of Kitty. She'd never received such a message from a pupil before – one filled with care for her as a person, not simply as their teacher. In fact, the only letters she'd ever received from pupils had been to thank her for helping them prepare for an examination or for writing a good-conduct reference when they left school – businesslike missives which, albeit cordial, were about educational matters. In missing school, did Ruby also miss Beatrice? Certainly, her letter seemed to suggest that she did. Beatrice had also never received a letter from a pupil signed off 'with love'.

November wasn't a 'disagreeable' month at all. And Beatrice was the happiest she'd been since before she'd lost everything.

Chapter Twenty

Monday, 18 November 1940

'Now we're out of quarantine and the school is reopening, I shall be glad to return tomorrow. Although it seems wrong to feel glad about anything, what with the dreadful news of Cromer being bombed again and the terrible destruction in Coventry.' Nell clicked her tongue against her teeth, and the three teachers fell silent.

Cromer wasn't far from Hazelbury and several of their pupils had family there. As for Coventry, the Luftwaffe's recent aerial assault on the city had been relentless. As bombs rained down, hundreds were killed and homes, businesses and transportation networks destroyed. The photographs in the newspapers showing the scale of destruction were appalling.

'What about you two? Are you looking forward to being back at school?' After a moment, Nell looked up from the heap of red fabric on her lap – part of a pre-war Father Christmas costume she was remaking for David – and gave Beatrice and Victoria a determinedly cheerful smile.

'I've missed the children, and school *will* be warmer.' Victoria grimaced and gestured to the fireplace in the teachers' sitting room at Hazelbury Manor, which was empty of logs. 'When I wrote to Louis yesterday, I asked if he could have a word with his great-aunts about lighting at least one fire during the day when it's so cold and damp. Despite the timber shortage, there must be enough wood on the estate to spare a little for their comfort. Given permission, I could cut it myself. I often helped my father chop and gather logs for the fireplace at our summer cabin.' A blanket covered Victoria's legs, she'd wrapped a shawl around her head and shoulders, and she'd made herself a pair of fingerless gloves to wear when knitting or sewing. 'If I'm feeling the cold, it must be so much worse for the Misses Grainger, unhealthy even.'

'I expect they're used to it.' Beatrice withheld a sigh. In winter, the servants had lit morning fires in most rooms of her family's home and kept them going all day. Oblivious to the labour and expense involved, she'd also taken the resulting comfort for granted.

For ladies in straitened circumstances like Miss Hetty and Miss Addie, fires were a matter of economy. However, with the national timber shortage, depriving themselves of adequate heat was also part of their patriotic wartime duty. Except for cooking and washing, fires would only be lit on the coldest winter days, in the evenings or during the daytime due to illness. Although Victoria had the kindest of intentions, coming from Canada – what Beatrice privately considered a 'land of plenty' – she could not understand the Grainger sisters' mindset or expect to change it.

'In winter, my mum kept the fire in the kitchen range going from morning to night.' Nell's cheerful expression dimmed. 'It was cosy.' She held up a piece of red fabric edged with black felt. 'Our Father Christmas will look quite smart, if I say so myself. From a distance, nobody would guess this felt came from inside an old hat, and it covers the moth-eaten places.'

'You're a marvel,' Beatrice said, admiring Nell's handiwork. Unlike Beatrice, Nell had learned to reuse and repurpose items since childhood, so it was second nature. 'Dr Stanley will be impressed.' She fidgeted with a pencil as Victoria and Nell both looked at her with knowing expressions. 'What?'

'I'm sure "Dr Stanley" is already more impressed with you than he will be with any Father Christmas costume, no matter how fine.' Victoria's brown eyes sparkled before she returned to the crocheted snowflake she was making from scrap white wool.

'All right, he did ask me to call him "David",' Beatrice said. 'But we're friends, nothing more.' She made a show of opening an arithmetic book to review a lesson for the next day.

A small smile tugged at Nell's mouth. 'He *is* lovely, though, isn't he? Most distinguished. And you're going to a dance with him, aren't you?'

'Yes.' Beatrice's mouth curved into an answering smile. 'But it's— Oh, there's the front doorbell and Marjorie left early. I'll go down.'

'You do that,' Victoria murmured, exchanging a look with Nell. 'But paraphrasing Hamlet, "methinks the lady doth protest too much".'

Nell chuckled and then covered her mouth with a hand – her old, frightened gesture – as if fearing she'd said or done something wrong.

'Behave. Both of you.' Beatrice gave them her most disapproving look as she gathered up her shawl. Yet, as she reached the corridor and descended the main staircase, she couldn't be cross and Victoria and Nell knew it. There was no harm in enjoying David's friendship… or something more.

The bell rang again as she neared the door. The Misses Grainger were resting, but with this racket, they would soon be awake and enquiring what was going on.

'Yes?' Beatrice stopped at the sight of a uniformed telegraph boy on the wide stone doorstep, his bicycle propped against a garden wall. *Not Louis, please not Louis.* Her heart raced and she pressed a hand to her throat.

'Telegram for you, Miss Wentworth.' The boy, whom Beatrice recognised as one of Mrs Yallop's sons from the village – a boy of fifteen or sixteen – touched his cap, a shadowy figure in the misty darkness.

'Thank you.' It wasn't Louis. If he'd been injured or killed, the telegram would have come to Miss Hetty or even Victoria. Beatrice took the slip of paper between trembling fingers. Had something happened to her mother? A second worry replaced the first. No, the office stamp was from London, not Oxfordshire.

'Beatrice?' Victoria's voice came from the bottom of the staircase as Beatrice closed the front door. 'What is it?'

'I don't know yet.' She held the telegram gingerly as if it might explode.

'Here, sit.' Victoria's face went pale and she led Beatrice to a chair as the longcase clock in the corner of the hall struck five sonorous bongs.

'Girls?' Nell appeared behind Victoria.

Beatrice sat and opened the telegram as Victoria and Nell sat on either side of her. 'It's from Miss Hopson.'

She scanned the brief typed message and drew in a harsh breath. 'Ruby's mother has been killed in the Coventry bombing.' Beatrice fumbled for her handkerchief before remembering she'd left it upstairs.

Wordlessly, Nell passed over a clean, starched square with poppies embroidered on one corner.

'Mrs Parker...' Beatrice gulped and gripped the handkerchief. 'She'd gone to Coventry to visit her mother, who was ill.'

'What about Ruby's stepfather?' Victoria asked, putting an arm around Beatrice.

'Miss Hopson didn't say. Here.' Beatrice set the telegram on Victoria's lap so she and Nell could read the stark missive. 'If only I could ring Miss Hopson straightaway, but she won't be at school.'

'Even if she were still there, it's too dark and wet for you to go into the village to use the telephone box,' Nell said. 'We'll have to wait until tomorrow for more news. A letter might follow, perhaps, or you can ring then.'

And tomorrow for Beatrice to tell Ruby. The poor child. She'd never mentioned additional family, but if her mother had been killed, and her grandmother was so ill, what about any other relatives?

Beatrice dropped her head into her hands as Victoria and Nell held her tight and made soothing noises.

Only a few hours before, she'd thought that, as bad as the situation in Coventry was, at least she didn't need to worry about their pupils' families.

But she'd been wrong, and now she had to deliver the worst news of all to a blameless child. One, moreover, who'd breached the fortress of her guarded, frozen heart and whom she cared for almost as if she were her own daughter.

Chapter Twenty-One

Wednesday, 20 November 1940

The next day, Beatrice replaced the receiver and, still inside the red telephone box near the village green, hesitated for several seconds. Sunlight sparkled like diamonds on the frost-tipped grass, and a flock of bright-coloured wild ducks soared high in the crisp blue sky. Winter had not yet hardened, and the scene was almost too beautiful. Beatrice placed a hand to her chest as if to ease the pain in her heart.

Since there was no one waiting outside, despite being in the small tobacco-scented space, she bowed her head, not so much in prayer as in an instinctive gesture of respect. When no letter from Miss Hopson had arrived with the first post, Beatrice decided she couldn't wait any longer. Leaving Nell in charge, she left her classroom to ring the headmistress at morning break.

Now, though, she had another dilemma: not only telling Ruby about her mother's death, but also when, where, and how best to break the news. Earlier, she could hardly bring herself to look at the girl who, as always, sat quietly at her desk absorbed in the lesson Beatrice had set. She certainly couldn't tell Ruby the entire truth. Beatrice pressed a hand to her stomach to quell a rush of nausea and then fumbled for the door. Fresh air. That's what she needed.

'Miss Wentworth?' David's voice reached her and then his hand gripped Beatrice's arm. 'Are you all right? What's happened?'

Beatrice shook her head as his voice seemed to rise and fall, receding and then drawing nearer through the encroaching blackness.

'Here you are. Let me help you to sit.' He eased her down onto the bench on the village green and pressed a handkerchief into her hand. 'No, thank you, Mrs Meldrum, your assistance is not required. Nor yours, Mrs Yallop.' David's voice was crisp and competent as it also was when he spoke to the matron or nursing sisters at the convalescent hospital.

'I'm sorry, I'll be all right directly,' Beatrice said. 'It's simply...' She raised her head and dropped it again after glimpsing the small group of villagers gathered nearby. As if things could not have been worse, she had also made a public spectacle of herself.

'Don't fuss. I'll deal with them.' David's whisper was for Beatrice's ears alone, then he raised his voice and spoke to the gathered crowd. 'Miss Wentworth appreciates your concern, but all is in hand. There, there, you'll be right as rain in a moment.' He might have been speaking to a child of Ruby's age rather than a grown woman, but it was unexpectedly comforting.

'Sorry.' She swallowed around the lump of emotion in her throat.

'There's no need to apologise. I'm glad I was passing and able to help.'

David's arm was around Beatrice's shoulders, almost hugging her. He was caring for her as a physician, as he would for anyone who, as Nell would put it, 'had taken a sudden turn', but the gentle pressure was also unexpectedly comforting and oh so reassuring.

When Beatrice raised her head again, the villagers had scattered, although she and David were likely still a focus of attention from behind net curtains and to anyone walking along the high street. 'My pupils. I must return to the classroom. I left Miss Potter in charge while I came here to ring our headmistress.'

'Miss Potter seems eminently capable,' David said. 'I am sure she will realise that you have been delayed.'

'True but...' Beatrice took a deep breath. 'There has been the most dreadful news about Ruby Parker's family. I must convey it to her but I... don't quite know how.'

'I see.' David clasped Beatrice's trembling hand. 'Would you like me to come with you? For us to speak with Ruby together?'

'Oh no, I couldn't prevail upon you to...' Beatrice stopped. For possibly the first time in her adult life, could she actually say what she meant and express what she truly needed? If she didn't do it now, when would she? 'Whilst I suppose I should say no, I would indeed appreciate your help with Ruby. She likes and trusts you, and if she is unwell after hearing the news, she may need medical attention.' The words had come out in a rush, but she'd said them, and David's presence would primarily be for Ruby.

'I don't have to be at the hospital until late this afternoon, so I can come with you now if it suits. We'll take my car. I parked it there by the ironmonger's shop.' David helped Beatrice to her feet. 'While we drive the short distance to the school, you can tell me what has happened to Ruby's family.'

Beatrice swallowed again. That lump of emotion seemed to have grown even bigger, but she couldn't let herself cry. Then they walked to his motor, where he helped her in and closed the door before settling himself in the driver's seat.

'Ready?' He gave her a quick but reassuring smile and started the engine.

'Not really, because you see…' Beatrice stopped as David turned the car out of the village. He evidently intended to take the long way around to the school via the lane that meandered behind the church and high street, like part of a snakes-and-ladders game.

'Go on.' After changing gear, he touched her gloved hand, the brief contact giving her courage.

'Ruby's mother was killed in the Coventry bombing. I received the telegram yesterday evening, but, having just spoken to Miss Hopson, I find the news is even worse than I could ever have feared.' Beatrice paused, marshalling both her thoughts and her composure. 'Mrs Parker was sheltering under the stairs in her widowed mother's home, along with her mother, sister and their family, and there is nothing left. Of the house or any of them. I gather it was as if fire rained down from the sky.' Her voice hitched. 'Mrs Parker's mother was seriously ill. That is why Mrs Parker had been given several days' leave from her factory job to travel to Coventry. When Miss Hopson tried to contact Ruby's stepfather, a message came back that his "whereabouts are unknown". Ruby told me he'd enlisted in the navy but perhaps he did not.'

David shook his head and when he glanced across at Beatrice, his hazel eyes were filled with tenderness. 'There is no other family?'

'Not in Britain, apparently. Miss Hopson spoke to one of Mrs Parker's neighbours, who said she had heard mention of an aunt in America – Ruby's late father's elder sister – but she did not have any other information or an address. I suppose someone will have to go through Mrs Parker's home and pack up her belongings so an address may be forthcoming but for now...' Beatrice rubbed her eyes in another desperate attempt to compose herself. 'I doubt her stepfather's absence will concern Ruby, but she will grieve the other deaths, and without bodies or a funeral, it will be made even more difficult.'

'I read in *The Times* that there is a mass funeral taking place in Coventry today with another to follow very soon.' David's voice was tight, and as he parked the car outside the school, his expression was grim. 'That poor girl. We shall have to tell Mrs Fisk as well.'

Perhaps they should have gone to Mrs Fisk's cottage first, but Ruby had been all Beatrice could think of.

'I am too used to delivering distressing news, but in this case, as you know Ruby best, I shall be guided by you.' With a gentle squeeze of Beatrice's hand, David got out of the car and came around to her side as Nell, evidently having heard them arrive, opened the school door and poked her head outside.

Beatrice nodded to Nell, who soon returned holding Ruby by the hand.

'Miss Wentworth?' Ruby shrugged into her warm coat – another item which Beatrice had bought for her – and hovered by the school door. 'Doctor?' Her jaw clenched, even as her bottom lip trembled.

'I'm afraid we have something very hard to tell you, dear.' When Beatrice reached the girl, she knelt at her side. There was no use drawing out the matter any further or beating about the bush. That had been her father's way, and she supposed it made sense.

'It's me mum, ain't it?' Ruby's blue eyes stared at Beatrice, unflinching.

'Yes, and I'm so very sorry.' Beatrice clasped Ruby's cold hand in hers. 'Also your grandmother, aunt and cousins. They were in the Coventry bombing. Miss Hopson contacted me. She was unable to reach your stepfather.'

Ruby made a small, choked sound and then she flung her arms around Beatrice's neck. 'All gone?' She looked up at David.

'Yes, duckie.' David's voice cracked and then the three of them were embracing with Ruby in the middle, her sobs muffled against the collar of Beatrice's coat.

Unlike Beatrice, who still had her mother, Ruby had truly lost everyone and everything – and so had many others. Anger and too many other emotions for Beatrice to distinguish engulfed her at the unfairness of it all. The loss, grief and devastation. The cruelty and horror.

Over Ruby's heaving shoulders, David's steady gaze met Beatrice's.

Despite what had happened to Ruby's family – despite this deadly war, where the carnage seemed never-ending – there was still goodness and hope. She only had to trust in it – and in him.

Chapter Twenty-Two

Friday, 22 November 1940

On Friday afternoon, having had another largely sleepless night with British and German bombers thundering overhead, Beatrice clapped her hands in front of the small stage in Hazelbury's village hall, where a school Nativity rehearsal was in progress. 'Mary and Joseph, stay where you are. Those of you playing sheep, move closer to the donkey. No, Leonard. You are meant to *hold* the star, not wave it around like a London policeman at a traffic crossing. Could you please help the sheep get into their places, Miss McKaye?'

Victoria nodded and gave Beatrice a small smile as she diverted two of her smallest infants from playing with the doll serving as baby Jesus.

'It's lucky we have Miss McKaye's cousin here to help, isn't it?' Nell's gaze followed Pilot Officer Richards, who had arrived the night before to spend forty-eight hours' leave in Hazelbury.

'It is – and with the boys especially.' Beatrice glanced at Stewart Richards, who stood beside Albert and Ralph, filling in for one of the kings who'd been kept home from school with a toothache. Dazzled by the glamour of the visiting Canadian flyer, even their most obstreperous lads had been awed, clustering around him at break to pepper him with questions about his squadron and the aeroplanes they flew.

'He's big, isn't he? Taller than even the largest of Jimmy Clarke's brothers. It does make me wonder what mums in Canada feed their children.' Nell took the copy of the Nativity play Beatrice held out but couldn't seem to drag her gaze from Victoria's cousin. 'He's not fat, but he's bigger all round.'

Beatrice understood what Nell meant. Stewart Richards's height, surely over six foot, plus his brawn, ruddy face and hearty manner, made him seem like a giant in a doll's house.

'He's near your age. You may wish to strike up a correspondence with him. I expect he'd appreciate a bit of cheer so far from home.' Beatrice hadn't missed the admiring looks Stewart had directed towards Nell, and this morning before breakfast she'd overheard him telling Victoria that 'Miss Potter was a real humdinger of a gal.'

'I shall be happy to include my best wishes when Miss McKaye writes to him, but nothing more.' Nell sniffed as she did when any young man was mentioned, in which disdain mixed with dismissiveness, and turned away to speak to a girl about the snowflake dance.

What Nell's life had been like before the war was none of Beatrice's business, but while she had no fault to find with Nell's work or conduct, for her age she seemed staid – almost old before her time. She also never attended local dances, ostensibly because her mother disapproved of dancing, but was there another reason as well?

As Victoria continued to guide the sheep and other animals into their places, a small hand crept into Beatrice's.

'Yes, Ruby?' She'd stopped questioning the rightness of Ruby taking her hand. The child needed comfort and Beatrice needed – wanted – to offer it.

'See the marble Mr Richards gave me? He let me choose first, so I chose blue. Isn't it lovely?' She held it out for Beatrice's inspection.

'It's beautiful, and most kind of him.' Along with several bars of chocolate and a quantity of tinned food, which were a welcome supplement to Hazelbury Manor's lean pantry, Victoria's cousin had brought a large bag of marbles and distributed one to each child.

Ruby nodded. 'Mr Richards is almost as nice as Doctor. I said I'd draw him a picture of Kitty before he leaves. He has a cat at home in Canada. She's called Boots.'

'That's very kind of you as well.' Beatrice resisted the urge to ruffle Ruby's hair. The child was quiet as always – but was she *too* quiet? Although Beatrice had proposed taking Ruby to one of the Coventry mass funerals, the girl had declined, saying she'd rather stay in Hazelbury. And after her initial outburst, she'd seemed to accept the deaths of her mother and the rest of the family with a stoicism of one much older.

To be truthful, it seemed unnatural and, as was so often the case, Beatrice's thoughts turned to David. Should she write to him for advice? Since his letter to her during the influenza quarantine, they'd exchanged regular notes and, while it had only been a few weeks, Beatrice had come to count on them. Although they mostly wrote about their work and the war, the correspondence was a bit of brightness amidst the dreary days.

'See Miss McKaye waving to you? She needs you to get back into place with the other angels. As we sing, imagine you're wearing the costume Mrs Fisk is making for you.' Beatrice guided Ruby towards the stage where Ivy waited to help children up the short flight of stairs, before moving to the piano where the carol book was already open at 'Silent Night'.

'Miss Wentworth?'

Nearing the piano bench, Beatrice stopped. 'Yes, Mrs Meldrum?' Whilst ostensibly Mrs Meldrum had 'dropped by' to see how 'poor, dear Ruby was coping' and how the Nativity rehearsals were coming along, Beatrice had soon learned that she usually had another agenda. 'Is there a problem?'

'Not at all. Everything seems to be going splendidly.' Mrs Meldrum pursed her lips and, as she darted a glance in the direction of the stage, the feathers on her hat shook. 'Diana is a natural actress, isn't she?'

'She is. Her mother hopes to be here for the performance.' It would be lovely to see Mary, Beatrice reminded herself, even though her visits unsettled Diana.

'Mrs Foster-Dalton's presence will depend on the bombing situation, I expect.' Mrs Meldrum tutted. 'Dreadful business. Coventry, Birmingham, wherever will be next? And Coventry Cathedral. Almost brought me to tears it did, seeing photographs of the destruction. Cromer as well with that—'

'Please, Mrs Meldrum.' Beatrice shook her head and put a finger to her lips, as she so often did when adult visitors brought war news into the school.

'Forgive me. I shall "keep mum" as that information poster says.' A wry smile creased Mrs Meldrum's face. 'All I truly wanted to say is you seem to have more than enough to manage with the children. If I could be of assistance in providing any necessary musical accompaniment, it would be my pleasure.'

'You?' Beatrice's mouth opened and snapped shut again before she said something inappropriate. 'I didn't realise you played the piano.'

'Not as well as you, but we must all do our bit mustn't we? I can certainly manage a few carols. Since Mrs Russell mentioned she was lending you records and the vicarage gramophone for the snowflake and other dances, I wouldn't have to provide accompaniment for those parts.' Mrs Meldrum's smile turned almost smug. 'Seeing Pilot Officer Richards up there with the children made me think that if such a brave boy can give of his time so unstintingly, I must not shirk my own duty.'

'No but...' Beatrice pressed her lips tight together again. She couldn't decline Mrs Meldrum's offer. It was welcome and would give her more time to focus on the performers. However, Mrs Meldrum was already involved in every village activity, whether related to war work or not. She also spent too much time meddling in school matters and now she'd wormed her way into the Nativity as well. 'Having you accompany the children for the carols would be a great help.'

Even as Beatrice spoke, Mrs Meldrum had settled herself on the piano bench, removed her gloves and was flexing her fingers as if taking to the stage at London's Royal Albert Hall instead of in a small, out-of-the-way rural village.

Standing in the wings with Ivy and Wilf, who was one of the Nativity's narrators, Victoria raised her eyebrows and gave Beatrice a strained smile.

As the children's voices rose in an off-key version of 'Silent Night', almost drowned out by the piano, Beatrice shrugged. They all had more than enough to cope with. She wasn't in the mood for an argument, especially in front of the children, who would carry a highly embellished version to the rest of the village. But Beatrice had also been taken off guard.

Mrs Meldrum might think she'd got away with whatever plan she was hatching, but she hadn't. Not for long, anyway.

Chapter Twenty-Three

Saturday, 23 November 1940

'It feels as if Stewart were hardly here before he had to leave again.' In Beatrice's bedroom at Hazelbury Manor, Victoria studied herself in the glass on the front of the wardrobe. 'Along with the war news, it also hardly feels right to be going to a dance without Louis.' She turned in a circle, the dark green floral-patterned dress her mother had sent in a recent parcel draping around her figure in elegant folds. 'If Stewart had been able to stay for the dance, it would be different.'

'If Stewart were still here, the village hall wouldn't have been able to hold the crowd.' From where she sat on Beatrice's slipper chair, Nell grinned. 'Women would have come from Whittleton, Cromer and all over.' Her smile slid away. 'But I know how you feel. I can't help thinking of all the lives lost. If you don't want to dance, stay behind the refreshment table with me.' Nell smoothed one of her school skirts, which she wore with a white blouse and hand-knitted blue cardigan.

Almost as if she wanted to disappear into the background. The thought had crossed Beatrice's mind before, but now it settled and took root. Although she had always been timid, Nell had an eye for fashion and the skill to remake garments into the height of style. Before this autumn, despite her limited means, Nell had been a regular fashion plate.

In the past few months, though, something had changed and Nell had become even more retiring than usual, including in her choice of clothing. When she went to the convalescent hospital at Whittleton Hall to work in the kitchen, she wore her plainest clothes as if she wanted to look as drab as possible. And while her beauty remained undimmed, as Stewart Richards's admiring looks and the attentions of the single local farmers since they'd been evacuated made clear, Nell continued to remain oblivious.

'Are you sure you don't want to borrow one of my dresses?' After studying her own smart reflection wearing a frock of Victoria's, Beatrice opened the wardrobe door and gestured to the hanging rail. 'My cousin Louisa's colouring is nearer to yours than mine, so the clothes she sent me would suit you better.'

Those once-regular parcels of hardly worn clothing had slowed and then stopped entirely at the end of the summer. Although clothing hadn't been rationed, even Louisa, usually profligate, had likely been forced to become more mindful of scarce resources – or her husband, a canny Scottish laird a good ten years older, had reduced her allowance. A move which Beatrice had long considered overdue.

'Thank you, but I'm fine as I am.' Nell buttoned her cardigan. 'I'm only going to the dance because Mrs Russell needed extra helpers and it's a church function. As I told my mum in my last letter, it's part of my duty, really, and it's not as if I'll be dancing myself.'

They all knew and had long ago accepted that Nell's mother 'didn't hold with dancing' or even being in places where dances were held, but surely, with the government encouraging dancing to boost morale, Mrs Potter wouldn't judge her daughter harshly.

'Should you ever want to borrow any items, you know the offer is there.' Being of a similar size, the three teachers sometimes shared clothing, but apart from smart frocks to change into for dinner with the Misses Grainger, they hadn't had reason to exchange other items except for school blouses and skirts when one of them had a mishap before laundry day.

Beatrice closed the wardrobe door and, in the lamplight with the blackout already up, studied her appearance once more. Whilst her own mother wouldn't disagree with Beatrice having a responsibility to go to this dance or any other, she would have a great deal to say about the man escorting her. However, that was her mother's snobbishness, not Beatrice's, and if Beatrice didn't write to her about David, her mother had no need to know. That was how she rationalised it. But was she still, even at her age, as mindful of her mother's opinion as Nell? Of course not. She wouldn't let herself think such a thing.

Beatrice turned away to find the evening bag she'd left at the end of her bed. 'Right, are we all set? David will be here shortly.' She checked her wristwatch. David had arranged to collect them in his car, which meant they didn't have to walk in the dark. It also, from Beatrice's perspective, made it seem less like a 'date' and so less likely to set tongues wagging.

'Nell and I are ready, but you aren't.' Victoria picked up her vanity case and took out several lipsticks and a floral-patterned enamel compact. 'A slick of lipstick, some blusher and powder will finish you off perfectly.'

'Oh, I couldn't.' Beatrice took an instinctive step back.

'Why not? Mrs Bertram wears cosmetics, and she's much older than you.' Victoria gently guided Beatrice to sit on the edge of the bed. 'Anything I do will be subtle. You can hardly object to some Vaseline on your brows, can you?'

'No.' Even when she was a girl, Beatrice had hardly worn any makeup, and in her mid-twenties she'd stopped entirely. Without suitable men or anyone else to impress, what was the point? She also didn't have the money for it, not while trying to ensure her mother's comfort.

'Go on with you.' Nell leaned closer. 'You want Dr Stanley to think you've made an effort, don't you?' Her smile was mischievous. 'Like Louis with Victoria, Dr Stanley would expect you to be well-presented.'

'I'm not Victoria.' And David wasn't Louis. Even without the class difference, he was older and a widower, for a start, and did not have what many women would consider the 'glamour' of a military uniform.

'No, you're you.' Victoria smoothed Beatrice's brows with Vaseline. 'As my mother always says, you must make the most of yourself for yourself, irrespective of others. It gives you confidence.'

'All right then.' Beatrice certainly needed confidence, and if makeup would help, she'd try it. Besides, David likely wouldn't notice her dress or how she looked. They were friends with similar interests, and whatever relationship they had was a meeting of minds, along with a united concern for Ruby – despite those tingles whenever David took her hand or arm.

Victoria's brown eyes softened as she took a clean towel from the washstand and wrapped it around Beatrice's shoulders to cover her dress. 'Don't look so worried. You'd think I was holding a stick of dynamite. Close your eyes.' Beatrice did as she was told, and Victoria brushed something – eyeshadow? – across her eyelids. 'Your skin is so lovely you don't need foundation, and only a touch of blusher. Powder to set and lipstick. Which pink do you think, Nell?'

'The palest one. Beatrice is an English rose,' Nell said. 'I used to read copies of *Country Life* in the library near my teacher training college. Pored over them I did. All the lovely frocks. You look like an elegant lady in one of those magazine photographs, Beatrice.'

'Thank you but you flatter me too much.' Beatrice kept her eyes closed and tried to maintain a neutral expression. Before Nell was even born, Beatrice *had* been in *Country Life*. Not like her mother who had merited a cover, but as part of an inside photographic spread about that year's debutantes. Most of them, like her, had ultimately either had their hopes dashed or, as Mary had done, married someone who, before the last war, would have been wholly unthinkable.

'Open your eyes and take a look.' Victoria produced a small hand mirror from her vanity case and held it in front of Beatrice.

'I hardly recognise myself.' It was her, but somehow more so, with the girl she'd once been shining through. Her eyes were more defined, her cheeks rosier and she looked… dare she think it, almost pretty?

'You're lovely.' Victoria put the cosmetics away and removed the towel. 'You always are, even without a bit of paint on your face. You just have to believe it.' She set aside the vanity and gave Beatrice a rose-scented hug. 'You shall be the belle of the ball, Miss Wentworth.'

Beatrice laughed. 'It's only a village dance. Don't get too carried away.'

'I've never been to any kind of dance *or* ball.' Nell joined the hug, her tone wistful. 'Only Sunday School Christmas parties.'

Beatrice's heart squeezed. She'd never much enjoyed the formal balls her mother had insisted she attend, but they had been yet another part of the privileged life she had taken for granted.

'It's not too late.' Victoria patted Nell's shoulder. 'Tonight is only the start.'

As the three of them left Beatrice's room and descended the wide staircase – which must once have been the backdrop for elegant balls – there was a new lightness in Beatrice's step.

When she reached the bottom of the stairs where Miss Hetty, Miss Addie and Lady were greeting David at the front door, his gaze caught hers.

And Beatrice's supposedly well-regulated heart skipped a beat at the expression in his eyes. He wasn't looking at her like a friend, but rather with the admiration reserved for a beautiful woman.

'Do be careful, girls, won't you?' Miss Addie fluttered about, distributing hats, scarves and gloves.

Beatrice dragged her gaze away from David. 'With Dr Stanley accompanying us, I am sure we will be quite safe.' David was the kind of man who would never shirk his duty of care, whether to family, friend or patient.

'Don't fuss, Addie.' Miss Hetty's tone was brisk. 'After Coventry and Birmingham, the Germans will have other, more important targets in their sights this evening rather than such an insignificant spot as Hazelbury's village hall. No, Lady, you are not going out again. You only went a quarter of an hour ago.' She took the dog by the collar and shook her head at Nell, who hung back. 'Go to the dance and enjoy yourself. There is no need to stay at home on our account.' She made a shooing motion.

As David retrieved Beatrice's coat and helped her into it, she took her hat from Miss Addie.

Inner backbone. By the time I realised I was wrong, it was too late.

Those words Miss Hetty had uttered that October evening, when they'd been alone in the library came back to Beatrice yet again.

Even amidst great loss, there was still hope if one was able to look for it. That's what Beatrice had to hold on to because if she didn't, what else was left?

Chapter Twenty-Four

Was there anywhere else Beatrice would rather be than in David's arms? She didn't think so. As they circled the village hall to a waltz played by a three-piece band from Whittleton, she glanced up at his strong, clean-shaven jaw. She hadn't noticed before that his long thick eyelashes were several shades darker than his hair, and there was a small white scar next to his left eye.

'You're a good dancer.' She tried to make ordinary conversation.

'Thank you. So are you.' David chuckled, then escorted her from the floor when the set finished. 'Did you not expect me to be able to dance?'

'Of course not.' Although Beatrice denied it, had a part of her instinctively assumed that a labourer's grandson from a Yorkshire village would lack social graces? 'I know that many people enjoy dancing, but with your work and, before that, medical studies, I'm surprised you had time to go to dances.'

That explanation was partly true, partly diplomatic. Although Beatrice had never been to a dance hall, after the last war they'd become popular with all social classes. It was only before the present century that dancing had been primarily the preserve of the more well-off.

'You are right that I didn't have a great deal of time for dances or other leisure pursuits, but my late wife loved dancing.' David's voice softened. 'I insisted I had two left feet, but Maud taught me to dance when we were courting.'

'She did a fine job.' Beatrice spoke around a lump in her throat. She couldn't ask David about Maud, but she could not help wondering about her. How she and David had met and what she'd been like. Why he'd fallen in love with her.

As the musicians announced a break, David guided Beatrice to a clear spot away from the crush of people near the main door. 'Would you care for another glass of lemonade?'

Although Beatrice was thirsty, she shook her head. She'd rather not venture to the refreshment table, where Mrs Meldrum and several other ladies had held court for most of the evening. Beatrice still had to decide how to tackle the matter of the Nativity music – but not tonight. This evening was special and not to be marred by any disagreeable school matters.

'Shall we get some air?' David gestured to Beatrice's coat where it hung from a hook next to his in the entryway. 'It's rather warm and stuffy in here.'

'Yes.' Beatrice held out her arms for her coat. The hall *was* hot but that wasn't the reason for the warmth flooding her body. No, that was due entirely to David's nearness. Except for one dance with the vicar, Beatrice hadn't circled the floor with anyone else for the entire evening. And even when she'd been with Mr Russell, Beatrice could hardly pay attention to him, her gaze still drawn to David dancing nearby with Mrs Bertram.

'There, that's better.' As he shut the hall door behind them, David tucked Beatrice's arm into his elbow and wrapped his hand around hers. 'November's been such a wet month but tonight the weather is beautiful. So clear and…' He looked up at the stars, then stopped and grimaced.

'Bombing weather.' Beatrice finished his sentence. She should have put on her gloves, but they were still in her coat pocket, and since she'd left her hat behind, the light breeze ruffled her hair.

'But the Luftwaffe is not here, and I suppose we must be thankful for some respite despite what may be happening elsewhere.' David's voice was low in the still evening air.

'We must.' As they rounded the corner of the hall, the village allotments were in front of them, backed by fields and woodland. If Beatrice hadn't known better, she'd have called the scene peaceful – pastoral even – with the harvested stalks silvered by moonlight and only the call of nightbirds to disturb the quiet. 'We can't go far from the hall.' Their footsteps crunched along the path between the allotments, and a rabbit darted in front of them, disappearing into the stalks of corn Victoria had planted with her infants. 'Not with the blackout – and we don't have a torch.'

'No.' David stopped on the far side of the allotments and the silence lengthened between them. 'Beatrice, I…' Still holding one of her hands, with the other he traced the curve of her chin. 'Although the war is changing things, changing all of us, perhaps that is not enough for someone like you. Perhaps *I* am not enough.'

She trembled as he drew nearer, his face blocking the moonlight. 'It… it doesn't matter.' More warmth swept through her and also swept her doubts away. 'I would like you to kiss me, please.' It was forward and unladylike – and, if they could hear her, her female ancestors would surely be spinning in their graves – but Beatrice knew she had to make her feelings clear.

'I would like to kiss you too, very much.' David's voice held amusement and then his lips were on hers – firm, masculine and possessive.

Beatrice lost herself in the sensations roaring through her. David's strong arms that held her tight. His kisses that made her weak at the knees. How time seemed to stop and nothing else mattered but the two of them here together in this moment. And how, without expecting or planning for it, Beatrice could lose her heart to him in a different way than she had with Alex.

–

An hour later, sitting in the front passenger seat of David's car in the drive at Hazelbury Manor, Beatrice licked her lower lip – the pale pink colour Victoria had applied long since worn off. He'd kissed it off. He'd likely kissed off the blush and face powder as well, even the colour on her eyelids, as he dropped kisses all across her face. Although they'd only been outside the village hall for less than a quarter of an hour before approaching voices warned them they were no longer alone, her entire life had changed.

'Good night.' David glanced over his shoulder at Victoria and Nell. 'I shall walk you all to the door.'

'No need.' Victoria had already opened one of the rear doors and was out of the vehicle before he'd finished speaking, tugging Nell with her. 'I have a torch, so we can go around to the scullery door.'

'Yes, we don't want to disturb the Misses Grainger. Here' – Nell thrust another torch towards Beatrice – 'we'll give you two a minute and then meet you at the door, shall we, Beatrice?' One of Nell's rare, teasing smiles blossomed and then she and Victoria almost scuttled across the gravel drive, neither of them glancing back.

Beatrice avoided looking at David. 'They could not have been more obvious if they'd tried, could they?' Still, her friends meant well, and from the moment Beatrice and David returned to the hall and bumped into Victoria and Nell near the door, any idea Beatrice might have had of keeping her new understanding with David a secret from them vanished.

'No, but they care about you. As do I.' David smoothed several loose strands of Beatrice's hair away from her face. 'I never thought I could care about anyone this way again.'

'Nor me.' Alex was in her past. He would always be a cherished memory, but David now had his own place in Beatrice's heart. 'I truly must go. Miss Hetty's bedroom is at the front of the house, and she's a light sleeper so she will have heard the noise of the car.'

'I understand.' Still, David leaned even closer and kissed Beatrice once more before they both reluctantly drew apart. 'But wait, I don't want you walking by yourself.' In a moment, he came around the car, opened Beatrice's door and walked with her to the corner of the manor house, the beam of his own tissue-shaded torch mingling with hers. 'I'm on duty at the hospital for the next four days but I'll see you on Thursday after school, won't I?'

'Thursday?' Beatrice could hardly let herself think beyond tonight.

'Yes, Nell asked me to come round to try on the Father Christmas costume. She said she needs me for a final fitting. I could meet you at the school. See Ruby as well? We could return to the manor together, and then I'll drive Ruby home. I told the Whittleton doctor I'd drop in on one of his patients who lives out that way. He asked me for my opinion on a tricky heart case. I also don't like Ruby walking such a distance, especially with it now getting dark so early.'

'Of course.' *The Nativity. Father Christmas. Ruby.* Beatrice's thoughts were as jumbled as if she'd been turned upside down and shaken. 'I'll tell Mrs Fisk at church tomorrow.' Beatrice had to be there early for an extra choir practice to rehearse Advent music. Like school, that was her ordinary life, quite separate from this delightful interlude.

'Good.' David's voice held affection and – maybe – love? 'I'll wait until I hear the scullery door close and the three of you are safely indoors.'

'Thank you. The air feels heavy, as if it's about to rain.' Beatrice pressed her lips together. Why was she mentioning the weather? He must think her a fool.

'Then get inside quickly, darling. *My* darling.' David's voice grew husky, and after one last kiss, Beatrice darted around the house to rejoin Victoria and Nell, her feet hardly seeming to touch the path.

Could this interlude become her ordinary life as well? With wartime shortages, there were now many married teachers, including one in Whittleton whose husband was stationed at the RAF base.

Beatrice couldn't let herself think such a thing. It was too soon to consider marriage, but the thought was also too tempting. *My darling.* As she almost skipped up the stairs to her bedroom, David's words reverberated in her ears like a caress.

Chapter Twenty-Five

Thursday, 28 November 1940

'You look right fine, Doctor.' On Thursday after school, in the library at Hazelbury Manor, Ruby walked in a circle around David. 'But you needs more of that white stuff for your beard. Otherwise your real whiskers might show through.'

From where she sat at a nearby table marking Jimmy Clarke's misspelled composition, Beatrice's breath caught at Ruby's adoring expression and the trust and affection in her voice. David was the girl's hero and maybe even the honourable father figure she'd never known.

'That "white stuff" is cotton and wool, Ruby.' David's engaging laugh rolled out as he ruffled the girl's hair. 'What do you say, Miss Potter? Do you have any more to spare?' He glanced at Nell, who was on her hands and knees by his feet as she pinned the hem of his red Father Christmas trousers.

'There's an end of cotton left from that old sheet.' Nell took several pins from her mouth as she spoke. 'Could you get it for me, please, Miss Wentworth? I left it on the bookshelf ladder. I daren't leave this measuring as we'll soon lose the daylight.'

'Certainly.' Beatrice mustered a professional smile. Although they had to be formal within earshot of Ruby,

Nell was much more to Beatrice than just another teacher. Against all her preconceived expectations, Nell had become Beatrice's closest friend, along with Victoria.

'No need to get up,' Victoria said as she came into the library with Lady. 'Here.' She retrieved the sheet and passed it to Nell. 'I can't stop as I'm fixing that stuck window in Miss Addie's bedroom. I only popped in to leave Lady with you and say that the butcher was out of sausages. I met Jimmy Clarke's mum outside the post office, and she said she had to queue half the morning at the fishmonger's only for him to sell the last cod and haddock as she reached the front counter.' Victoria frowned. 'Even foods that aren't rationed are in short supply.'

Such shortages did not bode well for the coming winter months. A familiar knot of anxiety tightened in the pit of Beatrice's stomach. As Victoria left, Beatrice patted Lady, who sprawled by her feet. 'There is still enough tinned ham to make you a sandwich, Ruby, along with honey biscuits, a small wedge of cheese and a glass of milk. You shall have a feast before Dr Stanley takes you back to Mrs Fisk's.'

'Honey biscuits?' David gave Beatrice a hopeful look. 'You made honey biscuits?'

'No, Miss Potter did, but there are enough for you as well.' Beatrice had never learned to cook or bake and had never needed to, since she'd expected to have a cook, as well as kitchen and scullery maids, in her own home, as there'd been when she was growing up. Then, as a teacher living in lodgings, her landlady had provided meals, so Beatrice had never truly had to fend for herself. She'd also never learned how to fix a stuck window or do any of the other domestic tasks Nell and Victoria managed with ease.

Had Maud, David's late wife, been a model house-keeper? From the scant amount Beatrice knew of doctors' wives, alongside family life, they often helped run their husbands' medical practices. Even if they had a profession of their own, none continued in it after marriage. Is that what David expected of a wife?

As she returned to Jimmy's composition – a short piece about what he wanted to do when he left school – several troubling thoughts which Beatrice had tried to avoid bobbed to the surface of her mind. Jimmy had never expected or wanted a life beyond farming. Was he content with his lot or, if given a chance, would he rather do something else? Before the last war, Beatrice had never considered teaching, but along with nursing and office work, it was one of the few respectable professions then open to women. Almost to her surprise, she'd discovered she enjoyed it and would now be reluctant to give it up.

Not the administrative work, though. If she could, she'd give that up in an instant. However, between keeping abreast of government educational policies, her responsibilities for pupil welfare and record-keeping, and informally supervising Victoria and Nell while also trying to manage with scarce classroom resources, the non-teaching part of her role had only increased since the school had been evacuated. As she finished marking Jimmy's composition, which, despite its numerous deficiencies, still showed striking improvement from his previous efforts, she set aside the exercise books, her thoughts drifting against the backdrop of Ruby's chatter.

If Beatrice became a headmistress, whether in wartime or not, she would have even more administrative duties, when really she'd rather be in a classroom with the children. Although that notion would have been unthinkable even a few months ago, she could freely admit it now. Yet, as a single woman, the extra salary that came with a headmistress's post would give her a more comfortable retirement, especially as so much of her current income went to secure her mother's well-being. Round and round in circles she went, never arriving at any answers, let alone the right ones.

She also hadn't reached any decision as to what to do about Mrs Meldrum and the Nativity. Beatrice had managed to avoid her so far that week, and rehearsals hadn't involved musical accompaniment, but she'd have to speak with her soon. Hazelbury only had one Mrs Meldrum, but as headmistress of a larger school in a bigger place, Beatrice would likely have to manage many more women like her.

'Miss Wentworth?'

A soft voice brought Beatrice back to the present. 'Yes, Ruby?'

'Doctor said you must be "away with the fairies". Were you?' Ruby tilted her head to one side and raised her eyebrows.

'I suppose I was.' Beatrice gave a light laugh. 'Did you know what "away with the fairies" meant or did Dr Stanley explain it to you?'

'I knows.' Ruby gave a solemn nod. 'Me gran were Irish.'

'I see.' Beatrice paused. 'Do you have any family in Ireland? Aunts, uncles or cousins?' She didn't want to pry, but anything Ruby could tell her about such connections would help in tracking down relatives. So far, no address had been found for the supposed aunt in America, and although Mrs Fisk was happy to host Ruby for as long as she was able, she was elderly and there was also that nebulous time 'after the war' to consider.

'Not that me mum ever said.' Ruby sat on the floor beside Lady and rubbed the dog's ears. 'I reckon they was all in Coventry.' Her voice hitched and she bent her head so only the parting in the centre of her fair hair was visible.

Beatrice rested a hand on the girl's shoulder. 'Do you know anything about your real father's family?'

'Only that his name were Smith and he were an orphan. "Smitty" is what me mum called him.' Her voice cracked. 'Parker's the name of me stepdad. He said I ought to take his name since Mum did. I were too young to choose for myself, but I'm bigger now and I'd have rather stuck with Smith. I don't want his name nor nothing else. I hope he's gone forever.'

'I could use your help with this last bit, Ruby.' Nell beckoned to her, but not before exchanging a worried look with Beatrice.

'Off you go, then.' Beatrice tried to keep her voice steady as Ruby darted across the room to join Nell and David.

From everything Miss Hopson had said, it was likely that Ruby would get her wish for her stepfather to be 'gone forever', but it would be wrong of Beatrice to say so. She should also have chastised Ruby for her rudeness, but Beatrice couldn't do that either. If Mr Parker had no interest in his stepdaughter and had treated her cruelly, good riddance to him. Ruby deserved a new family – one that could give her the kindness and love she deserved.

Beatrice's gaze settled on David and Ruby. The affection between them was obvious. Any child would be fortunate to have him as a father. And Beatrice had begun to care for Ruby as a mother might. If the girl had no other family, perhaps the three of them… Oh, gracious, she shouldn't let herself take such a wild leap of fancy – because that's all it was. A castle in the air, more nebulous than that retirement cottage by the sea. A cottage where she'd begun to imagine David as well. The two of them sitting in the garden in summer and by the fire in winter. Growing old together.

Whether with David or Ruby, though, she couldn't allow herself to think so far ahead. There were too many unknowns, including what might or might not happen with the war and finding a member of Ruby's real family.

'All done. Thank you, Ruby.' Nell stood and looked David up and down. 'You'll be a fine Father Christmas. You can get changed back into your own clothes.' She turned back to Ruby. 'What do you say we let Miss Wentworth get on with her marking and find that "feast" she promised? I expect Lady would like a snick of cheese. She can do one of her tricks for you. I've been teaching her to balance a treat on her nose.'

'Yes, Miss Potter.' Ruby got to her feet but lingered at Beatrice's side. 'You aren't going nowhere, are you?'

'No, Ruby. I shall stay here in Hazelbury for as long as Miss Hopson says I must.' It was now understood that Beatrice, Victoria and Nell would remain in the countryside as long as the war – or the government's school evacuation scheme – lasted.

'You promise?' Ruby's eyes filled with tears. 'I don't want you *or* Doctor going away.'

A promise was sacred, and Beatrice would never do anything to break Ruby's trust. However, the war made even the most everyday plans – like what would be available to eat on any given day – uncertain. She couldn't expect a child of Ruby's age to understand such complexities, and as a doctor at the convalescent hospital, David's life was even more in flux. 'Whilst I cannot speak for Dr Stanley, Ruby, I shall do my utmost to never let you down.' But for the foreseeable future, she was only Ruby's teacher, and as such, her role and influence in the girl's life were limited – despite Beatrice now wanting more.

'I s'pose that's all you can do.' Ruby's narrow shoulders slumped. 'It's all 'cause of bad Mr Hitler. That's what Mrs Fisk says any road. She'd have his guts for garters if she could.' With a mournful nod, the child followed Nell and Lady out of the now-silent library, David having already gone to the teachers' sitting room to change.

Beatrice understood Mrs Fisk's indignation. She'd felt that same fury herself both before the war broke out and in the early months of the conflict. And while she was still angry, especially when news reached them of yet another German atrocity and photos of bomb damage were splashed across the front pages of the newspapers, she tried to channel those feelings into other things. While she couldn't do anything to stop Hitler or influence the war's outcome, by teaching and trying to make life better for her pupils, volunteering at Whittleton Hall and with the Red Cross, W.I. and church, she was still making a difference.

And no matter how difficult, she'd keep doing it.

'All right?' A quarter of an hour later, David came back into the library, tightening the knot in his tie. 'You're all on your own, and it will soon be dark.'

At his voice, Beatrice looked away from one of the library windows, where the wind lashed the leafless tree branches into a frenzy. 'I'm meant to be either marking or reading yet another directive from the London County Council's Education Department.' She gave him a dry smile and gestured to the paperwork that surrounded her on the long table. 'I put up most of the blackout but left this one window uncovered. There's something about today's weather that both unsettles and inspires me. I can't stop watching it.'

She'd like to paint the scene, capturing the wildness of the gale in oil. She could picture it clearly: broad strokes of green, blue, brown and black on the canvas – the sky and landscape mixed together in an abstract quite unlike her usual precise pencil sketches or gentle watercolours.

'I understand that fascination. It's a reminder that no matter who thinks they may be in charge, nature still has the upper hand.' He paused partway to the window. 'Shall I?' He gestured to the remaining blackout curtain.

'Please. We can hardly see. I should light a lamp.' Still, there was something almost intimate about being here with him in what her Scottish nanny would call 'the gloaming' – that transitory time between the sun's setting and true night. 'Ruby will have finished her sandwich and be ready to go home soon, if she's not too distracted by playing with Lady. She has a real affinity with animals. Each day at school, she can hardly wait to tell me what Mrs Fisk's cat has done.'

'That's good for her. I often see it in my patients. An animal's unconditional love and companionship are frequently better than medicine when it comes to healing, especially those who've experienced the kind of distress we can't pop a bandage on.' With his back to Beatrice, David fixed the blackout curtain. 'Major and Mrs Bertram have begun bringing their dogs up to the Hall for visits, and already the difference in some of the men is remarkable. Let young Ruby spend as much time with Kitty, Lady and whichever other animals she likes.'

'I will.' Beatrice's face heated as David finished with the blackout, turned around and caught her staring. His shoulders were very fine, and she knew exactly how it felt to wrap her arms around them. Her stomach quivered. 'Did you have a pet as a child?' She changed the subject and, hopefully, since she hadn't yet lit the lamp, he wouldn't notice her embarrassment. She fumbled for the matches, and in the small yellow light David's gaze zeroed in as he sat across from her at the table.

'I did. Patches – a little terrier, he was. Maud and I thought we'd get a dog ourselves, after we had a family but…' He rubbed a hand across his face and in the lamplight, the lines between his nose and mouth were more prominent. 'What about you?'

'We always had dogs. My father and brothers had a pack of hunting dogs, but I also had several special pets of my own.' She paused. 'Although not since becoming a teacher.'

David reached across the table and took one of Beatrice's hands in his. 'I suppose you must wonder about Maud.'

'As you undoubtedly wonder about Alex.' Beatrice let out a soft breath. If there was to be anything more between them beyond a few kisses, it was important that they talk, at some point, about his wife and her fiancé.

'I do. That's if you're able to talk about him.' David's voice was gentle, and the clasp of his hand was comforting whilst also sparking that familiar tingle of excitement along her nerve ends.

'I am, but there's not much to tell. We grew up together until one day our childhood friendship turned to love.' The wind rose, shrieking about the old house, and rain beat against the windows behind their black shrouds. 'His death changed me, certainly, but I had to go on. As you did as well, I imagine.'

'I did.' David let out a long breath. 'She was also from Yorkshire, but Maud and I met in London. At a dance hall, actually.' His eyes twinkled. 'We'd only been married a year, never had a real chance to make a home of our own when… well, no need to go into that part of it.' His expression became shuttered. 'We expected we'd have a big family and would likely return to Yorkshire where I'd set up my practice, but it was not to be.'

'Because of the war.'

'Yes, because of the war.' David held Beatrice's hand more tightly.

As a result of that war, the two of them had also ended up alone. 'I suppose without that war – and this one – we'd have never met.'

David stared into the distance. 'It's unlikely you'd have exchanged the gentle, manicured fields of Oxfordshire for the wilds of Yorkshire. As for meeting in London, unless you had reason to call upon me in a professional capacity, it's safe to say we would not have mixed in the same circles.' His chuckle was without malice.

'I expect not.' There it was again, the social gulf between them which would once have mattered so much, but to Beatrice no longer did.

'I would not have dared to court you then.' His eyes surrounded by those thick lashes were intent on her.

'And now?' Beatrice's mouth went dry.

'I should have thought those kisses at the dance would have made it obvious.' He leaned closer, moving Beatrice's paperwork aside. 'But if there is any doubt, let me make myself clear. I should very much like to court you, Miss Wentworth.' His gaze gleamed with fun, giving Beatrice a glimpse of the boy he must have been.

'I should like that very much, Dr Stanley.' Beatrice half rose from her chair and then, as he did the same, their lips met in a kiss both urgent and sweet.

Chapter Twenty-Six

Saturday, 14 December 1940

In the small drawing room at Whittleton Hall, Beatrice opened one of the boxes of ornaments that Mrs Bertram had brought down from the attic. In emerald, gold, silver and cobalt, the baubles shaped like teardrops, fruits and birds had been made by skilled German glassblowers and were similar to those Beatrice remembered from her childhood Christmases. A time when anything German brought pleasure, not pain. 'Please be very careful, Ruby. These baubles are old and fragile.'

'Yes, Miss Wentworth.' At Beatrice's side, Ruby drew in a soft breath and her eyes widened as she took in the delicate shapes, each nestled in a bed of cotton wool. Less than a fortnight before Christmas, with Mrs Fisk confined to bed due to a heavy cold, the Misses Grainger had agreed that Ruby and her beloved Kitty could spend several days at Hazelbury Manor. Today, Ruby had joined Beatrice for her Saturday-morning volunteer stint at the convalescent home.

'Don't worry, Ruby. All these decorations survived my three rambunctious boys, so I doubt you'll cause any harm to them. Even my daughter wasn't as careful as you. She always tried to keep up with her elder brothers.' Mrs

Bertram's laugh was tinged with sadness. 'This Christmas is the first one that none of our four will be at home.'

'It feels like the first real wartime Christmas, doesn't it?' Beatrice set aside an angel tree topper, similar to one she remembered from childhood. It would be perfect on the spruce tree Major Bertram and two of the Land Girls had set up in a corner of the room earlier. 'Last year we didn't have food rationing, and it was, well… different.' She glanced at Ruby, who was showing a brown mohair teddy bear with black button eyes to a gruff army officer who'd lost an arm in combat in France.

Mrs Bertram nodded. 'If things don't let up in London and other cities, it's likely many will be spending Christmas Eve in shelters. As always, we must count our blessings.'

'We must.' While at first she'd resented being evacuated to the country, now Beatrice was grateful for Hazelbury's relative safety. Despite air-raid warnings, if any bombs fell in the vicinity it would likely be an accident rather than because the area was the Germans' intended target. 'Would you like to help us decorate the Christmas tree?' She turned to Flying Officer Brown, who had wheeled himself into the room but kept his back to Ruby and a small group of men clustered around a table playing chess.

He shook his head and stared at his hands.

'Aircraftman Griffiths will likely be back with us after Christmas.' Mrs Bertram spoke into the silence. 'Matron says he's made remarkable progress at the hospital in Norwich.'

'I'm glad to hear it.' As much as she wanted to, Beatrice couldn't save everyone, but because she'd been here when Griffiths had been brought in, she'd taken a special interest in him. 'I've got all the ornament boxes open. Shall we make a start?'

'I'd hoped a Christmas tree would bring some seasonal cheer to the men.' Mrs Bertram's face creased into a worried pucker. 'The staff did warn me it might be difficult but…' She stopped and her gaze drifted to the group desultorily playing chess and to Brown's vacant look, as if the most important parts of him had gone somewhere neither he nor anyone else could reach. 'Well, all we can do is try.' She forced a smile.

'We're making paper chains from newspaper at school.' Ruby, who'd rejoined them, held up one of the baubles – a plump gold pear – to Mrs Bertram, cradling it between her hands like she might a newborn chick. 'We're painting them red and green. Miss Wentworth is also painting us a beautiful frieze with deer and hedgehogs and snow and birds.'

'It sounds charming.' Over Ruby's head, Mrs Bertram gave Beatrice an approving nod.

'She's makin' pictures and scenery for our Nativity too. We're singing and dancing and doing all sorts to celebrate the baby Jesus being born.' Ruby clasped her hands behind her back as Beatrice unpacked a box of icicles crafted in intricate spun glass. 'I liked it better when Miss Wentworth played the piano for us to sing instead of that other lady. She's too loud.'

'That other lady?' Mrs Bertram raised her eyebrows.

'The one with a hat made from a poor animal.' Ruby gave a solemn nod. 'Mrs Drum.'

'Mrs Meldrum,' Beatrice interjected. 'She offered to help and I couldn't… decline.'

'I see.' Mrs Bertram's tone implied she saw more than Beatrice had intended. 'Do you know that Miss Grainger is quite a gifted musician?'

'Miss Hetty?' Beatrice paused. The piano in the drawing room was a fine instrument, but as far as Beatrice knew, she was the only one who ever played it. Yet it was kept tuned and a nearby cabinet held a wide selection of music. Whilst she'd never given it much thought, Beatrice had assumed that, like so much at Hazelbury Manor, the piano was a relic of another time.

'Yes indeed. Both Misses Grainger are musical. Miss Adelaide used to sing at concerts, some as far away as Norwich, and she also played the violin. On occasion, the sisters performed together. Only at house parties and such. Their parents would not have heard of them going on the stage.' Mrs Bertram paused. 'If you were to ask Miss Grainger to accompany the children as a great favour, and if you made her aware of the current situation, she might be most obliging.'

'Obliging' was not a word Beatrice would ordinarily use to describe Miss Hetty, but Mrs Bertram might have offered a solution to one of the problems keeping Beatrice awake at night. 'Thank you.'

'It is a pleasure, my dear. In one way or another, most situations can be managed, and people are more adaptable than you may think.' As she took an exquisite glass icicle from Beatrice, Mrs Bertram nodded towards Ruby, who was helping the army officer hang a trio of gold-painted paper stars. 'Old *and* young.'

'As my wife so often proves to me, it is indeed possible to teach an old dog new tricks. At least this one.' Major

Bertram came into the drawing room with David and two hound dogs gambolling at their heels.

'Sidney, really.' Mrs Bertram's cheeks went pink as she greeted her husband. 'Dr Stanley.'

'Doggies!' Ruby squealed and darted towards the animals.

'Hold on.' David scooped Ruby up as she passed him. 'These dogs are friendly, but you must never approach a strange dog without asking its owner first. Understood?'

'Yes, Doctor.' Ruby wrapped her arms around his neck as he balanced her on one hip.

'Mrs Bertram, Miss Wentworth.' David nodded and smiled, his gaze lingering on Beatrice several seconds longer than necessary. 'Haven't you done a good job on this tree! I'm impressed. What do you say, men?' He transferred his gaze to his patients.

'Bear.' The single word came from the depths of Brown's wheelchair, where the man sat huddled in blankets.

'Sorry, what was that?' David glanced around.

'Mr Brown said "bear". I heard him. Did you mean the teddy bear?' From her perch in David's arms, Ruby pointed to the bear which she'd left on a table near the tree.

'Bear.' Brown nodded and held out his hands, a lone tear trickling down his scarred cheek.

Hardly daring to breathe, Beatrice retrieved the bear and gave it to him. 'Here you are.' He'd spoken, finally.

'Thank you.' Brown's voice was rusty but still understandable. 'Good bear. Like mine was.' He set the toy on his lap and reached out to pat one of the dogs who'd come over to investigate. 'Little one should put angel on top of tree.' His mouth worked in the manner of one unused to forming words.

'I'm Ruby.' She looked from David to Brown.

'Ruby. The gem.' Another tear rolled down the young man's face. 'Yes, Ruby should put the angel on the tree.'

'That's a fine idea,' David said. 'Shall I lift you up, Ruby? Where's that angel, Miss Wentworth?'

'Here.' Beatrice caught her breath.

David took the delicate angel and, with Ruby's help, put it atop the tree.

The angel, the Christmas tree, David and Ruby swam in front of Beatrice's eyes as emotion rushed over and through her.

Clapping broke out, led by the gruff army officer as Major and Mrs Bertram and the rest of the patients joined in.

The world was far from peaceful but here at Whittleton Hall these broken men were finding peace and healing. They were also finding companionship and understanding.

Beatrice glanced at Flight Officer Brown, who was cradling the teddy bear and speaking softly to the dog, her chin resting on his knee. The chess game resumed, and the other dog settled in front of the fire.

As David, Beatrice, Ruby and Mrs Bertram added the last ornaments to the tree, Ruby's high-pitched chatter rising above the rest, Beatrice's heart swelled.

Hope and love. That's what all of them were finding here as well, perhaps her most of all. And with David and Ruby, she also felt as if she'd found a family.

Chapter Twenty-Seven

Sunday, 15 December 1940

'Will I do as a suitable accompanist for the Nativity?' The following afternoon, Miss Hetty looked at Beatrice over the top of her spectacles from the piano bench, the rousing finale to 'Joy to the World' reverberating in Hazelbury Manor's large drawing room.

'You will indeed. You're more than suitable, Miss Hetty.' From one of the dust-sheet enveloped sofas, where she sat between Victoria and Nell with Ruby on a small stool at her side, Beatrice stopped herself from giving a most unladylike whoop of pleasure mixed with relief. Mrs Bertram was right. In the matter of Mrs Meldrum and the Nativity music, Miss Hetty had been most obliging indeed.

'You're as good as a professional.' In a shaft of weak sunlight, Nell stared at Miss Hetty, goggle-eyed.

'The matron at Whittleton Hall mentioned getting up concerts after Christmas,' Victoria said. 'Some of the patients are musical, so perhaps you might consider—'

'Victoria' – Miss Hetty gave her a severe look – 'please restrain yourself. You would do well to remember that, in this country, we are not as forthright as you Canadians. We do not push ourselves forwards.'

Unless you were a Mrs Meldrum or a Mrs Yallop.

Beatrice exchanged a furtive glance with Nell and held back what would have been a most unladylike snort of amusement.

'Yes, Miss Hetty.' Victoria twirled her engagement ring and bent to pat Lady.

'It will be quite like old times, with Hetty playing for a concert.' As usual, Miss Addie, who stood beside the piano to turn pages for her sister, poured oil on troubled waters.

'*Two* concerts.' Miss Hetty's smile was magnanimous. 'One here in the village and the other at Whittleton Hall. It is certainly much more appropriate for me to assist you than Mrs Meldrum. I shall write to tell her of the change of plan.'

'But—'

'Do not trouble yourself, Beatrice.' Miss Hetty interjected with a regal wave. 'I will make it clear to Dot Meldrum that I shall be in charge of any music you require for the Nativity, so there is nothing more to be said about it.' Miss Hetty closed her music book with a sniff. 'Dorothea, indeed. She was christened Dorothy. It is only latterly that she has assumed such an affectation.'

'What's a "fectation"? Is it like Mrs Fisk being poorly?' Ruby looked up from tossing a ball of wool for Kitty.

'No, Mrs Fisk has an infection, Ruby.' Beatrice repressed another smile. 'When I spoke to one of her neighbours after church this morning, she said that Mrs Fisk is much improved. You and Kitty should be able to return to the cottage by the middle of the week.'

Beatrice would miss Ruby so very much – more and more, she caught herself thinking, *What if?* So many children, like Ruby, had been orphaned by the war, and each of them needed a family. If Ruby truly had no relatives left, would it not be better for her to be with those who already loved and cared for her? The girl was such good company, so sweet-natured and quick to learn. Both her speech and manners were improving, and while still not fully robust, she was almost unrecognisable from the spindly, wan child who'd arrived in Hazelbury in August. Whilst she couldn't show it or any other hint of favouritism, Beatrice had begun to take an almost maternal pride in Ruby's progress.

'I like Mrs Fisk, but I like being here too.' Ruby lolled against Beatrice's knee. 'Not only 'cause it's closer to school, neither.' She looked around the room, her gaze alighting on the piano. 'I don't suppose I could learn to play like you and Miss Grainger?'

'Why not?' Miss Hetty shut the piano lid. 'Even in this degenerate age, music is a suitable accomplishment for modest and respectable girls. Learning to play a musical instrument is far preferable to gyrating around a gramophone or the like. If you wish, I expect that Miss Wentworth would be pleased to teach you.'

'Me?' Beatrice tried not to gape at Miss Hetty.

'Who better? You may use the piano here. Ruby could practise after school, could she not? I expect some transportation to Mrs Fisk's cottage might be arranged. Didn't Dr Stanley say he thought the walk in winter was too much for Ruby twice a day?' Miss Hetty's eyes narrowed on Ruby as if she were a medical specimen.

'He did.' Beatrice's thoughts whirled.

'If you and Miss Addie were agreeable, I could perhaps use the motor to drive Ruby back to Mrs Fisk's?

Only when it's dark, of course, or the weather is bad.' Undoubtedly mindful of Miss Hetty's admonition about 'forthright Canadians', Victoria kept her eyes lowered and her tone respectful, almost diffident. 'We should have sufficient petrol. Especially if Dr Stanley were to recommend the journey, and if anyone in authority were to question us, such travel would be deemed necessary.'

Only because Beatrice knew Victoria well did she catch the whisper of a smile that quivered on one side of Victoria's mouth. The motor, which had belonged to the Misses Grainger's father, sat in what had once been a carriage house. It was driven only by their great-nephew Louis or by Victoria, who'd learned to drive in Canada, for occasional essential errands.

'Why not, Hetty?' Miss Addie's wrinkled face lit up with a smile. 'It's been lovely having a child around the place these last few days and that way we wouldn't have to truly say goodbye to Ruby. I could also continue working with her on her stitching. She has the makings of a fine needlewoman, and she told me she would like to learn to knit.'

'Please Miss Wentworth? I wouldn't be any trouble, I promise.' Ruby's expression was beseeching.

'Of course you wouldn't be, dear.' Beatrice hesitated. 'I would be happy to give you piano lessons, but let us try it for a month starting after Christmas and see how we get on.' If Ruby's initial enthusiasm waned, neither of them would feel compelled to continue.

She'd rather give her drawing lessons as Ruby had obvious talent, but she couldn't. Art was something to be nurtured in the classroom but not beyond, as it would be considered favouritism. However, formal music tuition, which wasn't offered at school, was different.

As Ruby beamed at her, Beatrice returned the girl's smile. Even before the war, Beatrice's work at school had meant she'd never considered offering piano tuition, but with Ruby, it would be special. Another way to help the girl thrive and possibly provide a distraction from her grief. Another way to spend time with her, too.

'Right, shall we go to the kitchen, Ruby?' Nell stood and held out a hand. 'Since it's Marjorie's day off, I promised to teach you how to make a bread pudding. You can have a slice for your tea. "Proper comfort food" is what my mum calls it.'

'Yes, Miss Potter.' Ruby hesitated. 'Do you know how to make bread pudding, Miss Wentworth?'

'No, I can't say I do.' Beatrice didn't remember eating it either, not even for nursery tea with her nanny. Although the servants might have eaten bread pudding, it was not a dish that would ever have been served upstairs.

'Miss Potter could teach you with me, couldn't she?' Ruby's blue eyes held a pleading expression.

'I could.' Nell worried her lower lip. 'But I expect Miss Wentworth has other things to attend to.'

'Doctor said he likes bread pudding because it fills him up. I 'spect he'd like it if we shared some of ours with him, 'specially if Miss Wentworth and me made it.'

Beatrice did have many other things to attend to. From finishing her Christmas cards to writing the weekly letter to her mother, completing a lesson plan and sewing a button on a school dress, Sunday was far from a 'day of rest'. However, all those tasks could wait, and she had to smile at the thought of making David something to eat.

And working alongside Ruby to give David a treat would make it extra special.

'If you and Miss Potter will be patient with me, why not?' If Beatrice wanted to have that imagined cottage by the sea, learning some basic cookery skills was long overdue. And if she ever shared that cottage with David… *Despite telling herself not to imagine such a thing, she couldn't seem to help herself.*

'A way to a man's heart is through his stomach,' Victoria murmured as the two of them followed Nell and Ruby out of the drawing room, leaving the Misses Grainger reminiscing about music popular in their girlhood. 'Louis certainly appreciates the food parcels I send him.'

Beatrice's face heated. 'That's different. Louis is your fiancé.' Although it would be kind to share some bread pudding with David. They were courting, after all.

Victoria gave Beatrice's arm a gentle squeeze. 'He is – and this time last year I could never have imagined any of what has happened. Apart from Louis himself, one of the nicest things about becoming engaged is wishing that same happiness for my friends.'

Happiness didn't come from wishing for it. Beatrice had learned that lesson well. Nor did she believe that bread pudding would influence David's feelings for her. But if she was honest with herself, she didn't want to live in that seaside cottage with anyone but him.

Chapter Twenty-Eight

Monday, 16 December 1940

'Thank you, Ralph and Albert. Please return to your seats and settle back to your work. The room should warm up shortly.' Beatrice nodded to the boys who had added coal to the fire at the front of the classroom.

Unlike Victoria, who relied on wood for heating in the village hall or at Hazelbury Manor, the school had an adequate supply of coal. Still, with ill-fitting windows and doors and its location on the northerly edge of the village near open fields, the building was never truly warm. On this blustery December day, Beatrice and many of the Londoners had kept their coats on following the afternoon break.

'I don't see the point in doing sums if we're all going to be blown to bits.' Albert slumped into his seat in the first row. 'No point to Christmas neither.'

Along with Beatrice reprimanding him to do as he was told, she should also tell him to raise his hand before speaking. Yet she understood why he'd said what he did. With hundreds more killed in the past several days from the bombs dropped on Sheffield, let alone the attacks on Southampton, Coventry and other British cities, it was difficult to summon enthusiasm for learning, let alone festive cheer. But it was up to her and the other teachers to keep things as normal as possible for the children and help them enjoy what should be a joyful season.

'Me dad says the Germans don't care if it's Christmas,' Leonard, one of the village boys, added. 'I bet Jerries come right here to Hazelbury on Christmas Day. Me dad also says we'll be speaking German soon, you'll see.'

'That's enough.' Beatrice rapped on her desk to restore order. 'Don't be absurd. The Royal Air Force is holding the Germans at bay, and they will not bomb the British people into submission. As for Christmas, the German people celebrate Christmas and Christ's birth as we do.'

Even if she didn't feel it, Beatrice had to seem brave. Undaunted and resilient. Except the war wouldn't be won by slogans, and if their British fighter pilots – young men who were *truly* brave – couldn't hold back the German aerial assault, where would they be? Maybe they would all have to speak German eventually. Oh, she couldn't let herself countenance such a thought.

'We have our Nativity performances to look forward to, and the party afterwards at Whittleton Hall and then Christmas Day itself.' She glanced at Diana who, usually a cheerful child, looked almost as morose as the rest. 'Christmas is a time to give joy to others, and our play will certainly do that.' Even to her own ears, Beatrice's voice sounded artificially bright. 'Yes, Ruby, what is it?' She nodded at the girl's raised hand.

'I see the Air Raid warden coming up the lane. To do our gas mask inspection like you said, Miss Wentworth.'

'Thank you, Ruby.' The warden's visit for his regular, required inspection of the children's masks would be a distraction from lessons that, so far today, had failed to capture the interest of even her most diligent pupils.

'Miss Wentworth, I… Oh…' At Diana's raised voice, Beatrice turned to see what the matter was, but whatever else Diana said – or intended to say – was drowned out by a series of rapid, building-rattling thuds.

'Get under your desks, children. Quickly and put your gas masks on.' Beatrice grabbed her own gas mask box. 'Stay where you are for the moment.' The noise wasn't loud enough to be from a bomb blast, not one nearby anyway, and there had been no aircraft sound or raid warning. However, it was also unlikely to be a drill as those were planned in advance.

Holding her gas mask, she stepped outside her classroom, meeting Nell in the middle of the small central hall.

'What's happening?' Nell's face was even paler than usual, and she had her gas mask half out of its box.

'I don't know, but I shall find out. Stay with the children and make sure they keep under their desks with masks on as we've practised.'

Nell nodded as someone hammered on the front door.

'Miss Wentworth? Miss Potter?' It was the ARP warden, known as Herb by most of the village but Mr Foulger to the children. 'All right in there?'

'Yes.' Beatrice moved to the stout wooden door.

'Good, good.' Mr Foulger's voice echoed from the other side. 'Thanks to those wind gusts, your sandbags have slid down off the roof ledge, front and back, and burst open.'

Hazelbury was near Whittleton's RAF base, and after a number of air-raid warnings, the authorities had recently decided to put sandbags around and atop the school and several other local buildings for what was termed 'basic protection'.

'It's not poison gas, then?' Beatrice's legs shook and she rested one hand against the door frame.

'Not at all.' Mr Foulger's voice was reassuring. 'I said it were a bad idea to put them bags up there, leastways until we got a hard freeze, I've been proved right, haven't I?' Although muffled by the wall of the building, he seemed to snort. 'Once I get the front and rear doors unblocked, can you spare several of your lads to help me clear up the mess?'

'Certainly.' Beatrice exhaled. 'It's fortunate you arrived at the school when you did.'

'Fortunate? No, I'd say it were right providence. Otherwise, you'd be having to break one of them high windows and climb out.'

'Thank goodness we don't.' Beatrice glanced over her shoulder at Nell who'd reappeared. 'It's fine. The children do not require their gas masks. There has been an incident with the sandbags, nothing more.'

'If Miss McKaye's infants were here, they'd have thought that there noise was Father Christmas come early.' Albert poked his head around Beatrice's open classroom door, swinging his gas mask box from its string. 'His sleigh on the roof like. Maybe trying to find us at school since we're not in London.' He sent her an endearing, gap-toothed grin.

'Albert' – having taken her gas mask off, Nell gave him a severe look – 'what are you doing out here?'

'I heard Miss Wentworth say it were fine and we didn't need no masks so I were curious.' Albert came into the hall, followed by several other boys. 'Besides, me dad says it's up to us men and boys to keep the girls and women safe. That's why I gave Ruby my last boiled sweet. She were scared.'

Beatrice gave a sigh of relief. She couldn't resist Albert's smile or well-intentioned chivalry. 'Thank you, Albert. That was very kind. Mr Foulger will also soon need your help.' The rhythmic thump of a shovel resounded against the front door. 'School is dismissed early today.'

Only an hour of the school day remained, and it was the last week before the Christmas holiday. There was little to be lost by giving the children some extra free time and much to be gained.

By leaving school now, she might cross paths with David on his way to the hospital. He'd have received the parcel of bread pudding she'd left for him at the vicarage before school. Or, if she didn't see David, there might be a note from him at the manor.

She could wrap her Christmas presents for Victoria, Nell and the Misses Grainger if they'd arrived from London in today's post. Enjoy a half hour with her sketch-book. Write to the music shop in Norwich to order several beginner piano books for Ruby's lessons. Oh, the possibilities were limitless and pleasurable.

As the front door swung open bringing in Mr Foulger and a shower of sand, Beatrice picked up the school bell to ring it.

For perhaps the first time ever, she welcomed a change in routine. Because she was ready to seize life, her real one, with both hands and hold tight.

-

'I can't properly look forward to enjoying Christmas until we get these two Nativity performances over and done with,' Nell said. That night, after the Misses Grainger and Ruby had gone to bed, the three teachers gathered in the small parlour across the hall from their bedrooms. Nell sat in the armchair with her mending basket, while Beatrice and Victoria strung popcorn kernels and cranberries into a garland. 'That said, it doesn't seem right to enjoy Christmas at all this year. Not with so many deaths and folk having lost their homes.'

'And with so many of us separated from our loved ones.' Victoria let out a heavy sigh. 'I'm grateful that Louis is safe, but it's still bad luck he can't get leave until the middle of January. Do you remember this time last year when we all hoped the war would be over soon?'

Beatrice had hoped for the best like the others, but privately, she'd been considerably less optimistic. Maybe they all were, but it was bad form to say so. The war wouldn't be over soon. In fact, all the signs indicated that it would last for years, so there was no use grumbling. Letting a sigh of her own escape, she tied a knot at one end of the garland and added it to Victoria's completed pile.

'Nevertheless, despite things being so grim, maybe it is more important than ever to celebrate Christmas this year. As Mr Russell says, the true meaning of Christmas is not parties and other such events, but to draw inspiration from our faith, which will give us hope as well as comfort and strength.' The vicar was one of those whom Beatrice considered a truly devout and godly man, but after his son's death he too seemed almost as worn down as the rest of them. Still, he was doing his best to boost morale and set an example, and in that and so many other ways, Beatrice looked to him for both inspiration and guidance. 'The three of us are together, at any rate.' And spending Christmas at Hazelbury Manor was far preferable to Beatrice than making the trek to Oxfordshire to listen to her mother's complaints.

Food rationing is so dreadfully tedious, darling. I can hardly let myself think what Christmas will be like. Only one bottle of wine left and not even a good vintage. And the women I must associate with in the Red Cross and W.I. are dreadfully common... Oh, it's all too awful. You can't imagine what I must endure.

Beatrice could imagine it all too well, but likely not in the way Clarissa Wentworth intended in her letters. Her mother had never been inclined to make the best of circumstances, so Beatrice should not have expected the war to make a difference. And, unlike the Misses Grainger, Mrs Bertram and Mrs Russell, she would always be more concerned with herself than with any greater good.

'We *are* together – and we've become like a family, haven't we?' With their popcorn garlands complete, Victoria took up her knitting – a pilot mascot toy she was making for her cousin Stewart from scraps of wool.

'We have indeed.' A family Beatrice would never have expected but one that gave her more support and care than the one she'd grown up with. Would this new understanding of what a family could be help her make one with David and maybe Ruby as well?

'A family for keeps.' Nell gave a decisive nod. 'Even my mum is starting to come round to that notion. In her last letter, she wrote that she put the Christmas cards you two sent her front and centre on the mantel next to the clock. She's showing them to all the neighbours. Quite proud, she is, that I have what she calls "such distinguished" friends.' Bent over her sewing, the lamplight picked up russet tones in Nell's dark hair and gilded her high cheekbones and thick, sooty lashes.

'I'm sure Miss Hetty and Miss Addie would agree that I'm hardly distinguished.' Victoria laughed. 'Still, they've accepted me with good grace for Louis's sake and for that I am grateful.'

'They've accepted you for your own sake – and don't dismiss it.' Beatrice's tone was sharper than she had intended and she softened it. 'Like Nell, you are a woman of fine and upstanding character, and you will make Louis a more than suitable wife.'

'Mrs Grainger has a nice ring to it, doesn't it?' Nell gave Victoria a sideways glance and grinned. 'Will you be asking me to make you a wedding dress in the new year?'

'Not as yet.' Despite her blush, Victoria's tone was prim. 'But I shall let you know when that time comes. I've resigned myself to marrying without any of my family, except you three and perhaps Stewart there.'

Nell took several strands of white wool and draped them across Victoria's hair in imitation of a bridal veil. 'Because there's a war on, you know.'

As the three of them broke into laughter at a phrase so oft-used it had become almost meaningless, Beatrice felt more warmth than from the dying embers of the weak fire.

There *was* a war on but despite its many hardships, the war also continued to enrich her life. And that meant sharing Christmas with friends who *were* family and made the hardships more bearable.

Chapter Twenty-Nine

Saturday, 21 December 1940

'Beatrice, my dear.' On the Saturday of the school's Nativity performance at the convalescent hospital, Diana's mother, Mary Foster-Dalton, greeted Beatrice at the front entrance of Whittleton Hall. 'After such a dreadful journey, I can hardly believe I am actually here. It was so kind of Major Bertram to collect me in Cromer.' Mary brushed snowflakes from her coat collar and russet-coloured feathered hat. 'Whilst I long to see Diana, I'm more than willing to lend a hand today.'

'Just… applaud as loudly as possible. After yesterday's performance in the village hall, I do not jest.' As Beatrice welcomed her childhood friend, she tried not to shudder at the memory of forgotten lines, an over-excited king sitting on the bejewelled cardboard crowns Nell had laboured over, and one of Victoria's infants having an attack of stage fright, darting offstage and taking the rest of the sheep with her. 'Diana has been longing to see you as well. Although she'll undoubtedly miss her father and brothers, it's lovely you're able to stay at the vicarage with her over Christmas Day.'

But would a longer visit from her mother make it even more difficult for Diana to settle again into village and school life? Beatrice made herself push the thought to the back of her mind. It was almost Christmas, and for the holiday she'd promised herself she would try to live more in each moment.

'Yes, but poor Edward will have to spend the day alone in the hotel. Still, with the boys not having leave and Edward having to return to work on Boxing Day, we could not have had our usual family Christmas anyway. Like everyone else, I am making the best of things.' For an instant, Mary's bright expression faltered. 'I'm a trained first aider and have become quite a stalwart of the local W.V.S. In the new year, I may even learn to drive an ambulance or take on some kind of paid war work. I expect Mummy will be horrified, but no matter.' Mary's shrug was dismissive. 'Since I'm not quite the full-time worker bee, I wanted to make the most of this Christmas for Diana. You and I will also have time to catch up. I've missed you, Beatrice.'

'I've missed you too.' Since reconnecting through Diana being evacuated with Beatrice's school, she and Mary had exchanged regular fortnightly letters. Still, such missives could not replace being together in person, which was needed to truly rebuild the once deep friendship between them. And while Mary had made several previous visits to Hazelbury, they had been fleeting. Naturally, Diana was Mary's priority, so she and Beatrice had never managed anything more than brief and rushed chats – and always in the company of others.

'Here, come through.' Beatrice guided Mary through the main hall and into the large drawing room where patients, nurses, other hospital staff and a group of the estate's Land Girls had already taken their seats in front of a blue velvet curtain strung between two poles. 'I saved you a place near the front.' She indicated a parlour chair at one end of a row and waited for Mary to settle herself. 'I'm glad you're here, truly.'

'I am as well.' Mary's gaze held Beatrice's and it was as if the years – and the distance – momentarily slipped away and they were girls again. 'You must dash – but give Diana my love before she goes on.'

'I shall.' As Beatrice slipped behind the curtain, exchanging a small smile with Miss Hetty, who was checking her music at the piano, there was a new fullness in her heart. Maybe, with Mary, she could build a bridge between her old life and this new one. It wouldn't be seamless. The gaps would still show, as in a piece of badly mended porcelain, but those breaks were part of Beatrice's history and her evolving life story.

'All right?' On the other side of the curtain, a hospital porter moved the rustic stable into place. Jimmy Clarke and several older boys had fashioned it from scrap wood and the sturdy cardboard box that Victoria's mother's W.I. branch had used to send Christmas presents for the schoolchildren.

'Yes.' Beatrice's voice caught. Except that David should be here by now, so where was he? No matter what happened at today's performance, she'd counted on it being all right because of David – not only since he was to play Father Christmas. In a way, Beatrice had only just realised that she needed his quiet support and encouragement. His work was important, certainly, but was it more important than her?

–

'The angels do look quite angelic, don't they?' From where they stood in the makeshift wings, Nell darted a glance at Beatrice as the Nativity continued on what was meant to be a stage – in reality, a large rug that had been brought down from one of Whittleton Hall's attics and laid at one end of the drawing room.

'They do indeed.' Beatrice took in the sight of the winged angels – Ruby included – gathered around Mary, Joseph and the baby Jesus. Behind them, and out of view of the audience, Leonard stood statue-like, holding a yellow-painted cardboard star aloft above the stable roof. It was the final scene, with all the performers gathering on stage together, and Beatrice could almost breathe a sigh of relief that, unlike yesterday, this performance had gone smoothly. Almost, but not quite. If only David were here. Once again, she glanced around. If he didn't arrive soon, what would she do? One of the porters could perhaps play Father Christmas – the costume was stored in the office – but it wouldn't be ideal. She forced her attention back to the performance. 'At a distance, the damage to those crowns won't be noticeable. Excellent work.'

At Beatrice's praise, Nell flushed with pleasure before turning to help Peter, one of the infants, fix his shepherd's cloak. 'Not to worry. Nobody will have noticed you were missing. There you go. See Ruby holding out her hand for you?' She gave the boy a gentle push back onto the stage as Miss Hetty played the incidental music before the final carol, with Miss Addie at her side to turn pages.

'Any word from Mrs Meldrum?' At Beatrice's other side, Victoria spoke out of one side of her mouth and into Beatrice's ear.

'Mrs Bertram said she's in the audience today and has taken charge of the W.I.'s Christmas party for the children, but otherwise, no.' Beatrice shook her head. 'I must speak to her later to make sure there are no hard feelings.' After Miss Hetty announced her intention to provide the musical accompaniment – given the Misses Grainger's higher social standing in the village – Mrs Meldrum would have had no choice but to defer, but it was still awkward. And from what Beatrice knew of Mrs Meldrum, like any seasoned general, she would have only made a brief, strategic retreat, not withdrawn from the fray entirely.

'Rather you than me.' Victoria made a face.

Beatrice turned at a tug on her arm to find David behind her, dressed in his Father Christmas costume, mostly hidden by another curtain drawn across one of the room's window alcoves. 'I'm here. There was an emergency with a patient and, well… I hope Nurse Sibley got a message to you as I asked?' he whispered in Beatrice's ear. 'I'd never let you down, but since I was too late to join you here, I saw most of the Nativity through a crack in the door in the main hall until I could sneak round. Couldn't risk the kiddies getting a glimpse of me before the big moment. Looks like it's gone over ever so well, though.' Behind the beard Nell had so painstakingly crafted, his mouth crooked into a familiar and reassuring smile.

Beatrice hadn't received any message, but knowing that David had sent her one made all the difference. Of course, he didn't want to disappoint the children, who'd begun singing the first verse of 'Silent Night'. With an answering smile, she turned back to the makeshift stage.

'Now for Diana's solo. She does have such a lovely voice.' Nell glanced from the prompt book over her shoulder at the curtained alcove where David waited for his cue. 'I knew he'd be here. No need to fuss.'

Beatrice nodded and let the music and Diana's high treble wash over her. Although originally written in German, to Beatrice's relief nobody had questioned having 'Silent Night' as the closing number in the school's Nativity. Music should transcend conflict. And, as in the Christmas truce of 1914, when British and German soldiers had come out of their trenches to sing Christmas carols in a brief break from the fighting, the message of peace and hope in 'Silent Night' prevailed.

Laughter rippled from some of the performers and then the audience.

'What on earth?' Beatrice exchanged alarmed glances with Victoria and Nell.

Although Diana continued singing, the girl's voice hitched, and above her Virgin Mary costume, her face flushed pink.

As Beatrice took a step forwards, a scuffle broke out by the stable, and the star jerked up and down as if Leonard had taken some kind of fit.

The laughter grew louder and drowned out the music entirely.

Wilf, the innkeeper, grabbed Leonard by one shoulder. 'What do you think you're playing at?'

Rooted to the spot, Beatrice let out a horrified gasp as Leonard flicked the tail end of a moth-eaten fox stole – borrowed from the amateur dramatics society for one of the small-animal costumes – towards Ruby and the other angels.

'See here.' Ruby took hold of the fox's head, raised a hand and spoke into the sudden silence. 'You's not spoiling

Miss Wentworth's Nativity or Diana's song or any of it. You's should be grateful for all these nice things. You're a bad boy, you are. Stop making silly faces with this here fox and behave.' She smoothed the stole's fur as if soothing the animal itself. 'Carry on.' With a note-perfect imitation of Miss Hetty, Ruby looped a consoling arm around Diana.

'That's right. You listen to Miss Ruby. Stop your laughing, fellows.' Flying Officer Brown spoke from where he sat in his wheelchair between Major Bertram and the vicar, both of whom had a hand over their mouths.

Behind the piano, Miss Hetty nodded and resumed playing 'Silent Night', the corners of her mouth twitching.

As the audience settled and patients and hospital staff tried to assume suitably solemn expressions, Beatrice pressed a hand to her stomach to hold back a belated laugh of her own.

It was dreadful, of course, and Leonard would have to be punished – given lines to write and an extra rota of chores. Yet, it was wonderful too, and amidst the daily horror of war, such real, heartfelt laughter was sorely needed.

As the carol ended, Beatrice, the other teachers and now David – in his well-padded Father Christmas costume with a sack of presents slung over one shoulder – joined their pupils on stage.

'Ho, ho, ho.' David's voice boomed out, ending with a chuckle worthy of St Nicholas himself. So quickly that Beatrice almost missed it, David winked at her before wishing the assembled children a 'Happy Christmas'.

The audience clapped and cheered, and those who were able to stood and stamped their feet.

And while the pupils took their bows, Beatrice placed herself between the angels and Leonard to prevent any further mischief, and Ruby's hand crept into hers and squeezed.

A little child shall lead them.

The Bible verse from Isaiah popped into Beatrice's head, and as she squeezed Ruby's hand back, she knew that despite the war, the message – and miracle – of Christmas would endure.

–

'That's the last of the children gone home with their families, and the Land Girls helped me put the drawing room to rights.' Beatrice sank into what she now thought of as 'her' chair in the office at Whittleton Hall's convalescent hospital and checked if any urgent telephone messages had come in whilst the Nativity and W.I. party had been in progress. Following the performance and children's party, she wanted to make sure her volunteer duties were complete. 'Mrs Bertram has taken charge of the money we raised for the Red Cross. Together with yesterday's collection at the performance in the village, it's a tidy sum.'

'You've done more than enough today.' From the other side of the desk, David held out Beatrice's coat. 'You should have left half an hour ago with the Misses Grainger and the others. Come, I'll drive you home.'

'Are you sure you can spare the time?' After sitting down, Beatrice didn't want to get up again. 'You were a wonderful Father Christmas, but it also took you away from your working day. I expect I can get a lift with someone else. And what about your patient? The one with the emergency?'

'He is doing well and under the capable care of Matron and the doctor I called to attend from Whittleton. Making that call and then waiting for the medic to arrive is why I was late but… I'm sorry, Beatrice. Truly. Emergency care isn't usually required here but sometimes… well, one never knows what may happen.'

Like that crashed aeroplane and the men who'd been brought here the day they met. 'It is forgotten.' Beatrice wouldn't tell David that Nurse Sibley had neglected to give her his message. The hospital staff were busy, so it wasn't surprising that a communication had been overlooked. She would think no more of it. David would always be there when she needed him. He'd even said he wouldn't let her down.

'In terms of a lift or anything else, I shall make the time. Not only for you but also for Ruby and Mrs Fisk.' Setting Beatrice's coat on the desk, David took Beatrice's hand to tug her up.

'They're still here?' Beatrice half-stumbled to her feet.

'Ruby insisted on waiting for you.' David's hand in hers sent a familiar tingle along Beatrice's spine. 'Quite fierce, she was.'

'She was "quite fierce" with Leonard during the Nativity too. I wondered what had come over her.' With David's help, her hat, coat and scarf were donned. 'I was about to intervene, but she spoke up before I'd even rightly seen what was going on.'

'The child has potential, that's for certain.' David's hands lingered on Beatrice's shoulders. 'She might make something of herself one day.'

If she had the right training, guidance and a loving family. Beatrice's heart twisted. 'There's still no news of Ruby's stepfather, and while an address finally turned up for her father's sister in America, we have no way of knowing if it's current. Miss Hopson has written.' When David took his hands away to put on his own coat, Beatrice's body chilled. She'd resolved not to let herself think about that letter and whether or not they would receive a reply. Or if they did, what it might say.

'It's a shame Miss Hopson could not be here today. I expect your headmistress would have been pleased with how you teachers did your bit for the men who needed cheer.'

'Despite Leonard's comic intervention.' Beatrice returned his smile. 'Fortunately, Miss Hopson has a sense of humour, so I expect, like everyone else, she would have seen the funny side.' While the headmistress had intended to make a brief Christmas visit to Hazelbury, several staff members from Park Road School in the West Country having been taken ill meant she needed to go there instead. 'However, I shall never be able to look at one of those dreadful animal stoles in the same way again. It was shocking, really.'

'That may be, but I suspect it made Christmas for many of the men here.' One of David's rich laughs rolled out. 'Leonard's an imp, no doubt about it, and when Ralph dared him to make that fox sing along with Diana, I can see the temptation.'

Beatrice did as well, but as to whether that made the situation better or worse she was in a quandary. 'Poor Diana.'

'Once she knew what was happening, Diana was good-natured about it, as was Mrs Foster-Dalton.' David took Beatrice's arm, the gesture almost possessive. 'Do not trouble yourself any further as to what you could, might or should have done. Certainly nobody is blaming you, not even Mrs Meldrum.'

'I suppose not.' At the W.I. party, as the children clustered around Father Christmas, Mrs Meldrum had been almost jovial, recounting some of the antics her own sons had once got up to. Yet, Beatrice still blamed herself. Some would say she was not strict enough with her pupils, so it was natural that Victoria and Nell would follow her example. 'Ruby did bring everyone together.'

'She did, even Brown. The change in that young man has been remarkable. Along with you, Ruby has been a large part of his healing.' David sobered and cupped Beatrice's chin with one gloved hand. 'However, you are the one whom Ruby and the others look to and rely upon.'

'I'm only a teacher.' Beatrice flushed under the intensity of his gaze. 'Compared to everyone else, I'm not doing anything of great importance in this war.' She read the newspapers and listened to the wireless. From bus conductors to those in the Forces, there were daily accounts of heroism, both large and small.

'Don't be so modest.' David's face drew closer to hers. 'Although it may not seem so at present, you and the other teachers have sacrificed as much as your lives for your pupils. Your ordinary lives, in any case, for as long as the war may last. And as Miss Hopson's deputy, you bear the brunt of responsibility for all aspects of these children's well-being.'

She did, and sometimes the weight seemed too heavy, almost crushing on Beatrice's narrow shoulders. 'It's my job, isn't it?' She tried to laugh.

'It is, but many would not take it as seriously or be as devoted to the work as you are.' David dropped a light kiss on Beatrice's cheek. 'I admire and respect you, Beatrice Wentworth. Now, let's find Ruby and Mrs Fisk and get the three of you home before it's dark. I'm on duty here until early afternoon on Christmas Day, but if I come round to the manor after my shift, shall we take a walk?' As he held open the office door for Beatrice to leave the room first, his smile was unexpectedly hesitant.

'I'd like that very much.' Beatrice put a finger to her cheek, still feeling the imprint of David's kiss.

'Good.' After another brief smile, he stuck his hands into his coat pockets. 'Why don't you wait here? I don't expect Ruby's gone far. Did I tell you I found a doll for her for Christmas?'

Beatrice shook her head. In the main entrance hall, once again surrounded by nursing staff and patients, the scent of cigarette smoke mixed with the pungent pine from a second Christmas tree propped in a bucket inside the front door. It still felt as if the two of them were in their own world.

'Not a new doll. Couldn't manage to get my hands on one with the shortages here, especially.' His expression was earnest. 'However, a fellow I worked with in London has a daughter who has outgrown dolls. When I mentioned Ruby, his wife posted me a doll their daughter had discarded, along with clothes and other bits and pieces. She has blonde hair and looks like Diana's doll. I'm making Ruby a doll cot as well. Mrs Russell found some scrap wood for me.'

'Ruby will be delighted. Mrs Fisk does her best but despite the money she gets for Ruby's keep, she doesn't have much to spare for necessities, let alone presents.' Emotion clogged Beatrice's throat. Except for the Christmas card she'd given to each of her pupils yesterday – the last day of school before the Christmas break – she couldn't give Ruby any other present. Such a gesture would rightly be seen as having a favourite – something no teacher could countenance.

'Right then. Take a seat.' David gestured to one of the hall chairs. 'I'll only be a moment.'

Beatrice sat as the hospital bustle continued on around her. *What did you do in the war?* On the rare occasions she let herself think about the future, if ever asked such a question she had always assumed she'd say, 'Oh, nothing much.'

But maybe her 'nothing much' was, in fact, everything.

Chapter Thirty

Wednesday, 25 December 1940

'Happy Christmas.' In the dining room at Hazelbury Manor, Beatrice raised her glass of fruit cordial in a toast.

'Happy Christmas.' The voices of Victoria, Nell and the Misses Grainger mingled around the table.

They'd decorated the room with ivy and other greenery, and despite the limited fare (a carrot-soup starter followed by a layered potato, vegetable and apple dish Nell called 'mock goose') it had been a happy Christmas. A warm one as well, since for today the Misses Grainger had consented to having daytime fires – perhaps induced by the coal delivery their great-nephew had arranged at Victoria's urging.

Beatrice glanced at the small stack of opened presents beside her plate. Soap from Victoria, knitted gloves from Nell, and books from Miss Hetty and Miss Addie. Even the dog, Lady, had given each of the teachers a handkerchief. None of the gifts were costly, but they meant more to her than any of the lavish presents she'd once been accustomed to receiving.

'Shall we leave the carrot pudding until later?' Nell had already begun stacking the empty plates, despite Beatrice and Victoria insisting she wait for them to clear up together. 'A treat for when Dr Stanley arrives?'

'Yes, please do.' From her place at the head of the table, Miss Hetty gave a gracious nod. 'Although this is the first Christmas without a turkey or indeed meat of any kind, I am mindful of how much worse off so many others are.' She bowed her head briefly, as if again acknowledging the dreadful Christmas bombing of Manchester, where several elderly Grainger cousins lived and of whom there had so far been no word.

'We'll have a rabbit when Louis visits in a fortnight,' Victoria said. 'Almost like a second Christmas. Besides, it's not the food that matters.'

'Indeed, it is not.' Miss Addie nodded in agreement. 'However, that carrot fudge you made, Beatrice, is surprisingly tasty.'

'Thank you.' Beatrice accepted the unexpected compliment. Under Nell's tutelage, she'd mastered a few simple dishes and, as a sweet indulgence for Christmas, she'd ventured to tackle carrot fudge. The recipe had been published in one of the newspapers, and Nell had assured her it would be easy enough to make, even for someone with what Beatrice readily acknowledged were limited cookery skills.

The front doorbell rang, and Lady, who had been allowed into the dining room for what Miss Hetty said was 'only for Christmas', cocked one ear.

'That will be Dr Stanley.' Nell paused in the doorway.

'I'll go. Please, excuse me.' Beatrice pushed back her chair. Although it still felt odd for her to answer the door in a family home, Nell wasn't a maid, and here they all did household chores.

'Enjoy your walk.' Was that a teasing note in Victoria's voice?

'We will, thank you.' Beatrice smoothed her hair, and as she reached the door she checked her reflection in the spotted mirror above the umbrella stand.

Her dress wasn't new, but despite being a pre-war hand-me-down from Cousin Louisa, the berry colour suited her and was festive. Nell had altered the collar and inserted a piece of old lace, so Beatrice felt more stylish than usual.

When she opened the door, David stood on the other side smiling at her. 'Hello. Happy Christmas.'

'To you as well, Beatrice.'

His deep voice and that gentle intonation on her name made Beatrice's stomach lurch. 'I'll get my coat on. How was your shift?'

'Uneventful, thankfully. Here' – he passed her a small basket – 'homemade jam and chutney. With Mrs Russell's and my compliments of the season to all of you at Hazelbury Manor.'

'Thank you.' Beatrice put the basket on the polished hall table. She'd got David a book and had tucked the parcel into her coat pocket to give to him if he had a present for her. But this basket wasn't an individual gift, so perhaps her giving him one in return would not be appropriate. The rules of etiquette she'd learned and followed assiduously from childhood onwards often seemed of little use in this new world.

'Shall we?' After sliding Beatrice's coat onto her shoulders and tucking her scarf around her neck, David left her to adjust her turban hat which had also come from Louisa and was near enough the same colour as the dress.

'Yes.' She took the arm he held out, and they went out into the crisp winter day and walked towards the garden.

'We kept Nell's carrot pudding for later in the hope that you can join us.'

'That's most kind.' David gazed into the middle distance, where the nearby woodland was topped by a silver-blue wedge of sky. 'There was a Christmas lunch at the hospital, and we toasted the King and family and friends at a distance. I can't say it was especially jolly but we all got through it.'

'As we did here.' Entering the garden, sunlight sparkled on frost, and the air was still, with not even a flock of birds to break the silence. 'I hope your mother didn't have to spend today alone.'

'No, she joins her sister, my widowed aunt, for such occasions.' David still hadn't met her gaze. 'Your mother? I hope she's well?'

'As far as I know, she is, yes.' Why was he so stilted? Their conversation might have been between casual acquaintances rather than a courting couple. 'My mother will be with our cousin and extended family. That is where I, too, used to spend Christmas before the war.'

While there hadn't then been the current wartime restrictions, such celebrations couldn't be described as 'especially jolly' either. Like Beatrice and her mother, their cousin's family lived in what might euphemistically be called 'straitened circumstances' or, perhaps more appropriately, 'genteel poverty'. However, they still tried to keep up appearances. So, along with a general air of strain, the whole affair carried a whiff of crumbling grandeur overlaid with a pungent taste of disappointment and regret.

'I see.' At the corner of one of the garden paths, David stopped by a wrought-iron bench half-encircled by holly, its glossy leaves and bright red berries like a Christmas card come to life. 'Beatrice. My dear, dearest Beatrice.'

'Yes?' Her breath caught.

'Perhaps you will think it too soon, but if that is the case, all I can say is that I would rather be too soon than too late.' He finally turned to face her. 'You may also think my feelings inappropriate, but I must confess them.' He took both her gloved hands in his. 'I asked you to walk with me today because… that is to say… I love you and would be most honoured if you would agree to become my wife. Would you… will you marry me?' His jaw seemed to clench, and he cleared his throat.

'Marry you?' Beatrice's voice wobbled as joy coursed through her. Had he truly said what she thought he had? 'You are asking me to marry you?'

'Yes, I am.' David clasped her hands tight. 'Although we haven't known each other long, it is wartime and, well, I'm old enough to know my own mind. I love you, Beatrice, and I hope you might feel the same way about me.' His eyebrows furrowed and, for such a usually decisive and confident man, he seemed almost uncertain.

'I… I love you too. And yes, I'll marry you.' Beatrice's legs trembled and she was glad of his hands holding hers and keeping her upright. 'It would be my honour to become your wife.' Excitement fizzed inside her, making the winter sunshine brighter and the frost on the trees and bushes dazzling. Then the world – the garden – disappeared, leaving only David and herself. Dear David, and the second chance she'd hardly let herself imagine, let alone believe in.

True, they hadn't known each other long, but she too knew her own mind. And she trusted herself – and him. Besides, nowadays, she'd heard of engagements and weddings happening in a week or less from start to finish. More than ever, people snatched whatever chance at happiness they could because no one knew what tomorrow – or even the next hour – might bring.

'Thank you.' He exhaled, his breath forming a misty cloud in the cold air. 'You had me worried there for a moment.' His mouth curved into a smile.

'I didn't mean to worry you.' Beatrice smiled back, her heart light. Despite the different places from which she and David had started out in the world, they had met here in the middle. 'You are a fine man. Upstanding and good. Oh, David, I do love you. So very much.'

'It is the same for me with you.' His smile broadened as if, like her, he could hardly contain his joy. 'I also enjoy spending time with you. I think of you often, even when we are not together. You are intelligent and gracious. Kind and loyal. You also accept me as I am, and more than anything, I can see us having a future together. A happy and fulfilling one.'

She nodded, too overcome with emotion to speak. That future stretched out in front of her, more wonderful than anything she could have ever imagined. And unlike Alex, David was settled here in Hazelbury. There was no chance of his going off to war. She raised her face to his, letting him see what was in her heart. The love and steadfast care. The spine tingles she got whenever he was near. A passion she'd never expected to feel again.

'I want to make you happy, Beatrice. That is both my vow and promise. One I have only ever made to one other woman, and I now make to you.' He dug into the pocket of his coat and withdrew a small brass box, topped with a floral design embellished with seed pearls. 'For you.' He took off his gloves and opened the box's lid. 'I hope you will wear this ring as a symbol of our love and commitment to each other. It is not new, but when I saw it in the window of a shop in Norwich a fortnight ago, I thought it would suit you.'

Beatrice's eyes widened at the ruby, surrounded by seed pearls in a simple rose-gold setting. Of course, David couldn't get her a new platinum engagement ring with a diamond, which had been the fashion before the war. Like most other things, engagement and wedding rings had also fallen prey to wartime shortages. 'It's beautiful.' And he knew her better than she expected. It was exactly the ring she'd have chosen for herself, even if presented with a tray full of them.

'Almost as beautiful as you. May I?' David tugged off Beatrice's left glove, took the ring out of its velvet nest and slid it onto her wedding finger. 'It's rather large but can easily be altered to fit.'

'Yes.' The central stone flashed like fire in the sunshine. 'Thank you.' She folded her fingers into her palm so the ring wouldn't fall off. 'A ruby.'

'The stone seemed to fit. After all, Ruby helped bring us together.' His hand clasped Beatrice's cold one, infusing her with love and affection.

'She did.' For which Beatrice would be forever grateful.

'And who knows, if Ruby doesn't have a suitable family, perhaps we could...Well, only if you agreed, of course, but we could consider giving her a home.' David's smile was gentle, loving. 'Adopting her after we are married.'

'Oh yes. Ruby would be delighted.' Just as Beatrice would be. How was it that David had been thinking the same way as Beatrice? That the three of them becoming a family was a real possibility. More happiness bloomed. 'A Christmas proposal.' She met David's steady hazel gaze. 'I only got you a book. But it's *How Green Was My Valley*. When we were quarantined for influenza, you wrote that you thought you'd enjoy it.'

'I will and I am touched that you remembered and acted on such a trivial comment.' He laughed, light and boyish. 'But you will also give me a lifetime of happiness. Or rather, that is what we shall give each other. And yes, a Christmas proposal.' His eyes softened. 'I know your life hasn't been easy, Beatrice, so what better time than Christmas, a day of love, to express *our* love for each other.'

'It's wonderful.' She hadn't thought it possible to be so filled with unfettered bliss. 'I love you, David. Truly, I do.'

'I love you too, and it will take all the days of my life to show you how much.' He still held her hand, the ring and its box between them, but bent his head so there was hardly any space separating their faces, their breath intermingling in the cold air of the winter garden.

Beatrice stood on tiptoes and then they were kissing – heat and urgency mixed with delicious languor and a sense of rightness, her once-guarded life disappearing and reshaping into something new and better.

-

'Congratulations.' Miss Hetty raised a crystal glass holding the last of their carefully hoarded sherry and gave her a slow, sideways smile. 'Your engagement is most welcome news. I only regret that we cannot toast with champagne. Still the wishes are no less sincere.'

'Thank you.' Beatrice smiled back and glanced at David, who was being congratulated by Victoria, Nell and Miss Addie.

It had been too cold to linger in the garden, so they'd soon returned to the manor. While Beatrice would once have felt compelled to first tell her mother and other family members of an engagement, now it was her friends with whom she wanted to share this special moment.

'I'm almost as thrilled for you as I was for myself when Louis proposed.' Victoria grabbed Lady's collar to stop the boisterous dog from running in circles around the morning room. 'And your ring is gorgeous.'

'Definitely.' Nell's approving nod was decisive. 'And I wish you a lifetime of happiness. I mean, I already did even before Dr Stanley – David – came along.' She corrected herself with a faint blush. 'But your engagement, well, it's the icing on the cake.'

'Not literally, though.' Victoria grinned. 'None of us can have icing on a cake at present. Not even for weddings. It's a reusable cardboard cover decorated with plaster or white paint.' Her smile turned into a grimace. 'I'd rather have a plain cake topped with a few garden flowers or leaves than pretend for show.'

'You and me both, but it's too soon to talk about cakes or anything else.' Beatrice glanced at David again and, as if he sensed she needed him, he drew Miss Addie across the room to join them.

'Will you keep teaching after you marry? You could, despite the marriage bar' here. Victoria's brown eyes were bright. 'If you wanted to stay on at work, I mean. I've looked into it and also wrote to Miss Hopson. She was most amenable to my continuing to teach, so I expect she'd say the same to you.'

'It would be up to you, Beatrice.' David looped an arm through hers.

'I'd like to keep teaching, yes.' Teachers were needed. The so-called 'marriage bar', which had previously prevented many married women from teaching, had been abolished by the London County Council before the war and relaxed by councils elsewhere due to wartime shortages – especially in rural areas like Hazelbury. Beatrice also enjoyed teaching and didn't want to give up her career. Still, for the first time, unease prickled.

What did David expect of a wife? He was a busy man, a doctor, and after the war, could she run a household and work as well? It was something they would have to talk about, but not now. He said he loved her and she believed him. He hadn't proposed any kind of marriage of convenience.

She was a mature woman, not a girl. And he was a mature man. From their work to everything else, they'd sort it out in due course, including adopting Ruby. While it was undoubtedly wrong to think such a thing, a part of Beatrice hoped the girl's aunt didn't turn up. She and David could give Ruby such a happy home.

All the things she hadn't had to consider with Alex. But her love for David was different. Even in the midst of her happiness and excitement, Beatrice understood that difference.

Despite those spine tingles when David was near, Beatrice didn't love him with the same unbridled, almost frightening fervour she'd once felt for Alex. This new love was steadier, softer and more measured. An adult love based on mutual respect, understanding and shared interests. One that was still passionate but would bring her contentment and stability rather than earth-shattering highs and lows – or profound grief, loss and the piercing disappointment of shattered hopes.

'Beatrice?' Miss Hetty's keen gaze settled on her. 'Are you quite all right?'

'Certainly.' There was no reason for the past to intrude upon the present.

And she wouldn't let worries cloud this happy Christmas Day because, despite the war, her future was bright. When Miss Addie and Nell began shepherding them to the dining room for carrot pudding, Beatrice moved closer to David and smiled up at him.

Their future. Together.

Chapter Thirty-One

Friday, 27 December 1940

'So there you have it, Mary. Our meeting and courtship, such as it was, and engagement.' In the spare room at Hazelbury's vicarage, Beatrice sat on the cushioned window seat and looked out onto the gravel drive. David was at work at the hospital, and after her Christmas visit with Diana, Mary would soon leave to catch a bus from the village crossroads to travel to Norwich – the first part of what would be a long, undoubtedly crowded and delayed journey back to Wales.

'I am delighted for you.' Mary folded a forest-green shirtwaist dress into her case and then rolled her dressing gown, sliding it in along one side. She packed with the same methodical precision Beatrice remembered from their boarding school days.

A place for everything and everything in its place. That had been Beatrice's nanny's stricture, and before the last war, it had applied to people as well as belongings. But the world was upside down and inside out, and many of the 'old ways' no longer made sense. If people still had a 'place', the lines were blurred. As for belongings, even if a person hadn't been bombed out, almost everyone's lives were in flux, their roots torn up or badly stretched.

Beatrice worried her bottom lip. When she and David had returned to Hazelbury Manor and announced their engagement, everyone had been elated for them. Beatrice had joined in the happy celebration, not letting herself think about what 'being engaged' would truly mean. A wedding, certainly, but how and when? And telling her mother, to whom she'd never even mentioned David – let alone that the two of them were, as Nell put it, 'stepping out together'.

'You don't think it's too soon or too… I don't know.' The vicarage drive was enshrouded in mist, the bare trees rising like ghostly figures amongst stone garden statuary.

'Indeed not.' Mary closed her case and sat on the edge of the bed nearest the window seat. 'Alex would want you to be happy, as do I.' She laced her thin fingers together, her narrow yellow-gold wedding ring sliding against her love-knot-style engagement ring with its trio of small diamonds. 'As long as you are happy, that is all that matters.'

Beatrice hesitated. Despite her closeness to Victoria and Nell, unlike Mary, they didn't come from Beatrice's world. Also unlike Mary, she hadn't grown up with them. Of all people, Mary was the one person Beatrice could speak to honestly and without artifice about matters of the heart. Unburden herself in as much as she could ever do. 'Your family… with Edward. Is that situation any… easier?'

More than twenty years later, Beatrice remembered the horror that had greeted Mary's engagement to Edward Foster-Dalton as if it were yesterday. The whispers and sidelong glances. The unfashionable wedding, held on a Thursday afternoon in London rather than at their

Oxfordshire parish church. The bride wearing a travelling suit in navy wool and a simple flat-brimmed sailor hat, rather than white satin and a diaphanous veil held in place by the Athill family tiara. Only Beatrice and one of Mary's cousins were in attendance, along with Edward's parents and younger sister.

Oh, Edward was quite respectable. As the son of a solicitor and a prosperous Hampshire farmer's daughter, he'd served with distinction in France, and after the war, had taken a senior administrative position in the civil service. Yet, as Beatrice's mother was wont to say, 'He is not like us, dear. Swans do not mate with jackdaws, do they?'

'If "that situation" as you so diplomatically put it *were* easier, Diana would not have been evacuated to a rural village school. Indeed, she would not have attended Park Road School in the first place.' Mary gave a short laugh. 'Still, we have made a happy life together despite my family's censure. While Edward's family did not disapprove of *me*, things have always been awkward between us. We are rather like Switzerland at present, you understand? Edward's mother was widowed five years ago, but even if she did not live so near Southampton, I could not have sent Diana to stay with her, either.'

Beatrice did understand. Mary and Edward were neutral but nevertheless prepared to defend themselves and their family – an island, as it were, between opposing factions. And from the outset, their marriage had been complicated and rife with undercurrents – like submarines lurking beneath what, on the surface, appeared to be a tranquil blue sea.

'I'm sorry.' Beatrice clasped her hands together.

'Don't be.' Mary's blue eyes, so much like Alex's, softened. 'If I hadn't married Edward, I likely would not have married at all. I would not have had Diana and the boys.'

Although Mary hadn't said it, she would have ended up like Beatrice. Alone, childless and working to earn her living. But Beatrice had a second chance at love and, in some ways, life. She wouldn't waste it.

'Besides, you don't miss what you don't have.' Mary took a handkerchief from her cardigan pocket and smoothed the delicate linen square. 'If our lives had turned out as we once expected, yesterday would have been the Boxing Day hunt. Remember how it used to alternate between your home and mine?'

Beatrice nodded. She'd hated hunting and hadn't even much enjoyed riding but had never been able to say so, even to Mary.

'Dreadful business. Even before the last war, I didn't like hunting, but now it seems barbaric. The same goes for my father's shooting parties.' Mary grimaced. 'There are advantages to being beyond the social pale. I did not have to subject my sons and Diana to the life they would otherwise have been expected to lead.'

'I didn't know.' Beatrice's breathing sped up.

'How could you have?' Mary's sweet smile flowered like a shaft of sunlight to brighten a gloomy day. 'I never told you.'

'As I never told you I felt exactly the same. I told Alex, though. He promised me that our children would never hunt.' The memory of what might have been still pierced Beatrice's heart, but time had dulled the sharpness to leave it bittersweet.

'My brother was always more outspoken than me. More sensible as well. I still often wonder what he would have made of his life if he'd had the chance.'

'I do too.' Although she'd long ago packed away Alex's letters and the engagement ring he'd given her, Beatrice still thought of him and likely always would.

'Daddy managed to cling on to the estate and one of my cousins runs it. Mummy and Daddy live in the dower house with my youngest sister. We write for birthdays and such – they never cut me off entirely – but I only ever see them at funerals. When I married Edward, I made a new life for myself. It was the only way.'

Except unlike Beatrice, Mary didn't have to support her mother financially or in any other fashion. Beatrice's situation was different.

'Have you written to your mother about your engagement?'

'Not yet, but I will do so later today.' It was unlike Beatrice to avoid anything unpleasant, but on this occasion she'd wanted to enjoy being engaged without having to think about how to explain that engagement to her mother. 'David said we'd write the letter together. We'll write to his mother at the same time.'

David had also said his mother would think it 'lovely news', but would she? Beatrice couldn't imagine that she was the kind of woman Mrs Stanley would have chosen for her son. From what David had told Beatrice about his mother, she was a pragmatic, unpretentious Yorkshirewoman. She'd be more likely to warm to housewifely Nell than to career girl Beatrice, who didn't know how to run a home without help.

'Remember that although you and David, if I may call him by his Christian name, are not yet married, your first loyalty is now to him and the life you will make together.' Mary scrutinised Beatrice, her expression intent. 'He, not your mother, is the one whose good opinion matters. I know your mother, like mine, can be rather… pronounced in her opinions.' One corner of Mary's mouth quirked into a faint smile. 'And whilst you will always give her the kindness and respect that she is due, do not let your mother influence you. Dr Stanley is a fine man, and the world is so different from how it was in our mothers' day. Irrespective of how the war ends, when it is over, the world – *our world* – will be different once again. I have had to make my own peace with that, and by marrying David, you will as well.'

'Goodness, you sound rather forceful.' Beatrice tried to laugh. 'I've made my peace with the world being different. I did so long ago.' However, before being evacuated, Beatrice recognised that she'd only given lip service to those changes, accepting them because she had no other choice. In the last year, though, she'd come to embrace her new life and the opportunities it offered, cherishing who and what she was and the future she was making.

Looking back to when this war had been declared, she'd almost prided herself on her pragmatism. She'd set aside her personal feelings and made the best of things because she had a job to do and pupils, fellow teachers and a school depending on her. But in not acknowledging her emotions, in pretending they didn't exist, she'd been as false as those wedding cakes with their plaster tops. It was only through her friendship with Victoria and Nell that

Beatrice had come out of herself – indeed, had grown to believe that she could be different.

And now she saw Mary in a new light too. Mary, who had been distraught that day when Beatrice, Victoria and Nell had visited her on behalf of the school, urging her to evacuate Diana to the countryside with the other children. Then, she truly hadn't understood Mary's agony. How unfeeling Beatrice had been. How constrained – believing that any display of emotion was unseemly and that she must, indeed could, only show calm endurance, no matter the circumstances.

While Beatrice had given up her London life, unlike Mary, she hadn't had two sons who'd enlisted nor a daughter who'd been evacuated because there was nowhere else 'suitable' for her to go. She also wasn't trying to make a home for her husband and cobble together a life in a hotel room in North Wales, with their three children scattered in all directions.

She curled her hands inwards and tucked them against her stomach. Even though she'd never said it aloud, inside she'd judged Mary. But Mary was the one who, without a hint of judgement and with only Beatrice's best interests at heart, had helped her see an additional truth. In some ways, despite how she'd grown and changed, Beatrice was still cossetted in the same world she always had known. But with David, she was fully stepping out of that world and into another new one where nothing would be the same.

'Good. It is only by making peace with change that you can rightly embrace it.' Mary nodded and then her resolute expression eased. 'In this quarter of an hour before I must leave, let us speak of pleasanter things. Like your wedding. No German, not even Hitler himself, shall prevent me from being there. Despite wartime privations, I shall also make it my mission to find you a proper wedding dress. I've always regretted having to marry in that terrible suit.'

'It wasn't terrible at all.' Beatrice managed a genuine smile. 'Besides, you married in wartime too.'

'I did – but I want you to have the wedding I didn't.' Mary's eyes glistened with unshed tears. 'Diana is already asking pointed questions about being a bridesmaid. Between you and Miss McKaye, she has weddings very much on her mind.'

'Diana's a dear child, and I'd be delighted for her to be a bridesmaid.' *With Ruby.* Two girls who each had a special place in Beatrice's heart. 'Although I've only been engaged for less than two days and we've not yet discussed a date, Nell and Victoria are already planning how they might divvy up our rations to make a somewhat fitting wedding cake. I suggested they consider a cake for Victoria's wedding first, but they would not be deterred. Of course, Louis must secure leave from the navy, so their wedding date is not so readily fixed.'

'Like me, Miss McKaye and Miss Potter love you and are happy for you.' Mary stood and collected her handbag from the end of the bed. Between her faint floral scent, smart leather case and jaunty hat atop the dresser, she brought glamour to the utilitarian spare room – undoubtedly more used to hosting sober visiting clergy. The same glamour she'd always brought to Beatrice's rather dull life. 'You never know, your mother might surprise you.'

She might – but Beatrice wouldn't count on it. 'I'm glad you came here for Christmas, Mary.' And even more glad they'd found their way to being true friends again. They couldn't turn back time, and Beatrice didn't want to because she had all sorts of wonderful things to look forward to.

Which Mary, her oldest and dearest friend, would be part of.

Chapter Thirty-Two

Saturday, 4 January 1941

'Happy New Year.' In the corridor outside Whittleton Hall's kitchens, Beatrice nodded and smiled at several staff carrying breakfast trays. 'Yes, let us indeed hope that 1941 is better than 1940.'

While there had been good news in that the elderly Grainger cousins in Manchester were safe following the bombing there, after a devastating German raid on Cardiff only two days earlier, it seemed – if not foolish – then almost as if inviting bad luck to exchange the usual 'Happy New Year' greetings.

After climbing the stairs to the main hall and going into the office, she took off her coat, hat and gloves and hung them up behind the door. Today, following the Christmas holiday, she was glad to return for her regular volunteer shift. Or was it the prospect of seeing David? He was working today and had left a note for her at the manor suggesting they have lunch together.

Humming 'Only Forever' under her breath – the Bing Crosby hit for which she'd recently bought the sheet music to learn to play on the manor's piano – Beatrice sat behind the desk and checked the list of tasks Matron had left for her.

She wouldn't mull over why she hadn't received a reply to her letter to her mother announcing her engagement. The post might have been delayed in either or both directions. David's mother had written, offering her warmest congratulations. She'd also tucked a beautiful handkerchief, hand-embroidered with yellow roses, into the envelope as a present for 'dear Beatrice' and expressed her 'fondest wish' that the two of them should meet soon.

As Beatrice went down Matron's list line by line, she forced her thoughts away from anything but the job at hand. If Griffiths had returned, she might squeeze in a visit to him after she finished filing the accumulated paperwork. If—

'Oh, Miss Wentworth.' Mrs Bertram came through the half-open office door. 'Good, you're here.'

'Where else would I be?' Beatrice looked up from the list with a smile. 'Weren't you expecting me back today?'

'I was but…' Mrs Bertram's face seemed to crumple. 'You've not heard the news, then?'

'No, what news?' A cold chill slithered along Beatrice's spine. There was nothing out of the ordinary on Matron's list, and apart from the kitchen staff who'd wished her a Happy New Year, Beatrice hadn't spoken to anyone else since arriving at the Hall a quarter of an hour earlier.

'I'm so sorry.' Mrs Bertram came around the desk. 'You remember Aircraftman Griffiths, of course?' Beatrice nodded, fear stuck in her throat and making speech impossible. 'He returned here from Norwich by ambulance yesterday, but when Sister Morton went to rouse him for breakfast, she found him dead in his bed.'

Beatrice put a hand to her mouth. *No, no, no. Not Griffiths.*

'As you might expect, Sister Morton is most cut up. We all are. That young man was such a favourite.'

'But he was doing so well.' The words felt like cotton wool in Beatrice's mouth.

'He was.' Mrs Bertram nodded. 'However, in such cases I suppose one never knows. Possibly there was some kind of dormant internal injury from the crash? Dr Stanley has rung Norwich Hospital, and the undertaker from Whittleton is on his way, but there was nothing in Griffiths's chart to suggest… Oh, my dear. I expected you'd take it hard, so I wanted to tell you myself but—'

'Thank you.' Beatrice blinked back the hot burn of tears. 'His poor mother. She must have been so hopeful.'

'Yes.' Mrs Bertram's voice cracked. 'He was her youngest child of six, only turned nineteen on Christmas Day, and his three elder brothers are also in the Forces. If you don't feel able to complete your shift, I shall speak to Matron and—'

Beatrice swallowed hard and waved away Mrs Bertram's well-meant offer. 'You're most kind, but I am here to do my work, and I won't let anyone down.' *Least of all myself.* 'I expect that the other patients will need me more than ever.' Beatrice's duties had gradually expanded, when time permitted, beyond office work. Rather than being daunted, she'd found she rather enjoyed the change of pace and camaraderie that came with these additional tasks, which ranged from taking Flying Officer Brown on walks to playing board games and doing crafts with patients.

Like the men in his care, David might need her too. Doctors' wives often helped run their husbands' practices, but such women could have an even more important role as someone to confide in when their husband lost a patient or had a difficult day. Until now, she'd never rightly thought about the burdens a doctor must carry – burdens David was unlikely to be able to share with anyone but a wife. How alone he must have felt all these years. They weren't married yet, but it wasn't too soon for Beatrice to begin as she meant to go on.

'Our patients will be grateful you are here, Brown especially.' Mrs Bertram touched Beatrice's shoulder. 'As you are aware, he was also doing very well, but Sister Morton said he refused to eat his breakfast and hasn't said a word since Griffiths's body was discovered. The two of them were on the same ward and, well, it's such a shame.'

'Yes, it is.' Beatrice took a deep breath and picked up Matron's list. She couldn't let herself think about Griffiths or she'd break down. 'If you see Dr Stanley, could you please let him know that I'm here? He suggested we meet for lunch later.'

'Certainly. Oh my goodness. I haven't even congratulated you on your engagement. I'm delighted for you both – and what a beautiful ring!' Her gaze darted to Beatrice's left hand. 'You must let me know when you set a wedding date. I'd be happy to assist with any plans. The men were so cheered to hear your news when Dr Stanley told them on Boxing Day. I'd intended to write, but one of our sons got leave and came home unexpectedly.'

'How lovely.' As Beatrice acknowledged Mrs Bertram's good wishes, it was almost as if she were outside herself, detached and observing from a distance. She was an engaged woman. David's fiancée – as it should be, she was being drawn into his life. She wasn't alone in her grief for Griffiths. It was a grief David undoubtedly shared.

She would get through the next few hours as best she could and mourn poor Aircraftman Griffiths later. *With David*. For the first time since Alex was killed, Beatrice didn't have to face life alone.

-

'Dealing with death is part of my work.' At a table for two in what had previously been Whittleton Hall's breakfast room – where the hospital's staff took their meals when on duty – David spooned up the last bit of watery vegetable stew from his bowl. 'Like everyone else, I did my best for Griffiths.'

'I know you did. I was there, remember?' Beatrice drained her cup of now lukewarm tea and, since David continued to avoid her gaze, stared out through one of the long windows into the frosty afternoon. He'd sent her a message via Mrs Bertram saying he'd be late, so to go ahead and eat without him. Beatrice had done so, choking down the tasteless stew and a slice of dry bread, but she'd still hoped they'd have a chance to talk. However, since he now only had ten minutes for lunch anyway, it was insufficient time for a meal, let alone to remember Griffiths.

'Of course you were there at my side. I'll never forget it.' He gave her the ghost of a smile. 'So you must also understand that no doctor, no matter how skilled, can save every patient.'

'I do understand, but that doesn't mean I'm not sad about Griffiths.' As a V.A.D. in the last war, she'd tried – largely unsuccessfully, as it turned out, given the memories which still lingered – to detach herself from the terrible injuries of the men she'd treated. The deaths too.

But Griffiths was different. She couldn't distance herself because she'd got to know him.

And care for him. She felt his death as if he were a friend. Once again, she'd lost someone important to her.

Emotions rolled over her, past and present colliding, and she willed herself not to cry.

'You have a kind and loving heart, Beatrice.' David touched her hand briefly before setting his crockery and cutlery aside. 'But in wartime especially, there are so many fatalities that none of us can give in to our emotions.'

How could he be so matter of fact? Beatrice found her handkerchief and gripped it between her hands, hiding them out of sight beneath the table so David wouldn't see them shake.

'I said as much to Sister Morton earlier.' His voice was firm and professional, with no hint of the tenderness it usually held when he spoke to Beatrice. 'Like you, she was most affected by Griffiths's death, but we must move on. Focus on the living. There is no other way.' His expression held none of its usual warm-heartedness either.

Beatrice swallowed a lump of the emotion David seemed so easily able to guard against. 'But you don't have to shoulder your responsibilities alone. Perhaps I can help. I'd most certainly like to try. Not the medical part, naturally, but if you are worried about a patient… The weight of your responsibilities must be heavy indeed. As a teacher, I understand the importance of discretion.'

'Certainly you do.' With a brief smile, he stood. 'I'm sorry but I must dash. Matron asked me to check on a wound. She fears infection. There are also sutures needing my attention.'

Beatrice nodded, even as David had already turned away. Had he heard what she'd said? Clearly, his mind was elsewhere.

I need your attention too. Aren't I important?

He was busy and it was no wonder. The hospital and its staff were always overstretched and understaffed. But once they married, would David be too busy for her as well?

Round and round the thoughts circled as she collected her things, left Whittleton Hall and cycled back to Hazelbury.

Three-quarters of an hour later, when Beatrice arrived back at Hazelbury Manor, Victoria met her inside the front door holding a telegram. 'I hope it's not bad news. I'm not being nosy, but it was sent from Henley. Knowing your mother lives near there, I couldn't help but worry. Mrs Yallop's boy delivered it half an hour ago.'

'Thank you.' Beatrice took the thin slip of paper. What was that saying about bad things coming in threes? Griffiths, and now a telegram. What might be next? No, she mustn't let herself entertain such thoughts.

'Here, sit down.' Victoria patted one of the hall chairs. 'Miss Hetty and Miss Addie are still at the W.V.S. clothing exchange, but Nell's back from tutoring Jimmy. When we saw you at the end of the drive, she went to make a cup of tea.'

Nell was always making cups of tea, and while at first Beatrice had found it uncomfortable – almost an intrusion, much like Victoria's easy friendliness – she'd come to appreciate that it was one of the many ways her friends showed care and concern.

Beatrice sat on the chair and opened the envelope as Victoria hovered by her side. 'It's not bad news as such. My mother is in good health but… She will be here on Wednesday to see me.'

'Here? Gosh.' Victoria sat on the chair next to Beatrice's as if her legs all of a sudden couldn't hold her up.

'Not exactly here, but close enough. Near Norwich.'

'Does she say why?' Victoria stared at Beatrice wide-eyed.

'No, but I understand why she's coming.' A lump of dread lodged in the pit of Beatrice's stomach. 'She wants to dissuade me from marrying David. Oh, she doesn't mention him, but I know my mother.'

'But you're not a young girl, and with the government discouraging unnecessary travel, how is your mother getting here? And where does she plan to stay?' Victoria shook her head as if in disbelief.

As Nell arrived, Beatrice took the teacup and saucer from her and returned to the telegram. She indeed wasn't a 'young girl', and as a decidedly middle-aged woman, whom Beatrice married was no concern of her mother's or anyone else's. 'She's staying with a school friend and as for her travel arrangements…' Beatrice sipped tea, the hot liquid warming her chilled body. 'She has managed to secure transport with Colonel Beauchamp.'

'Who's he when he's at home?' Nell sat on Beatrice's other side. As always, when surprised or in the grip of some strong feeling, Nell's East London accent became more pronounced.

'Colonel Beauchamp has always had, if I dare say so, rather amiable feelings for my mother. But then she married my father, and the colonel, who wasn't a colonel then, bestowed his affections elsewhere. Since he, like Mother, is widowed, I gather they have begun to correspond. He has a home near Oxford, not far from where my mother lives with our cousin.'

'Oh.' Nell sounded like a party balloon from which the air had been let out. 'Nevertheless, I expect your mum's longing to see you.' She gave Beatrice the kind of bracing smile that Beatrice was more accustomed to dispensing than receiving. 'The poor lady must still be bereft what with losing your dad and brothers. And living with someone else, no matter how welcoming, isn't the same as having the comfort of her own home and things round her.'

Beatrice's mother had never, of course, said anything about the situation in which she had found herself. It would not be seemly. However, was it possible that Beatrice had misread her mother's intentions, even in part?

Clarissa Wentworth had lost everything too, but unlike Beatrice she'd not been of an age to be able to start again. Maybe that's why she clung to the past as if it were a lifebelt and she were adrift in a choppy sea. Apart from the money Beatrice provided for her keep, in her mother's mind that vanished Edwardian world might be the only security she had.

Even though Beatrice had not truly considered it before, a woman such as her mother would find it, at best, awkward and, at worst, humiliating to be supported by her daughter instead of her husband or sons. She'd always felt so judged by her mother that she'd never stopped to consider Clarissa Wentworth's point of view.

'Beatrice?' Victoria put a hand on her arm. 'You were saying about Colonel Beauchamp?'

'Yes, I was, wasn't I?' She dragged her mind away from that new and surprising train of thought. 'Colonel Beauchamp is retired but has returned to military service in an ad hoc capacity. To "lend a hand at this moment of national crisis" is what Mother said in one of her letters before Christmas.' A phrase Beatrice had taken hardly any notice of, being more concerned with the Nativity than her mother's friendships. 'The colonel is coming to RAF Whittleton, and with a driver and transport provided, he is bringing my mother with him in the staff car.'

'How nice for her.' Victoria patted Lady, who'd wandered into the front hall as if wondering what the three of them were doing sitting out there rather than staying cosy in the morning room.

'Indeed.' Surely that wasn't sarcasm in Victoria's voice? Unlike Beatrice, who could be too prone to think the worst of people, Victoria didn't have a mean or spiteful bone in her body. 'Even if she is, as Nell said, "longing to see me", Mother has not given any consideration to what I shall be doing on Wednesday. I can't leave my pupils for a jaunt into Norwich – actually, outside Norwich. Her friend lives in the country, closer to Whittleton than here. I expect I'd have to take several buses and then walk to get there.'

'It would be an imposition to the Misses Grainger to invite your mother to come here.' Victoria worried her bottom lip.

'Yes and it wouldn't be right at all.' Beatrice didn't want her mother at Hazelbury Manor or anywhere in its vicinity. She'd built a new life here. One in which her mother had no part.

'Why don't you suggest your mother meets you at Whittleton Hall after school?' Nell leaned forwards. 'It's close to the RAF base, so likely wouldn't inconvenience Colonel Beauchamp or his driver. And if Dr Stanley, David—' Nell paused, even though David had told both her and Victoria to use his first name. 'If he's working there that day, your mother could meet him. The Hall has that pleasant room overlooking the fountain where patients sit with their visitors. The kitchen's always bringing up tea and small cakes of an afternoon. I expect you could use it.'

'And we'll be there as well. Nell and me,' Victoria added. 'Wednesday's Nell's regular volunteer shift, and I'm doing an extra one that day so as to be free for Louis's leave. The two of us could casually drop by. Not that I expect you'll need moral support, but it would be lovely to meet your mother.'

Lovely for Victoria, Beatrice supposed, because Mrs Wentworth wasn't her mother or, from the sounds of it, anything like Victoria's own mum – a woman who seemed to be unfailingly kind, generous and accepting, three things Beatrice's mother wasn't.

'Having Mother come to Whittleton Hall would be an ideal solution, and I expect she would enjoy meeting you both as well.' Unlikely, because her mother had never expressed any genuine interest in Beatrice's fellow teachers. But although she wasn't about to admit it, Beatrice did need moral support, and Victoria and Nell would also be a distraction.

Beatrice straightened her shoulders and drained her cup of tea, her friends' staunch backing giving her fresh resolve.

If she hadn't misjudged her mother's intentions, Clarissa Wentworth might think she'd boxed Beatrice into a corner – but she hadn't. Beatrice could marry whomever she wanted, with or without her mother's approval.

As for David, although he hadn't admitted it, Griffiths's death must have affected him too. That's why he hadn't been as attentive as usual. She was fretting unnecessarily.

Chapter Thirty-Three

Wednesday, 8 January 1941

'Mother.' After school on Wednesday, Beatrice stood as her mother, escorted by a young nursing sister, entered the small visitors' parlour at Whittleton Hall. 'I hope your journey wasn't too tiresome.'

'It was rather but Colonel Beauchamp – William – is a most entertaining travelling companion.' After the nurse scurried away, Beatrice's mother greeted her with a dry peck on one cheek. 'He has also put his car and driver at my disposal. The driver is in the kitchen waiting for me.' She gave a small smile, almost a simper.

'I'm glad you were able to come here.' Ignoring her mother's comment about the car and driver – few but Clarissa Wentworth would accept such a courtesy as their due – Beatrice gestured to an armchair across from hers and nearer the fire. A tray on a small table between them held tea things and slices of condensed milk cake. 'I was, naturally, at school today, so Whittleton Hall is considerably more convenient than your friend's home. I hope you received my letters?' Following the one announcing her engagement, she'd sent another letter as well as a telegram, but had only received a brief telegram acknowledging today's meeting in return.

'I did. In fact, I discussed both letters with William on our way up.' Her mother draped her fur coat – one Beatrice remembered their cousin wearing before the war – across the back of the chair, removed her leather gloves and settled herself as Beatrice poured tea for them both.

'Why would you do such a thing?' Albeit determined to give her mother the benefit of the doubt, Beatrice still felt herself bristle. He might be her mother's friend, but to her, Colonel Beauchamp was almost a stranger.

'There are times when one needs a man's advice, aren't there?' Beneath her hat, in the same black fur as her coat, her silvery-grey hair lay in beautifully crimped waves, suggesting she'd either visited a hairdresser – a luxury that should be beyond her means – or prevailed upon their cousin's sole remaining maid to do her hair. 'In the absence of your dear father and brothers, there is no one else suitable with whom I could consult.' Before she picked up her teacup, her mother fluttered one hand in the helpless gesture that had always infuriated Beatrice – a pretence of softness encased in a manipulative steel glove.

'I shouldn't think you would need to consult with anyone. I'm marrying David and there is nothing more to be said about it.' Best to get the purpose of today's visit into the open from the start. Otherwise, her mother would undoubtedly circle around it with veiled allusions and hidden threats.

Beatrice picked up her own teacup and, as she did so, was struck by a new realisation. While she'd known that the past year and a half had changed her, until this moment she hadn't appreciated how much. In speaking to her mother so directly, she'd sounded a great deal like Victoria. Polite but nevertheless decisive.

'Naturally, darling, you are free to marry whomever you choose, but all the same, you cannot have thought this decision through.' Her mother leaned closer as if to impart a confidence. 'Alex's death was a great tragedy, and whilst your heart, as it should be, has always been buried with him in France, it is also not surprising that, after all these years, you should consider sharing your affections, such as they may be, elsewhere.'

Such as they may be? What on earth did her mother mean? 'As I wrote, Dr Stanley is a fine man.' Beatrice picked up a fork and one of the plates with a thin slice of cake. 'He's currently on his rounds seeing patients, but he promised to come and meet you shortly. As have my friends and colleagues, Miss McKaye and Miss Potter, who are volunteering here today.' Best to insert those details into the conversation from the start as well.

'I am disappointed in you, Beatrice.' Her mother's expression was pinched with disapproval. 'Whilst war naturally brings new associations, except for the Misses Grainger, Major Bertram and his wife and, I suppose, the family at the vicarage, one is not required to make so much of them as you appear to have done. Such friendships and now an engagement... You have evidently forgotten yourself. Do you not remember Mary Athill?'

'Perfectly. Mary was recently here to visit her daughter, Diana, who, as I have mentioned previously, is one of my pupils. Diana is a charming girl, and Mary, with whom I've renewed my friendship, has found great happiness with Edward Foster-Dalton.' After only a mouthful, Beatrice set the plate with the cake aside.

'Whilst that may be true, Mary's children will never be received in society, will they?'

'What does that matter now? Besides, the Foster-Dalton family is eminently respectable and certainly considerably better off than we are.' Beatrice tried to steady her breathing.

'Society *does* matter, and it is vulgar to discuss money.' Her mother's face went red, then paled.

'I was only stating facts.' Facts which her mother preferred to avoid – sheer hypocrisy on her part, since without Beatrice's salary, the two of them would be destitute. 'I'm sorry to cause you distress.' At her mother's pained expression, Beatrice forced herself to adopt a gentler tone. Society – and her place in it – was the foundation of her mother's life. Now it was also likely the only reminder of the person she used to be. 'But don't you see? If Mary had not married Edward, who else *could* she have married?'

'No one, I suppose.' Her mother's voice faltered, perhaps the first time she'd ever shown any genuine emotion in front of her daughter. 'But that doesn't mean that she – or you – should forget who you are. Where you come from. The standards and customs we must uphold.'

'I haven't forgotten any of those things.' Even though Beatrice often wanted to. 'However, given my age, and since David and I are unlikely to have children at all, the question of their social acceptance will not be a concern, will it?' This conversation was rather like one of the youthful tennis matches Miss Hetty had recounted to Beatrice, with her and another opponent batting the ball back and forth across a net. However, here, love meant everything, not nothing.

'You need not be indelicate, Beatrice.' Her mother put a fine lawn handkerchief, like a filmy cobweb, to her mouth.

'I did not intend to be.' She tried not to grin. If her years of teaching pupils from all backgrounds in the melting pot of inner London schools hadn't ripped away the last shreds of girlish delicacy, the war and evacuation had finished the job. An image of poor Ruby and 'something in me knickers' in the school lavatory popped into her head.

Her mother gave a stately nod. 'I only have your best interests at heart. That is why I must protect you.' She put the handkerchief to her eyes, and for an instant, her voice sounded almost choked. 'You are all I have left. William's eldest son is recently widowed and has been left with five children. I have already spoken of you to him, and he looks forward to renewing your acquaintance. Henry would be much more suitable. If you were to make yourself pleasing—'

'No.' Beatrice was not about to make herself 'pleasing' as her mother put it, to try to attract the attentions of odious Henry Beauchamp. She'd been forced to dance with him once – at a ball during her first season out – and it had been more than enough. 'I understand your apprehension, but I'm a grown woman.' Nell's comment about the magnitude of her mother's loss also echoed in Beatrice's mind and she softened her tone. 'While I appreciate your concern, the world is changing. It changed after the last war, and with this one, class distinctions are even less important than they once were. Although David's father was a self-made man—'

'And his grandmother a parlour maid who married a common farm labourer.'

'How—?'

'I have made enquiries. William's father's grandmother was from Yorkshire. Her family seat is near Whitby.' Her mother sniffed. 'Really, Beatrice. You may no longer concern yourself with our family's reputation, but I do. For people such as us, women in particular, taking up with the lower classes never ends well. Have you not thought about how your engagement announcement might appear in *The Times*? Once it is besmirched, one's good name can never be restored. After my eldest sister, Elinor, ran away with a coachman, my father never spoke her name again. It was as if she had never existed.' Her mother's mouth worked. 'Even when Elinor was on her deathbed, Father would not permit any of us to go to her, not even Mother.'

'He must have been a very cruel man.' Her mother's father had died before Beatrice was old enough to remember him. As for her aunt Elinor, her mother had only mentioned that sister once before, when Beatrice had asked about a family photograph she'd found in an old chest before their home and its contents were sold.

'Father did what he thought best.' Her mother's expression was pinched. 'He had two other daughters and could not risk Elinor's foolishness damaging our prospects. Elinor thought she was in love, but practicalities are more important. She did not live long enough to rue her choice, but living in a cottage, no better than a hovel—'

'I can assure you that David and I will not live in a hovel,' Beatrice interjected. 'And he is not a coachman. With the growing number of motor cars, coachmen are becoming almost an endangered species.' She tried to smile.

'Do not jest.' Her mother's tone was anguished. 'Is it not better to remain single than to make an unsuitable marriage?'

'I find David eminently suitable.' Beatrice tamped down her irritation. 'He also makes me happy.'

'I *do* want you to be happy, but I also don't want you to marry in haste and repent at leisure. Before the letter announcing your engagement, you had not mentioned Dr Stanley to me at all. Just like poor Elinor. Not a word to any of us and then… I lost her but I cannot lose you as well.'

'I should have mentioned David; that is true, but I also expected you would disapprove.' Beatrice pressed a hand to her forehead. 'However, I am not your sister, and you won't lose me.'

'You say that now but how can I trust—'

At a knock on the parlour door, Mrs Wentworth stopped.

'That must be David. Or Miss McKaye and Miss Potter.' Beatrice hesitated.

'I suppose you need to answer it, seeing as any staff seem few and far between.' Her mother tutted. 'This must once have been such a delightful home.'

Beatrice got to her feet, went to the door and opened it, almost fearing who might be on the other side. How could she bring David or Victoria and Nell into this situation?

Clearly, she couldn't hope to change her mother's mind, but she had new sympathy for her too. Beatrice often struggled with who she was and where she fit in this changed world, but it must be so much worse for her mother.

'Hullo there.' David's smiling face greeted her, with Nell and Victoria close behind him. 'The three of us met on the main stairs. I hope we're not intruding?' His smile slipped as if sensing Beatrice's unease.

'Not at all.' She opened the door wider. 'Please, do come in and sit with us.' The world Beatrice had grown up in had made her adept at lying and donning the appropriate social mask, whatever the occasion. 'Mother.' She made the necessary introductions – noting her mother's narrowed eyes, stiff posture and tone – and then David and her friends took their seats.

Clarissa Wentworth was too well-bred to express her displeasure in any overt way. Instead, her disapproval – or could it also be fear? – was cloaked in social niceties.

Enquiring about Victoria's Canadian family as if they mattered to her. Giving Nell a benevolent 'lady of the manor' nod as she had been wont to do when dispensing Christmas 'boxes' to the estate's servants on Boxing Day. And to David she made a particular moue of her mouth whilst chatting about the weather (a damp chill, frosty, with intermittent mizzle), his work (expressing her horror about the 'truly dreadful' injuries he must see amongst the 'poor, brave boys'), Colonel Beauchamp's staff car and other general but inconsequential matters.

Sitting beside David, with her mother taking charge of the conversation as Beatrice had seen her do so many times before, Beatrice's heart pounded like the blacksmith's anvil at the rural village forge she remembered from childhood. That 'moue', which some might see as verging on a flirtatious pout, was nothing of the kind. Rather, it was the face her mother used to show both petulance and distaste. A sign of endurance rather than enjoyment. One which indicated that she was performing her duty under duress rather than with any real pleasure.

'Nell.' Her mother's sharp tone broke through the fog of Beatrice's distress. 'Fetch more hot water. This tea is so cold it is undrinkable.'

'Mother.' Beatrice gasped, her gaze darting to Nell who was already halfway out of her chair. 'Do not speak to Miss Potter that way. She is not a kitchen maid nor any kind of servant.' Beatrice waved towards Nell to remain seated. 'But even if she were, there is no need to be discourteous. I shall fetch hot water myself.' With a clatter, she put her teacup on its saucer, stood, and then David did the same.

'It's all right. I'll go and ask for hot water,' Victoria interjected. 'With Miss Potter. We must both return to our duties and will be passing the kitchen anyway.' She gave Mrs Wentworth a stiff smile which didn't reach her eyes.

Then, behind their backs and out of view of her mother, David's warm hand crept into Beatrice's cold one and gave it a gentle squeeze.

A touch of consolation, reassurance and love, reminding her she wasn't alone, no matter what Clarissa Wentworth said or did.

Chapter Thirty-Four

Thursday, 30 January 1941

'If not for young Ruby making such good progress on the piano, I'd hardly know where this month has gone.' As the three teachers walked home from school on a Thursday afternoon at the end of January, Nell shivered and tucked her snood more closely around her ears. 'You'll continue to give Ruby lessons, won't you? If David says they aren't too much for her?'

'I shall – and David is most pleased with Ruby's progress. The dreadful nightmares she experienced in the wake of her mother's death have lessened, and along with Mrs Fisk, we both continue to keep a close eye on her.' Despite the visits being brief – a few minutes after school or before Ruby's piano lesson or practice time, when David was on his way to or from the convalescent hospital – him popping in to check on Ruby and ask Beatrice about her day increasingly made the three of them feel like a real family.

Pride, satisfaction and gratitude filled her. 'Ruby works hard at the piano and shows talent.' And Beatrice enjoyed spending time with the girl. Was that how a mother felt? She had no way of knowing, but those times with Ruby – and David – were highlights of her week. Somewhat to Beatrice's surprise, from learning scales to other basic exercises, Ruby had accepted the reality of learning to play the piano without complaint. And in addition to her lesson time, she came to the manor most days after school to practise faithfully for half an hour. 'Miss Addie is also pleased and says that Ruby is coming along well with her sampler and has a natural knack for knitting.'

The younger Miss Grainger doted on Ruby and was a good influence on her. And, although Miss Hetty kept her distance from the child, she was noticeably less acerbic when the girl was at the manor.

'Ruby's becoming a lovely girl, but apart from Louis's visit, between the war news and the weather January's been awfully dreary.' Victoria's voice was glum. 'I keep thinking about poor Miss Hopson being bombed out of her flat. I still can hardly imagine it. All her cherished possessions… gone.'

Unlike many Londoners, Miss Hopson could stay in a fellow Park Road teacher's spare room for as long as she needed to. It was also fortunate that their headmistress had been safe in a shelter and hadn't lost her life. Still, the levelling of an entire block of mansion flats was shocking and made the war feel both more immediate and intimate.

Beatrice also knew precisely where January had gone. Following the upset of her mother's visit, the war news had become increasingly dire, and with the Germans' continued bombing of London and other British cities, they'd spent several nights each week in the manor's basement shelter owing to alerts. And across Europe and North Africa the fighting continued. Tanks, aeroplanes and ships everywhere, all of them united against a common enemy.

What if Britain and her allies didn't win? Nobody wanted to entertain that possibility – certainly not in public – but in private, Beatrice considered it foolish not to. She gripped the handle of her school satchel more tightly.

During his seventy-two hours' leave, Louis Grainger, a lieutenant commander in the Royal Navy, hadn't said much, but bound by the Official Secrets Act, he couldn't have been forthcoming even if he'd wanted to. Instead, they tried to forget the war, maintaining a forced jollity, but the German advance all the while lurked in the background, its malevolent tentacles extending even to their small, rural circle.

'Sorry, what did you say?' Aware of a heavy silence, she turned back to Victoria. Together with worry over the war situation, Beatrice couldn't set aside the unease her mother's visit had provoked. She'd stood up to her mother over her rudeness to Nell, but that didn't mean the underlying issues had gone away. Was her background too different from David's for them to be happy together? Beatrice loved him – of course she did – but practicalities *were* important.

'Your engagement party will be a bit of brightness, won't it?' Victoria waved at several of their London pupils who lingered at the village crossroads, chivvying them homewards. 'Mrs Meldrum dropped by the hall today for what she called a "final reconnaissance". Personally, I suspect she was just passing and wanted to have a nosy round. The children were being rather boisterous. It was morning break, you see, and I'd had to keep them indoors because of icy patches in the playground.' Victoria's laugh was mixed with a sigh.

'Don't fret about Mrs Meldrum,' Nell said. 'When I wrote to my mum about her, not naming names, Mum said she reckoned the poor soul is lonely and heartsick. Who wouldn't be with four lads in the Forces? Bless her.'

Like Victoria, Nell was charitable by nature, and what Mrs Potter had said about Mrs Meldrum made sense. However, despite the lady's good works for the war and other village affairs, Beatrice still found her difficult to warm to. 'Not that one is needed, but it's most kind of Mrs Meldrum to organise an engagement party for David and me.' They were hardly a young couple beginning their lives together, but Mrs Meldrum would not be dissuaded. What had started out as a small gathering hosted by Mrs Russell at the vicarage had, once Mrs Meldrum seized the helm, evolved into a village event, including a dance band coming from Cromer for the occasion.

'We want to celebrate the two of you,' Victoria said. 'You're a person of consequence in Hazelbury, and while David isn't the village doctor, he's certainly quickly become a local favourite. When I was queuing at the butcher's yesterday, Mrs Yallop was telling all and sundry how he as good as cured her indigestion. He was marvellous with Mrs Green's bunions too. A "font of medical knowledge", she called him. Word has also got round about his many kindnesses to Ruby and Mrs Fisk.'

As they walked along the lane leading to Hazelbury Manor, the fields on either side were etched silver with frost, leaden clouds scudded across the pale blue sky, and the fast-darkening winter afternoon closed in on the frozen world.

'Even so, there wasn't a village party to celebrate your engagement to Louis. Only an announcement at church and tea and biscuits afterwards,' Beatrice said.

A more subdued gathering which Beatrice, not wanting to be the centre of attention, would have preferred. However, Mrs Meldrum had dismissed Beatrice's tentative objections and forged ahead.

Is that what her life would be like as a doctor's wife? Feeling as if she were somehow 'village property' solely by virtue of her husband's profession? She and David hadn't spoken about what he'd do after the war. Would he return to London and work in one of the big hospitals there? Or set up a village practice? If she chose, she could likely work as a teacher anywhere, but what if the currently lax 'marriage bar' on teachers were later enforced? Except for London, any regulations were likely to be stricter than here in the countryside.

And what would she do about supporting her mother if she gave up work? She had to speak with David about the monthly stipend she provided to her. Did he do something similar for his mother? However, since he was always at work, and she'd hardly had a moment alone with him in weeks, there hadn't been an opportunity to raise the subject.

Familiar loneliness crept around her heart. Wartime was different, but after the war would her life as a doctor's wife also be lonely and isolating? If so, how would she cope? As a wife, she expected to share her life with her husband, not to be left on her own, almost as an afterthought.

'There wasn't a party because Louis is a Grainger.' Victoria's voice held both resignation and pride. 'Miss

Hetty said it wouldn't be suitable. Their family is part of the village, but it has always been their custom to keep somewhat at a distance from it. I suppose it stems from the time when most of the villagers worked on the manor estate in one way or another. If there were to be a party, Miss Hetty also said it should be hosted at the manor by the Grainger family. Which isn't appropriate at present. Although I don't understand it, I have to accept it as the way things have always been done.'

Turning into the manor's drive, Beatrice straightened her shoulders. Unlike her mother, she wasn't stuck in the past. She also wouldn't let her mother's disapproval – which had lingered long after her visit like a heavy, sulphurous fog and continued to be expressed in frequent letters – or her own occasional prickles of unease and anxious imaginings of 'after the war' dim her happiness.

You must not dismiss Henry Beauchamp out of hand. Not only is he a member of parliament but he will one day inherit Beauchamp House. There is hardly a more agreeable property in the whole of the county. Henry was exempted from military service due to his eyesight, poor fellow, but that does mean you would never have to fear for his safety.

On and on her mother's last letter went, never mentioning David directly, of course. That was not Clarissa Wentworth's way. But in urging 'dear Beatrice' to be 'reasonable', and with the multiple references to Henry, her mother's intent was clear.

Henry Beauchamp of the wandering hands. The sort of man around whom a woman was advised to keep a sharp hatpin handy.

Inside Beatrice's left glove, her engagement ring encircled her finger, a talisman of David's love for her and hers for him. A love that would be faithful, loyal and enduring.

Henry Beauchamp indeed.

Beatrice had a party to look forward to, which would, as Victoria had said, 'be a bit of brightness' they all needed. She had to put everything else out of her mind.

Friday, 31 January 1941

'As W.I. president and on behalf of all of us in Hazelbury, please join me in offering our warmest congratulations and good wishes to Miss Wentworth and Dr Stanley on this most happy occasion of their engagement.' At the front of the village hall, standing beneath pink, white and blue gingham bunting strung from one side of the room to the other, Mrs Meldrum raised her glass of fruit cordial in a toast.

'Hear, hear.' Major Bertram's voice boomed out as glasses clinked, a chorus of voices from the village and convalescent hospital congratulated Beatrice and David, and several of Beatrice's pupils, led by Jimmy Clarke, clapped.

'It's rather touching.' David glanced at Beatrice, who stood by his side in front of what was usually Victoria's desk when the hall was used as a schoolroom. 'I haven't lived here long but you're very much a part of Hazelbury, aren't you?'

'I suppose I am.' Beatrice returned his smile. It had happened gradually – not like Victoria, who seemed to have jumped headfirst into village life – but Beatrice felt she belonged here. Certainly, seeing the crowd of well-wishers who'd braved the blackout and icy January weather to come to their engagement party was heart-warming. 'However, you are liked here for yourself, not only because of me.' Good humoured, engaging and kind, David was the sort of person who would make friends wherever he went. From timid Ruby to dignified Major Bertram and everyone in between, he had an innate way with people that seemed to make class distinctions irrelevant.

Except when it came to her mother. Despite the fire burning brightly, a frigid gust of wind seemed to go right through Beatrice, chilling her to the bone. David, Victoria and Nell continued to reassure Beatrice that her mother would eventually come around, but Beatrice wasn't so sure.

As she glanced around the room, her gaze settled on several young nurses, including Miss Sibley, part of the group who'd arrived in two military lorries from Whittleton Hall. While it was understandable that Mrs Meldrum had invited some of David's colleagues to this party, Beatrice had detected a certain frostiness in the nurses' greetings. Had they had thoughts of marrying David themselves? And on the day of the Nativity, had Nurse Sibley intentionally neglected to pass along the message from David, letting Beatrice know that he'd been delayed? Her manner was not only 'frosty' but decidedly frigid, and Beatrice hadn't missed the woman's sidelong looks – nor how she'd smoothed the lapel of David's jacket when greeting him, her hand lingering under the guise of removing a bit of fluff.

'Miss Wentworth?' Ruby stopped in front of them, holding Diana's hand with Jimmy and Albert close behind. 'We made you and Doctor presents.'

'How lovely.' Beatrice turned away from the nurses – who were now talking and laughing behind their hands, with Miss Sibley in the middle – and smiled as she took the small parcel wrapped in newspaper that Ruby held out. 'What do we have here?' Holding the parcel, she opened one end as David did the same with his larger bundle.

'Yours is to put your engagement ring in when you're doing the washing up or working in the garden.' Ruby pointed out the features of the keepsake box fashioned from wood and painted a soft, creamy yellow.

'But you—'

'It's beautiful and will be most useful.' Beatrice shook her head at David who had undoubtedly been about to point out that her ring had come in a box – one he'd chosen.

'Jimmy gave me and Diana the scrap wood, cut it for us and showed us how to put it together to make a box,' Ruby continued. 'Mrs Russell had paint left over from when the dining room at the vicarage was redecorated.'

'Lovely.' Beatrice's throat thickened with emotion.

'Very fine indeed.' David acknowledged Beatrice's gentle interruption about the ring box with an understanding smile. 'See here?' David displayed his present: a wooden rack to hold ties, painted the same pale yellow as Beatrice's box. 'It's just what I needed. Thank you.'

'I cut wood for the girls as well. It weren't only Jimmy,' Albert said. 'And painted. It was also my idea for the ties. I made one for Mr Russell for his birthday.'

'Excellent work. All of you.' Beatrice thanked her pupils. 'We shall treasure your charming presents.'

'As we will also treasure this delightful cake knife and plate from the W.I. and village.' David raised his voice, presumably to make certain Mrs Meldrum and the other women clustered around the tea urn heard him.

Those gifts had been presented earlier, before the toast, and David had offered thanks on behalf of himself and Beatrice then as well. Along with an elaborate crocheted tray cloth made by Jimmy's mum, the cake plate and knife were displayed on the desk alongside numerous cards.

As the band from Cromer began setting up, Beatrice glanced around the hall once more. The long tables, where the infants usually sat, had been moved along one wall and draped with white tablecloths on loan from various village homes. They were topped with a miscellaneous collection of 'best dishes' holding cakes, biscuits, sandwiches and pickles, while a tea urn borrowed from the church steamed at one end. A brown paper banner from the school's stock, its other side previously used as a backdrop to one of the Nativity scenes, hung above the table with wobbly uppercase letters spelling out 'Congratulations'. Surrounding it were drawings of flowers and wedding bells.

'I drew them poppies.' Albert pointed to the banner.

'I did the daisies,' Ruby added. 'Everyone in school helped make pictures for you.'

'How ever did you manage without my noticing?' Beatrice looked between the children.

With her rosy cheeks and bright eyes, Ruby was an entirely different girl from the one who'd arrived in Hazelbury last August and now looked almost as robust as Diana. After Ruby's mother's death, the two girls had struck up what at first Beatrice had considered an unlikely friendship. However, like Miss Addie, Diana was a good influence on Ruby. Her kindness to someone less fortunate was, as Mrs Russell had said to Beatrice privately, 'an example of true Christian charity of which certain of her elders might take note'.

'We mostly did it that day when nurse came for health check.' Jimmy, who'd so far remained silent, gave Beatrice a bashful smile. 'We were all in the hall here with Miss McKaye and Miss Potter, and you were at the school doing your paperwork.'

'I remember now. You all seemed most excited when you returned to your classrooms.' At the time, Beatrice had wondered why the nurse's visit had been the cause of such merriment, but it had been lovely to see her pupils, who had so little amusement, happy.

'Miss McKaye said we had to keep the secret.' Jimmy made a zipping motion across his mouth.

'Well, you did a wonderful job. If you'll excuse me, children, I must find Miss McKaye and Miss Wentworth to thank them.' But first, Beatrice needed to tidy her hair before the dancing started. David had been drawn into conversation with Major Bertram, the vicar, and several other men, so Beatrice gave him a discreet wave before – being sure to avoid the nurses now looking daggers at her, Miss Sibley chief amongst them – making her way to the rear of the hall where a small mirror hung on the wall in an alcove near the kitchen.

From using precious ration coupons for the food, to taking up a collection for the silver cake knife and pretty floral cake plate, as well as the borrowed dishes, tablecloths and various other items, a great deal of effort had gone into this party. And it was for *her*. David, too, but she was the bride-to-be.

Despite what hopes Miss Sibley and those nurses might have harboured, they were too young and flighty for a man with David's life experience. Outside their professional capacities, they would have nothing in common, and he'd never give them a second glance. Their jealousy, if that was indeed what it was, was foolish. Since Beatrice didn't work with them, she wouldn't let their looks or whispers disturb her.

Reaching the alcove, she bent to look in the glass and smoothed her flyaway hair. Victoria had done it for her in a new way – a style she'd seen in a magazine – and between the soft waves that framed her face and the berry-red dress she'd worn at Christmas, which David liked, Beatrice hardly recognised herself. Like Ruby's, her eyes sparkled more than they once had, and her cheeks were rosier. It wasn't only because of the makeup Victoria had applied, either.

Smiling to herself, she tucked a stray wave behind one ear and tilted her head to one side. As Victoria often said, it wasn't 'vain' to want to look nice. Looking one's best did give a person confidence, and nowadays, it was also part of helping to keep up morale.

'Dr Stanley obviously needs a wife. Have you seen the state of his shirts? Shocking!' The voice came from the kitchen, but combined with the clatter of pans and crockery, Beatrice couldn't distinguish which of the village women it belonged to.

'I can't see Miss Wentworth troubling herself with his shirts, can you?' That was Mrs Yallop. From the schoolroom to village shops, Beatrice had heard its strident tones often enough for there to be no mistake. 'Likely thinks herself above mucking about in the laundry tub.'

Beatrice drew in a sharp breath. When Marjorie, the manor's daily help, was on holiday or had too much regular work, Beatrice had to launder her own clothes. All three teachers did. Heavy and laborious work it was too, what with heating water in the copper over the fire, using the washboard and mangle in the scullery, and pegging out the washing – either on a line outdoors or, when the weather was bad, on one strung up in the old orangery. Although Nell had had to show Beatrice how to use the copper and mangle, Beatrice had learned and had never shirked her part of the chore.

'Now, now.' The first speaker laughed. 'Miss Wentworth's not so bad. For all her book learning, she's got a knack with the children. My Mavis likes her.'

Mavis Kett. The speaker was her mother. A wiry woman with a gimlet-like face and a sharp tongue, she was known in the village as a model housekeeper – as much feared as she was emulated.

'That may be, but she has that "lady of the manor" air about her, don't she? Leastways with the rest of us.' Mrs Yallop laughed too. 'Above us lot and looking down her nose. It'll be a come-down when Dr Stanley expects her to help in his surgery. I reckon that's the real reason he all of a sudden decided to take a wife. Looking ahead to after the war, he'll have a nice setup for himself. Being a widower for so many years, why else would he take notice of Miss Wentworth otherwise? She's not much to speak of as far as looks go – too pale and mousey – but with her family connections, he'll be going up in the world, that's for certain.'

'And she'll be going down.' Mrs Kett tutted. 'I can't see her being a skivvy for him, though. She's too proud.'

'Yes, indeed.' Mrs Yallop's tone was amused. 'Him and Miss Potter would be a much better match. She can cook and doesn't have any airs and graces. Unlike Miss High-and-Mighty Wentworth, she'd be proper grateful for his attentions too.'

The two women dissolved into raucous laughter.

'Are there any more of Mrs Russell's sweet pickles?' Brushing past Beatrice's alcove without seeing her, Mrs Meldrum went into the kitchen. 'Major Bertram is especially fond of them, so I told him I'd check. Aren't you two finished with those pans yet?'

Beatrice pressed a hand to her throat, her hair forgotten, and left as quickly and silently as she could. She hadn't intended to eavesdrop, but the proverb 'listeners never hear any good of themselves' was true. Those dreadful women! Knowing what they truly thought of her, how could she face them or anyone else in the village again? The nurses had only looked disgruntled and been rather cold in their manner, but were they saying something similar?

And David. Her heart seemed to drop into her stomach like a rock tumbling from a high cliff into the sea. He loved her, didn't he? He didn't only want a wife to keep his shirts tidy, cook and clean for him, and manage his surgery. He knew she wanted to keep teaching and, maybe even still, become a headmistress one day. Anything else was just gossip, wasn't it?

Swallowing tears, she forced a smile and stepped out into the main part of the hall towards David's outstretched hand, the band music – Tommy Dorsey's hit, 'I'll Never Smile Again' – swirling around her like a taunt.

'I thought I was going to have to mobilise a search party for you. Everything all right?' David's hazel eyes were shadowed with concern, and he drew her close onto the makeshift dance floor.

Beatrice nodded and lowered her head to hide her face. She couldn't tell him or anyone else what she'd overheard. That would give those carelessly spoken, cruel words more importance than they deserved. She had to put them out of her mind and not let herself entertain any doubts. She couldn't let herself doubt David, either.

Which might be easier said than done.

Chapter Thirty-Five

Friday, 14 February 1941

'Class dismissed and make sure you walk home quickly. No dawdling. It's dreadfully cold.' Beneath the clatter of books being put away and excited Friday afternoon chatter at the prospect of two days without school, Beatrice sighed. Despite the roaring fire, the schoolhouse had been cold all week, with the wind slipping beneath the doors and under window frames and snow drifting on the sills.

She looked out one of the long windows into the grey afternoon, where low-hanging clouds scudded across the bleak, wintry landscape. There was no use grumbling. David was on duty at the convalescent hospital, so, like many couples, they had to spend Valentine's Day apart. It wasn't the day that mattered; it was the feelings.

With a nationwide hospital bed shortage, Whittleton Hall was now not only for convalescing patients and some more acute cases ended up there as well. Since David had several such seriously ill men, Beatrice hadn't seen him in almost a fortnight, except briefly when he stopped in to check on Ruby. However, his letters were as loving and devoted as ever. There was no reason for the unease that dogged her, nor for her to second-guess herself or their relationship.

She urged the last of the children from the classroom, picked up a stray gas mask box to reunite it with its owner, and went across the hall to find Nell. 'Are you ready, Miss Potter? The weather looks to be worsening. Like the children, we too must hasten home.'

'I'll be with you in a moment.' Nell's voice was muffled as her head bent over her school satchel.

Returning to the entryway, Beatrice found her coat, hat and overshoes and put them on. 'What do you say to—?' She stopped as Nell came out of her classroom, brushing her face with one hand and tucking a crumpled handkerchief into her skirt pocket with the other. 'Is something amiss?'

'No, I'm fine, thank you.' Nell gulped.

She clearly wasn't fine, but Beatrice knew Nell well enough not to press the matter. 'The children were rather dull today, weren't they?' While Nell put on her outdoor things, Beatrice chatted about desultory things. 'It's not surprising, I suppose. One needs to be warm to learn – and teach.' She forced a light laugh. 'Since it's Friday evening and Valentine's Day, I thought we might… Oh, my dear, there *is* something wrong.' She put a gentle hand on Nell's arm as several tears rolled down the younger woman's cheeks.

'Nothing more than usual.' Nell's ordinarily cheerful expression was a picture of misery. 'The children *were* dull, and I suppose… I'm dull too. I can't seem to engage them in lessons at all. What would Miss Hopson think of me if she were here? She said I was a good teacher and had the makings of a first-rate one, and I smile in the classroom like she told me to, but it doesn't make one bit of difference.'

'Of course it does.' As they left the schoolhouse and Beatrice locked up, she considered how best to console Nell. 'Teaching is rewarding but it's jolly hard work. You're feeling low, as we all do at times. I expect the children are learning more than you give yourself credit for.'

'It's also… oh… do you know what Ralph said to me when I was on afternoon playground duty?'

'I can't imagine.' Victoria had warned Beatrice about Ralph, having taught him in her infants' class, but in all her years of teaching, Beatrice hadn't met a child quite like him. Yet, despite Ralph often testing her patience, she always tried to recognise each child's uniqueness rather than forcing them into a single mould.

'He said that since I don't have a fiancé, he'd find what he called a "good 'un" for me. I only had to say the word.' Nell's voice was despairing, and she raised a gloved hand at the sombre sky in a helpless gesture. 'I'm happy for you and Victoria, but I don't want a fiancé or even to walk out with anyone. Ralph said it on his way to retrieve a ball, and several other children were close by and likely heard him. I expect they'll tell their families, and then, at church on Sunday, people will be looking sideways at me and whispering.'

'I suppose Ralph thought he was being helpful.' As she and Nell left the small playground and walked along the track towards the village proper, nearby buildings sheltered them from the worst of the bitter wind. 'He's not a malicious boy, but he's impulsive and doesn't think before he speaks or acts.' The incident with the fox stole at the Nativity popped into Beatrice's mind. 'What did you do?' Despite her numerous charms, Nell seemed oblivious to masculine attention. If approached by any of the remaining local single men, she firmly but politely rebuffed them. Respecting her privacy, Beatrice had never enquired as to Nell's personal circumstances, but that didn't mean she hadn't wondered why her friend was so reticent.

'I tried to stay calm.' Nell sniffed. 'I took Ralph aside and told him it wasn't right to comment on such things. Then he said he'd heard his foster mum say it was bad luck Miss Potter would be alone on Valentine's Day.'

'Oh.' Beatrice stopped herself from saying more. Even before she'd overheard Mrs Yallop and Mrs Kett at her engagement party, she'd suspected that she and the other teachers were subjects of village gossip. Why wouldn't they be? Hazelbury was a small community, and despite the war, the London school evacuation and the nearby air base widening what had previously been a limited social circle, it was natural people talked. They did so in London as well, but there it was easier to remain anonymous. 'I wouldn't worry over it,' she added. 'If you say anything else, it will only spark more talk. You dealt with Ralph as well as could be expected, so you must put the incident from your mind and rise above any heedless chatter.'

Just as Beatrice was trying to do with the careless comments that had wounded her to the core. *'Pale and mousey', indeed!* The hurtful words continued to rankle.

'I shall do my best, but it grieves me folk would say such things.' Nell nodded and her chin trembled. 'Let's go round to the manor by the footpath instead of through the village crossroads. I can't face anybody else at the moment.'

'I understand.' More than Nell realised. After the engagement party, once she was safely back in her bedroom at the manor, Beatrice had shed silent tears into her pillow. What should have been such a happy occasion was tainted, and her joy diminished. She hadn't even wanted to go to school the following Monday morning, fearing what could have been said about her in her pupils' hearing over the weekend. 'Here.' Beatrice gestured to a stile leading to the path that ran along the edge of a field. 'Going this way, we must walk more quickly. It's longer and the day is drawing in.'

'I don't mind how fast we walk as long as we don't meet anyone.' Nell tucked her head down, her face half-hidden by her scarf.

Beatrice did the same, the two of them walking into the wind. She glanced at the darkening sky where, in the distance, the cloud-banked horizon blurred into snow-covered fields.

'Watch your step. It's slippery with those ice patches under the snow.' Beatrice took Nell's arm and then stopped, forcing Nell to halt too. 'Look over there by the trees.'

'What did you say?' Nell's eyes narrowed in puzzlement.

'Look over there by the trees.' This time, Beatrice hissed the words into Nell's ear. 'It's a man.'

Nell put a hand to her mouth. 'He's in uniform, so he's not a farmer.'

Beatrice nodded, fearing to say more in case the gusty wind carried her words across the field to the figure making his way furtively out of the woods. A faint curl of smoke rose above the leafless trees, and the air had an acrid smell of burning.

It didn't appear to be a British uniform. Even at a distance, and with her admittedly limited knowledge, Beatrice could make out that detail. The man's gait was also uneven, one leg seeming to drag in the snow, and he kept an arm pressed against his chest.

She tugged Nell, who stood still as if frozen in place, away from the path and behind a plough undoubtedly left there by a farmer or his Land Girls, either doing maintenance work or in preparation for spring planting. 'Here.' The two of them crouched low, and Beatrice tried to steady her breathing.

'He's coming closer.' Nell's voice was a murmur, and her eyes were wide with fright.

'Go to the farmhouse.' Beatrice pointed to the reddish-orange roof tiles poking up through a copse on their side of the field. 'Get the farmer, the Home Guard, Constable Smith, anyone... then call RAF Whittleton.' She picked up a long digging fork that had been left beside the plough, its sharp, silver-coloured tines glinting in the fading light.

Nell hesitated. 'I can't leave you here.'

'You can and you will. Run.' Beatrice gave her a rough shove. Nell hadn't seemed to notice, but the man had already spotted them. This way, one of them could escape and raise the alarm. 'Now.'

With a startled gasp, Nell stumbled into the trees, snow and branches crunching under her feet, the cracks reverberating in the cold, crisp air.

Slowly, Beatrice stood, one hand gripping the fork, still staring at the figure coming ever closer, red stains dotting the snow in his black-booted wake.

He wore a pilot's winter uniform: a flying jacket, light brown with a fur or sheepskin collar. Blue-grey trousers. A brown leather helmet with flaps covering his head and part of his face. She squinted. Although she needed spectacles for reading, sewing and other close work, her distance vision was still good. Now what she'd known and feared from the start came into focus. The German eagle insignia on the right breast.

He was an injured *German* pilot, and she was alone with him in this windswept Norfolk field.

Chapter Thirty-Six

After glancing all around, and with no sign of Nell, the farmer or anyone else, Beatrice took several cautious steps towards the German pilot, who'd stopped about fifteen feet away from her, nearly in the same spot he'd been ten minutes earlier.

Where was the Home Guard when she needed them? Formed almost a year earlier, the motley group of volunteers practised drills and other exercises each Thursday evening on Hazelbury's village green. Made up of men either too old or too young to be called up for military service, or farmers, bakers and others in so-called essential jobs, they were, one and all, excluded from conscription. Even David joined the drilling when he could, saying he needed to do his bit. Like them, Beatrice couldn't defend herself – or the country – against a member of Germany's mighty and well-trained military. However, since this one was hurt, perhaps she could slow him down sufficiently until reinforcements arrived.

But was he truly alone? Given his uniform and that he was on foot and presumably hadn't yet been spotted by anyone else, his aeroplane must have crashed nearby. Likely in the trees where she'd seen that wisp of smoke. Were there additional crew lurking in the woods, ready to strike? Why hadn't the plane been identified on radar at RAF Whittleton and their own aircraft dispatched in pursuit?

So many questions and no answers. If there was no one at the farmhouse, Nell should surely have reached the police house or the pub and raised the alarm. Although usually officious and puffed up by the gravity of his helmet and badge, even Herb, the ARP warden, would be a welcome sight.

The seconds ticked by, each one seeming as long as an hour, and cold sweat trickled down the back of Beatrice's neck beneath her coat and scarf.

Alex. He'd died on a French field, cut down by a German sniper when he was still almost a boy. All these years later, here was another German – this time in an English field.

Beatrice held the fork in a vice-like grip – the cold, her initial fear and everything else, even David, forgotten. Anger surged through her like a red mist. Who did that fellow think he was, bringing the war here? The one place where she'd almost felt safe and had begun to truly rebuild her life.

'*Hált*.' Her accented voice came out in a croak.

Enchanted by German Romantic music and literature, she'd studied German rather than French at school. Before the First War, she'd even travelled to Bavaria to spend a month with her father's elderly great-aunt, who'd married a minor German noble. Then, the Germans were friends, not foes, and their country, with its beautiful scenery and rich culture and history, was much admired. Nowadays, Beatrice couldn't even play Bach or Beethoven without guilt stabbing at her, each note like a sharp point of accumulated misery, despite their having nothing to do with Hitler.

'*Hált.*' She raised the fork and spoke more loudly, even though the pilot hadn't moved as much as an inch.

Please stop. Alongside her anger, a small voice inside Beatrice pleaded with him. This boy – for that's what he was, with his face as pale as snow, thick blond hair and wide, staring eyes – hadn't killed Alex or her brothers.

But his father or uncles or family friends could have. Some of them would have been part of that war, which had taken everything from her, including the ability to bear sons and daughters of her own. It was because of men such as them that Beatrice was in this field at all.

She sucked in several harsh breaths. *An eye for an eye. Revenge.*

The vicar preached forgiveness. She encouraged her pupils to forgive and be kind to one another. But that was when it concerned small and trivial matters. A playground game. A dispute over a pencil. Not an invader intent on destroying her home and the British way of life.

'Jerusalem'. The hymn they often sang at church. *England's green and pleasant land.* She must protect it at all costs. They all would. That was why those road signs had been removed. Why the Home Guard had been formed. Each and every Briton was prepared to defend their country to the death.

She advanced towards the pilot, and he still stared at her unmoving, red blood darkening the snow and seeping across his flying jacket and that terrible eagle – a symbol of everything she both feared and despised.

Then he raised his left arm in a gesture of surrender, while the right still hung limp at his side. '*Ich werde dir nicht wehtun*.'

I will not hurt you. Beatrice mentally translated what he'd said.

'*Danke schön*,' she spoke through cold lips. *Thank you very much*. The phrase she'd once used to express gratitude in a cake shop and to Great-Aunt Edwina's seamstress for mending a rent in her frock. Not one she'd ever expected to utter, or even in her darkest moments imagined uttering, in a situation such as this. 'Where is your aeroplane?' In the recesses of memory, she searched for the long-unused German words.

'Over there.' He pointed to the woods.

'Is there anyone else with you?'

'The other… dead.' He swayed and pressed what must be his good hand to his chest and the spreading blood stain. 'You speak German?'

She nodded, conflicting emotions making further speech impossible. Was this how Alex had died? Or her brothers? A wound to the chest that had turned out to be mortal? Her eldest brother's body had never been found. Like poor Gilbert Russell's. The gossip about the whereabouts of his remains had taken months to die down. What would his fiancée do if she were Beatrice?

She couldn't know what a young woman she had only seen in church at Gilbert's memorial service – and with whom she hadn't exchanged even a few words – would do, but David… His steady, hazel gaze, more frequently serious than teasing, swam into her mind as clearly as if he stood in front of her alongside the German pilot. A doctor, he'd dedicated his life to healing and saving lives.

He'd certainly done his best for Griffiths, Brown and so many other injured men. Even when confronted with this enemy, she knew what David would do.

Slowly, Beatrice lowered the fork and set it aside. 'Here, let me help you,' she began.

Then, as if in slow motion, the pilot slid onto the snowy field, landing with a dull thud on a small hillock near her feet.

'I am Karl… Schneider.' His blue eyes, the same colour as her favourite forget-me-not flowers, fluttered half-closed. 'From Munich. Please tell…' He stopped.

'No, you can't die.' Beatrice crouched at his side and yanked off her scarf to press it to his wound.

'My mother, Minna, and my sisters. Elsa and Beatrix. My father. Hermann Schneider.' The names came out in staccato bursts. 'Tell them… I love them. Wotan too. Dog.' His pale lips curled in what Beatrice guessed was an attempt at a smile.

'I will – but you shall tell them again yourself.' *Beatrix*. Her heart gave an agonising thud at the thought of that unknown young woman. A loving sister, as she had once been. 'I am Beatrice too.'

'Beatrix. Golden hair. Also like my sister.' He tried to raise one hand again but could not, his gloved palm lying unmoving on the frozen dirt.

Frantically, Beatrice administered basic first aid, still pressing the makeshift tourniquet to Karl's chest. Would it be enough to prevent one or both of his lungs from collapsing? If it had been Alex or her brothers, she would have wanted a German woman to do the same for them. For David as well, if he were ever to be hurt in combat which, thankfully, he wouldn't. He was doing his duty at the convalescent hospital. He wouldn't be called up for front-line military service.

If Beatrice's life had unfolded differently, Karl would be the same age as one of her own sons could have been. He might have gone on a cultural exchange or tour – an English youth meeting his German counterpart. Meeting the golden-haired Beatrix. A party of young people seeing the sights. Eating decadent cream-filled cakes at a *Konditorei* and laughing together. Playing with Wotan, the dog. Listening to music at a beer garden on a summer evening or boating on a lake.

Oh dear God, she didn't want revenge; she wanted this boy to live. He'd be a prisoner of war, but the Red Cross could get a message to his family. Like so many British boys who were also caught up in this dreadful war, he was only following orders from his superiors. A boy playing at being a man.

An image of Jimmy Clarke taking charge of the snake when the school inspector visited skittered across Beatrice's panic-stricken, conflicted mind. If the war went on for several more years, Jimmy could be like Karl. Several of Jimmy's elder brothers had already joined up. Her stomach rolled at the thought of Jimmy – with his teasing smile, light-hearted jokes and gentleness to all living creatures – taking his place in a bomb-laden aeroplane. The machine plummeting to earth, and his body breaking into pieces. *Like Gilbert Russell and Aircraftman Griffiths.*

'Stay still. More help is coming.' As she pressed on the wound as hard as she could, in the distance men's voices shouted and an ambulance klaxon sounded. 'I visited Munich once. It is a most beautiful city.' Was it still?

The RAF had bombed Munich just as the Luftwaffe was bombing British cities. 'I love music, the great German composers.' She was babbling, anything to keep Karl with her, despite his eyelids flickering and his breathing becoming more laboured. 'Lady. That's our dog's name.' She looked up as footsteps thundered across the field. 'David.' She gasped his name. Medical bag in hand, he led the group of men, which included the police constable, several members of the Home Guard, and Herb, the ARP warden. 'Thank God Nell found you.' When he reached Beatrice's side, her body trembled and she sat back on her heels, letting him take over.

'You should have come with Nell. What do you think you were playing at stopping here on your own?' Two orderlies from RAF Whittleton ran towards them carrying a stretcher. 'If he'd hurt you—'

'He didn't.' Explanations could wait. German or not, Karl was a patient who needed attention. 'I applied pressure to his wound. See? His name is Karl. Karl Schneider.' Briefly she introduced them and told David what kind of treatment she'd administered. Karl was loaded onto a stretcher, and officers and men from RAF Whittleton fanned out into the woods and across the surrounding fields, but she stayed by the boy's side.

Like Beatrix, Karl's sister, would have. His mother too.

Almost blinded by tears, she hurried alongside David and the orderlies until Karl was bundled into an ambulance.

Herb, the ARP warden, grabbed her arm to hold Beatrice back from following Karl or David any further. 'You're in shock, Miss Wentworth, and no wonder. Ever so brave you were. Let's get you home, shall we?' Another man joined them. The grandfather of one of her pupils – but which one?

'Gone swoony, has she?' Leonard's grandfather. He sat in one of the back pews at church. An image of his solemn, jowly face and bald head above a stiff white collar rose in Beatrice's mind.

'I certainly don't feel faint.' She tried to stand upright but now the men held both her arms as the field shifted around her and the sky, land and trees slid together.

Her satchel with the school's logbook. She had to keep that book safe. It was her responsibility, but had she dropped the satchel somewhere? Behind the plough? How could she become a headmistress if she lost the logbook?

Then everything faded, leaving only fuzzy, terrifying darkness.

Chapter Thirty-Seven

Wrapped in a blanket and sitting in an armchair in front of a blazing fire in the morning room at Hazelbury Manor, Beatrice cradled a cup of tea and scanned the worried faces surrounding her.

Miss Hetty and Miss Addie sat side by side on the high-backed sofa covered in a faded floral Liberty print. Victoria was in the dark red armchair which matched Beatrice's, and Nell perched on a small stool with Lady at her feet.

'What time is it? I seemed to have misplaced my wrist-watch.' She glanced at her bare arm beneath the sleeve of her dressing gown. The journey back to the manor in Constable Smith's police car had been something of a blur, as had Victoria and Nell insisting on helping her out of her dirty, wet and bloodied clothes. While Beatrice bathed, the two of them had warmed her nightdress and dressing gown in front of the fire, which had been lit earlier than usual especially for her.

'Just gone seven,' Nell said, proffering a plate holding a stack of golden-brown toast drenched in what must be most of their butter ration for the week. 'Your watch is on top of the chest of drawers in your bedroom. I cleaned the strap as best I could, but between the dirt from the field and that German lad's blood, you're likely to need a new one.' She wrinkled her nose.

'Constable Smith was most kind, wasn't he?' Memories of the past few hours returned. The walk from school across the field. Karl's frightened blue eyes. The patches of his blood on the snow. 'I didn't faint for long, you know.' She'd come to, sputtering, with Herb and Leonard's grandfather – usually at loggerheads due to some decades-old dispute over a cricket match – putting snow on her face and neck beneath her coat collar. Hazelbury's chemist, another member of the Home Guard, had retrieved her school satchel with the precious logbook and directed proceedings with Churchillian gravitas.

'Long enough to worry us.' Miss Hetty's crisp voice brooked no argument. 'Thank goodness tomorrow is Saturday so you can rest here at home. Constable Smith was indeed kind. Surprisingly efficient as well. One might say that he and everyone else rose to the occasion.'

'They did – and magnificently so. You and Nell most of all.' Miss Addie's knitting needles clicked as she worked on a long navy-blue sock for Louis. 'How that aeroplane slipped through radar detection is anyone's guess. I expect there are some red faces at RAF Whittleton this evening.'

'There should be,' Miss Hetty added. 'It was far too close a call for comfort. A proper investigation must be launched immediately.'

'Quite so.' Miss Addie echoed her sister. 'When Nell rang the air base from the pub, at first some junior WAAF, full of her own importance, tried to put her off, but Nell insisted on speaking to the station commander and wouldn't take no for an answer. Simply because nobody was aware of a German aeroplane crashing in the vicinity didn't mean one hadn't.'

'Good for you.' Beatrice smiled at Nell. A German aeroplane coming down on the outskirts of the village, and one of its pilots roaming about nearby, would certainly divert any gossip from Nell's lack of a suitor. 'How *is* Karl? The German boy? Has anyone heard? And what about the one in the aeroplane?'

Dead. Tot. Karl's shaky voice echoed in Beatrice's head as she forced herself to nibble some toast.

'Mrs Meldrum came round with the latest news while you were upstairs,' Victoria said. 'Karl was taken to hospital in Norwich under military escort. The word is he's likely to survive, so he will be transferred to a prisoner of war camp as soon as possible. The other poor fellow will be buried in the churchyard. Mrs Meldrum said the vicar insisted on there being a funeral for him with full military honours.'

'It's right and Christian that he should have a proper service and resting place.' Beatrice's breath caught in her throat, and when tears threatened, she reached for her handkerchief. The whole experience had left her badly shaken – more so than she could acknowledge even to her friends.

'Mrs Meldrum and several others were returning from a W.V.S. meeting in Whittleton when Nell reached the village crossroads,' Miss Hetty continued, discreetly averting her gaze – and at the same time diverting the conversation – from Beatrice's display of emotion.

'In all the uproar, and Nell shrieking about a German pilot and you going after him with a digging fork, Mrs

Meldrum almost collided with Dr Stanley, who was travelling in the opposite direction,' Victoria said.

'I wasn't shrieking. I merely raised my voice so as to be heard above the two motors,' Nell said, her posture stiff and with an affronted air. 'When nobody answered my knock at that farmhouse, I ran straight to the village.'

'I also didn't "go after him with a fork". I merely took the fork to defend myself if necessary. However, the chap was so badly injured he would not have been a threat to me or anyone else.' At first, though, her mind fixed on vengeance, Beatrice had intended to stab him. She might even, to her shame, have taken pleasure in those lethal tines going clear through Karl's slender body. Thank goodness she'd stopped herself before acting on such a dreadful impulse.

'When you told me to run, we didn't know he wasn't a threat,' Nell said. 'You would have sacrificed your life for mine. If that isn't the act of a real heroine, I don't know what is.'

'I'm not a heroine.' Beatrice finished her tea, glad that the blaze from the fire would hide any flush on her face. David certainly didn't think she was a heroine. Her insides clenched at the memory of his anger and impatience. Almost like the day they'd met. Was that how he'd treat a wife managing his surgery if she did something he disagreed with?

'You *are* a heroine,' Nell insisted and the others murmured agreement. 'You should have come with me to the village, but you didn't. In fact, you pushed me away and were quite fierce about it.'

'I'm the senior teacher. It is my responsibility to look out for you, no matter the circumstances.' Along with having the same responsibility for her pupils, it was one which Beatrice took seriously. 'Please, let us not speak of it any further.'

'All right we won't, but Dr Stanley was ever so worried about you,' Nell said. 'He didn't say much, but as soon as he heard you hadn't come back to the village with me, his face went real pasty. Then he got back into his motor and went off like an entire German platoon was pursuing *him*.'

Beatrice stilled. She'd wanted to protect Nell who was younger and had more of life ahead of her. She'd also wanted to protect any of their pupils who might still have been walking home from school nearby. However, had David wanted to protect *her*? Like he'd done that day of the air raid when they'd sheltered in the cellar of the pub with Ruby and the other children.

Maybe he'd only been angry and impatient because he feared for her. Beatrice had thought the worst, but she was probably wrong, and he was working overnight at the hospital. She had no way of reaching him to explain – on Valentine's Day, as well. Oh, it was all too dreadful.

'Beatrice?' Miss Hetty's usually sharp voice was soft. 'You must get some rest.'

'Yes.' She tugged on her dressing gown cord. Although it was fruitless to disagree with what amounted to an order, Beatrice couldn't rest – not with everything in such a muddle.

'I'll bring you up a hot water bottle.' Nell stood, and Lady roused from her slumber. 'I'll also make more potted beef sandwiches if anybody wants some. Since none of us has had a proper tea, I expect I could rustle up other victuals from the pantry. There are still four savoury potato biscuits left.'

'There is no need to trouble yourself. My sister and I are eminently capable of making sandwiches and retrieving biscuits should we require any. We soon shall have to fend for ourselves, for the immediate future anyway.' Miss Hetty paused, and in the firelight, the gossamer spider's web of lines on her face appeared deeper. 'Marjorie gave us her notice today. She's off to work in one of the Norwich factories. It's not unexpected but I'd hoped… well it will be a minor inconvenience until we find another daily, won't it?'

If they found anyone else. With its lack of indoor plumbing and other modern conveniences, Hazelbury Manor was not what would be described as a 'desirable place' under any circumstances, but especially so in wartime. Not when the world and opportunities were opening up for girls and women of all ages. Having recently turned eighteen, and no longer needed at home to help care for her younger brothers and sisters, it was natural for Marjorie to want more excitement.

Amidst Victoria's and Nell's dismayed exclamations, Beatrice's heart seemed to sink even further. After full days of teaching and the myriad tasks she and the others performed outside the classroom – from lesson preparation and marking to visiting the children in their foster homes, letter writing, and, for her, the extra administrative work associated with the school's evacuation – taking on additional domestic tasks would be a major, not minor, inconvenience.

'Oh, and Beatrice? There's a parcel and other post for you on the hall table,' Miss Addie rejoined the conversation. 'No, don't go out into that draughty hallway. I'll fetch it.'

'Thank you.' Her chest constricted. Today, everyone in Hazelbury had pulled together, petty politics and grievances forgotten in the moment of crisis. The same was true here at the manor. Against the odds, the three teachers and Misses Grainger had become a family of sorts.

Miss Addie's gentle blue eyes sparkled as she paused by the morning room door. 'Whilst it is not in my nature to pry, when I took the parcel in, I could not help but notice that it appears to be a box of chocolates, presumably from Dr Stanley.'

'There's also a letter from your mother,' Victoria said as she gathered up their cups and saucers and put them on a tray. 'I recognised her handwriting on the envelope.'

'The "rough with the smooth" may spring to mind?' As Beatrice went to stand, Miss Hetty took her arm, speaking quietly so her words were for Beatrice alone. 'Much like life itself, is it not? Still, chin up, my dear. I expect Dr Stanley will call round in the morning. As for your mother, each of us is fearful, but many will not acknowledge it. You were most brave today, but perhaps you still have other fears to face?'

Chapter Thirty-Eight

Saturday, 15 February 1941

'I am indeed sorry to have caused you such worry.' The next morning, Beatrice and David wound their way along the garden paths at Hazelbury Manor. A pair of birds circled high above, and although it was still cold, the sky was a pale blue after weeks of dreary grey. Together with the white snowdrops poking through the frozen soil, there was a new softness to the air – one that heralded the promise of spring.

He gave her arm a gentle squeeze. 'All is forgiven, if not forgotten. Initially, I could hardly make sense of what Nell was saying, but when I did, I was consumed by fear that you'd put yourself in great danger.'

'In the heat of the moment I didn't think.' Their footsteps crunched on the gravel path. 'I suppose I also instinctively wanted to spare Nell from realising the true nature of the threat.'

'Nell, although quiet and retiring, is far from unworldly, my darling.' David drew Beatrice closer. 'She immediately knew "what was what", she said, and while she admirably kept her head, she was well aware of the danger you were in.'

'How do you know so much about Nell?' As far as Beatrice was aware, the two of them hadn't exchanged more than a few words, and those had always been in a group, either at school or in a social setting.

'I don't. I hardly know her.' David hesitated. 'However, I recognise much in Nell that is like me. Or rather, as I once was. The two of us have, as some would say, "bettered ourselves", and there are also some who are loath to let us forget it.'

Beatrice's face heated. She'd never said it aloud, but privately she'd certainly thought of Nell as 'bettering herself'. Beneath the surface was Beatrice as bad as gossips like Mrs Yallop and Mrs Kett? Much as she tried, along with the nurses' pointed looks and Miss Sibley's particular disdain, those women's ugly words lingered and still made her stomach churn. Nevertheless, along with what Miss Hetty said about Beatrice still having 'fears to face', she also had prejudices to overcome.

'I admire both Nell and you for what you have made of yourselves. It is inspiring and speaks not only to your intelligence but also to your strength of character and hard work. You are to be applauded, not looked down upon. What I mean to say is…' Had she sounded superior? She hadn't intended to. 'I began life with many advantages, it is true, but I also know what it means to make a new life for oneself.'

'You do – and here we are.' David's voice held a tinge of something that might have been wistfulness.

Several aircraft from Whittleton roared overhead, and Beatrice shivered. 'After the war, I expect everything will be different once again.'

'After the war.' He let out a heavy breath. 'I can't let myself think so far ahead. But yes, everything *will* be different. How could it not? However, will it be better and more equitable? Despite all the talk about equalisation of classes, I am not so certain. I would like to see a fairer society. One where a child such as Ruby has the same chance for good health as one like Diana, irrespective of their family's ability to pay.'

Beatrice murmured her agreement. It was sensible and fair and, as a doctor, David would be at the forefront of such changes. 'What do you see yourself doing after the war?' There, she'd been direct and put one of the things that was worrying her out into the open.

'You mean if the Germans don't win?' He gave her a wry smile.

'They can't win. Can they?' The possibility of a German victory was something she tried not to think about, but it nevertheless lurked at the corners of her mind like a snake waiting to strike.

'Of course they can, although it's not patriotic to say so. Germany has already laid claim to most of western Europe, and they're on the move east and in Malta and North Africa.'

'Yes, but Britain and her allies are holding firm.' Beatrice couldn't let herself think otherwise.

'Only just, if one is being honest. That aeroplane yesterday was a reminder of many things, not least that we're in a precarious position. I don't mean to frighten you—'

'No, it's right that I know the truth.' She'd never shirked from it and wasn't about to start now.

'I'm not serving in the Forces, nor do I have any connection with the government, but Major Bertram looks grim enough. He can't say anything, naturally, but he had a look inside that crashed aeroplane yesterday after our fellows got the flyer out. So did the top brass from Whittleton. Rumour is that it was eye-opening. All the latest gadgets and bells and whistles, apparently.'

'Britain has first-rate aircraft too. The Spitfire, for example.'

'True.' David shrugged. 'However, will it be enough?'

'It has to be.' Fine words – but even as Beatrice uttered them, there was a sour taste in her mouth. So far, the Americans have shown no signs of joining the war, leaving Britain and her empire to fight alone.

'Anyway, returning to your question about what I see myself doing after the war?' He wrapped his arms around her. 'First and foremost, it's making a home with you.'

'Yes, but where and how?' If Beatrice didn't press David now, when would she? 'In Yorkshire, London or here even?'

'I don't know.' His eyebrows knitted together as he frowned. 'I miss medical research so London perhaps, but I also enjoy general practice. What would you say to settling down in a village, with a cottage near the sea? Might be a nice way to grow older.'

Although she'd never told David about her erstwhile dream, he'd still captured it almost verbatim. 'It sounds wonderful. I used to imagine such a thing for when I retired but now, with you, it would be even better. We could have a garden. Perhaps even travel a bit.' The happiness the prospect of this new life with David brought made Beatrice feel almost as if she were floating. The blue sky, the faint sound of birdsong, the sunshine and the fresh scent of the earth in the garden. Each of her senses was heightened.

If she had a chance to be a headmistress first – or… did she even still want that job? The pleasant fancy dissolved like a soap bubble, and she returned to reality with a bump. 'I do like London, though, so maybe there first and then a cottage by the sea.' She gathered her scattered thoughts. She had to ask him about that general practice and whether he expected his wife to manage it. And how, between the two of them, they'd support her mother. Her worries about him working too much. Her fears of being lonely and overlooked. One thing at a time. 'About that GP's surgery—'

'I'll only have it if we're not dancing attendance on the Germans by then,' David interjected. 'I didn't know you spoke the language.'

'Not well, but I learned German at school and visited family in Germany before the last war.' Such things weren't unusual in her circle, but maybe they were to David. Or, even more likely, would it be yet another source of village gossip? 'I didn't know you heard me speaking German to Karl.' When David arrived, Beatrice had focused more on him, relieved that Karl would receive proper medical care rather than her amateur efforts.

'You introduced the two of us. As proper and composed as if you were receiving callers of an afternoon at home. I half expected a uniformed butler to toddle up bearing a silver tea service.'

'Stop it.' Beatrice put a gloved hand to her face.

'I'm teasing, darling. And some of the chaps at Cambridge spoke German, as well as several other European languages.' At the joining of two of the garden paths, David drew them both to a halt. 'You were wonderful. I was cross because of the danger you'd put yourself in. I wanted to take you away from that field as fast as I could, but instead I had to attend to my patient. He's German, but he's also a human being who needed my help.'

'Despite what the Germans have done – *are* doing – I couldn't leave Karl to die knowing there was something I could do to try to keep him alive.'

Still, guilt pricked at Beatrice because initially she'd certainly wanted him dead. She'd pictured, in detail, herself killing him – and not in self-defence either. She dropped her chin to her chest, unable to meet David's eyes as hot shame turned her insides over. It was only at the last minute, when she'd considered what David would do, that she'd shifted course.

'Because of your efforts, Karl is very likely to live.' David twirled a stray curl of Beatrice's hair sticking out from beneath her hat around one finger. 'In a prisoner of war camp, he will owe that good fortune to you. Prisoners are likely to have a longer life span than fighter pilots.'

'Such a thought also crossed my mind.' She paused. 'Karl told me a bit about his family. He has a sister, Beatrix. I thought of her and then the fact of Karl being German and my mortal enemy didn't matter.'

'That's the way of war. It's often illogical and contradictory. When we see that the enemy isn't faceless but is instead much like us – someone who might have been a friend under other circumstances – they become human and we can show them compassion.'

'As in Wilfred Owen's poem "Strange Meeting" from the last war.' Beatrice's breath quickened. 'His verses are as pertinent today as then. We are meant to be friends, but war takes away our humanity and makes us enemies.'

'Yes.' David's voice was rough. 'But enough talk of conflict, past or present. It is after Valentine's Day and I have not yet kissed you.' He drew Beatrice even closer.

'You have not. Nor have I kissed you.' She couldn't let herself think about the future because today was all they had. She couldn't let herself think of Karl, either. Since they'd undoubtedly never speak of him again, David didn't need to know the truth of what she'd almost done. It was over and forgotten.

'We must rectify that lack of kiss, don't you think?' One of David's gentle smiles flowered across his face.

'We must indeed.' Their eyes met, followed by their lips, and Beatrice gave herself up to the sensations David evoked, shutting out the world and everyone and everything in it for these few precious but all too brief moments.

Chapter Thirty-Nine

Monday, 3 March 1941

'When will Miss McKaye come back?' Peter, one of Victoria's infants, tugged on Beatrice's cardigan sleeve, while Diana and Ruby helped another infant find her lost reading book.

'Soon, I hope.' Beatrice dredged up a stiff smile. Victoria had returned from school on Friday afternoon with the onset of a heavy cold and now, on the first Monday morning of March, she was confined to bed.

'Miss Potter said I could, so never you mind.' Leonard's voice rose above the hubbub, and he swung his gas mask box, clipping Albert's ear.

'Children.' Beatrice rapped on Victoria's village hall desk. 'Return to your seats immediately and check your assigned work. And Leonard' – she waited until the noise subsided – 'bring me your gas mask box, please.'

Having slipped and fallen on a patch of ice, Nell had a badly sprained ankle and wasn't at school today either. Beatrice had left her on the sofa in the morning room, one leg propped up on a needlepoint footstool, with Miss Addie and Lady trotting between her and Victoria, administering cups of tea and comfort. With no replacement for Marjorie, Miss Hetty and Miss Addie tried to manage the cooking and housework, with Beatrice giving what assistance she could before and after school – which, this week, would have to be held here in the hall to accommodate all the children.

She took the battered cardboard gas mask box from Leonard. 'What did Miss Potter say you could do?'

'Don't matter.' Leonard studied his boots.

'If it doesn't matter, why did you tell the other boys it did?' She glanced across the now silent hall, where Ivy Byrne – who wasn't a teacher at all, only a helper – had gathered the youngest infants to read them a story. Despite numerous absences, the room still held more than eighty pupils, ranging in age from five to almost fourteen.

'I dunno.'

'It is "I don't know" and please look at me when I'm speaking to you.' Beatrice tamped down her irritation and opened the gas mask box. Correcting Leonard's speech would not make any practical difference and would undoubtedly make him even more defensive. With Victoria and Nell away, Beatrice had fallen into old habits. Far better to focus on truly important matters. 'Where is your mask?' She fished out a sandwich in greaseproof paper, several marbles, a *Biggles* adventure story and a tin aeroplane. There was no sign of the gas mask, which everyone – children and adults alike – was expected to carry with them at all times. 'What would you do if I were to shout "gas, gas"? You cannot expect such an alarm to always be one of our daily drills.'

'Sorry, Miss Wentworth. My mask's at home. Maybe under my bed?' Leonard raised his head and shrugged. An apology in name only.

'I have an extra one which you may use for today, but please remember to bring your mask with you to school.' Leonard wasn't the only child to forget or lose his gas mask, so the teachers had prevailed upon the warden at Whittleton's ARP station to issue them an additional one. 'Your gas mask box should also not take the place of a school satchel.' She studied the items on her desk. 'With the exception of your sandwich, which you may have at lunchtime, I shall keep hold of these other things until the end of the day.'

Leonard shrugged again but the gesture was half-hearted, now not so much belligerent as defeated. 'Why does carrying a gas mask matter anyway? The Germans will get us no matter what.'

Murmurs broke out around the hall.

'The Germans will not "get us no matter what".' Beatrice suppressed such rumours with the same regularity with which she dispensed arithmetic problems, composition topics and the daily bottles holding a third of a pint of milk the government provided for each of her pupils. It could not be denied that the war news was bad. From the recent Swansea Blitz, which left hundreds killed and wounded, to British ships being sunk with depressing regularity, it was difficult to be cheerful, but she couldn't let herself doubt or give up hope – especially at school.

Leonard gave another half-hearted shrug before his shoulders slumped entirely. 'I knows what I knows. Those two Germans falling from the sky in that aeroplane were only the beginning. Me dad says all the men are going to be called up soon, young *and* old, boys even. Doctors and all the rest to go and fight, but it still won't be enough to stop Hitler. Me dad also says least you'll be able to speak to them Germans when they gets here. Not like rest of us. You'd be one of 'em.'

There it was. The comment Beatrice had dreaded. No matter how imperfectly she spoke German, in Hazelbury, knowing the language at all marked her out as different and, possibly, a person of suspicion. Was that what Leonard's mum and several other women had been talking about in the post office last week? All conversation had ceased when Beatrice had entered, and at the time, she'd put it down to the usual village gossip neither the teachers nor the Misses Grainger would ever be part of. However, now she considered it, the same thing had happened after church two Sundays running. Was it suspicion she'd seen in the eyes of Mrs Kett and Mrs Yallop, in the centre of a group of parishioners who'd lingered in the churchyard after the service? The same women whose cutting words Beatrice had overheard at her engagement party.

The murmured voices rose in volume, and several smaller girls broke into muffled sobs.

While Beatrice had no control over what was being said in pupils' homes and in the village, here at school she could put a stop to any talk – whether malicious rumours about her perhaps having German sympathies or to do with the war itself.

'You have evidently been listening to silly stories. Remember that I will not countenance such talk in our classrooms. That aeroplane flew off course and crashed due to a mechanical problem. There is no need to cry, girls.' She gestured to Pauline, the oldest girl in school, to take charge of the weeping infants, while Ivy separated two boys tugging a homemade catapult between them.

'Our British and allied forces are defending us with all their might, and we must put our trust in them.' Beatrice made her voice firm and encouraging.

As the vicar had said at church yesterday, they were also to put their trust in God. He meant it to be comforting, and while Beatrice had accepted it as such, the question of where God was in this war, as it had in the last one, nevertheless kept her awake at night.

'I speak some German because I studied it at school. It was then a not unexpected choice as a second language for pupils who continued their studies beyond the primary level.' Apart from Diana, though, there were few amongst her pupils here who would stay on at school after fourteen, either by choice or family circumstances. 'While not used in everyday British life, German is often spoken in university and scientific circles. Like the German and Austrian refugees at present sheltering from Hitler here in Britain, those German speakers, myself included, are as opposed to Nazism just as everyone else is. Do you understand?' Beatrice took a steadying breath, which sounded loud in the now quiet hall. Had she made her point sufficiently clear?

'Yes, Miss Wentworth,' Jimmy Clarke said and then other voices, even Leonard, muttered agreement.

'Good.' Beatrice nodded. Many of her pupils would tell their parents what she'd said, so any gossip would likely soon die down. Still, it was another matter she would have to record in the school logbook and mention in her weekly letter to Miss Hopson. 'Here in Hazelbury, we're all contributing to the war effort to defeat the Germans. Can you give me some examples? One at a time – and raise your hands before you speak.'

Despite her best efforts, it had already, at only mid-morning, proved impossible to hold regular lessons today. With Victoria and Nell absent, the children were more unsettled than usual, and Beatrice's usually ordered classroom life had descended into chaos.

'Yes, Ruby?'

'We're helping the war by finding scraps of metal, glass, paper and food so they can be used again.' Ruby gave Beatrice a cherubic smile.

'Yes, indeed. Thank you, Ruby.'

Surely doctors of David's age wouldn't be called up to serve on the front lines? The other part of what Leonard had said – momentarily set aside by Beatrice's greater worry over possibly being considered a German sympathiser – returned to prickle at her. Doctors were needed on the home front. And David had already been called upon to do his duty at the convalescent hospital.

At Beatrice's nod, Albert spoke next. 'We're raising money to help build munitions. And me and Wilf and Diana are "Diggin' for Victory" by helping Mrs Russell in her vegetable garden.'

'Yes, you are, and you'll soon have loads of wonderful fresh vegetables to enjoy.'

So far, the hint of spring that Saturday, when she'd walked with David in the garden at the manor, was just that – fleeting. But spring would be here before they knew it. Following such a cold and dreary winter, the season of renewal would be even more welcome. Beatrice was feeling low only because of the weather, taking to heart gossip that she would usually dismiss and, except briefly in the village and at church, not seeing David since that day over a fortnight ago.

'Most of you are helping your families with gardening at home too, and we'll shortly be doing the same in our school allotment. We are *all* doing our part to help win the war and together, even if only in a small way as individuals, we will defeat Hitler's Germany.'

The outer door banged, and then there was a knock on the inner one, and eighty-plus pairs of eyes swivelled towards the rear of the hall.

What now? As Beatrice hurried to the door, albeit trying to think positively, she couldn't help but wonder what new catastrophe might have befallen them.

'Mrs Meldrum.' After opening the door, she gave the woman on the other side a stiff smile. 'Oh, and Mrs Bertram and Mrs Russell.' She greeted the two women standing behind Mrs Meldrum more cordially. 'I hope nothing is amiss.' She looked between them, searching for signs of distress or anguish.

'Not at all.' Mrs Bertram stepped forwards. 'We gather that you may be having rather a trying day, so are here to help.'

'You are?' Beatrice put a hand to her throat as shouts rose from the hall.

'Yes.' Mrs Meldrum's voice was brisk. 'Amongst the three of us, we've had eleven children, ten of them boys.' Beneath a navy-blue feathered cloche hat, her expression was resolute as well as surprisingly compassionate. 'We all three also have ample experience teaching Sunday School and working with children in other capacities.'

'We do,' Mrs Russell interjected. 'Whilst we are in no way questioning your ability to manage a large number of pupils, it must be difficult with Miss McKaye and Miss Potter unfortunately both struck down at once. If we might help, we are happy to do so and will follow your direction, Miss Wentworth.' She said the last with a pointed look at Mrs Meldrum.

'Albert Glover. Return to your seat immediately and no more nonsense.' Ivy's pained voice rose above the growing mayhem.

'Yes, please. I should be most grateful.' Beatrice exhaled. It didn't matter what Miss Hopson might say or do. The headmistress wasn't here, and Beatrice was doing the best she could.

'Leonard, you must not pull Ruby's plaits. Just because you have to sit on the floor is no reason to—'

A pencil whizzed towards them, and Beatrice jumped forwards – only to be overtaken by Mrs Meldrum who caught it in mid-air, as sharply as a cricketer fielding a ball.

'To whom does this pencil belong?' Mrs Meldrum held the pencil aloft and spoke into the sudden silence, the feathers on her hat quivering as if echoing their owner's outrage. 'Leonard?' Her gaze zeroed in on him.

'Yes, Mrs Meldrum. I weren't aiming for you, Mrs Meldrum.' Leonard's face turned scarlet.

'It does not matter for whom you were aiming,' Beatrice said, reasserting her authority. 'You should not have been aiming at anyone, do you understand me?'

He nodded, shamefaced.

'Good. I will assign you five extra arithmetic problems as your punishment. You will also apologise for being the cause of such a disruption.'

After Leonard mumbled an apology, Mrs Bertram squeezed Beatrice's arm. 'We're all in it together, remember?'

'Of course we are.' Mrs Meldrum took off her coat with its mink collar, which was the source of almost as much talk in the village as her mink hat.

'I may also have a solution to the matter of domestic help at Hazelbury Manor,' Mrs Russell added. 'Ivy has a younger sister who will be leaving school soon, and her mother is most keen to remove her from London. Stella could stay with Ivy at the vicarage, but if the Misses Grainger were willing to employ her on a trial basis to start… What would you think of my proposing such a scheme to them?'

'Please do so.' It would be the answer to a prayer Beatrice hadn't dared to utter.

'Tell us what to do and we shall do it.' Mrs Meldrum rolled up the sleeves of her belted bottle-green day dress and donned a bib apron she'd taken from her capacious handbag. 'Not all battles are fought on a field, on the sea or in the air. Those of us here at home – we women in kitchens, classrooms or village halls – are rarely recognised in the wider sphere, but we are winning this war as much as any of the men, and don't you forget it.'

'I won't.' Beatrice tried not to laugh as Mrs Meldrum fixed Leonard and several of her other most lively pupils with a stern glare.

'Don't fret, love.' Mrs Meldrum turned back to her as, at Beatrice's direction, Mrs Russell took charge of the infants with Ivy, and Mrs Bertram collected the younger junior pupils into a group near the hall's stage. 'There are times when we all have too heavy a cross to bear, but that is when we must take things one step at a time. It is also when we women must rely on each other more than ever.'

As relief flooded over her, and irrespective of having been called 'love', Beatrice flashed Mrs Meldrum perhaps the most genuine smile she'd ever given the woman. Whilst she'd never considered hugging Mrs Meldrum, just now she could nevertheless have hugged her, and Mrs Bertram and Mrs Russell as well.

The wider world was breaking apart into pieces, jagged shards of pain spreading outwards from individuals to families, communities and countries. But here, in her village hall classroom, balance and order had been restored. For now, that had to be enough.

Chapter Forty

Friday, 7 March 1941

'I never knew there was such a thing as fish-oil factories before our British commandos attacked those Nazi-occupied islands off Norway this week.' From her seat on the morning room sofa, Nell looked up from her sewing as Beatrice came in with the post after school on Friday. 'The Germans use fish oil to build explosives. I've been reading about it in the newspaper.' She gestured to a copy of *The Times* folded neatly by her side. 'Did you know that Britain has also officially severed ties with Bulgaria? Oh, and Mr Churchill has appointed a "Battle of the Atlantic Committee" to oversee something called "wartime logistics" in that area.'

'No, but we're all learning things we never expected. I've been so busy this week I haven't kept up with the war news or anything else.' Beatrice also had a fresh appreciation for the invisible work required to run a household, and for those women in the village who did it unaided. 'I knew that Mrs Meldrum was efficient, but I've discovered she has capabilities I never imagined. She only has to glance in Leonard's direction, and he settles to his work.' Beatrice sat in the armchair across from Nell. 'Give me a minute to sort this post, and I'll go and make tea and then help Miss Addie and Miss Hetty get started on our supper – such as it will be.'

'While Miss Addie was laundering the sheets, Miss Hetty got a small portion of fish but she had to queue for ages for it,' Nell said. 'I peeled the last of our potatoes and we have carrots again as well.'

'Stella Byrne can't arrive soon enough. Even though Ivy says her sister's not a "proper domestic" – having never had a place in service – her willingness to learn and, I hope, her energy will more than make up for any deficiencies.' At any rate, she would do better than Beatrice and the Misses Grainger, none of whom had any experience with real housekeeping, only flower arranging and tidying their bedrooms.

'From what Ivy's said of her mum, Mrs Byrne sounds an excellent housekeeper, so she'll have trained up her girls the same way,' Nell said, nodding her approval. 'The doctor from Whittleton called, and my ankle is much better so I can go to school on Monday as long as I don't run round after the children. He also said Victoria's bad chest is improving, and if she keeps on the way she's going, with rest and care, she should be able to come back on Monday too. She didn't go into pneumonia like he first feared.'

'Thank goodness. Even with Mrs Meldrum and Mrs Bertram, and Mrs Russell coming in when she could spare the time from parish duties, this past week is not one I want to relive.' Beatrice turned to the post, organising it into piles on a small side table. 'Still, as I wrote to Miss Hopson, we've managed and survived – if not entirely thrived. The older girls enjoyed the needlework and domestic science lessons with Mrs Bertram and Mrs

Meldrum, and several of the Home Guard coming in to give the boys some training in drilling and woodworking helped keep them occupied and direct their excess energy in productive ways.'

Most of all, the additional classroom help had enabled Beatrice to deliver some of the usual lessons in rotation, so the week wasn't as great a loss as it might have been.

'There are several letters for you from your family.' Beatrice handed them to Nell. 'Along with another one with a typed address. The ribbon on that typewriter certainly needed replacing. I can hardly make out your name. There's also a letter from Miss Hopson for me, and one from David as well.' She'd save his to read as a treat after Miss Hopson's, which was undoubtedly a continuation of the one about school administration concerns that had arrived the day before. Beatrice stood, still holding her own letters. 'Do you need anything? I can… Nell, what is it?'

'Nothing.' Nell stuffed a sheet of paper back into its envelope. 'Only a circular.'

'You looked as if you'd had bad news. For an instant, you went quite pale.'

'I turned my ankle the wrong way and had a twinge of pain.' Nell picked up the letters from her family and avoided Beatrice's gaze. 'There are still some honey biscuits in the tin in the scullery. I'd quite fancy one of those with my cuppa.'

'All right. Stay there. I'll bring you a tray.' Leaving the morning room, Beatrice pressed her lips together. Whatever was in that envelope with the typewritten address was none of her business, and she wouldn't

– couldn't – ask any more questions. However, it didn't stop her from wanting to do whatever she could to help Nell.

Reaching the empty kitchen – the Misses Grainger presumably having a lie down as they usually did at this time of day – Beatrice put water on to boil for tea and opened Miss Hopson's letter.

Dear Miss Wentworth,

She scanned the headmistress's handwriting and then took out a second, smaller piece of paper enclosed within it. 'Oh no.' She read the two letters more closely, her breath quickening.

> *Not in a position to adopt the girl. Haven't ever met her. No money to spare. New life in America. Orphanage would be best. Give the child the care she needs.*

The misspelled and ink-spotted missive from Ruby's aunt, who'd turned out to be her father's much older half-sister, swam before Beatrice's eyes.

Ruby wouldn't go to any orphanage. Not if Beatrice had anything to say about it.

-

Later that evening, after the rest of the household was in bed and the most pressing chores were complete, Beatrice finally crawled between her own covers, putting a cardigan on over her nightdress and tucking a stoneware hot water bottle at her feet. She curled her sock-covered feet around its welcome warmth and took David's letter and her spectacles from the bedside table. In the circle of light from her bedroom oil lamp, she propped herself up against the plump feather pillows and pulled the eiderdown to her chin, ready to savour the only time she'd had to herself since getting out of bed more than twelve hours before.

Opening the precious letter, she drew out the single sheet of blue paper and squinted at David's spidery handwriting. *Doctor's writing*, she'd teased him, illegible to the ordinary person.

> *It has been too long since we've seen each other properly.*

Beatrice had been thinking the same. Although her life before the war had never seemed like one of leisure, even when teaching, she'd certainly had more free time than she did now.

> *I have something important to discuss with you. Since I shall be at Whittleton Hall when you are there for your shift tomorrow, shall we meet up afterwards?*

She had something important to discuss with David as well. *Ruby*. Beatrice's heartbeat sped up as anticipation mixed with trepidation.

Surely David would want to adopt the child just as much as Beatrice did. He'd mentioned it the day they became engaged, and while he'd never said anything further, that was because they'd been waiting for word about Ruby's family. His feelings would not have changed. And the three of them making their own family together was all Beatrice had been able to think of since reading that letter from Ruby's aunt. Like Beatrice, David wouldn't want Ruby to go to an orphanage – not if the two of them could give her a loving home.

Except in general terms, early summer perhaps when the weather was better for David's mother to travel down from Yorkshire, they hadn't talked about a wedding date. However, unlike Victoria and Louis, there was no reason for them to wait, because David wasn't serving in the regular forces. He wouldn't be either, despite what Leonard had said about all men being called up to fight. That was another rumour, nothing more.

There were more pressing considerations, such as where they would live after marrying. Although housing was at a premium, surely they could find something small. Perhaps there was an empty cottage on the Whittleton Estate. It would be more remote, though, so how would Beatrice and Ruby get to school each day? What had once been the teacher's house beside the school would be ideal, but it was currently lodging two expectant mothers and an elderly couple who'd been bombed out in London. However, they were only there temporarily until more permanent accommodation closer to home became available. If Beatrice and David applied to the authorities…

She shook her head and smiled to herself. As always, she was trying to plan things too far in advance and now she had David to consider as well.

Returning to the letter, she read the last few paragraphs.

I made an enquiry to the hospital in Norwich, and you will undoubtedly be pleased to hear that Karl Schneider was recently released from medical care and has been sent to a prisoner of war camp in Canada. It is somewhere in Ontario along the northern shore of Lake Superior and sounds a very remote place, but labour is needed in a logging camp, so most of the prisoners are put to work there.

Where was Lake Superior exactly? Beatrice tried to picture the map of Canada in her head. Victoria was from Manitoba, the province immediately to the west of Ontario, but given the country's vastness it was unlikely Karl would be anywhere near her town. Still, if the ship carrying him made it safely across the Atlantic Ocean to Halifax, he'd be out of harm's way and reunited with his family after the war.

Through the Red Cross, he could send letters to them and receive their messages in return. Would he tell his sister Beatrix about the Beatrice he'd met in an English field? She'd likely never know, but she hoped he thought of her with the same fondness she felt for him.

You saved Karl's life. The Norwich doctor was most emphatic on that point. If not for you applying pressure to Karl's chest, he'd likely have bled to death before I arrived. Although you gave me a great fright, I am terribly proud as well. There is such dreadful suffering and loss of life on both sides in this war, and your kindness to that injured German airman is a reminder of our shared humanity. It is one of the many reasons I love you with my whole heart, darling, and hold you in the highest possible esteem.

With all my love, always.

David

Setting the letter aside and taking off her spectacles, Beatrice felt her insides coil into a tight knot.

Consumed with rage and grief, the only thing she had been able to think of at first was making at least one German pay for the devastating loss his countrymen had caused her. If she hadn't been able to kill him herself, she would have wanted him to die alone, as Alex and her brothers had.

If David ever learned the truth – that it was only thinking about what he would do in the same circumstances that had stopped her – he wouldn't hold her in 'the highest possible esteem' or be 'terribly proud'. Instead, he might despise her – and with good reason.

Usually so mild-mannered and retiring, in that moment she would have gone against basic human decency as well as the lessons of the church – all those sermons she'd heard – without thinking twice. The Biblical principle of kindness and compassion to others, which she'd absorbed since childhood, had meant nothing in that moment.

She blew out the light and lay in the darkness, wrestling with her conscience as thoughts unspooled in her head like thread from a bobbin.

Since she'd thought Karl would never be mentioned again, she'd put the whole experience from her mind. It was easier to forget it than to confront that part of herself, let alone acknowledge it to anyone – David especially.

But now she had to explain. She couldn't marry David without telling him the truth. She couldn't be Ruby's adoptive mother either. Her thoughts whirled, all the new confidence she'd had in herself crumbling as previous doubts and the way she used to second-guess herself came to the fore. She hadn't acted on the thought of killing Karl, true, but she couldn't keep it a secret either.

Usually scrupulously honest, she'd kept her friendship with David a secret from her mother until they were engaged and look how that had turned out? Her mother had not only disapproved but, rightly, also felt deceived. As his wife or Ruby's mother, it wouldn't be right for David to think Beatrice was someone she wasn't.

No, if she was to deserve happiness, she had to unburden her mind to him. All of it – not only about Karl. The nurses and Miss Sibley. The village gossip. She had to ask David what he expected of a wife, how they'd manage their work – his especially – and the question of supporting her mother.

She wouldn't feel honourable and proper in herself otherwise.

Chapter Forty-One

Saturday, 8 March 1941

'Here you are, Beatrice. Right where Matron said I'd find you.' On Saturday afternoon, David stuck his head through the half-open door of what had once been a dressing room, now transformed into a medical supply cupboard. 'That was after I looked for you in the office. Your shift is over, is it not?'

Beatrice tucked the last roll of bandages in with the others. 'Yes, it finished a quarter of an hour ago, but one of the nursing sisters needed help here, and there was no one else available.' She moved towards him. 'I'm free now.' As she untied her apron, his kiss landed on her jaw rather than on her lips. 'I got your letter. I have something to discuss with you as well.'

If Beatrice were honest with herself, she'd taken on this extra job to delay seeing David. She still didn't know what she'd say to him, but after a largely sleepless night, her thoughts spun faster and faster until she almost felt dizzy.

'I'd hoped we could go for a walk to the sunken garden, but it's still so cold and wet I don't want you to get a chill.' David tucked one arm into hers. 'And when it's not wet, it's dull. Or perhaps that's only me feeling dull because of not having seen you to actually talk to for so long. I've missed you, my dear.'

'I've missed you too.' She tried to smile as he led her into a long wood-panelled corridor. Portraits of men in starched ruffs flanked by hunting dogs and stiffly posed women in silk gowns lined the walls, interspersed with bare patches where the presumably more valuable pictures had been removed and stored elsewhere.

A long gallery. Beatrice, who usually spent her shifts in the ground-floor office or recreation room, hadn't been in this part of Whittleton Hall before, but she recognised it – Hazelbury Manor had one too, although it was less grand. Her family home had one of these long, narrow rooms where portraits and other art were displayed. On cold and wet days, she'd played in the long gallery, running from one end to the other with her nanny in pursuit. Grown older, she'd walked along it with Alex and Mary, their heads close together, sharing secrets.

'While some of the men take their exercise here, just now they're having luncheon either in the mess hall or on trays in their rooms, so we won't be disturbed.' They walked, and David held Beatrice closer. 'You look tired. I hope you aren't doing too much.'

She'd been working all hours because there was no other choice, but his concern was touching. 'Victoria and Nell will return to school on Monday, and Ivy Byrne's sister will hopefully arrive shortly after Easter. Life at school and home should become easier.'

'Good' – he squeezed her arm – 'I worry about you.'

'I worry about you as well. You look tired too. I fear you're overworking.' David's eyes were purple-shadowed, the lines between his nose and mouth seemed deeper, and each time she saw him, his hair had more silver strands mixed in amongst the brown.

'We are always short staffed, and the men's needs, already great, continue to increase. It's meant I've neglected you. I am indeed sorry. You are more important than my patients.' When they reached the tall windows at the far end of the gallery, by unspoken agreement, they sat down side by side on an elaborately carved sofa. Tufts of horsehair poked through tears in the gold upholstery, and a burn mark marred one armrest. 'However, several local doctors are shortly coming out of retirement to assist.'

'I'm glad for you.' Beatrice dragged her gaze away from the circular, discoloured patch of wood. Was the burn the result of a carelessly held cigarette? Whatever the cause, it was another scar of war in what had once been the Bertrams' cherished family home. 'As I said, I wanted to talk with you—'

'Me first.' David's voice rasped as he turned away to look out the window into the misty rain and low-hanging clouds. From this first-floor vantage point, the Whittleton Estate spread out in front of them. Nissen huts nudged against the stable block, and several Red Cross vehicles crawled up the gravel drive.

'All right, then.' Beatrice clasped her hands together to stop herself from fidgeting. 'What is it?'

'It's…' He stopped and turned back to face her. 'You know that as a doctor, I was initially exempt from conscription?'

'Yes, medicine was a reserved occupation.' She stared at him, unease making her skin prickle. 'And rightly so.'

'I was also exempt because of my particular skills and training but now… You know that since April last year, all male doctors have potentially been subject to being called up?' Again, he hesitated.

'Of course, but you... you were called up to work here. In a convalescent hospital with injured servicemen. Surely you can't be expected to do anything else?' Beatrice's heartbeat sped up, and her palms grew clammy. She'd managed to dismiss what Leonard had said – but amidst the rumours, had there been a kernel of truth?

'It isn't only at Whittleton that there's a shortage of doctors and other medical staff. Both the Emergency Medical Service, mobilised to care for civilian casualties, and the armed forces are in urgent need of help.' He let out a heavy breath. 'Personnel from Canada, Australia, India, America... they're all being recruited to work in this country temporarily. If they meet particular requirements, even Jewish refugee doctors are being brought into service.'

'But what does all that have to do with you?' Fearful of what David was about to say, Beatrice resisted a childish urge to cover her ears.

'I've been called to serve elsewhere. I'll be working in London initially, but thereafter I'll be sent overseas with the Royal Army Medical Corps. My name was on a national register, you see, as a volunteer. I can do so much more, Beatrice, whether at a field hospital or a mobile surgical unit. Even treating prisoners of war. I can't stand by and watch—'

'Aren't you too old?' Desperately, as David's words crashed over her, she clung to a last shred of hope. 'You're forty-two, almost forty-three and—'

'I'm still fit enough.' He gave her a strained smile. 'Besides, because the need is so immense, some doctors considerably older than me are already serving.'

'Wait, you volunteered? You said your name was on a register?' Conscious that her voice was rising, she instinctively modulated it.

Ladies do not raise their voices and displays of emotion are both unseemly and ill-bred. Why did those strictures, imbued in childhood, still haunt her?

'Before the war, long before I met you, yes, I did volunteer. I served in the Medical Corps before, remember? The last time round?' His hazel eyes were as serious as Beatrice had ever seen them and pleaded with her to understand. 'However, even if I hadn't offered, I *was* called up to work here and… well… with more doctors coming out of retirement, it's been deemed that I can be more useful elsewhere. I won't shirk my duty.'

She buried her head in her hands so he wouldn't see her tears. Naturally, she wouldn't want him to shirk his duty, as she would never shirk hers. However, she'd never expected that 'duty' would mean him serving on the front lines. The men here needed him. *She* needed him. Ruby did too.

Ruby. So soon after losing her mother and the rest of her family, how would Ruby cope with David's departure? Ruby didn't yet know that her aunt didn't want her. Beatrice had hoped to soften that blow by telling her she could have a new family, one who did want her, with David and Beatrice.

'Beatrice, darling.' He rubbed a hand across her heaving shoulders. 'You must see it was inevitable? Besides, in London or elsewhere, I can put my Home Guard training to better use than marching around Hazelbury's village green. It's as good as playing at being a soldier.'

'Don't joke.' She raised her tear-stained face to his. 'I worried about you wanting me to manage your GP surgery and holding me back in my work… in becoming a headmistress if I had the opportunity. I also worried about you working too much and leaving me alone but…' She gulped back a sob. 'You might not have a GP practice at all.' *Or that cottage by the sea where they'd grow old together.* 'You might not come back.'

And she might lose another fiancé.

Oh, how could she bear that kind of loss twice? She'd let herself fall in love with David in part because she thought she didn't have to worry about him being injured or killed by a German bullet.

'Yes, I might not come back, but if you calm yourself and think about it sensibly, there's every possibility I could be killed or harmed anywhere – even here.' He scrubbed a hand through his short hair. 'A traffic accident, a German pilot dropping the last of his bomb load before heading out over the North Sea. Cromer has been bombed twice, the last time in November, if you recall.'

'Certainly, I recall it.' She wrung her hands and then clenched them into fists. 'A girl of eleven was killed. The same age as some of my pupils. As for "calming" myself, I… you… I don't want to lose you.'

'I would never intentionally leave you.' David leaned towards her, his expression earnest. 'But I also can't promise—'

'Nobody can promise anything in wartime.' She hugged herself.

Alex and her brothers had promised they'd come back but she'd lost all three of them, along with every part of the life she'd expected to have. Her gaze darted from one side of the long gallery to the other. Those portraits represented centuries of tradition, but the war had upended the world yet again. She had to adapt or be left behind, but that didn't mean giving up everything once more.

Love. A family. The new life with David she'd let herself believe in.

'Wartime or not, a promise is a commitment, a sacred trust.' David's voice was almost as stiff as his posture. 'When I asked you to marry me, I told you that I loved you and those feelings will never change. You must believe me.'

'I do but I can't lose you. I can't lose another fiancé. It would be torture for me. I think it's better if we end things now.' Beatrice was usually so measured but the words burst out as if they'd been spoken by someone else. Yet, it was her worst fear, losing the love and life she'd counted on. Her happiness… gone like a puff of smoke. She gulped back a sob.

'If breaking our engagement is what you truly wish, I must accept your decision.' David hesitated and hurt flashed in the depths of his eyes. 'I also do not want you to worry about me or indeed for us to marry against your mother's wishes.'

'I never said that my mother—'

'You did not have to.' His laugh was bitter. 'How could a woman like your mother approve of a man such as me?'

'She… I…' Beatrice wanted to say that it didn't matter, but it did. She was still responsible for her mother and had to support her, maybe even bring her to live with her at some point. Their cousin was growing older, and Beatrice couldn't expect her or her family to house Clarissa Wentworth indefinitely. How could Beatrice ask David to share that responsibility for a woman who, whether rooted in fear for Beatrice or herself, had made no secret of her dislike for him?

And maybe Beatrice had deluded herself. Not only about the kind of person she was – one who might have killed a German airman without a second thought – but also about who David was. A man who'd leave her like Alex had, and whose duty to King and country was greater than his love for her.

David stood. 'I shall arrange for someone to take you back to Hazelbury. It is too wet for you to cycle.' He gestured to the rain coming down in sheets, and the grey mist which swirled around the treetops like mournful wraiths. 'You may be assured that I shall not trouble you further. I leave for London on Tuesday at midday. There is no longer any reason for me to seek to delay my departure.'

Beatrice stared at him for several seconds, momentarily stunned into silence. *She couldn't lose him. She couldn't let herself love and then be hurt again. She didn't deserve to be happy.* The words ricocheted inside her head, back and forth with dull thuds, as rhythmic as the metronome atop the manor's piano. She tugged at her engagement ring. The ruby, with its circlet of pearls, she'd been so proud and happy to wear. 'Here.' The word was thick in her mouth, as if she spoke through cotton wool.

'Keep the ring.' David shrugged. 'I have no use for it.'

Then he turned and walked away, his dignified footsteps echoing on the wooden floor, leaving Beatrice alone with the portraits and loss rolling over her in waves.

Chapter Forty-Two

Half an hour later, Beatrice tugged open the front door of Hazelbury Manor and entered the hall, shaking water from her coat, hat and rain hood. After leaving her bicycle in the carriage house, she'd lingered there before coming into the house, trying to get control of herself.

'No, Lady. We're not going for a walk.' She bent to pat the dog, who greeted her with a wagging tail and wriggling body.

'Dr Stanley will be missed, won't he? Such a fine man.' The chatty WAAF who'd driven Beatrice to Hazelbury, on her way to collect several officers from a base further inland, had been keen to talk about David's impending departure. 'Handsome too. So distinguished looking, don't you think?' She'd simpered and darted a sidelong look at Beatrice.

Beatrice, who'd said something non-committal in reply, had been thankful that the girl, who must have been all of nineteen, hadn't known there was anything more personal between her passenger and Dr Stanley.

But she couldn't keep up a front any longer. As soon as she reached the privacy of her bedroom, she would—

'Beatrice. I heard the door. Did you get very wet?' At the top of the stairs, Victoria greeted Beatrice as she hung her coat, hat and hood on the hall tree.

'No, I got a lift.' Beatrice fussed with Lady.

'So did Nell. Mrs Meldrum collected her. The church is too far for her to walk and risk slipping and turning her ankle again, and since she's singing a solo at that wedding this afternoon, she had to be there. We spent half the morning wondering what the bride would be wearing.' Victoria came down the stairs, a book in one hand, talking all the while. 'Whether she'd be in uniform or have a real wedding dress. It's good of the vicar to allow a wedding during Lent, but it was the only time the bride and groom could get leave, and he's soon to be deployed to North Africa.' Victoria reached Beatrice's side. 'Have you given any more thought to *your* wedding dress? That magazine Nell borrowed from – what is it?'

'There will no longer be a wedding.' Beatrice forced herself to say the words which would make her broken engagement real.

'But why?' Victoria took Beatrice's arm and hustled her past the dining room and large drawing room towards the rear of the house. 'Surely you—'

'I ended our engagement. David has been called up again and this time he will soon be sent overseas.' Beatrice twisted her ring, still on the fourth finger of her left hand. She'd have to remove it. She should have done so before leaving Whittleton Hall, but she'd been a coward.

'Called up again?' Reaching the kitchen, Victoria pulled out a chair from behind the table and gently lowered Beatrice into it.

'With the Medical Corps. He'd volunteered before coming here, but even if he hadn't I gather… with the doctor shortage… he needs to do his duty.' Beatrice tried to make herself sound brisk and businesslike.

'Yes, but why does him being called up have anything to do with you breaking your engagement?' Victoria collected two cups and saucers and poured tea from a pot covered in a knitted pink-and-blue cosy. 'The tea's fresh. I made it before going upstairs to get my book.' She gestured to the D. E. Stevenson story, a recent present from Louis, which she'd set in the middle of the table. 'This kitchen is the warmest room in the house at present.'

The book's title swam in front of Beatrice's eyes. *Rochester's Wife*. One of those so-called 'light romances' Victoria enjoyed, and Beatrice and Nell often teased her about.

Beatrice would never be a wife, and an empty future stretched in front of her once again. As an unmarried woman, it would be much harder for her to adopt Ruby – maybe even impossible. Beatrice would be alone and when her mother died… no, she couldn't let herself think of it.

Yet it had been her decision, and when those impulsive words had come out, David had been a perfect gentleman. More gentlemanly, in fact, than some men who had been born as such. But there was that flash of pain in his eyes and face. Hurting him would haunt Beatrice until her dying day.

'If you can't talk to me, who *can* you talk to?' Victoria sat at Beatrice's side and looped an arm around her tight shoulders. 'Diana's mother, I suppose, but Mrs Foster-Dalton isn't here. And Nell…' Her voice trailed away.

'She's too young.' Beatrice cradled her teacup. With almost twenty years between them, she and Nell were from different generations. But how could Beatrice expect any of her friends, even Mary, to understand her current predicament when she hardly understood it herself?

'Nell's young, but she's wiser than her years.' Victoria's tone was thoughtful. 'However, we're not talking about Nell, we're talking about you.'

'I can't lose another fiancé. I was upset when David told me he'd be sent overseas so I said it was better to break things off.' If Beatrice didn't look at Victoria, she wouldn't cry. She'd already cried in front of David and that was once too many. Tears, on the rare occasions she let herself shed them, were reserved for the privacy of her bedroom. Just as, when a child, it had been the back of the nursery cupboard, hidden behind abandoned toys.

'Oh, my dear.' Victoria's voice, already gentle with compassion, softened further. 'I take it that he accepted your decision, didn't question it?'

'I was rather forthright.' Beatrice drank tea without tasting it. 'He also said he didn't want us to marry against my mother's wishes.' Of course, her mother shouldn't matter, but had Beatrice actually said so? No, she hadn't. She'd only considered David having to share in Beatrice's responsibility for Clarissa Wentworth and, in that moment, had decided she couldn't expect him to do so. What man would? 'I suppose… I didn't know David as well as I thought I did.'

'You can still try to fix things. You love David and he loves you. Besides, you can't avoid loss. It is a part of life, but you can't always let yourself think the worst. *Carpe diem*. Seize the day.'

Beatrice tried not to shudder. Victoria had British parents, but she was, to use that dreadful expression, more 'free and easy' in her outlook and opinions than any

British person would ever be. She was also more naturally optimistic.

'I'm not like you.'

'No, and that's a good thing.' Victoria chuckled. 'Sometimes I wish I were more like *you*.'

'You don't.' Beatrice raised her head from her teacup.

'I do, because if I were, I'd understand Louis better.' Victoria sobered. 'Oftentimes, it's as if the two of us are speaking different languages. We grew up in different worlds. All this...' She gestured around the kitchen. 'The Graingers' way of life is foreign to me – quite literally.'

'David and I also grew up in different worlds.' But it wasn't about the class difference. Months ago, she'd realised that the perceived divide was immaterial. Instead, it was the fear of losing him, but now, thanks to what she'd said in the heat of the moment, she'd lost him anyway.

'See? Like Louis and me, you meet in the middle.' Victoria gave Beatrice's hand a consoling squeeze.

'It's not so straightforward.' Not for Beatrice anyway, who was both a product of the same world as the Grainger family and, with Alex, had experienced a loss she thought she'd never recover from.

'I think I understand. You're older than me too but...' Victoria hesitated, as if reluctant to say anything more. 'War brings all kinds of fear. Of course, we worry we'll be blown to bits at any moment. We also worry about our loved ones. In his last letter, my cousin Stewart wrote that each time he gets into his aeroplane, he worries less about himself and more about our family at home. Still, although he's never said so, he must be afraid for himself. How could he not be? Everyone fears the unknown.'

If they were like Beatrice, they also feared that which *was* known. 'I—'

She stopped as the air-raid siren wailed. Since last autumn, the siren hardly ever went off during the daytime. The Luftwaffe had instead turned most of their attention to bombing Britain at night, coming across the sea under cover of darkness to unload their deadly cargo when people should have been safe in their beds.

'We must get the Misses Grainger and Lady and go down to the shelter.' Victoria picked up the teapot and called for the dog. 'Only you can decide what you want, but if you truly love David, you have to accept the risk that comes with that love.'

Like Victoria must do with Louis.

The words she didn't say hung between them, seeping into Beatrice like water on parched soil.

Chapter Forty-Three

Monday, 10 March 1941

'Doctor's leaving.' On Monday morning, before Beatrice had rung the school bell, Ruby ran into the classroom and skidded to a stop in front of Beatrice's desk. 'Why didn't you tell me?'

'I only found out myself on Saturday.' Beatrice tucked her left hand into her right to hide the bare space where her engagement ring had been. She'd only worn the ring for a few months, but she'd soon grown accustomed to it. A constant reminder of the promise she and David had made to each other. During the brief, thankfully uneventful, air raid and thereafter, she'd thought of that promise all weekend, turning it over in her mind this way and that, assailed by new thoughts and feelings.

'Doctor came to see me and Mrs Fisk yesterday afternoon.' Ruby's tone was laden with importance. 'To tell me specially and say goodbye.' She gulped. 'He promised he'd write. We can write to him together and send parcels. I expect he'd like it if I drew pictures for him. He said he'd miss me and Kitty.'

Like the daffodils that had apparently sprung into bloom overnight, their yellow heads bobbing in the breeze, the spring sunshine streaming through the classroom windows seemed to mock Beatrice. While she was in the depths of unhappiness, the world around her was coming to life, full of renewed hope and promise.

'I'm sure that Dr Stanley will miss you very much.' With an effort, Beatrice kept her voice steady. Pleading a headache, she'd stayed home from church and, except for a short walk with Lady – when she'd been sure to head away from the village – she'd stayed at the manor all weekend.

She had to get through each day, each hour at a time, but at school she didn't have to face the silent sympathy of the Misses Grainger or Victoria's pointed looks. Here, she only had Nell, who'd appeared at Beatrice's bedroom door on Sunday morning with a handkerchief edged in delicate crocheted lace.

'In case you need an extra one,' Nell had said before pressing the handkerchief into Beatrice's hands. Nell hadn't referred to the matter directly or indeed again, but she'd made Beatrice's favourite potato and cheese pie for Sunday's supper, and a small brown paper bag of pear drops – a sweet both Beatrice and Nell favoured – had appeared on Beatrice's pillow before bed last night.

'Doctor will miss you most of all so we hafta' be brave together,' Ruby continued. 'Mrs Fisk says everybody misses someone. Like she misses Mr Fisk even though she says he's been "yonder in the churchyard for many a year".'

'I must ring the bell, Ruby. Go to your desk, please. See? There's Diana waiting for you.' The two girls who were meant to be her bridesmaids. Beatrice pushed that thought into the dark recesses of her mind where it belonged.

All day, beginning with the regular gas mask drill and continuing through each lesson, she focused on her pupils with grim determination. Despite the headache still pounding behind her temples and the dull ache in her heart, Beatrice couldn't let herself forget that these children needed her.

There were upcoming examinations to prepare for. Letters to write, including one to Miss Hopson about Ruby. It should be possible for the girl to stay with Mrs Fisk until the end of the war – but what then? Cousin Louisa and her husband had not been blessed with children. Might they be interested in adopting Ruby? If they were, Ruby could still be a part of Beatrice's life, albeit not in the way she'd dreamed of. *A mother and daughter. And with David, the three of them making a family.* A sharp pain shot through her, briefly replacing the ache.

'Yes, Jimmy. What is it?' Beatrice nodded to the boy who'd raised his hand. It was the middle of the afternoon, when all her pupils were absorbed in the lessons she'd set. The classroom was blessedly silent except for the squeak of pencils and the soft rustle of pages turning in reading books.

'It's the Home Guard and the warden, Miss Wentworth.' He pointed out the window beside his desk. 'They're comin' this way, Miss,' Jimmy added.

'I suppose they're on some kind of training exercise.' Beatrice peered where Jimmy had indicated and saw the group, headed by Herb, the ARP warden, marching along the road towards the school. Was that David behind them in the distance? No, it couldn't be. If not already at the hospital, he'd be on his way there. Despite herself, she couldn't help but remember his familiar routine. Another, sharper pain, shot through her.

'Quiet, children.' She raised a hand to quell the chatter that had broken out. 'Please return to your work.' After the early sunshine, the day had turned cloudy, and light rain now spattered the windowpanes.

Moments later, a vehicle's engine rumbled and chatter erupted again. 'Children. Silence, please.' Would this day never end? 'I shall see what is going on.'

Leaving the classroom, she went to the outside door and opened it. Nell was leading her pupils in a music class, so in the midst of a rousing patriotic song and the banging of saucepans with spoons, she and her children were oblivious to whatever was happening. 'Constable Smith.' The village policeman stood on the doorstep looking grave. Although younger than Beatrice, likely only in his mid-thirties, in the past year he'd lost most of his hair.

'Miss Wentworth.' He acknowledged her greeting. 'I do not mean to cause undue alarm, but you and your pupils must leave the school immediately. There has been a…' He cleared his throat. 'A German parachute bomb was dropped, presumably by mistake, during that brief raid yesterday afternoon. It is caught in the trees several hundred feet or so behind the school lavatory. One of the Land Girls working at Lower Yarrow Farm spotted it and raised the alarm. The bomb has not gone off,' he hastened to add. 'Otherwise, you would have heard it.'

Heard it? Beatrice suppressed a wild and inappropriate shriek of what, if she'd allowed it to come out, would have been hysterical laughter. They'd have all been blown to smithereens with the force of such a blast. 'Of course, Constable.' She kept her expression as grave as his. 'We shall be with you directly. I expect that is why the Home Guard and warden are here as well?' She gestured to the small party that had almost arrived at the school. The figure she'd spotted in the distance had disappeared. Of course it wasn't David. Her mind was playing tricks on her.

'Yes, a local state of emergency has been declared and the surrounding area placed under an evacuation order,' Constable Smith continued. 'The warden and Home Guard will escort you to the shelter. RAF Whittleton has also been informed of developments.' Since Beatrice had last seen him, Constable Smith had grown a moustache, and the ends twitched, rabbit-like, on his upper lip.

Nell and the children had moved on to singing 'Rain, Rain, Go Away', and the voices and clatter of pots and spoons seemed to rise in volume.

The vibration... any sudden movement... A bomb nearby...

Galvanised into action, Beatrice went to Nell's classroom and then returned to her own. 'School is dismissed for the day because we must evacuate this area.' She kept her voice as calm as she could. 'In your pairs, please go outside as quickly and quietly as possible where you will be met by Mr Foulger, Hazelbury's Home Guard, and Constable Smith. No talking or shouting, and leave your books and everything else except your gas masks behind.' She picked up her own mask, handbag and the school logbook and class lists from behind her desk, then stood at the classroom door as the pairs of silent, white-faced, wide-eyed children filed past her.

Since the London evacuation day in September 1939, the three teachers had grouped the children into pairs as a means of keeping them organised and ensuring that no pupil was ever left behind or alone. Although those pairs had changed over time, their usefulness was now proven once again.

'What about our coats and umbrellas, Miss Wentworth?' Holding Ruby's hand, Diana's voice was a whisper.

'Take them only if you can do so easily when passing your peg in the entryway.' She mustered what she hoped was an encouraging smile. The children getting wet or catching a chill was nothing compared to what a parachute bomb could do to them or anyone or anything else in the vicinity.

Yet one had been nearby for almost twenty-four hours, and Beatrice had gone about her day oblivious to the danger. Over their pupils' heads, she briefly caught Nell's gaze, her colleague standing at the other classroom door marshalling the rest of their children out of the school. Fearing their pupils would overhear, she had only told Nell that a state of emergency had been declared and that they had to leave the school since it was in the evacuation zone. However, her friend was no fool, and Nell had immediately grasped the urgency, if not the details, of the threat. Now the fear and dread in Nell's brown eyes must surely mirror those in Beatrice's own.

She'd read about parachute bombs in the newspaper. First used at sea as naval mines, the Luftwaffe had adapted them to hit targets on land. Each bomb was attached to a parachute and dropped from an aeroplane. She tried not to shudder, remembering the photos accompanying the article. Light-coloured parachutes floating from a plane with the black Iron Cross of the German Air Force on the underside of its wings. A cylindrical bomb dangling from each parachute, powerful enough to destroy an entire street. Designed to detonate when they reached roof level, they maximised the force of a blast across a wider area.

'Here we are.' Closing the classroom door behind her, as she did at the end of each school day, Beatrice buttoned her cardigan and, joined by Nell, went outside into the misty rain.

'Do you—' Beatrice stopped by the schoolhouse steps, unheeding of Nell, their pupils and everyone else.

'Oh, Dr Stanley.' Herb waved at David from amongst the Home Guard men assembling the children into place. 'Are you joining us or rather—'

David shook his head, patted his medical bag and for several endless seconds, his gaze locked with Beatrice's.

He was a member of the Home Guard but... No, no... For an instant the world seemed to spin around her. *The unexploded bomb.* He wouldn't be part of the bomb-disposal unit, but as a medic... Like everywhere else, RAF Whittleton was short of medical staff, so David could have been pressed into service.

Or he'd volunteered. The dreadful thought hit Beatrice, and she put a hand to her chest. It was like David to have done such a thing. Placed himself in danger to help others.

What had she done? She'd feared losing him on the frontlines, but he'd been right. He could just as easily be killed here.

'Good, good.' Constable Smith, who appeared to be overseeing matters from the school steps, rubbed his hands together. 'Miss Wentworth? That's the last of the children.'

'Yes, right.' Her pupils. She made herself focus, her own fear almost forgotten in the face of David's even greater danger. David, who was now crouched at Ruby's side, reassuring her. Trying to lessen her fear. As always, thinking of someone else before himself.

An RAF lorry pulled up. Two uniformed men in steel helmets sprang out and, with a smile to Ruby, David joined them.

'Move along, children. Follow Mr Foulger where he directs you.' Nell's voice was firm without even a hint of a tremor. 'Stay in your pairs in line, that's right.'

The children walked in orderly twos behind the warden, with members of the Home Guard flanking them on either side.

'Come with me, Miss Wentworth. Miss Potter.' Constable Smith gestured to his police car. 'We shall be at the shelter under the pub in a jiffy. We must go there as the village trench is also in the evacuation zone.'

'And leave our pupils? Certainly not.' Beatrice would never forsake her pupils, not even if part of her wanted to run after David. As if her mere presence could keep him safe. Which it would not. Regret, loss and too many other emotions to name surged through her as she brought up the rear of the group of silent children – even the most rambunctious were undoubtedly rendered mute with fear. Were they also remembering that first evacuation when they'd had to leave their families and everything familiar behind?

'We wouldn't think of abandoning our post. Not ever,' Nell said, joining Beatrice. 'Besides, don't you need to wait here for the rest of whoever's coming from RAF Whittleton?' She gave Constable Smith what, for usually gentle Nell, was a hard stare and gestured towards a convoy of vehicles rumbling up the track to the school and across the nearby fields.

'Yes, I suppose I do.' His cheeks reddened.

'Not the most imaginative or perceptive of men' was how Miss Hetty described Constable Smith. Still, like everyone else, he tried to do his best and was bound to make mistakes, so who was Beatrice to judge?

One of her shoes caught on a rough part of the track, and she stumbled and almost fell before righting herself.

Nell grabbed Beatrice's arm to steady her and then kept hold of it. 'Not far to the pub from here.' Nell's voice was low and as they came into Hazelbury proper, she gave Beatrice's arm a comforting squeeze.

'No, we're almost at the shelter.'

Who was she to judge? That random thought, which had popped into Beatrice's mind in relation to Constable Smith, settled and took root. As far back as she could remember, she'd judged others and been judged accordingly.

Them and us. Our kind. Not our sort. Beneath them. A maid who was getting above herself. An impertinent footman.

At first, before knowing better, Beatrice had judged Victoria and Nell, assuming she would have nothing in common with such women. Yet they had become friends as dear to her as Mary Foster-Dalton was. Dearer in some ways because, unlike Mary, the three of them were seeing out the war together – and relying on each other no matter what.

Despite trying not to, she had judged David too. Her insides quivered as shame engulfed her. That judgement hadn't been so much because of the class difference. No, she'd judged him for volunteering and being called up to serve in the Army Medical Corps only in terms of what it meant to *her*.

She'd been so afraid of loss that she couldn't truly embrace love. She'd even convinced herself she didn't deserve happiness, when in reality she was too fearful to embrace it. Passing the post office and village shop – ordinarily bustling but now shut up – it was as if she was seeing herself for the first time.

Whether it was fear of invading Germans or concern for the fate of loved ones serving in the Forces, everyone had to live their lives as best they could. Which meant opening themselves fully to joy as well as sorrow. What had Ruby said about Mrs Fisk?

Everybody misses someone.

And Miss Hetty. She'd remained devoted to her Montague's memory but at what cost?

By the time I realised I was wrong it was too late.

That's what Miss Hetty had said that night in the library so many months ago. Beatrice had thought she'd moved on and adapted – but had she truly?

As the first of the pairs of children reached the pub where Mrs Russell and Mrs Meldrum stood outside to guide the boys and girls down into the basement shelter, Beatrice's heart constricted in her chest so hard she thought it might burst.

In the ways that counted most, she hadn't adapted at all. Caring what the villagers might – or might not – have been saying about her speaking German. Her mother's disapproval of her marrying David. That silly gossip when Mrs Yallop and Mrs Kett had speculated about why he wanted a wife. The nurses' frosty manner and looks, and Miss Sibley perhaps not passing on David's message. Even David, doing his duty and going where he was needed.

His working all hours, and Beatrice expecting him to guess how she felt. Oh, she'd been so dreadfully wrong.

'Down you go, Ruby. Stay with Diana. I'll join you shortly.' She patted the girls' shoulders.

She loved both Ruby and Diana. And she loved David. Loved him as a woman should. Her love for Alex, whilst precious and dear, had been that of a girl for a boy, cut off before it had a chance to grow into full maturity.

Her love for David would sustain her for a lifetime. And he loved her – all of her. He wouldn't judge her for wanting to kill Karl, having to support her mother, or lacking confidence. Everyone felt uncertain at times. And if he worked too much, she'd be honest about it making her feel lonely. He'd apologised for being neglectful, and reassured Beatrice she was more important than his patients. She'd got herself worked up in knots over nothing, and she somehow had to make it right. It couldn't be too late, not even with him accompanying that bomb disposal unit. In those few seconds when they'd looked at each other—

'Miss Wentworth?'

'Oh, Mrs Meldrum.' Beatrice took a deep breath. 'The children are safe?'

'Every last one of them.' Mrs Meldrum's usually sharp expression was almost soft. 'Only you and me left to pop down. And Herb.' She jerked her chin towards the warden, who stared skywards as if expecting another parachute bomb to drop at any moment. 'I can't say I like being beneath the ground in that dank dark. Sometimes it gives me quite a turn, but I'm not alone down there, so I make the best of it and go forwards. That's all you can do, isn't it?'

'Yes.' Truer words had never been spoken, and it was as if a lesson Beatrice hadn't realised she needed to learn had finally become clear. 'I don't like it down there either. Shall we go together?' Beatrice held out her arm, and Mrs Meldrum took it.

David wasn't leaving until midday tomorrow, and if he was safe after today… The alternative was too awful to contemplate… While Beatrice had thought she didn't have a choice, maybe she did. A choice she'd never let herself consider.

Chapter Forty-Four

'More toast?' The next morning, Nell came into the dining room at Hazelbury Manor holding a teapot in one hand and a silver toast rack in the other.

'No, thank you.' Even though David and the other men were safe – news that Herb had come round with the night before – Beatrice had barely managed to choke down one slice of toast.

'I'm hardly surprised there's no school today,' Victoria said. 'Removing and detonating an unexploded bomb must be a tricky business. It's no wonder Whittleton had to call resources from London to help. But despite being outside the evacuation zone, I can't truly relish the unexpected holiday either.' She held out her teacup for Nell to refill it. 'I think I was more frightened afterwards than in the actual moment of crisis. Knowing you two and our pupils were so near that bomb and waiting until you arrived at the pub…' She shook her head and drank some tea. 'I had to stay calm for the infants but inside, well, it was another matter indeed.'

'I expect the village is talking of nothing else.' Miss Hetty took another piece of toast and added a scrape of the precious butter and sweet jam made from the blackberries they'd picked last September from the bushes in the lane behind the church. A day which, to Beatrice, seemed like a lifetime ago. 'I wrote to Louis last night so the dear boy wouldn't worry over us. Oh, here's Addie back with the post.' She greeted her sister, who had gone to answer the postman's knock.

'Not many letters this morning,' Miss Addie said. 'Like everything else, the war is also disrupting the postal service, but there's a card for you from Louis, Victoria.' She handed it over with a smile filled with sweetness and kindliness.

Why had Miss Addie never married? Having seen photographs of her when she was young, Beatrice knew that Adelaide Grainger had been a beautiful woman. She was still beautiful, albeit somewhat faded. Had she loved and lost like her sister or had her family not approved of her intended? Either way, there would have been disappointment.

She took the letter Miss Addie held out, addressed in her mother's familiar handwriting. Although yesterday, in what Victoria called 'the moment of crisis', Beatrice thought she knew what she needed to do to make things right with David, in the light of day she was less certain. Since they had all slept late, it was after nine, and midday was fast approaching.

Opening the envelope, she glanced at her wristwatch – a new one with a dainty gold bracelet she'd bought to replace her old timepiece. Although she could have just had a new strap for the latter, she'd decided she was overdue for a change, and this wristwatch was prettier and more feminine than anything she'd bought for herself in years.

David likely wouldn't be at Whittleton Hall. He would have said his farewells there yesterday. However, she didn't want to turn up at the vicarage either. In the hurry of leaving the school, Beatrice hadn't had time to put on her gloves. When she reached the pub, she hadn't missed how Mrs Meldrum and Mrs Russell zeroed in on her bare ring finger. Both ladies had been admirably discreet, but if news of her broken engagement wasn't already out, it soon would be. Oh, the gossip would be dreadful, but even worse, she would be an object of pity.

Taking out her mother's letter, she made herself read it. What recriminations and complaints would it hold this time? Clarissa Wentworth was never short of grievances. How would Beatrice tell her that she was no longer going to marry David? That confession would be the worst of all.

'Goodness.' She put a hand to her mouth.

'What is it?' Nell pushed back her chair as if about to take flight.

'It's…' Beatrice dropped the letter by her plate. 'My mother has written that Colonel Beauchamp asked her to marry him and she has accepted. She says…' Beatrice pulled the letter back towards her and slid her spectacles further up her nose.

'*I expect this news may come as rather a shock but when William proposed, I was pleased to accept. As well as Beauchamp House here in Oxfordshire, he has a townhouse in Mayfair, a hunting lodge in Scotland and villa in Bermuda. It is bad luck that we cannot travel to the latter at present – it would make such a wonderful honeymoon spot – but I expect to take up residence in Beauchamp House as soon as we marry. William still has staff there, thank goodness, though not as many as he once did.*'

At a choked sound, Beatrice looked up to see Miss Hetty covering her face with her linen napkin.

'Henrietta.' Miss Addie gave her sister a sharp look.

'Forgive me. Do continue.' Removing the napkin, Miss Hetty fussed with the jam pot.

> 'Although our wedding will be a small affair – the Saturday after Easter in London – I hope you will be able to attend. Perhaps the Misses Grainger may like to accompany you? Henry will naturally be there and would be delighted to escort you.'

Beatrice stopped reading aloud and shuddered as she took in the next part of her mother's letter, which included more fulsome praise for Henry Beauchamp and several references to his 'poor motherless children'.

'Flipping Nora. Not exactly subtle, is she?' Nell flushed. 'I'm sorry, Beatrice, but really.'

'Quite.' A small smile played at the corners of Miss Addie's mouth. 'I take it that Henry is Colonel Beauchamp's son?'

'Yes and he is of no importance to me and never will be.'

'So your mother is settled, then?' Miss Hetty met Beatrice's gaze.

'It seems so.' Beatrice stuffed the letter back into its envelope, not bothering to read to the end. All these years she'd been tied to her mother, needing to support her financially and in every other way, but that bond had finally been severed. Her mother would still need her – but not as she once had. From now on, Mrs Wentworth, soon to be Beauchamp, was the colonel's responsibility.

Her mother hadn't been afraid to seize whatever chance of happiness she could, and at long last, she had moved forwards in her life. Unlike Beatrice, she hadn't been the architect of her own misfortune. Rather, she'd been the driver of what she undoubtedly considered her great 'good fortune'. And whether she truly loved the colonel or had accepted his proposal for security, Beatrice had no doubt that she'd make him exactly the wife he both wanted and needed.

'Even if I had been invited, I wouldn't go to that wedding if you paid me.' Nell began gathering up the breakfast crockery with a clatter.

'Do be careful, Nell. That breakfast set belonged to my mother.' Miss Hetty raised a hand, but her admonition lacked its usual vehemence.

'I wouldn't go to the wedding either,' Victoria said, folding her napkin.

'It is up to you, my dear, but in these times, a journey to London would be so dreadfully taxing.' Miss Addie picked up the empty toast rack.

'It would indeed.' Was that laughter lurking in Miss Hetty's eyes? 'A jaunt to Cromer, however… The sea air would be most restorative, don't you think?'

'Cromer?' Beatrice's breath stuttered.

'That is where Dr Stanley departs from. His train to Norwich leaves from the beach station around noon, Mrs Bertram said.' Miss Hetty stood. 'She called on us yesterday morning and left some magazines her daughter had sent from London. I enquired about Dr Stanley's travel arrangements, and Mrs Bertram was most forthcoming. It was almost as if she wanted to make sure I knew he'd be at the station several hours beforehand. A vehicle from Whittleton should be collecting him at the vicarage about now. The driver will drop him off before continuing on to a location where the RAF is constructing a new base. I can't remember the name at present. We must all, even in the Forces, be so mindful of petrol, mustn't we?'

The longcase clock in the hall struck half-past nine, its melodious chime echoing in the sudden silence.

'There's sufficient petrol for me to drive to Cromer and back.' Victoria reached for Beatrice's hand and squeezed it.

She'd ordinarily have pulled away, but Beatrice left her hand in Victoria's. 'Could you take me there, please?' If there was a chance for her to speak with David in person, she had to try. She'd rather say what she needed to him directly than in a letter which she'd have to prevail upon his mother to send on to him. 'It will only take me a minute to be ready.'

'Of course I shall take you to Cromer, but you must look your best. You can't set off in that old house dress.' Victoria stood and tugged Beatrice up with her. 'Come. Let us rummage in my wardrobe. The weather isn't warm enough for your pretty blue shirtwaist dress, but I have a suit that would be ideal.'

'It will hardly take me a moment to freshen your hat and best gloves. Even if you hadn't left your other pair at school, they wouldn't do at all.' At the sideboard, Nell stopped loading the almost translucent, floral-patterned breakfast dishes onto a tray.

'But there's the washing up and—'

'There is always the washing up or some other dreadfully tedious task.' Miss Hetty came around the table to Beatrice's chair. 'We shall do whatever needs to be done together when we return.'

'We?' Beatrice gulped.

'Yes, we,' Miss Hetty said. 'All of us.' Her gaze drifted to Nell, poised to scurry towards the scullery. 'Lady, too. Although the pier is closed off, I expect we can still walk along part of the promenade. It looks to be a fine day, and we must make the most of it.'

Beatrice stared at the Misses Grainger, then at Victoria and Nell. No matter what happened with David, all four of them would be steadfast and loyal. True friends of the sort she hadn't known she'd needed.

Beatrice's vision blurred. Would David forgive her or would she be too late?

'You are only too late if you let yourself think so,' Miss Hetty said as if she'd read Beatrice's mind. 'It also would not hurt for you to wear lipstick. Dr Stanley may be less concerned with fripperies than some, but he's still a man and Victoria is right. That house dress is not only dreadful but also makes you look rather bilious. He'll be more inclined to think you need a tonic instead of a kiss.'

Chapter Forty-Five

Over an hour later, Beatrice took a deep breath and got out of the Graingers' motor at Cromer Beach railway station.

In Victoria's navy-blue suit with its white piping and stylish nipped-in waist, along with her own gloves and shoes she wore to church, and an almost-new blue pillbox hat which Nell had 'sponged' to 'freshen up', she felt much smarter than usual.

'I only tacked up the ends of those jacket sleeves, so don't make any sudden moves. Your arms are shorter than Victoria's.' About to shut the car door behind Beatrice, Nell issued a last reminder.

'And don't look so fierce,' Victoria added like an anxious mother. 'You don't want David to think you're nervous.'

Although Beatrice *was* nervous – more than she'd ever been in her life – Victoria was right. 'Thank you. All of you.' Beatrice rubbed Lady's ears as the dog, who sat between Miss Hetty and Miss Addie in the rear seat, clambered across Miss Hetty's lap to stick her head out the half-open window.

Miss Hetty gave her a regal nod and then tapped Victoria's shoulder. 'Do park the car so we can get out.

If there is hope of finding a cup of tea, I need one. You drive much too quickly, and the way you take corners…'

With a grin, Nell shut the car door, causing Beatrice to miss whatever else Miss Hetty had to say. Then she was alone, looking towards the empty platform.

What if David's plans had changed or Mrs Bertram had been mistaken? Beatrice made herself walk towards the platform. The sea beyond was a soft, misty blue, and the town perched on the cliffs above with the great tower of the parish church rising above the scene. If she didn't let herself think about the barbed wire on the beach, the dark blots of ships on the horizon, or the group of men in naval uniform clambering down from an army lorry, she could almost trick herself into believing they weren't at war at all, and that she'd come here on holiday to stay at one of the hotels lining the seafront.

Except they *were* at war and today David was going off to it. Beatrice touched her engagement ring, its bump visible beneath her left glove. She'd put the ring back on and never wanted to take it off again.

Reaching the platform, she glanced around, but apart from a white-haired porter pushing a trolley to the goods yard, it remained empty. Had David gone into the town, or was he inside the half-timbered-style station building? She would ask the porter if he'd seen a man matching David's description, and if he had not – although she shrank from the thought of seeing David again in front of other travellers – she would go into the station and look for him there.

As she walked towards the porter, brakes squealed and another military vehicle pulled up behind the army lorry.

Amidst a cacophony of voices, a door on the far side slammed.

'Good luck.' A young fellow in RAF blue leaned over one of the vehicle's open sides. 'Maybe see you over there.'

'Chippy's likely to crash, and you'll have to patch him up,' a second chap called out, followed by guffaws and more teasing.

Beatrice stopped as the porter continued past her. A tall figure, wearing a civilian suit and hat and carrying a small case, came around the rear of the lorry, shaking hands and joining in the joking.

David. Her breath caught as he saw her, and after a brief hesitation, he came towards her. He was familiar, dear and the man she loved with every part of herself.

'Beatrice.' He touched his hat. 'What are you doing here? Is your mother ill or—'

'I've been waiting for you.' She'd been waiting for him for almost her entire life, although she'd only this minute realised it. 'When I broke our engagement, you accepted it – but I should not have ended things between us in the first place. I should have told you how I genuinely felt. Yes, I shall worry over you, but I shall do so whether we are engaged or not. That worry is the price of love. A price which, if you can forgive me, I will gladly pay. I love you, David, and I always will. I know you have to leave but if—'

'I love you too. Oh, my darling. Dear, dear Beatrice.' In two steps, David had taken her in his arms and held her as if he never wanted to let her go. 'Yesterday… I feared for you, but I couldn't… So today, before leaving Hazelbury, I went to the manor to try to see you and when there was no one there, I thought it too late.'

‘Yesterday, I feared for you too. So very much. But it’s never too late. Not if you don’t think it so.’ Resting her head on one of David’s shoulders, Beatrice repeated what Miss Hetty had said.

‘But I have so little time. I unexpectedly have to take an earlier train and it will be here any moment. I waited for you in Hazelbury as long as I possibly could.’ He gestured to the lorry where the boys whooped and cheered. ‘I didn’t want to leave without trying again.’

‘I was so very wrong.’ Beatrice raised her head to stare into his beloved face.

‘It doesn’t matter. All that matters is that we have another chance.’

‘Yes, but I was foolish and I’d…’ Tears threatened and she swallowed. ‘I’d convinced myself of all sorts of things that weren’t true, and my mother… What she thinks doesn’t matter, and I don’t need her approval to marry, but I still have somewhat of a responsibility to her and didn’t want to ask you to take it on.’

‘Your responsibilities are mine, sweetheart.’ David traced the curve of Beatrice’s jaw with a gentle hand. ‘But are you sure you want to make a life with me? If, God willing, I return. What about becoming a headmistress? I don’t want to hold you back. Mrs Meldrum told me that there has been some ridiculous talk in the village. About me only marrying you because I need a wife to manage my surgery, and then your speaking German. Doubting your loyalties. Nobody could be more loyal than you. I also gather that our engagement put several noses out of joint amongst the nurses at Whittleton. As if it would ever be the case that I wanted a surgery manager, or I’d have been making sheep’s eyes at nurses young enough to be my daughter. I want you to be my wife because I love you. The kind of love I never thought I'd find again, but even more.'

Happiness rushed over Beatrice like waves crashing onto the shore. 'Miss Hopson said there is such a desperate need for school staff that I could not only keep teaching anywhere, not only in London, if I married, but I'd likely be able to become a headmistress as well. But right now, all of that is insignificant. I don't want to wait for us to make a life together, not too long at any rate. The war could drag on for years.'

A whistle blew, and a train chuffed into the station, clouds of steam billowing.

'I know you must leave, but you also need to know the truth. Karl, that German flyer? I wanted to kill him at first. Truly, I did, but then I thought about you – what you would do – and I couldn't.' Beatrice's words tumbled out, and as people streamed out of the station, David shielded her from the crowd with his broad frame. 'I'm not as good as you think I am.'

'Of course you are.' David's eyes held their familiar love for her. 'But you're also human as we all are, and I look forward to getting to know every part of you. We've only just begun, Beatrice, and together… well…' He took her left hand in his and drew off her glove. 'You're wearing my ring.'

'Yes, for always. I was so afraid of losing you, I pushed you away. But I lost you anyway, and so whatever life brings, I want to face it with you at my side. And Ruby, I hope.'

'What about Ruby? Is there news of her family?'

'Yes, it's a terrible thing, but her aunt in America doesn't want her and says she has to go to an orphanage. I can't let that happen. I haven't told Ruby yet but…' She stuttered to a stop.

'We must adopt her, then, as we spoke of before.' David's laugh was boyish. 'A doctor and a teacher, possibly a headmistress, should be suitable enough parents to satisfy even the most demanding of authorities. What do you say? Will you marry me, Beatrice? Make a family with me?'

'Oh yes.' Oblivious to the bystanders, she flung her arms around David and kissed him, showing him what was in her heart and soul – that she would be his, and they would be each other's, for always.

-

Standing alone on the once again silent and empty platform, Beatrice waved her handkerchief until the train was no longer even a speck in the distance. David was gone, but he'd return on leave and for the next few months he'd only be in London. She couldn't let herself worry about what might happen beyond that.

Where had the Misses Grainger and Victoria and Nell got to? Miss Hetty had mentioned wanting a cup of tea, but Beatrice should have arranged to meet them somewhere. No matter, she'd find a bench and wait for them here. They couldn't have gone to one of the hotels, not with Lady, so they'd undoubtedly be back soon.

She thought about the letter she planned to write to David. Amongst other things, she needed to tell him about her mother marrying Colonel Beauchamp. Yet, as a measure of the man David was, he'd shouldered the responsibility of Clarissa Wentworth without question.

And maybe with her own impending nuptials, Beatrice's mother would be less concerned about her daughter's.

When she turned away from the tracks to make her way to the ladies' waiting room, one of the station doors opened and Victoria came out with Lady – Nell and the Misses Grainger following behind.

'All right?' Victoria asked as they reached Beatrice. 'We stayed in the station in case you needed us.'

'Yes.' Beatrice clutched her handkerchief – the one with the lace edging that Nell had given her. She'd promised herself she wouldn't cry. 'We have renewed our engagement.'

'As if we expected anything else.' Victoria beamed and gave Beatrice one of her exuberant hugs.

'It's lovely news,' Nell said as the Misses Grainger added their congratulations. 'But good gracious, look at those jacket sleeves! The left one has fallen right down and the thread's dangling. It's white thread since, in the rush to leave, I couldn't find any navy. It's dreadful.'

'It doesn't matter. I didn't notice, so David would not have either.' Emerging from Victoria's hug, Beatrice laughed and patted Nell's shoulder as the three of them linked arms.

'It certainly does matter. I take pride in my work.' Nell gave an aggrieved sniff.

'Don't fuss. I expect you'll soon have a wedding dress to make and use all the white thread you wish.' Victoria tugged on Lady's lead so that, in the dog's excitement, she wouldn't knock Miss Hetty and Miss Addie over.

'I heard of a bride in London who made her dress from parachute silk.' Miss Hetty's expression verged on smug. 'I shall have a word with the station commander at

Whittleton. There must be sufficient silk in the parachute that came down at Lower Yarrow Farm yesterday.'

'But that was a German parachute.' Nell's eyes went wide.

'It's still silk, is it not? In wartime one cannot be overly fussy.' Miss Hetty's eyes danced with mirth. 'If Beatrice, or Victoria for that matter, do not want that silk for their dresses, I expect underwear could be made of it – enough for every woman in the village and beyond. Now let us find a proper cup of tea. That one I had in the station was like washing-up water.'

'Do you think she's actually drunk washing-up water?' Nell darted an anxious glance between Beatrice and Victoria as the Misses Grainger marched ahead of them, Miss Hetty chivvying Miss Addie along.

'Of course not.' Beatrice shook her head. 'It is an expression, nothing more. Surely these eighteen months of teaching have taught you not to be so literal?'

'They have but Miss Hetty is… well, she's not one of our pupils.' Nell's brow still furrowed.

'No but like our pupils – like each one of us – Miss Hetty is unique. Come on, I fancy a bun, don't you?' Victoria gestured towards the town. 'We could find a place on the prom to sit and eat, and then we'll give Lady a walk. Since she wasn't allowed further inside, I stood with her at the station entrance. A porter kept giving me disapproving looks, but I ignored him.'

Eat outside? The weather was not yet suitable for a picnic, and Beatrice had never eaten outdoors otherwise. 'Why not?' she said instead.

She'd kept her life on hold too long, but now, despite the war, she could truly start living it.

Author's Note

Welcome back to North Norfolk and my fictional village of Hazelbury. While *A Christmas Proposal* follows the first book in the series, *The Teacher Evacuees*, it also stands alone. If you're a new reader, you should soon feel at home in my early 1940s British home-front world.

Taking place between late August 1940 and early March 1941, *A Christmas Proposal* spans a momentous six months in the Second World War and includes the start of the London Blitz and Germany's wider aerial assault on so many other British cities and towns up and down the country. Fears of a German invasion had not truly subsided either and living near an air base, the war is very much on the doorstep for my fictional teachers and their pupils, much as it was for those living in rural Norfolk at that perilous time.

Still, everyone went on with life as best they could, including celebrating Christmas to try to bring cheer to those dark days. In writing *A Christmas Proposal*, I drew on some of my own memories of British and family Christmas celebrations, including lunch with a carrot pudding. Growing up, I didn't realise that my grandmother's traditional carrot pudding was a wartime legacy and now cherish her handwritten recipe even more.

Another incident in this story drawn from my own life is a child's comic intervention with a fox-fur stole during a Nativity play. I was the pianist for a Sunday School concert when laughter broke out during an otherwise solemn rendition of 'Silent Night' – for the same reason it does in *A Christmas Proposal.*

Many of you will note that this book is dedicated to Flight Lieutenant Gordon Stewart Richards, a World War Two pilot in the Royal Canadian Air Force. Killed in action at only twenty-three, he was my late mother's older cousin whom she looked up to and admired.

Visiting his grave together at Chester (Blacon) Cemetery, UK, was a special moment and, as my mother spoke about Stewart's short life, I wanted to ensure that he – and his sacrifice – weren't forgotten. That is also why a fictional Stewart Richards, a cousin to my Canadian teacher, Victoria McKaye, features in this story too.

At its heart, *A Christmas Proposal* is senior teacher Beatrice Wentworth's story. Since many readers have told me that they enjoyed reading about an older character, in her early forties, in *The Teacher Evacuees*, as Beatrice takes centre stage here, I hope I've given her the happily-ever-after – and lovely hero, Dr David Stanley – she deserves.

As Beatrice and David show us, love isn't only for the young, and their life experience and past heartache might just make this new love even sweeter.

I hope you have a happy wartime Christmas in Hazelbury, carrot fudge (for which I also have a wartime recipe) and all.

Acknowledgements

Thank you to my UK literary agent, Kiran Kataria of Keane Kataria Literary Agency, for guiding me through career ups and downs, and her incisive editorial feedback, wisdom and advocacy.

At Canelo, I owe sincere appreciation to Editorial Director Emily Bedford and Commissioning Editor Pauli Roos for helping me shape this story and for loving my fictional characters as much as I do.

Materials held by London's Imperial War Museum (IWM), the Home Front Museum in Llandudno, North Wales, and RAF Oulton Museum at the National Trust's Blickling Estate in Norfolk helped me deepen my understanding of British wartime life. Thanks to helpful research staff at each museum for answering questions and sourcing primary documents.

As always, thank you to my family and friends, who understand when I'm immersed in my fictional world and, in particular, my husband, who makes delicious meals to ensure I eat when on deadline. I'm especially grateful as well to my friend and fellow author Susanna Bavin (who also writes as Maisie Thomas and Polly Heron), who never doubted that I could write sagas/historical women's fiction and is so generous with advice and research material.

Not least, thanks to the readers, reviewers and bloggers who have embraced my 'teacher evacuees'. A particular shout-out to Vicki Eddison and Beverley Ann Hopper, whose bookish support on social media and elsewhere is much appreciated.

It is readers who make an author's career possible, and whether it's women's historical/saga fiction as Rose Warner, or sweet contemporary romance as Jen Gilroy, I write stories to bring readers' hearts home. From my heart to yours, thank you for being part of my writing journey.